Marrying
MR. RIGHT

THE BRIDES OF HILTON HEAD ISLAND

BOOK 3

international bestselling author

SABRINA SIMS MCAFEE

Marrying Mr. Right
The Brides of Hilton Head Island
Book 3

Copyright © 2015 by McAfee Publications & Entertainment

Formatting: Inkstain Interior Book Designing
Editor: GWE

Sabrina Sims McAfee can be contacted via her website:
www.sabrinasimsmcafee.com

To my dedicated readers: Once again, thanks for your support. Because of you, I'm able to fulfill my writing passion. From the bottom of my heart, I can never thank my readers enough. Mwah!

xoxo,
Sabrina

For my mother in law, Helen McAfee.

I'm blessed to have you as a mother in law

And to be a part of such a beautiful family.

With open arms you welcomed me into your family.

Made me feel like a daughter, your flesh and blood.

Thanks for your love.

Loving you always,

Sabrina

Chapter One

LAVENDER HUES SETTLED AROUND THE clouds in the early evening sky. The fading reddish-orange sun lowered behind huge oaks. Earthly scents of nature permeated the humid air of the dense forest. Green leaves scattered the grounds.

"Where are we going, Zeke?" Sixteen year old Taylor Spelling wondered as she followed her handsome boyfriend, Zeke Balfour, further into the woods. On the other side of town. More like, the luxurious side of town. Or as some would say, Hilton Head Island's filthy rich side of town.

Branches crunched beneath Zeke's new white sneakers as he traipsed through the forest, gently holding Taylor's hand. Leading Taylor around a burly oak, Zeke's sexy lips pulled into a handsome smile, showing off his straight white teeth. "It's a surprise, Taylor." His deep voice echoed throughout the forest, stirred her girly senses.

Traipsing beside Zeke, Taylor's stomach churned with fear because she had a big secret to tell him. What she had to tell him would change his life forever. Scared to divulge her secret to Zeke, anxiety spurted through Taylor. *How do I tell him this? How? Oh God, I hope he doesn't hate me after I tell him.*

Overwhelmed, Taylor ducked beneath a thick branch to avoid it from scraping her right cheek. "A surprise? What kind of a surprise, Zeke?" she asked, nervous tension spreading through her bones.

Zeke chuckled. "If I tell you it wouldn't be a surprise. Now stop asking so many questions and just be patient. Where're almost there, my love." A senior in high school, at eighteen years old Zeke had big bulging biceps, a hard muscular chest, and everything about him looked so incredibly scrumptious. Just delicious.

Darkness descended down on them. Nets flew in the air. A green grasshopper jumped about the slender grass then over Taylor's brown, flat sandal.

Clasping Zeke's big hand with her small one, Taylor admired her boyfriend's manly sex appeal. Silky dark brown hair, deep brown eyes, and white tanned skin, Zeke had dimples buried in his jaws. A star quarterback football player at Island Bay High School, all the girl's on Hilton Head Island loved themselves some Zeke Balfour, especially her. And from what Zeke showed Taylor, he felt the same way about her. According to him, he had eyes for only one girl——her. Hopefully after she shared her secret with him, he'd still feel the same way about her.

Knowing she had to tell him today, fright rushed through Taylor's veins. Wandering farther away from Zeke's parent's mansion, an evening summer breeze sailed over her natural curly hair, blowing unruly strands across her lips.

Kicking at the wooden sticks and leaves along the way, Taylor's heart beat at the base of her throat. Zeke clench her hand harder. Severely distraught, she lowered her gaze to the dried burnt grass. Her troubled mind drifted. *I'm nothing but trouble. My mother is so disappointed in me. I can only pray that Zeke won't hate me.*

Momma says I need to tell Zeke tonight. If I don't she's going to speak with his mother. For all I know, momma may be telling Zeke's mother about me now. Overwhelmed about her biggest mistake, Taylor felt her eyes water. *Ohmygod, how do I tell him I'm—*

"We're here!" Taylor's gaze snapped up to find a wide lake surrounded by trees in the near distance. To her left a long rope with a black tire attached at the end dangled from a thick branch.

Smiling his behind off, Zeke pointed upward. "Do you like my surprise?" Taylor's eyes left the makeshift tire swing and hiked up the big tree. A small tree house sat at the top of oak. "I built us a tree house so we can have some privacy. This my love is just for the two of us." Proud, he patted his rigid chest. "I built it myself?"

Shocked, Taylor's mouth parted. Eyes roaming over the wooden treehouse, she covered her heart. "Did you really build this, Zeke?" she asked, transferring her gaze from the nice surprise to him.

Zeke's dark brown eyes sparkled. He lifted his shirt revealing a book tucked between his stomach and jeans. He drew the book from between the band of his clothing and extended it to Taylor. Reaching for the book, she read the title. *How to Build Treehouses.*

Smiling, Zeke folded his arms across his chest. "Yes, I built it all by myself. Other than you and me, no one is allowed in our treehouse."

Our treehouse. Her insides beamed with appreciation. That was just like her Zeke—always so good with his hands. Those big hands of his was exactly the reason why she was now in all this freaking trouble. His talented hands had moved all over her body. His big hands had touched and fondled her. Had teased her. Pleased and pleasured her.

Taylor's eyes lowered to Zeke's big hands now resting at his sides. Oh my how she loved his big, powerful looking hands. Her gaze climbed up the length of his body. And she loved his big powerful looking body, too. And Lord knows she shouldn't, but she loved his big powerful manhood between his muscular thighs as well. Thinking about all the big things Zeke had, heat coursed through Taylor's veins.

"I'm so impressed with your talented skills, Zeke." Taylor's eyes once again hiked up the wide tree, stopping when they reached the top. Deep purple hues highlighted the dark sky. A soft glow gleamed from the carved window of the tree house. *Zeke built this just for us.* Taylor cupped Zeke's jaw. "Thanks Zeke. It's so beautiful." *I'm so sorry I've ruined your life. Ohgod. Ohgod.* Frightened, Taylor's eyes burned as she fought to hold back her tears.

Zeke's eyes roamed over Taylor's face. Taking the book from her hands, he pecked her lips. "Because my father is in charge of my allowance, the treehouse is all I can afford right now. But one day I'm going to build you a big house. It's going to be a mansion. Bigger than my parent's home."

Filled with utter sorrow, Taylor's lips curved into a bland smile. "I'd never need a home as big as your parent's house. All I'll ever need is you." *And our—* she couldn't even bring herself to say the word inside her head.

Zeke's lips pulled into a handsome smile. Staring at her like he loved her, he tucked a piece of curly hair behind her ear. "With all the children I plan on having with you, we might need a home bigger than you think. As soon as I graduate from college, I'm going to get you pregnant every year until I'm twenty-six." *It's too late for that.* Zeke continued. "Now come. Let me show you the inside." Turning away from her, he held onto the handmade wooden ladder tacked to the tree, and began climbing upward.

Watching Zeke climb toward the top of the treehouse, Taylor cupped the lower part of her belly. A big wasp flew by her head,

4

buzzed in her ears. Curious to what the inside of the treehouse looked like, Taylor mounted the ladder behind Zeke. When she reached the top, Zeke extended his hand palm up towards her. She placed her hand is his, and he gently pulled her inside.

With her hands and knees pressed into the blue rug covering the floor's wooden planks, her eyes combed over the small inside area. *Wow.* A woodsy pine fragrance sailed up her nose.

Zeke had the inside of the treehouse decorated like a small, cozy cottage. A red checkered blanket, two fluffy white pillows, a few books and two flashlights stashed the right corner. A bright lantern glowed in the left corner beneath the carved out window. On the center of the blue rug lay a handful of white daises with long green stems. *Oh Zeke, is so romantic. I can't believe he built this all by himself. Just for me. Just for us.*

Sunny cheerfulness swarming through her soul, Taylor sat on her rear, crossed her legs Indian style. Zeke picked up the white daisies, handed them to her. Nose on the pedals, she sniffed the delicate perfumed flower. "You're so romantic, Zeke." Fingers holding the long green stems, she lowered the flowers to her lap.

Gazing into her eyes, he reached into his back pocket, pulled out a silver band with diamonds, and held it up in her face. The gorgeous piece of jewelry sparkled. Thinking Zeke was about to propose to her, Taylor gasped. *Yes Zeke. I'll marry you.*

Zeke's Adam's apple bobbled up and down in his throat. "Taylor, this ring belonged to my birth mother. As you already know, my birth mother's name was Bridget. My father gave this ring to my mother on Valentine's Day of the same year she died. After she passed, my father gave this ring to me. He told me to give it to the woman I fell in love with. Well, that girl is you, Taylor. You're the girl I'm madly in love with."

Joy bubbled in Taylor's heart from Zeke's heartfelt love admission. Staring at the sparkling diamond band, she covered her heart with her hand, then linked her gaze with his.

Love glittered in his dark coffee eyes. "Oh Zeke. It's so beautiful." Thrilled at how much Zeke truly loved her, Taylor's words came out soft as a caress. The love of her life took her hand in his, and slid the ring up her wedding finger. Swallowing, she blinked sporadically. "So does this mean we're getting married?"

Zeke chuckled. "Not right away. But we will get married someday. Until we do, I want you to wear the ring as a promise ring. As a symbol of my undying love for you." Zeke clenched her chin between his index finger and thumb, tilting her head back. "Taylor Spelling...I promise to always be good to you, my love. I promise to love you now. Forever...and ever." Smooching his lips together, Zeke dropped his lips close to her mouth.

Tell him now Taylor! Tell Zeke Balfour that you're pregnant with his child! Ignoring the thoughts screaming inside her head, Taylor clutched Zeke's broad shoulders, pressed her lips into his, and let his mouth take hers on an exciting journey.

Tongues twining, Zeke's mouth felt so good on Taylor's. From his charming ways to his great personality and loving heart, everything about Zeke Balfour seemed perfect. Too good to be true. Seemed so right. *One day I'm going to marry Zeke Balfour—my Mr. Right.*

As Taylor's lips meshed with Zeke's, his hands explored her entire body. His talented hand sneaked beneath her shirt, slid under her bra, and then over her tender breast. Groaning inside her mouth, he tweaked her sensitive nipple with his fingers. A light moan squeezed from her pursed lips into his mouth, and Zeke drank it.

Plucking her tingling nipple with one hand, Zeke's other hand fondled the crotch area of her cheap jeans. Moisture formed inside her center. Curling her tongue with his, she winced. *Hot in the panties, this is why you're pregnant now.*

Once her mother had learned of her pregnancy, she'd warned her not to have sex with Zeke anymore. But Taylor just couldn't help herself. She loved Zeke, and he loved her. Just because they were young didn't mean their love was fake. No. It was the real thing.

Whenever Zeke and she got together, chemistry ignited. Magic filled the air. Desire and fire exploded.

Zeke released Taylor's mouth. Left it burning with fire. Breathing raggedly, he huskily suggested, "Let's go skinny dipping!" Before Taylor could reply, Zeke jumped to his feet, hastened over to the door. Glancing down at the ground, he jumped from the treehouse.

Ecstatic, Taylor quickly crawled over to the door. On her hands and knees, she poked her head from the opening of the tree house and peered down at a smiling Zeke. Her lips smiled. "Zeke Balfour you must be crazy if you think I'm getting in that cold lake!"

Zeke quickly removed his shirt, then hurried out of his jeans and underwear. Zeke's white, hard erection pointed straight out. Gliding her tongue over her lips, Taylor's heart thudded harshly beneath her ribcage. Gosh, his shaft was so big. No wonder she loved him. No wonder she'd been stupid and let him get her pregnant.

Naked as the day he was born, Zeke threw his arms up in the air. "I'm not crazy, Taylor Spelling. I'm madly in love! Miss all the fun if you want!"

Zeke's bare feet scampered along the slender grass as he ran towards the lake. Picking up his speed, his rod swung like Tarzan. When he reached the edge of the land, he hopped high in the air. Feet kicking, arms flailing, Zeke dove his naked behind straight into the lake. The sound of splashing water resounded through the early evening air.

Unable to contain her excitement, Taylor climbed down from the treehouse, and ran toward the lake. Standing at the edge of the land, she watched Zeke do back strokes in the lake. "Take off your clothes. I want to see your pretty, brown tits."

Keeping her eyes attached to his, she quickly rolled her shirt over her head. Anxious to join him, her fingers loosened the button on her jeans. Kicking the jeans from her feet, she removed her bra, flung it to the ground. She yanked her panties down her legs, tossed them to the side as well.

Cool soil pressed into her bare feet. The summer night air clung to her clammy skin. Her hard nipples tingled. A dull ache formed in her center. Wishing she could refute Zeke's sexual advances, she yearned to join him for a romantic swim.

Floating on his back, her man smiled at her. "You have the prettiest tits I've ever seen."

A tinge of jealously crept up inside Taylor at Zeke's remark. She fisted her hips and pouted. "Considering you're only eighteen, how many tits have you seen? I hope not that many."

Feet treading in the dark water, Zeke chuckled. "I've only seen two. You're right one, and you're left one." He got to his feet, held out his hands.

"You better had said that!" Giggling, Taylor hopped in the air, and then plunged into the depths of the lake. Gravity sucked her to the bottom. Kicking her feet and flinging her arms, she swam back to the top. Immersed in darkness, she popped her head up from the cold water, and looked around for Zeke. Staying afloat, she turned to find him behind her. "This water is cold!"

"I'll warm you up." Zeke swam over to Taylor. Putting his wet muscular chest to her breasts, he wrapped his strong arms about her shoulders. Teeth clattering, she shivered. Her nipples felt like frozen peas. "I'm c...c...cold, Zeke."

Keeping one hand to her shoulder, Zeke reached down between them. "Let's see if this will warm you up," he said, gliding his steely tool across her pregnant belly.

Turned on, her heart clenched. "Zeke there's something I have to tell you." *Tell him you're pregnant, Taylor,* she thought, chastising herself. *Stop being so freaking scared.*

Chapter Two

ZEKE'S EYES CARESSED TAYLOR'S AS he draped his arms around her waist. "Not now, Taylor. Tell me later. Tell me after I make love to you, okay?" Rubbing the pad of his wet thumb across her lips, his sensual eyes kissed her face.

Wanting him just as much as he wanted her, Taylor nodded in assent. Why ruin the moment? she thought, the pit of her stomach twirling with butterflies. "Okay."

Zeke slipped his shaft inside Taylor. Feeling him stretch her walls, she twined her arms around his neck. Wrapped her legs around his waist and rode him. Driving into her, Zeke slanted his mouth over hers, and tongued her down.

As usual, Zeke set her insides aflame. Bucking on him, Taylor lolled her head back, and glanced up at the dark sky. Bouncing up and down on Zeke's tool, water rippled along her spine.

"Look at me, Taylor," Zeke requested. Hair soaked and matted to her skull, Taylor rolled her neck forward to meet his deep, sensual gaze. "I love you Taylor." He softly bit her bottom lip then released it.

She sucked his bottom lip into her mouth then spit it out. "I love you, too, Zeke."

"Are you about to come?" Zeke asked her. Taylor nodded. "Good. Me too. Let's come together." He twirled her creamy walls and Taylor's sex exploded. And so did Zeke's. Like he'd wanted, they'd come together.

After Zeke and Taylor made love in the lake, they swam to the edge of the water. Zeke climbed out first. Knees pressed into grass, he hooked his arms beneath Taylor's armpits, and pulled. Taylor somehow ended up on top of him.

Laying on his back with her on top of him, Zeke smiled. His member grew hard on her stomach. Gazing into his handsome eyes, she threaded her fingers through his wet wiry hair. He clenched her hips with one hand, raised her from his lap. He slipped inside her again and they ended up making sweet tender love in the grass.

Long moments later, Zeke and Taylor lay side by side in the grass, gazing up at the sky. He pushed up on his elbows. He scooped her wet hair up in his hands, brought it up to his mouth, and kissed it. "I'll never forget this night for as long as I live."

"Me either." Taylor stood and walked over to the make shift tire swing. Holding onto the sides of the tire, she slid inside the circular part of the rubber, and then gripped the twinned rope. Batting her lashes at Zeke, she smiled. "Push me, Zeke. Push me as high as you can," she said, wildly kicking her feet.

"Hold on!" Zeke lifted the sides of the tire up to his chest, then gave her a hard push. Giggling hysterically, Taylor went flying in the air. Her wet hair whipped at the sides of her smiling face.

Suddenly, a voice rang out through a bull horn. "Zeke!"

Taylor shrieked. "Someone's coming, Zeke. Stop the swing. Stop the swing."

Zeke gripped the tire bringing it to an abrupt halt. "That's my stepmother, Katherine. How in the hell did she find me?"

Touching the tips of her toes to the ground, Taylor writhed her way out of the circular whole of the tire. Covering her breasts, she ran and snatched up her clothing. "Oh God, I'm really in trouble now," she said, quickly pulling her shirt over her head, then shoving her arms through the sleeves.

"What do you mean you're in trouble?" Zeke questioned, observing fear in Taylor's wide eyes.

"I'm so sorry Zeke—"

"Zeke! Where are you?!" Katherine's loud voice echoed through the dense wooded area.

"Your stepmother sounds mad, Zeke." Taylor prayed like crazy that Katherine hadn't somehow found out she was pregnant before she had the chance to tell Zeke herself. *Oh God, I should've told Zeke sooner.*

Zeke's brows drew close together. "You're right. She does sound angry."

Taylor yanked her jeans up over her hips, grabbed her brown sandals. "I'm going home. Call me later."

Zeke clutched Taylor's arms. "You don't have to hide from my stepmother, Taylor. You're my girl and I think it's high time that Katherine finds out about us. I love you, my love."

Moisture wet Taylor's pupils. "Oh Zeke. She probably already knows about us. I'm so sorry. So, so, sorry." With her worn sandals clenched to her chest, Taylor took off running through the forest. Breathing erratically, she ran as fast as she could past all those trees.

"THERE YOU ARE!" GRIPPING THE handle of a bullhorn in one hand and pointing a bright flashlight in the other, Zeke's stepmother, Katherine, marched toward him with a noticeable frown on her white, round freckled face. Wearing a long ivory dress and her red hair pulled into a low bun, Katherine pinched her lips together. "I've been looking everywhere for you?" Her eyes lowered to his bare shaft then back up to his face. "Where are your clothes? Have you been out here fucking that girl?"

"What girl, Mom?" Although Katherine wasn't his birth mother, his father insisted he call her that. At times he hated he had to refer to snobbish Katherine as his mother. But considering his birth mother, Bridget, had had an affair with his father while he was married to Katherine, she probably hated it, too.

Right after his birth mother Bridget had died, his father Colton had brought Zeke to live with him and Katherine, and their other two children—Antonio and Bane. From the very first day that Zeke had stepped inside their mansion, Katherine had despised his mere existence. Despised him for being born. Despised him because he was the result of an affair.

Katherine narrowed her eyes at Zeke. Pointing her finger in his face, she barked through clenched teeth, "Taylor. Taylor Spelling. Have you been out here fucking that girl again?!"

How does she know about Taylor? His mother's, well not his real mother, but Katherine's harsh tone irked him. Made him angry. His face scrunched as he snatched his jeans from the ground and put them on.

Hooking his gaze on Katherine's furious green eyes, Zeke sucked his teeth. "As a matter of fact, I have. What's it to you?" he asked snidely, buttoning his jeans.

Katherine threw her hands up in the air. "Dear Lord! It's true! It's true!"

What the hell she screaming about? Bemused, Zeke gave his stepmother a dumbfounded stare. He shrugged. "What's true?"

"Taylor's pregnant! You got that hot little bitch pregnant!" Stunned, Zeke's heart clenched. His stepmother continued spatting, "Now she's going to ruin the family's name. Everything your father has worked so hard to protect, you've destroyed it,

Zeke. You and Taylor. Other than you, we've never had a bastard born in this family. Never." Hatred dulled her green eyes.

Zeke's face turned beat red. Seemingly confused, his brows lifted. "Taylor's pregnant?" *This is what she wanted to me. She wanted to tell me she was pregnant.*

"Yes. She's pregnant." Still holding the bullhorn and flashlight, Katherine's green eyes narrowed. "Taylor's mother just paid me a visit and told me out of her own darn mouth." Taking a step closer to him, her eyes roamed over his face. She fisted her hips. Head tilting, her eyes stretched wide. "Oh. My. God. Your little supposedly girlfriend didn't even bother telling you, did she?" Zeke shook his head. Katherine continued. "These little sluts around here been trying to get their hands on the family's fortune for years. For all I know, the baby may not even be yours. Taylor's getting an abortion, and that's all to it."

Folding his arms across his chest, Zeke gave Katherine a brutal stare on purpose. *Like hell she will.* "No, Mom. If Taylor's pregnant, she's keeping my baby."

Katherine slapped Zeke! Face stinging, his mouth dropped wide open. Lips twisting, she clutched his shoulders and shook him. "There's no way in hell I'm letting another bastard child come into this family. Into my house. No way in fucking hell! Do you understand me? Do you?"

This lady is crazy. Knowing he had every intention of keeping his baby, Zeke nodded yes just to appease red head Katherine. "Yes ma'am."

Gently patting his face where she'd slapped him, the corners of Katherine's lips lifted. "I'm glad you agree with me, Zeke. You let me handle Taylor and this stupid pregnancy. Now let's go home and have dinner. Don't argue with your brothers tonight while at the table. I'm not in the mood for anymore drama tonight."

Lady, you put the D in drama. And you put the D in damn fool if you think my girl is getting an abortion. Zeke shrugged on his shirt then followed his stepmother through the forestry. Thinking about how Taylor was pregnant with his child, warmth infused his heart. Smiling inwardly, he couldn't wait to talk with Taylor and let her know of his new plans.

Walking behind Katherine and heading home, a mild smile touched Zeke's lips. *I'm going to make sure Taylor and my baby don't ever have to worry about a thing. As soon as I graduate from high school, I'm going to convince Taylor's mother to sign papers stating she can marry me. But even if she don't sign them, we're going to get married as soon as we can. If anyone tries to stop us from being together, we'll run away, and raise our child together. Yes. I'm going to be a father. Yes! Oh God, I love myself some Taylor.*

Trailing closely behind Katherine, Zeke finally reached the back of his parent's red brick mansion. Katherine fisted the sides of her long dress, and marched up the steps of the back desk.

So glad Taylor was pregnant, Zeke felt like jumping up and kicking his damn heels. However, knowing that action would piss Katherine off, he decided to keep his excited emotions on the down low, and just clambered the steps behind the stuck up woman instead.

GAZING DOWN AT THE SPARKLING promise ring that Zeke had given her, Taylor crossed the railroad tracks leading towards her home, and smiled. *Zeke said this is a promise ring. A token of how much he loves me. He said we're going to get married one day.* Placing her hand to the bottom part of her belly, Taylor's heart sang with delight.

Feeling blissful and hopeful about her future with Zeke, Taylor wondered if he knew she was pregnant by now. His stepmother's voice had sounded quite angry about ten minutes ago. Maybe she should've just stayed and faced mean behind Katherine head on. It wasn't like the lady could do anything about her situation. If anything, Katherine should be happy that she loved Zeke more than life itself.

Close to her home, the sky had grown even darker. Almost pitch black. Burning wood wafted up her nose. Gazing down at the ground, she kicked at a rock, and looked at her sparkling promise ring again. *Oh Zeke is so sweet. And good looking. And ooo, he's so fine.*

Suddenly, Taylor felt a shadow behind her. Just as she whirred, someone covered her head with a sack. Clawing at the hands squeezing her neck, the locket necklace around her neck snapped, and fell to the ground. Losing her breath, she plummeted to her hands and knees.

Scurrying away with the bag covering her head while on her hands and knees, the crazy man yanked her off the ground. Unable to see, Taylor screamed. Terrified, she kicked and punched. Jerked harshly in the strong man's arms. "Let me go! Let me go!"

"Shut up. You should've thought about your consequences beforehand."

Crying her eyes out, she heard bleeps from a car as if her abductor was unlocking a vehicle. The strong man tossed her, and she landed hard on something. *Bam!* Sounded like the trunk of a car had slammed close.

Frightened on wits end, Taylor snatched the bag from her head to find herself trapped inside the truck of some man's car. Laying on her back, surrounded in sheer darkness, she felt the car rock and shimmy over the railroad track. Short moments later a train's whistle resounded throughout the night's air, and sailed into the dark trunk of the horrible monster's car.

Kicking and banging on the trunk's roof, Taylor wailed. *He's going to kill me and my baby. Oh God, please help me.* "Somebody help meeee!"

Chapter Three

INDULGING IN A VERY BLAND meal, Zeke sat in silence at the long, wooden dining table. Along with him sat his stepmother Katherine, and his two half-brothers—Antonio and Bane. Forking green beans into his mouth, Zeke's eyes traveled to the empty chair at the head of the table where his father normally sat. His workaholic father, billionaire Colton Balfour, was still at work.

Hating the tension stabbing the air, Zeke's eyes left the vacant chair to glimpse Katherine's round, red freckly face. When their gazes connected, Katherine shook her head in disgrace then rolled her eyes.

Sitting across from him making mean faces, Katherine's long ivory dress bunched with ruffles over her breasts area. *Who gets dressed up just to stay in the house all day? She swears she's an actress on the soap operas.* Dark red hair, striking green eyes, and pink lips, Katherine was attractive on the outside. But on the inside she was ugly. *Past ugly. Way ugly.*

Always prime and proper, Katherine worked hard to maintain a perfect image for her family, especially her marriage. Because

Zeke was the result of a secret affair, Katherine felt embarrassed by him. Part of him couldn't blame her, but then again, it wasn't his fault that his mother had had an affair with his father and had gotten pregnant with him.

Everybody makes mistakes. I can't wait 'till dad gets home. Katherine's evil stare is driving me nuts. When I leave here I'm never coming back. Taylor and I are going to get married and move far, far, away. Raise our son or daughter, together.

With his older brother Bane to his left, and his other older brother Antonio to his right, Zeke spooned a heaping tablespoon of dry mashed potatoes into his mouth. Yuck! Katherine's cooking was horrible. He'd be glad when their chef named Delbert returned. But what he really couldn't wait for was to speak with Taylor.

Happiness filled Zeke's insides. *Oh Taylor. You're having my baby.* As soon as he finished his dinner, he was going to go upstairs and call her. Longing to speak with Taylor about the pregnancy, Zeke forced himself to swallow the disgusting food inside his mouth that Katherine had cooked.

When Taylor said she was in trouble earlier, he had no idea she was trying to tell him she was pregnant. Right before she'd taken off, she'd even apologized. As far as he was concerned, she didn't have anything to be sorry for, he thought, dragging a napkin across his mouth.

Zeke's older brother Antonio nudged him in his side with his elbow. Chuckling, Antonio shook his head. "Heard you gone be a father, Dude."

Holding a glass to his lips, Bane's tea flew from his mouth. "Damn dude, you got somebody pregnant?! What the fuck?!" Bane laughed.

Dabbing at the corners of her mouth, Katherine's napkin went flying in the air. "Watch your mouth Bane!" Her eyes narrowed at Antonio. "And you. How do you know about this?"

Reddish-blonde hair, blue eyes, Antonio looked a lot like his mother Katherine. Antonio's blue eyes became flat as he pondered what to say. "I overheard you talking with Taylor's mother, Veronica, a little while ago."

Shoulders pushed back, Katherine jutted her chin. In her famous proper tone she spoke, "What did I tell you about getting in grown folks business, Antonio? That wasn't polite, you know?"

Antonio met Katherine's dark green gaze, and shrugged. "Well, it's not like I was trying to hear you speak, Katherine. All that yelling you were doing with Veronica, I couldn't help but over hear you."

"Please, don't address me as Katherine. I'm your mother Antonio. Anyhow, I'm going to tell you just like I told Zeke...no baby is coming into this house. Veronica and I discussed this situation. And we both agree that it'd be in Zeke and Taylor's best interest if she had an abortion."

Zeke tried to give Katherine a black angered glare. Fuming, he scooted his chair back and jumped to his feet. His angry gaze held Katherine's hateful glare. "Taylor is not having an abortion." His tone came out bold and icy. Just the way he felt.

Katherine's red eyebrows dipped. Her pink, thin lips twisted with disdain. "Don't you dare speak to me in that manner," she ordered through clenched teeth. "You're too young to have a baby, Zeke. You've been accepted into some of the most prestigious universities, colleges in the world—Yale, Howard, Princeton, and even Oxford just to name a few. If you have a baby, you can forget about going to college. You'll be stuck here raising a baby. And the last thing I need is for you to stay here in Hilton Head."

Shaking his head, Zeke's fists balled. He tossed his head back and released a throaty fake laugh. Meeting Katherine's evil stare again, he retorted in cold sarcasm. "You've never wanted me here. Have you Katherine? Don't worry, I won't mess up your plans to get rid of me. I'll find a place of my own. And I will take care of my baby and Taylor all by myself." *Suggesting Taylor has an abortion, Katherine is one nasty woman.*

Katherine rose to her feet and fisted her hips. "If you and Taylor decide to have this damn baby, you and she will take care of it!" She roughly thumbed her chest. "Not me!" Hands back on hips, she gave her head a hard shake. "And not your father! Your father has invested too much money in you for you to go out and mess up like this! You—"

"What's going on in here?" Zeke's father, Colton Balfour, emerged from the kitchen and stood beneath the framed arch. Wearing a navy blue suit and loosening the red speckled tie at his neck, Colton stalked toward his seat at the head of the table. "I can hear you screaming all the way outside, Katherine. Please, lower your voice."

Katherine huffed. Her eyes were filled contempt, and she looked like she hated him. Just hated him. "Are you going to tell him, Zeke or should I?"

Silence hung in the air like black smoke, suffocating Zeke.

Both Zeke and Katherine sat back down in their seats.

Colton stood at the head of the long wooden table shrugging his arms from the sleeves of his suit jacket. Clearing his throat, he draped the jacket on the back of the wing back chair, then plopped down in his seat next to Katherine. Waiting for Katherine to fix his plate like she always did whenever the chef Delbert was absent, Colton clasped his hands.

Expressionless, Colton's dark brown eyes went from Katherine to Bane, then to Antonio and lastly to Zeke. "Well, is somebody going to tell me what the hell is going on or what?"

Zeke's heart palpitated wildly in his chest. *He's going to be pissed.* Mustering up the courage to drop the bombshell on his father, Zeke inhaled deeply. "My girlfriend, Taylor…well…she's pregnant."

"This is just horrible. Horrible," Katherine mumbled.

Colton's eyes rounded in disbelief. He opened his mouth to speak then zipped his lips shut. Straightening his back against the chair, he folded his arms across his thick, burly chest. As his father sat thinking, silence loomed in the air. Waiting for his father to say something, tension coursed through Zeke's veins. *I don't care what anyone says, I'm going to support, Taylor. She's having my baby, and that's that.*

Suddenly, Colton's eyes brightened. Looking at Zeke, his full lips pulled into a big wide smile. "Well, congratulations my son. I'm looking forward to being a grandfather. It's going to be fun having a little one running around here. Please invite your girlfriend Taylor over so I can tell her face to face how happy I am for the two of you."

Holy shit! He's not mad. Shocked at his father's response, Zeke's heart swelled. "Thanks, dad."

Katherine threw her hands up in the air. "You've got to be kidding me. Is that all you have to say, Colton? Really? Really?"

Colton nonchalantly shrugged his shoulders. "Yes, Katherine. That's all I have to say. Having a baby is not the worse thing that can happen to Zeke. He's not on drugs. Has a four-point-eight grade point average, smart as a whip. About to go to college. Got accepted into some very prestigious schools I might add. I'm very proud of Zeke." Colton held his right hand up to his chest level. "I'll admit, having a baby this early in the game isn't the best situation to be in, but what's done, is already done. And there's no need to mope about it. We'll just have to make the best of an unexpected, challenging situation."

Bane slapped Zeke on the back, and chortled. "Congratulations, my brother. I'm going to be an uncle."

Antonio jabbed his fork into his steak then sliced it with his knife. Holding a chunk of meat to his mouth with his fork, his bottom lip folded under. "I bet she got pregnant on purpose."

Glowering at Antonio, Zeke balled his hands beneath the table. "You better watch what you say about my girl, bro."

Antonio bolted to his feet. Zeke hopped to his. Standing face to face, Zeke was tempted to throw a punch at his idiotic brother's face. Antonio jutted his chin. "And if I don't. What are going to do about it?"

Zeke spat, "I'm going to beat your face in with my fist until it becomes a bloody pulp." *And fuck your ass up.* "Now say something so I can make good on my threat."

Colton ordered in a husky tone, "Alright you two. Stop—"

The doorbell rang, interrupting the chaos taking place inside the Balfour's home. Ordering both Antonio and Zeke to sit their behinds back down with one look of his cold eyes, Colton rose to his feet. "Everyone needs to calm down and be happy for Zeke. I don't want to hear another negative word out of anyone's mouth about this here situation. Everyone here is going to be happy for Zeke. As a family, we're going to support both Zeke and Taylor, and welcome their baby into our lives with open arms." Colton's dark gaze bounced back and forth between Katherine and Antonio. "For the record, I'm not asking. I'm telling everyone at this table, that we *WILL* be supportive of Zeke. Period. End of discussion." *Ringringring.* The doorbell rang repeatedly, signaling a sense of urgency. "Now if you'll excuse me, I'm going to go get the door."

Halfway to the front door, Colton yelled out, "Katherine fix my plate!"

Rolling her eyes, Katherine strolled toward the kitchen. "I swear, he can never do any wrong in that man's eyes," she murmured beneath her breath, but Zeke heard her loud and clear.

Stop hating.

Antonio stated, "Don't ask me to baby sit because the answer will be no. Good luck."

Bane exclaimed, "Dad said no negativity. I'll help you with the baby as best as I can, Zeke."

The corner of Zeke's mouth lifted in appreciation of Bane's kindness. "Thanks bro. At least someone has my back—"

"Zeke get in here! Now!" Colton shouted.

Glad that his father and his brother Bane was supportive of him, Zeke trudged through the living room, and headed for the front door. When he reached the living room, he instantly recognized Taylor's mother, Veronica Spelling. Red stained eyes, and bright red nose, Veronica's brown face held a sullen expression. Short straight haired bob, Veronica looked like she'd been crying.

Nervous, Zeke swallowed. "Hi, Ms. Spelling. I guess you're here about Taylor. I'm—"

"Have you seen Taylor?" Veronica blurted. Water filled her eyes. "She's normally home by seven, but she hasn't come home yet."

Zeke's heart dunked. "We were together earlier today not far from here. We split around six, right after it got dark. She said she was going straight home."

Veronica's lips trembled. A tear streamed down her left cheek. "How was she right before she left you? Did she seem sad?"

Oh God, Taylor. Where are you? Terrified, Zeke shook his head. "I wouldn't necessarily say sad. More like, scared. Yeah, she was scared. She said she was going to be in big trouble."

Veronica swiped at the tear falling from her right eye. "Was she scared because of the pregnancy?"

When Zeke nodded his head, his bang fell from the hair on top of his head to his brows. "I didn't know at the time that she was pregnant, but yeah. I think she was scared to tell me she was pregnant."

Curiosity rounded Veronica's red stained eyes. "She never told you that she was pregnant?"

Having a bad feeling about Taylor's unknown whereabouts, Zeke swallowed. "No, Taylor never told me. Right when she was about to, Katherine came looking for me, and interrupted her." *Darn, Katherine. She always mess things up for me.*

"Now Zeke," Katherine said, strolling inside the room up behind him. Looking ever so elegant in the long ivory dress she wore, Katherine had the nerve to caress his spine like she really cared for him. Like she really loved him. Boy, she could fake it good. "What did I tell you about calling me Katherine?" The only person who *regularly* addressed her as Mom was Bane.

Zeke swallowed his frustration. "Sorry. Mom."

Katherine questioned, "What's going on in here? Why does everyone look so sad?"

"Taylor's missing, Mom," Zeke murmured, hating to refer to Katherine as his mother. Katherine was *not* his mother. She'd never treated him like a son. Not ever. Wanting his girl to have an abortion. Tonight Katherine proved she didn't care about him. Not. At. All.

Katherine gasped. "Dear Lord. What do you mean Taylor's missing?"

Veronica replied, "Taylor hasn't come home yet. I've looked everywhere for her. So has my neighbors."

Colton asked, "Veronica, have you called the police yet?"

Veronica's lips quivered as she nodded. *Dripdripdrip.* Tears streamed down her face. "Yes. The police knows she's missing. She always come home by her curfew. Always. And if something comes up, she always, always calls me to let me know." Black purse strapped to her shoulder, Veronica put her hand to her ample breast. "I'm terrified."

"Me, too. Me too." Worry bubbled at the surface of Zeke's stomach.

Katherine took a few steps forward and cupped Veronica's hands. "Veronica, I'm sure Taylor is fine and will show up soon. I know it's hard, but try not to worry. We'll call you if we hear anything. Okay?" Releasing Veronica's hands, Katherine moved back beside Zeke, in front of Colton.

Nodding her head, Veronica sniffed. "Thanks——" Veronica's cell buzzed. She reached into the purse strapped across her shoulder to answer it. She placed the cell on her earlobe. "Hello." As she listened to the person on the line, Veronica's trembling fingers touched her quivering lips. "Where?" Silence. "By the railroad tracks? Oh God. Oh God. I'm on my way home now." Veronica pressed the end button on her cell phone. Angst filled her glassy black eyes as a sorrowful wail pressed from her lungs.

Panic coursed through Zeke's veins. Gaging the horrid expression on Veronica's face, he asked, "What's wrong? What's wrong Ms. Spelling?"

Colton gripped Veronica's shoulders. "Did they find Taylor?"

Veronica's shoulders shook up and down as she cried. Shaking her head, she mouthed, "No. She's still missing. They found the locket she wears on the ground by the railroad tracks."

"Jesus Christ." Zeke rounded Veronica, flung open the front door.

"Where are you going?" Katherine asked.

"To look for Taylor," Zeke responded.

Shaking her head, Katherine placed her hands on her hips. "No you're not. It's past your curfew young man."

Zeke glowered at Katherine. "Taylor's in trouble. There's no way in hell I'm going to just sit here and not do a damn thing."

Katherine clasped her hands together. "Watch your mouth, Zeke. Please don't curse in front of Ms. Spelling. Go upstairs and get your homework done," Katherine's stated in a curt, sophisticated tone.

Colton gave Katherine an icy stare. "Could you at least for once in your life have a little empathy for someone other than yourself? His girlfriend is in trouble. Only an irresponsible man wouldn't go searching for his woman?" Colton fixated his gaze on Zeke then retrieved his keys from his pants pocket. "I'm coming with you. Let's go, Zeke."

"But Colton, you haven't eaten your dinner yet?" Katherine whined.

Unspoken irritation stultified Colton's brown eyes. "You're pathetic, Katherine. Don't wait up for us. We'll get back when we get back," Colton barked as he crossed over the threshold with Veronica and Zeke walking behind him.

Sitting in the passenger's side seat of his father's black Cadillac Escalade, Zeke's heart thudded at the base of his throat. Horrified, Zeke put his hands in a prayer symbol, brought it up to his nose, and closed his eyes. Straining not to cry, his nose burned. His heart ached. *Please God. Please help me find Taylor. Please keep her and the baby safe. I love her and I promise if you bring her and the baby back to me, I'll take care of them for as long as I live. In Jesus name, I pray. Amen.*

Chapter Four

BANGBANGBANG. BANGBANGBANG. "GET UP! THERE'S work to be done around here!" Laying on her side sleeping inside a cramped room, Taylor's eyes fluttered open to find darkness surrounding her. Feeling the twin size mattress metal springs pressing into her side, Taylor's body ached all over. Blinking against the darkness, a mothball stench crept inside her nostrils. The door slowly cracked open with a resounding creak. "I know you're not sleeping. Get up! Now!" Old lady Mildred's tone echoed inside the tiny, cold room.

Trying to awake from a deep sleep, Taylor kept her back to the mean woman named Mildred who'd kidnapped her seven months ago. Clenching the thin, raggedy bedspread to her chin, Taylor reclosed her eyes, and pretended as if she didn't hear the criminal Mildred.

Nine months pregnant, Taylor was tired. Didn't feel like getting up. Always having to do all of Mildred's housework, she needed to rest for once. If Mildred wanted work to be done, she should ask her son, Kelvin.

When Mildred further opened the door to the chilly room, the light bulb in the ceiling's hallway glowed down on Taylor as she remained lying on her side. Mildred sighed harshly. "Oh so it's like that today, huh?" Ruffling sounds of Mildred's feet dragging against the floor assailed Taylor's ears. *She's coming. She's coming.* Keeping her eyes closed, Taylor felt Mildred towering over her, breathing heavily. "Mmmph. Mmmph. Mmmph. You're just as lazy as they come. Don't get any lazier than you." Mildred insulted her on a regular basis. *Apparently you haven't looked in the mirror dumb lady.* "I saaiiddd...get up!" Mildred yanked the covers off Taylor. A cold chill engulfed her.

Standing beside the worn bed, Mildred fisted the back of Taylor's long hair, and yanked it. "Ouch!" Taylor's eyes shot open. She slapped a hard palm to the back of her pained scalp.

"Bet you get your little ass up now," Mildred spat.

Taylor rolled over to her back, scooted up in bed, put her back against the brown, cracked headboard. Scalp burning, she tried her hardest to give Mildred a pitiful stare. Maybe if she treated her kidnaper nice and obeyed her, maybe someday she'll let her go. "I miss my momma. Please let me go, Mildred? Please?" Longing to see her mother, and Zeke, and her friends from high school, she studied Mildred's face intently.

Wearing a flowery dress, gray haired Mildred had pink rollers in her hair. Chubby face, she squinted her eyes at Taylor. "No. I'm never letting you go. You and the baby are going to spend the rest of your lives here with me and Kelvin. The four of us are going to be one big happy family."

Dissatisfied with Mildred's answer, Taylor felt water sprang into her eyes. "But I already have a family." *And a boyfriend, Zeke.* "They probably think I'm dead. Please let me go home? I'll do anything. I promise I won't tell the police about you if you let me go. I promise." Unsure if she was having a boy or a girl, Taylor's big pregnant belly cramped. Wondering if the sharp pain was a contraction, she cupped the lower part of belly. "I want to go home Mildred! Let me go!"

Mildred slapped Taylor's face so hard until her head snapped sideways and now she was looking at the wall instead of the mean lady standing beside her to the left. She huffed. "Look at me," Mildred ordered in a throaty voice. Breathing harshly, keeping her head sideways, tremors shook Taylor to the core. When Taylor refused to look at her, Mildred reached over, and pinched her cheek as hard as she could.

"Oww. Oww." Cheek stinging, Taylor turned her head and met Mildred's hateful gaze.

Wagging a bony finger in her face, Mildred leaned into Taylor, their noses almost touched. "Don't you ever ask me about leaving here again. If you do, there'll be consequences. Kelvin and I are hungry. Go make us some dinner," she ordered, her breath foul, smelling like bowels.

"Oww. You're hurting my face, Mildred." Finally, she let go of her burning cheek. *I hate you Mildred. I hate you.* Tears gushed from Taylor's eyes. Shifting in the bed sideways, she flung her shackled feet to the floor. "It's hard getting around the kitchen with my ankles chained like this, Mildred. Will you please take the shackles off?"

For a brief moment Mildred didn't respond, only stared at her. She reached into the pocket of her shabby flowery dress, pulled out a key, and held it up to Taylor's eyes. "Okay. I'm going to unlock them. But if you try anything stupid like you did the last time you tried to run away, I'm going to make your life a living hell." *You've already done that. This is hell. You're hell. Your son Kelvin is hell.* Mildred bent over, stuck the key in the shackles lock, clicked it open. Freed her bound ankles. The metal shackles clinked when they hit the wooden floor. "Thanks Mildred."

"Make something good to eat tonight."

"Okay. I'm coming. Just please give me a second." *Oh God. Why me? Why did Mildred take me? I'm going to die in this cold basement.* More tired than she'd ever been, Taylor glanced around the eerie room. A brown board covered the single window inside the room. An ugly burgundy carpet lay on the wooden floor near the foot of the bed. Other than a twin bed and a tiny bathroom, the room remained isolated. Didn't even have a television. Just nothing.

No one knew she was there. Mildred and her son Kelvin had her hidden from the world. They'd kidnapped her. Stolen her from her mother. Taken her away from Zeke. *Oh Zeke. I miss you so much. I hope you haven't forgotten about me.*

"Well, don't just sit there. Get a move on." Mildred fisted the top of Taylor's grey t-shirt, and roughly pulled her out of bed. Belly round and hard, Taylor put a hand to her lower spine, dragged her feet along the cold wooden floor.

Walking behind her, Mildred swatted Taylor's behind with her hand causing it to burn. "Walk faster!"

Rubbing her hand over her pregnant protruding belly, Taylor wobbled out of the basement's bedroom, and walked down the narrow hallway in front of Mildred. A sharp pain developed in her abdomen and she grind her molars. Coming to the stairway, she gripped the handrail, and began mounting the staircase toward the top. The worn planks creaked beneath her cold bare feet. *I can't let my baby grow up in this filthy house with these evil people. I have to escape. God, please help the police find me. Please don't ever let my mother stop looking for me. Please don't ever let Zeke stop looking for me either. Zeke will find me. He will. He will. He loves me.*

Right when Taylor reached the top of the staircase, the door to the basement swung open. Mildred's son, Kelvin, stood in the doorway looking down at them. The tall skinny man had brown scraggly hair, blue eyes, and one of his front top teeth was missing. "She giving you any trouble this morning, Ma?" Kelvin asked.

Holding on to the wooden handrail, Taylor glanced back over her shoulder at Mildred then back up at Kelvin. Mildred exclaimed, "She tried. But after I slapped the shit out of her she straightened up."

Eyeing Taylor wickedly, Kelvin's head tilted. "I hope she wasn't mouthing off, Ma."

"Ah just a little. I took the chains off her feet so watch her carefully. You never know about this one—she may try something." When Mildred swatted Taylor's behind again, she clenched her butt cheeks. "Get in there and cook me and my son something to eat."

"Yes ma'am." *Darn right I'm going to try something as soon as I get a chance. I don't care if I have to kill Mildred and Kelvin, I'm getting out of this freaking hell hole. They got me locked up in a dungeon. Treating me like a prisoner. I'm not letting my baby grow up like this.*

Kelvin stepped to the side so Taylor could enter the kitchen. "Let her try something, Ma. I'll be on top of her faster than she can blink her eyes." Kelvin grinned at Taylor, displaying his missing front tooth then went and took a seat on the couch inside the den.

"Don't be lolly-gagging around in the kitchen. Taking all night to cook me something to eat," Mildred complained as she headed for the den to join Kelvin on the couch.

Searching for a way to escape like she did every morning, noon, and evening, Taylor's eyes traveled over the musky scented, old house. Just like the basement, boards covered the windows in the den, kitchen and living room. The front door and the back door had big black chains on them.

Knowing she'd never give up trying to escape, Taylor's eyes traveled up the wall and stopped when they reached the small window almost to the ceiling. Glittering stars perched around the glowing half-moon. There was no way she could climb out of that small hole, especially not with her big belly. Feeling trapped and doomed, bile scratched the back of Taylor's throat.

Nauseated, she headed straight to the refrigerator, and yanked it open. Gazing over the dirty fridge, she hefted a package of raw chicken, milk, and eggs. With all the ingredients in her hands, she headed for the stove to make the batter for the fried chicken.

Moments later as Taylor stood over the stove frying drumsticks, the sound of a plane flying over the house resounded in her ears. All day everyday she listened to the planes flying to and fro. This house must be near an airport or something, she thought, turning just in time to see a plane flying past the window high above her head.

Wishing she was on a plane flying home to Hilton Head Island, Taylor picked up the tongs from the counter, and began removing the greasy chicken from the frying pan, transferring it to the white paper towels sitting on the counter beside the stove.

Suddenly, a series of sharp pains stabbed her stomach. Taken by surprise, her mouth dropped open. She gripped the sides of her balled stomach, her spine arched. Pinching her lips together, she swallowed the outburst threatening to erupt from her lungs. *Oh Jesus. I'm in labor. Oh God. This hurts. So bad. Give me strength Lord. Strength.* Not wanting Mildred or Kelvin to know she was in labor just yet, she mustered up some strength, and stood erect.

Looking at the back of Mildred and Kelvin's heads as they sat on the couch watching Family Feud on television, horrid thoughts ran inside Taylor's head. *Oh God what are they going to do with my baby? Keep it? Sell it? Kill it? Oh God. Please tell me what to do.*

Kelvin stood from the couch, pulled a pair of keys from his back jean pocket, and looked down at Mildred. "I'm going outside to chop some wood, Ma."

Keeping her eyes glued to the television, Mildred kicked her feet up on the coffee table. "Good. I can use a hot fire in this here fireplace."

After unlocking the back door and removing the chains, Kelvin pulled open the door leading to the backyard, and stood with his back turned to Taylor. He grabbed his parker from the coat rack beside the door and shrugged it on.

It'd been so long since she'd seen the outdoors. Longing to inhale the scent of the outside air, pain ricocheted through her stomach, threatening to bring her to her knees. *It's now or never. Now or never.*

Kelvin's head snapped in her direction and he glared at her. "It's real cold out here. But as cold as it is, I bet you'd like to get out here wouldn't you, Taylor?" With her belly in excruciating pain, Taylor nodded. "Too damn bad." Laughing, he walked outside, and closed the door behind him. Taylor listened intently for the sounds of the door locking, but she didn't hear anything. Could Kelvin have left the door unlocked?

Suddenly, a thought struck up in her mind. She poured more grease into frying pan, turned it up to high, and waited. Taylor caressed her stomach, tried to soothe it. Tried to make the pain subside. *I'm getting out of here. Just wait to come, my baby.*

The scorching hot grease in the pan boiled. Taylor gripped the handle of the frying pan in one hand, and grabbed a sharp knife in the other. Ready to turn Mildred's life upside down, she left the kitchen, walked inside the living room, and hid behind the wall.

Please God let this work. Terrified of what she was about to do, Taylor kept her back to the wall, and inched only her head out into the den. "Mildred," she cried. Mildred turned her gaze from the television to look at her. Taylor's face contorted. "Hurry. I'm in labor."

Mildred's face split into a big greedy grin. "Hot damn. It's payday!" She jumped off the couch and hurried in Taylor's direction. Taylor's fingers squeezed the heavy handle of the frying pan with the still burning oil.

Right when Mildred reached the living room, Taylor threw the hot grease in Mildred's face. Mildred's facial skin curled like fleshy cottage cheese. Tortured screams erupted from Mildred's throat. Grabbing her face, she ran around in circles, then plummeted to the ground on her knees. "Kelvin! Kelvin! Aagggh! My face! My face!"

Gripping the handle of the sharp blade, Taylor sprinted into the den, and hid behind the couch opposite the window. Crouching down on teetering limbs, her heart beat escalated as she waited for Kelvin to burst through the door.

"Help! Help! I can't see! I can't see!" Mildred hollered.

The back door flung open and Kelvin appeared. "Ma! Ma!"

"I can't see! I can't see!" Mildred's boisterous screams tore through the entire house.

Panicked, Kelvin ran toward the living room. "What happened, Ma?! Where's your face, Ma?! That bitch did this to you!"

Sharp knife handle gripped in her hand, Taylor quickly lurched from behind the couch, and bolted out the back door into the backyard. Pressured pushed against her pelvis. Clenching her aching belly, her eyes rolled over the wide wooded area. Trees surrounded the house.

Where in the hell was she? Did they have neighbors? "Help! Help!" Light drops of rain began falling from the sky, pelting her scalp. The cold air made her shiver. Freezing, she took off running into the woods.

Sprinting through the dense forestry, Taylor's bare feet froze from the cold muddy ground. Ragged breaths escaped her. Running for her life, Taylor's lungs constricted and expanded. Clueless to her surroundings, the navy dress she wore snagged on a branch, ripping the thin material. Her stomach balled, and cramped, and ached. Felt like the baby's head was pressing on her vagina. *Oh God. Guide me in the right direction. Lead me Lord. Lead me.*

The light drizzles of rain turned to fat droplets, pounded Taylor's head. Her contractions grew closer and closer, slowing Taylor's feat to escape. Barely able to withstand the sharp pain, she became lightheaded. Nauseated, vomit threatened to escape her.

"Taylor!" Kelvin's voice resounded through the woods. "I'm going to kill you!"

Suddenly, a gun shot rang out.

I got to keep running. Keep going. Oh God. Scurrying as fast as she could, white sheets of rain drenched her. Taylor glanced back over her shoulder, and tripped over a thick log. Screaming, she fell flat on her face in a pile of grimy mud. Sharp pains coursed through her belly as her face lay smothered in the wet soil.

Pressing her hands into the damp earth, Taylor rolled over to her back. Rain pelted hard on her face. Neck. Body. Her stomach burned like fire. Water gushed from her entrance. "Aaahhh!" Taylor cried. Looking up at the sky, she parted her thighs. She felt the baby's head slipping from her entrance. "Aaahhh!"

Kelvin burst from behind a thick oak with a riffle in his hands. "There you are!" Aiming the riffle at her, he bustled over to where she lay on the ground. Pointing the gun at her face, his lips twisted with anger. "I should kill you!"

Eyeing the barrel of the black weapon, Taylor's head motioned side to side as the pain overtook her young body. "Please, help me. The baby's coming." Her body stiffened. She leapt up and pushed.

"Agggh! The head! The head's coming!" Writhing in severe pain, Taylor pushed again.

Kelvin dropped the weapon to the ground then plopped down on his knees in front of Taylor. He hiked her dress up to her hips, and looked between her parted thighs. Giving her a hateful stare, he removed her underwear.

Biting her bottom lip, Taylor closed her eyes, and gave one final hard push. The fetus popped from her entrance out into Kelvin's waiting hands, and started screaming.

Out of breath, Taylor's eyes shot straight to the baby's genital. She quickly reached out and touched his penis. *It's a boy. It's a boy.* Rain steadily soaking her, tears drenched down Taylor's quivering cheeks.

Kelvin cradled Taylor's son to his chest, grabbed the rifle from the ground, and then rose to his feet. A satanic glare darkened his eyes. "After what you did to my mother, you can stay out here and rot for all I care." He spit on her before turning on his heels and walking away with her son.

"Give me my baby! Give me my baby!" Taylor cried her heart out as she watched Kelvin disappear beyond the trees with her new born son. "Help! Help!" Overcome with grief, she became weak. Too weak to move. Too weak to speak. Too weak to fight for her life.

Feeling blood pour from her womb, she lay on her back, gazed up at the moon. Rain impounded her face. Cold air froze her arms. Her thighs, and legs. Tears slid from the cracks of her eyes, dripped toward her ears. *I'm dying.* Although her life was over, at least she fought till the end. At least she didn't die inside Mildred's house. And at least she finally got to inhale the outdoor air. But more than anything, at least she got to have a fine baby boy from a fine young man like Zeke—Zeke Balfour. Her heart and soul. Her everything.

Cold chills spread through Taylor's bones. Shivering, she slid her hand into her dress pocket, and pulled out the ring that Zeke had given her seven months ago. Barely able to move, Taylor slid the silver ring on her wedding finger, and closed her eyes.

The lovely words Zeke had said to her on the day he'd given her the promise ring while inside the treehouse sailed into Taylor's mind. Zeke had said, "Taylor Spelling...I promise to always be good to you, my love. I promise to love you now. Forever...and ever."

The hard rain eased up, turned back to light drizzles. Taylor's eyes drifted closed. Life slowly slipped from Taylor's body as her breathing slowed. *I love you momma. I love you, Zeke. I love you so much, my baby boy. My darling son.*

"Roofroof. Roofroofroof." Loud barks emanated from a wild dog. Terrified the dog would eat her alive, fear rushed Taylor.

"Butch get back here!" Hearing the sound of a man's voice and a loud barking dog, Taylor prayed hard inside her head that help had finally arrived. That the dog wasn't alone and had an owner. *Help. I'm over here. I'm over here. God, send him this way. I'm over here.*

Shoes squished the leaves on the ground then came to an abrupt stop. The man's sharp gasp resonated in her ears. "Dear God! I knew I heard something!" A hard hand touched the side of her face. *Patpatpat.* "Wake up." Taylor felt two fingers press into her neck near her jugular vein, then she felt her body lifting. "Hang in there little girl. Help is here." At the sound of the man's strong voice, Taylor forced her eyes open to find a Caucasian man with a thick mustache and beard toting her. Despair shown in the man's blue eyes. "Who did this to you? What's your name?" Holding her tight in his strong arms, he darted through the woods. Vapor puffed like smoke from his nose and opened mouth.

Saturated in blood, Taylor parted her lips. "My name is Tay ...
Tay ... Taylor Spelling. Kelvin...took...my baby," she whispered,
then rolled her eyes closed.

"Don't you die on me!" The Caucasian man shouted.

Chapter Five

Oxford, England

CLOTHED IN A HOODIE AND a pair of sweat pants, Zeke strapped his athletic sports bag over his shoulder, and hiked up the steps of his dormitory at the University of Oxford. Grasping the doorknob to his building, sweat piped from his pores from the strenuous workout he'd had moments ago inside the gym on campus. Exercising and getting fit for football season challenged him, and he loved every minute of it. For starters, it relieved stress. Kept his mind occupied. Temporarily kept his mind off Taylor.

It wasn't that he wanted to forget Taylor. Because he couldn't forget Taylor Spelling even if he tried. It just hurt so bad to remember the day she'd been kidnapped. Hurt so bad to relive the pain. He'd never accept she may never come back to him. Never accept that he'd never hold her again. Or kiss her again. Or never get the chance to hold his baby in his arms. *Fuck. Life isn't fair.*

Walking down the hallway towards his dorm room, Zeke's heart squeezed at the remembrance of the last day he'd made sweet love to his girl, Taylor. He'd built a treehouse for her so they'd have somewhere to go when they needed some privacy, and some time alone in.

On that particular day, he'd even given her a promise ring, too. The look in her eyes had been one of pure joy. While many may thought his love for Taylor had been puppy love, it'd been the real thing. He still loved her with all his heart. His soul. His everything thing. And he'd do anything to have Taylor back in his life again. Anything. *God, I hope Taylor and my baby isn't dead. Please send them back to me. Taylor Spelling is the only girl I'll ever love.*

Heading down the hallway towards his dorm room, Zeke waved at a guy named Thomas, then rounded the corner. Still depressed about Taylor, his eyes got moist as he fought to push the ugly remembrance from his brain. Standing at the door of his dorm room, he wiped the tear from his eye, twisted the doorknob, and entered.

His roommate, Brad, sat at the desk looking at the computer. Fingers rasping over the keyboard, Brad glanced back over his shoulder to look at him then stopped typing. "What's up?" Brad swiveled the chair toward Zeke, crossed his legs at the ankles, then steepled his hands to the back of his head.

Zeke tossed his backpack on his twin side bed against the wall to his right. "I'm dreading my Business exam tomorrow. Dr. Webber's tests are tortuous. No matter how hard you study, man, he makes it damn near impossible to pass his tests." Zeke plopped down on the mattress, rolled his hoodie from his head, then began untying his sneakers.

"So I've heard." Brad hit the power button on the computer turning it off then stood. "I'm going to a party tonight. Want to come?"

Inwardly sulking, Zeke shook his head. "Nah man. I'm going to stay here and study for my test."

Brad sighed. "But it's Friday night man! Your test ain't till Monday. Everybody's going to be at the party. Some fine ass girls with big boobs. Lots of alcohol." Brad splashed some cologne on his neck before stalking over to Zeke. "You should come and have some fun for a change," his roommate stated, standing over him.

Brad, on the wild side, didn't understand him in the least bit, Zeke thought, sliding a sweaty sock from his left foot. He wasn't interested in any of the girls on campus, or off for that matter. Only one girl had his heart—Taylor. In his mind it'd always be that way, too. *I wonder if Taylor had a boy or a girl. Do I have a son? Or do I have a daughter?*

Zeke glanced up at Brad to meet his daunting stare. "What?" Zeke shrugged. "I'm not going. You should know by now that I'm not into partying, man."

Brad rolled his eyes toward the ceiling. "It's her again, isn't it?"

"What are you talking about?" Zeke asked, but already knew.

Brad's eyebrows slanted into a frown. "Taylor. The kidnapped girl. You need to get over her. Get on with your life."

A cold, congested ache formed in Zeke's chest. "I am getting on with my life. I'm here at one of the finest universities in the world, studying Finance. Making new friends, playing football. Just because I don't like partying doesn't mean I'm not having fun. Okay?"

Brad threw his hands up in the air. "But you haven't even had any pussy since you've been here. Girls are all over you, dude. Your father is one of the wealthiest men in the world. Owning hotels and shit. With your kind of money you can have all the pussy you want. But all you do is study. Study. Study. Study."

Tired of Brad's constant blabbing about his sex life or their lack of, Zeke stood. "And I'm fine with that. Getting laid doesn't mean squat if it isn't with the right girl. There's only one girl for me." *Taylor.*

"Maaannn Taylor's dead!"

Rage flooded Zeke's bones. He fisted Brad's shirt, drew back his fist, and barked, "Say it again! If you do, I'm going to smash your fucking face in! Taylor is not dead! Do you understand?! She's not dead! She's alive!"

Brad positioned his hands over his face. "Calm down. Damn man, I'm sorry. You ain't got to get all sensitive."

Zeke shoved Brad, causing him to stumble backwards. "You better not ever say that Taylor's dead again. She's alive. Her and my baby are alive. And I'm going to find them one day." Zeke struggled to tamp down his boiling anger.

Brad snatched his wallet from the desk against the window, stuffed it in his back jean pocket, and made his way toward the door. "Again, no harm intended. Sorry," Brad uttered, closing the door behind himself.

At the sound of the door clicking close, Zeke fell back on the mattress to his back. Glancing up at the ceiling, his head ached at the temples. Smelling musk emit from his armpits, he pulled his cell from the pocket of his sweats, and dialed.

On the third ring Katherine answered. "Hello."

"Hi, Katherine. Is my father home?"

"I guess you're just going to insist on calling me Katherine instead of mother, huh?" Uncomfortable, Zeke didn't respond. "Suit yourself. No. You father isn't home. As always, he's at the hotel working. And to answer your question. No. There hasn't been any word on Taylor. If we hear anything, we'll make sure to call you. I promise, you'll be the first to know."

Zeke sighed. "Thank you, Katherine. Please let my father know I called."

"I will, Zeke. Good night."

"Good night, Katherine." Zeke ended the phone call. Still laying on his back, he reached inside his pillow case, and pulled out a picture of Taylor. She'd given him this picture the last time they'd been together in the woods. Glancing at the photo of Taylor, a smile ruffled his lips.

Taylor's pecan colored skin glowed on her face in the photo. Caramel brown eyes, her brown, curly hair hung past her shoulders. *Jeez, she's so beautiful. Wife material. When I find you Taylor, I'm going to marry you right away. Provide a good home for you and our baby.*

Grieving, Zeke kissed the picture of Taylor. Wishing she was at Oxford with him, he placed the photo over his heart area, and prayed for God to please send her and their child back to him. Mourning the loss of the only girl he'd probably ever love, his lids drifted closed, and he fell into a deep slumber.

The full moon glistened in night sky. Hound dogs sniffed the ground. Bats flew overhead, all throughout the forest. Sticks broke beneath Zeke's shoes as he along with his father, and his brothers, and Taylor's mother, and people from all over the world searched for his girlfriend three days after she'd went missing from Hilton Head Island.

"Taylor. Taylor," Zeke muttered beneath his breath, inwardly dying inside. Never in a million years could he have predicted something so horrifying as this.

"Don't you think it's time we get home?" Katherine asked.

"No," Zeke responded.

Katherine sighed. "We searched this area already haven't we?"

Zeke paused in his tracks and gave Katherine a disgraceful look. "Look Katherine. If you're tired of looking for Taylor, then just leave."

Katherine released a frustrating sigh. "I never said I was tired of looking for Taylor, Zeke."

"You don't have to say it for me to feel it." Zeke snapped.

Katherine shook her head. "Aren't you ever going to forgive me for what I said? I've apologized a million times for suggesting she have an abortion—"

Colton's finger flew to his lips silencing Katherine. "Not here, Katherine. You should've never suggested such a thing in the first place. Anyhow, please don't rehash that here. In front of all these concerned people. In fact, don't ever bring it up again. Now let's get a move on. There's work to be done. Taylor is depending on us to find her."

"Over here! Over here!" A policeman shouted.

Zeke's stride picked up as he walked in a hurry toward the shouting police officer. "What is it?" Zeke asked, coming to a stop in front of several officers.

Clad in a navy blue uniform, one of the officers gripped young Zeke's shoulders. "You don't want to see this, Zeke," the officer stated.

Bracing himself for the worst, Zeke inhaled deeply. "Yes ... I...do." With his family, friends, and searchers standing behind him, the officer stepped to the side. Heart pounding in his chest, Zeke slowly stalked toward the white sheet laying on the ground.

Breathing increasing, Zeke knelt beside the white sheet. Clenching the ends of the fabric, he rolled the fabric downward. Zeke gasped. Breath left his body.

Taylor lay dead on the ground on top of scattered leaves and grimy dirt. Crying his eyes out, Zeke gathered Taylor in his arms. Someone had killed her. Someone had murdered her and his baby. Holding his dead, pregnant girlfriend to his chest, he kissed her forehead, and suddenly, her eyes shot open.

Zeke bolted up in his bed. His pulse beat sporadically at the base of his throat. Sweating profusely, he glanced around his dorm room. *Jesus Christ!* Thank God, it was just a stupid nightmare.

Dread ripped Zeke's heart to tiny little pieces. He lifted the picture of Taylor from his chest, held it over his eyes. Using his index finger, he traced the outline of her beautiful brown face. "I'm going to find you and our baby, Taylor. I promise." He kissed the photo. Rolling to his side, he slid the picture back into his pillowcase.

As Zeke headed down the hallway towards the bathroom to take a very much needed shower, knots pained his shoulders. *I'm going to hire a private investigator to help me find her. Yeah, that's what I'll do.*

Chapter Six

Hilton Head Island

KATHERINE BALFOUR STOOD IN FRONT of the mirror inside her luxurious bathroom brushing her long red hair. Thinking about her stepson Zeke, her expression grew taut and derisive. *Oh Zeke. Spoiled ungrateful, Zeke.*

Zeke had been given everything he'd ever wanted since the day he'd been born. Never having to work hard for anything, her husband Colton cherished the ground Zeke walked on. Colton acted as if Zeke could never do any wrong. However, when it came to her sons—Bane and Antonio—all Colton did was complain.

Colton constantly complained about how her sons were too lazy. Too irresponsible. Just the other day, he'd reminded them of how neither of them had gone to college after graduating from high school. Why in the hell would they go to college when they were already wealthy? Not to mention, their father was a freaking billionaire. Her sons didn't need money that was for sure.

With her hair looking straight and silky, Katherine lay the brush on the counter. Hefting the toothbrush in one hand, she lathered it with toothpaste with the other, and began brushing her teeth.

So what Zeke had been the only son out of three to go to college? That didn't mean Zeke was any better than her own children. Although Zeke had graduated from high school with a four-point-nine grade point average, he wasn't any smarter than her grown sons Antonio and Bane. The children she'd pushed from her body. Her own flesh and blood. *I was a fool for letting Colton talk me into taking Zeke into my home. Every time I look at him I'm reminded of Colton's ugly affair with Bridget. Well, Zeke will never get his hands on the fortune that my sons deserve. Never.*

Katherine knew she'd been a damn fool to take Zeke into her home after his mother Bridget had died. Considering Zeke's mother had had an affair with her husband, Katherine felt she didn't owe Zeke a thing. She didn't owe him love. Damn sure didn't owe the bastard any money. She owed spoiled Zeke nothing. Zilt. Zero.

Back when Bridget was alive, had she known the little bastard Zeke would end up living with her perhaps, just perhaps, she would've never killed Zeke's mother.

Katherine rinsed her mouth, gargled it with Scope, then wiped her mouth with a white washcloth. Breath minty fresh, she stared at her reflection in the mirror. "Messing around with my husband and getting pregnant from him, Bridget deserved to die. I'm glad I killed her," she mumbled.

A wicked smile tilted Katherine's lips. She hefted the bottle of expensive perfume from the counter and sprayed her neck. Wearing a red, long silk nightgown, she strolled out of the bathroom, and into her luxurious bedroom. Standing beside her king size bed with a diamond headboard, she turned back the silky comforter, and climbed on top of the mattress.

She hefted the remote from the pillow and clicked on the television. Flipping through the stations, sexual desire for Colton zapped through Katherine's veins. Aroused, her clitoris tingled. Shaking her head, she lowered the remote back to the pillow that

Colton slept on. "All he does is work, work. Work. It'd be nice if he came home and made love to me sometimes. Hell, for all I know he may be impotent." Katherine shrugged. Thinking about how she lived in one of the finest subdivisions in Hilton Head Island, her eyes roamed over her spacious master suite made for a Queen.

Married to a very wealthy man, living in a twenty-five thousand square foot home, and driving a Mercedes, she definitely didn't have anything to complain about. "Well, at least I'll get Colton's money when he dies. I may not be getting any sex, but I'm damn sure going to get every single dime he has after he's dead and gone."

Wishing Colton would come home and make love to her for once in his boring life, Katherine pulled the string on the lamp, the room darkened. Growing hornier by the second, she slid beneath the covers, closed her eyes, and tried to fall asleep. The light on the television dimmed the room.

"Breaking news. Breaking news." The news anchor voice caused Katherine's eyes to open. Glancing up at the ceiling, Katherine loved the way the six hundred and fifty thread count linen made by Martha Stewart felt against her skin. "Good evening," the reporter said. "I interrupt your program to bring you some astonishing news. A missing girl has been found."

Shocked, Katherine leapt up in bed and glued her eyes to the television. *This can't be. This can't be.* The news reporter continued. "At the present time the girl has been identified as seventeen-year-old Taylor Spelling. Taylor's been missing for seven months now. According to our sources, it's been reported that a man walking his dog through the woods in Walterboro South Carolina found her. She's alive. I tell you what a happy ending to a sad, disturbing story. I'm Shelly Cooper with WNXB—"

Panicky, Katherine flung the covers off her legs, and hopped out of bed. Chewing her thumb nail, she nervously paced back and forth. *Taylor is alive. She got away. This has to be a mistake. Just has to be.* "How did this happen? How?"

Scared about what she'd done, Katherine hastened over to the other side of her bedroom, pulled open the doors to her walk in closet, and got dressed in a hurry. *If you want something done right, I guess you have to do it yourself. Damn.* Horrified that someone may find out her secret involving Taylor, she snatched her purse off the nightstand, grabbed her keys. Katherine fled from her home like a thief in the night to go see the one person that may just have destroyed her life.

TWO DAYS LATER, CLAD IN an elegant emerald dress, Katherine's black high heels clicked against the marble flooring inside her kitchen as she walked toward the window while speaking with her accomplice via telephone. Pressing the phone to her ear, she pulled back the sliding glass door and stepped onto the deck. "Yes, I'm sure. Why do you always question me? I've been nothing but good to you."

"This is not about how good you've been to me. It's about what's right and wrong," Taylor's kidnapper stated.

"Are you going soft on me?"

"No. I want Taylor gone from here just as much as you. However, we have to be smart about this. If anyone finds out what we did to her, our lives will be over. We'd end up in prison. Now. I know that I don't want that. Do you?" She heard a heavy dose of sarcasm in his voice.

Rolling her eye, Katherine said through clenched teeth, "Of course I don't want to go to prison." Looking out at the trees behind her home, the cold outdoors air made her shiver. A family of ducks waddled past her deck then got into the lake. Turning away from the immaculate scenery behind her mansion, she walked back inside the house. "So you'll take care of it. Right?"

"Yes. I'll take care of it."

The last time she'd entrusted her accomplice to take care of things regarding Taylor, he hadn't done exactly as she'd told him. In short, he'd messed up big time. At least in her opinion he had. But considering how much she loved him, she wasn't going to hold his mistakes against him. "Call me when it's done. And——" The doorbell rang interrupting her sentence. "Someone's at the door. I'll call you back."

"Check to see if it's the police." Worry laced his deep voice.

A sliver of panic crept up inside Katherine. "Dear God. Did you do what I told you to do after I came to visit you the other night?"

"Yes. I did. I took care of it."

Katherine took her time walking towards the front door. *Dear Lord. Who's at my door?* "Then why in the hell would you think it's the police?"

He retorted, "I never said I thought it was the police. I just asked that you checked. Now, you need to calm down and trust me. The minute we stop trusting each other, all hell can break loose. You should know by now I'll do anything you tell me to do."

Katherine placed her eyeball over the peephole. Her heart dunked. "My Lord. She finally came."

"Who?"

Katherine inhaled a deep breath then let it ease from her lips. "Taylor."

He grunted. "Taylor! Damn. Remember what we talked about. You've always been good at acting, so pretending to be happy about seeing Taylor should come easy for you. Call me when she leaves."

After Katherine hung up the phone with the one person she loved more than life itself, she placed the phone on the decorative table in the foyer, checked her makeup in the mirror, then pulled open the front door.

When her eyes connected with Taylor's, she gasped. Pretending like she was glad to see Taylor, Katherine parted her lips. "Taylor. I'm so glad to see you. Thank God. Thank God you're alive." Katherine threw her arms about Taylor's shoulders. Then came the tears. Oh how she fake cried. *He's right. I'm a very good actress.*

Taylor's mother, Veronica, stood behind her daughter, rubbing circles on her back. Veronica said softly, "Yes. The good Lord brought my baby back to me. I prayed every day, all day for this." She sniffed. "One day God is going to find my grandson, too."

Like hell he will, Katherine thought, tears slipping from her squeezed eyes. *That baby is far, very far away from here.*

Taylor pried herself away from Katherine's tight embrace. Pity rested in her round squirrel eyes. "Is Zeke here? I need to see him."

Holding the door open, Katherine stepped to the side. "Please. Come in." Taylor walked inside the house first with her mother Veronica following her. "Please, have a seat." Katherine gestured towards the couch by the huge bay window.

Gazing around the house like she'd never seen a mansion before, Taylor's hands fidgeted near her lap. "Zeke. Is he home?"

Shaking her head, Katherine caressed Taylor's arm. "He's not here Taylor. He's in school. College."

Nodding her head, water filled Taylor's eyes. Her eyes left Katherine's face and transferred to her mother. "He's gone. He didn't wait for me to come back."

Veronica swallowed. "Oh baby, don't take it personal. I was with him when he searched for you. The look in his eyes was one of devastation. Staying here after what happened to you, was probably too much for Zeke to bare."

"You're probably right." Taylor returned her gaze back to Katherine. "Can you call him for me? Please? I need to hear his voice."

"Sure. No problem." Katherine hefted the cordless phone from the end table and pretended to dial Zeke, but she'd dialed her own cell instead. Listening to her voice stream through the speaker into her ear, she gave Taylor a sad face. "Hi Zeke. This is Mom. Someone you deeply care about is here to see you. Call me when you get this message. Okay. Love you." She hung up.

Gloom shone in Taylor's brown eyes. She sniffled. "Thanks. When Zeke calls, please tell him I miss him. Please tell him to come home and see me." Looking thin, Taylor stood.

Katherine stood and gently patted Taylor's shoulder. "I will."

Veronica stood and headed towards the front door.

Taylor's shoulders sagged as she walked back towards the front door. Gripping the door knob, she looked sideways at Katherine. "I had a boy. Zeke has a son. We have a son. He was beautiful," she said on a shaky voice.

"Oh Taylor, don't cry." Katherine patted her upper right shoulder. "Like your mother said, the police will find your baby." Katherine had done a lot of pretending in her lifetime, but this was the hardest of all. Harder than she could've ever imagined.

"I'm never going to stop looking for my baby." With her mother by her side, Taylor headed for her mother's car.

Katherine stood in the doorway watching Veronica back her raggedy, beat up Camry out of her driveway. From where she stood she could see Taylor still crying her eyes out while sitting in the front seat. As much as she hated putting Taylor through what she had, she didn't have a choice. If Taylor's son would've been born into the Balfour family, her generous husband would've undoubtedly left Zeke's son in his will. And the last thing she needed was to have to split Colton's fortune with another bastard child. One bastard in the family was enough.

Waving goodbye to Taylor and Veronica, Katherine shut the door. Just then, the phone rang. Hoping it was her accomplice, she spied the caller ID and frowned. "Hello."

"Hi Katherine. It's me, Zeke. Is my father there?" Zeke asked, as he did every other day.

Katherine rolled her eyes. "No, Zeke. He's at work. Like always."

Zeke queried, "Oh. Any word on Taylor?"

"No Zeke. I'm sorry. I haven't heard a thing about Taylor. She's still missing," Katherine lied, all the while wondering who had Zeke's and Taylor's son been sold too.

Chapter Seven

Paris, France

TEN YEARS LATER, TAYLOR SAT on an elegant golden chaise beside the opened window inside her luxurious apartment, holding a hot mug, and peering down at the breathtaking scenery below. White sail boats cruised the glistening river. People walked to and fro along the bustling sidewalk. Athletic cyclist sped through the city riding their bicycles. Never in a million years did she think she'd end up in Paris. The way she ended up in Paris still blew her mind till this very day.

Many weeks after an angel by the name of Scott Beringer had found her dying in the woods, she'd returned home to Hilton Head Island only to find out that Zeke had moved on with his life. According to Zeke's stepmother Katherine, Zeke had left the small town, and had moved to England. In hopes that Zeke and her would someday reunite, she'd left all her forwarding information for him with Katherine. Unfortunately, she never heard from him.

Taylor tried to keep the memories of Zeke and her pure and unsullied. *Guess he went on with his life. Probably met another girl while attending college.*

Bright sunrays streamed through the opened window, heating Taylor's face. She released a heartfelt sigh. She'd waited weeks and weeks and weeks for Zeke to call her and to come home, but he never did. She'd also waited weeks, months, and years for the police to find her son, and unfortunately that day never came either.

Devastated, Taylor had become severely depressed. She'd lost so much weight until she'd turned bone thin. Looked like a bag of bones. While many people, including her, found her weight loss unattractive, someone had found it beautiful. Strikingly beautiful.

While roaming the shopping mall in Hilton Head one day with her mother, a gentleman had come up to her, and told her that he was a talent scout looking for models. Because of what'd happened to Taylor, she didn't in the least bit trust the supposedly talent scout. And she definitely didn't believe someone that looked like her could actually become a model back then. Oh heck, no.

Well, to her surprise, the talent scout, Mr. Pierre de Givenchy, had invited her along with her mother to his top notch Agency located in Paris. After showing Taylor and Veronica around and introducing them to some of the most elite people in the fashion industry, Pierre de Givenchy made Taylor an offer she couldn't refuse. She'd signed with Pierre's multimillion dollar talent agency right away.

Like magic, modeling jobs by the dozens came Taylor's way. One after the other, after the other. To her blessing, Taylor now lived the life of a well-respected, wealthy model. She made so much money until it was impossible to spend it all. But her mother, Veronica, on the other hand, tried to spend every single dime she gave her. Thinking about her mother's wild spending excursions and her own blessings, Taylor smiled.

Even at the age of twenty-seven the people in the fashion industry here in Paris treated her like royalty. Like a Princess.

Looked at her like she was the most beautiful woman in the world. Gave her whatever she wanted, and things she didn't need.

Yet with all the money and the success Taylor had, she still felt empty inside. Had a hole in her heart. Felt like something was missing from her life. Her emptiness had nothing to with not having a man. Because if she wanted one, she could definitely have one. With very few friends, from time to time she dated. But every time she got close to having sex with a man, she couldn't go all the way. Before she knew it, all of her relationships ended because of her inability to give herself completely. Not just because of the sex though, she struggled with giving in to her emotions as well.

Zeke's name echoed in the black stillness of Taylor's mind. *The only man for me probably was Zeke. A girl only gets love like that once in her lifetime. What is your life like now, Zeke? I'm sure he's happily married with three kids or more by now.*

Reminiscing about Zeke, an image of what her ten year old son she'd named Zavier may look like came to Taylor's mind's eye. *Oh Zavier, who has you? I'm sure my little Zavier looks just like his father Zeke, only light brown complexioned. Probably has Zeke's hair texture, and my eye color.*

Gazing out the window, Taylor brought the hot cup of peach tea to her mouth, and sipped. Longing for the return of her son, she savored the warm beverage as it glided down her throat. A cool breezed rolled off the river across the street, sailed through the window, and prickled her scalp.

Just as she rose from the chaise, her cell buzzed on her fancy dresser inside her bedroom. Sipping from the mug, she crossed the room to answer her phone. She glanced at herself in the mirror before lifting the phone to her ear. God she could use a facial. "Hello."

"You're up early I see, honey. Good. Good. I have some great news for you." Pierre's chipper French accent immediately perked up Taylor's spirit.

Walking back toward the window, Taylor smiled. "I'm always up early Pierre, you know that."

"True. True." Pierre clucked his tongue. "I tell you this darn dog I have is becoming a nuisance. Prissy, stop hunching on my leg! Horny dog. Anyway, what was I saying?"

Giggling, Taylor flopped down back on the chaise lounge. Elbow perched on the window sill, she extended her legs in front of her, crossed them at the ankles. "You had some—"

"Oh yeah. Revlon called and they want to book you for a hair commercial. There's only one problem, though."

"Uh-oh. What?"

Pierre cleared his throat. "They want you to color your hair this god awful red."

A picture of Zeke's red head stepmother, Katherine, popped inside Taylor's head. "Red? Not red, Pierre. No."

"Honey, what do you mean, no?"

Having red hair would remind her every second of the day of Katherine. "I mean no I'm not doing it. I've reach a point in my career to where I'm only taking on jobs that makes me happy. And coloring my hair bright red won't make me happy. It'd only make me look like—"

"A damn fool! I agree, honey. Okay. I'll let them know. Tootles." Without further speaking, Pierre clicked her off.

Coloring my hair red, like hell I'm doing that. A few moments later, Pierre called her again. "Yes Pierre," she answered after spying the caller ID.

Pierre stated, "I spoke with the casting director at Revlon and you're not going to believe how much they offered to pay you if you agree to do the commercial shoot!"

"How much?"

"Three hundred and fifty thousand dollars." Pierre's voice pitched.

"Umm. For that amount of money, I think the red will look great!"

Pierre light chuckles came through the phone. "Me too, honey. Me too."

Hilton Head Island

ZEKE PUSHED THROUGH THE GLASS door of Balfour Resort & Hotel located on the ocean with a huge frown on his face. Wondering why in the hell his father had called a mandatory meeting at the last minute so late in the evening, Zeke stalked past the concierge desk, and headed for the elevator. While he loved working for his father at the hotel, and loved Colton with all his heart, he just wished his workaholic father hadn't interrupted him this evening, he thought, pushing the button to the elevator.

As Zeke waited for the elevator to arrive, his mind traveled back to what he'd been doing moments prior to his father calling him. He'd been at the group care facility with Braylon and Richmond tutoring under privilege boys. Giving back to his community meant so much to him, and there his father had to go and interrupt it. The gold elevator doors swished open and Zeke stepped inside. "Interrupting my pastime, this better be good, father."

A few seconds later Zeke stepped off the elevator and headed toward the conference room at the end of the hallway. Photos of his ancestors clung to the wall to his left. To his right, expensive sculptures aligned the walls. For their protection only certain people had access to the twenty fifth floor where the executive offices and boardrooms were located.

Coming to the end of the hallway, Zeke stopped when he reached the closed door to the conference room. Colton held only important meetings in this room. Knowing this, and considering the urgency that'd been in his father's voice a little while ago, curiosity piqued Zeke's interest. Zeke turned the doorknob to the big spacious room and pressed the door wide open.

Katherine, Bane, and Antonio were all present inside the conference room overlooking the ocean. Zeke's father, Colton, sat at the head of the table, and Katherine sat beside him. Bane sat to his father's left while Antonio sat to his right.

Antonio brought his watch up to his face. "About time you get here," he spat, giving Zeke an unjust look.

Ignore foolish Antonio. "I got here as fast as I could," Zeke remarked, feeling as if he shouldn't have to explain himself. *Some of us have important things to do for our communities after work.*

"Close the door," Colton ordered. Zeke closed the door then plopped down in the leather seat next to Bane. Colton's serious eyes grazed over Katherine's face first, then Antonio's, then Banes, and lastly Zeke's. Colton cleared his throat. "Thank you all for coming on such short notice. As soon as—"

The door flung open and his father's attorney, Gar Grainger, stormed in. "Got stuck in traffic. Sorry." Gar plopped down in the vacant seat next to Zeke.

Colton continued. "As I was saying before Gar came in. Thank you all for coming this evening, especially on such short notice. The reason I called you here is because there's something important I have to tell you. What I have to tell you will affect each and every one of you."

Katherine cupped Colton's hands. "Why do I have the feeling I'm not going to like this, Colton?"

Colton nodded. "You're right, Katherine. You're probably not going to like what I have to say. In fact, there may be several of you in this room that may not like what I have to say. But just know this...my decision has been made. And it's final. There's nothing no one can do to get me to change my mind. So don't even try." His deep firm made everyone sit up straight and take notice.

Katherine caressed the back of Colton's hand. "What's going Colton?"

Colton's brown eyes grew darker, and sad. "I've been diagnosed with prostate cancer."

Jesus Christ. Cancer? Zeke felt like someone had stabbed him in the heart with a sharp blade. Keeping his emotions intact, he swallowed. He inwardly prayed for his father.

Katherine's jaws dropped and a loud gasp flew out. "Cancer! You dying?!"

Colton shook his head. "Calm down, Katherine. Don't go over reacting on me."

Tears shot to Katherine's eyes. "Oh my God, Colton. Are the doctors sure? What does this mean?"

Colton explained, "It means, I'll be undergoing extensive medical care, and will be unable to work for a while. As of tonight, I'm relinquishing my duties, and have no idea when I'll be returning to Balfour Enterprises."

Zeke looked across the table at his reddish-blonde hair brother Antonio. A huge smirk displayed on Antonio's face. His blue eyes were lit up. *It's going to be hell working for Antonio,* Zeke thought, knowing Colton would probably make Antonio in charge. Antonio was the oldest after all. However, working for Antonio's arrogant ass would be downright hard. Almost impossible.

Colton continued. "That being said, I need someone I can trust to take over Balfour Enterprises while I'm out. Someone reliable. Someone that works their ass off just like me. Therefore, I've decided to make Zeke the new CEO of Balfour Resort & Hotels." Colton looked at Zeke. His lips turned upward into a smile.

SABRINA SIMS MCAFEE

Astounded, Zeke's eyes widened. "Whoa. Whoa."

"This is fucking absurd!" Obviously angry, Antonio jumped up from his seat. "I'm the oldest, and I should be in charge."

Colton glanced up at Antonio and shook his head. "Please don't take this personal, Antonio. I think the best of all my children. But Zeke, he's a lot like me. He'll run the company the way I run it. And he—"

Anger blazed Antonio's blue eyes. "Zeke's always been your favorite son! And I want to know why? Do you feel sorry for Zeke because his mother was murdered when he was just a kid? Or do you favor him because you feel guilty for cheating on Katherine, and bringing a bastard into our home?!"

Colton leapt to his feet and leaned into the table. He growled. "You watch your got damn mouth Antonio! I don't care how mad you are, Zeke is still your brother, and I'm still your father." Colton's jaws shook. "You will not speak to me in that nasty tone, son." Colton pointed at Antonio's chair. "Now, please. Sit back down so we can finish the meeting in a pleasant tone."

Muscles flickered in Antonio's jaw muscles. "How could you do this to me, father? How?" Breathing harshly, Antonio balled his fists, then stormed out of the room.

Colton barked, "Don't you walk out of here. I'm not done!"

Tears dripped from Katherine's eyes. "Antonio feels betrayed. I don't blame him. He's the oldest, Colton. The oldest. If anyone is going to run the company and handle all that money, it should be your oldest son."

Zeke's muscles tensed beneath his collared dress shirt. *God, please heal my father,* he thought, sitting quietly. Trying to absorb everything going on around him.

Bane shook his head negatively. "Mom, who runs the company should be the least of any of our worries. Our main concern should be daddy's health." Keeping a stern face, Bane looked at his father.

62

"I'm sorry to hear about your health. Please let me know how I can be of any help, dad."

Hearing his father had cancer, sadness filled Zeke's heart. Determined to remain positive, he shifted in his seat, and gazed Colton's sullen eyes. "Same here. When's your next appointment? I want to go with you."

Colton nodded at the attorney Gar. "Paperwork, please." Gar reached inside his briefcase, extracted some papers, and extended them to Colton. "The only thing I need for you two to do is see to it that Balfour Enterprises keeps thriving. Zeke you will run this company while I'm away. If he accepts, Antonio will be second in charge. This is the contract." Clenching the contract in his hands, Colton's eyes roamed up and down the extensive lettering. He then laid the contract on the table, retrieved an ink pen from his shirt pocket, and then scribed his name on the dotted line. A smile developed on Colton's face as he slid the contract towards Zeke. "You've worked hard, Zeke. You deserve to run Balfour Enterprises. Sign the contract and make it official, my son."

Zeke lifted the contract in his hands. "Are you sure?"

Colton nodded. "I wouldn't be doing this if I weren't sure."

A sense of achievement sparked inside Zeke as he wrote his signature on the dotted line. "Thanks for believing in me," he said, sliding the signed contract back towards Colton.

Colton signed his name beneath Zeke's, and now the contract was signed and sealed. He then handed it to Gar. "Here Gar. It's official. Zeke is the new CEO of Balfour Enterprises."

Gar took the contract, overlooked it, and shook Zeke's hand. "Congratulations, Zeke."

Katherine grabbed a tissue from her purse, dabbed the corners of her eyes. "I can't help wondering if this is a mistake. Antonio is your first born, Colton. Your first born. Antonio should be the CEO, not Zeke," Katherine whinned.

Seemingly irritated, the line of Colton's mouth tightened a fraction more. "Just because Antonio is my first born, it doesn't mean he's equipped with the right skills to run a billion dollar organization. From my perspective, Antonio has demonstrated that he's an irresponsible, pompous ass." Putting a hand to her chest, Katherine gasped. "He's never worked hard for a thing in his life. Everything Antonio has have been given to him and not earned. You can thank yourself for his behavior. You've spoiled him rotten, Katherine. Zeke and Bane on the other hand, they work hard. Put in way more hours than Antonio. They speak with the customers. Keep the finances in order. The renovations. From the maids and butlers all the way to the executives, Zeke gets shit done. Conversation over."

Katherine's face contorted then turned bright red. She hopped from her seat, snatched her purse from the chair next to her, and ran out of the office.

Colton cleared his throat. His lips turned up into a smile as he extended his hand toward Zeke. "Congratulations on your new position at Balfour Enterprises, my son."

Zeke gripped his father's hand and gave him a firm shake. "Thanks Dad. I'm going to make you proud."

Colton released Zeke's palm. "You already have. The first thing I need for you to do though, is go to Paris."

Surprised, Zeke shifted in his chair. "Paris? We don't have any business in Paris. So why there?"

Colton clasped his hands. "We don't have any business there yet. One of your grandfather's greatest wishes was to someday build a hotel in Paris. Before I die, I want you to make your grandfather's greatest wish come true. Have a hotel built in Paris. And do it quick. I want to see it done before I leave this earth, Zeke."

Is this cancer worse than he's telling us? Zeke wondered, the pit of his stomach churning with apprehension. Zeke wanted to ask his father if the cancer had spread, but decided the time to inquire about it was all wrong. "You're going to live a long time. However, your wish is my command. I'll to Paris and look for sites to build upon next week."

Colton shook his head. "Why put off next week what you can do tomorrow?"

Knowing this was important to his father, Zeke agreed. "I'll make some contacts with some realtors in Paris tonight. If anything sounds promising, I'll leave for Paris first thing in the morning."

Colton and Zeke stood at the same time. Colton threw his arms about his son's shoulders, and gave him a big bear pat on his back. Clutching his shoulders, his father released him. His eyes showed proudness. "I love you, Zeke. Your mother, Bridget, would be so proud of you. Now go make your calls."

"Thanks again, dad. Good night." Smiling, Zeke turned on his heels, and stalked out the conference room. Already imaging how he wanted the hotel in Paris to be built, he smiled harder. The hotel was going to be one of the tallest and grandest in the whole entire world.

Feeling good about his father's decision to make him CEO of Balfour enterprises, Zeke pushed the elevator button. The golden doors slid open, Zeke stepped inside. With his back to the wall, the door glided closed. *Look out Paris. Here I come.*

Chapter Eight

Paris, France
Three Days Later

PEOPLE PACKED THE INSIDE OF the Parisian eatery, Ladurée Bakery & Coffee shop. The bakery looked more like an elite jewelry store instead of a bakery. Chandeliers hung from the ceiling. Stainless steel chairs accompanied the circular glass tables. Diamonds outlined the glass displays containing the beautiful assorted pastries and desserts.

Sitting at the circular glass table by the window across from Pierre, Taylor brought her hot cup of coffee to her lips, and sipped. Gazing at the delicious pastries inside the glass display, Taylor's stomach growled. Seasonal winter pastries lined the shelves displaying like fine works of art. Deciding she'd better past on the red velvet cupcake that kept calling her name, she gazed back at Pierre.

Holding a pamplemousse macron to his lips, Pierre tore his gaze from the crowded sidewalk filled with people, looked at Taylor, and bit into his parisian pastry. "Mmmp. This is so delicious," Pierre spoke around his food. "Want a bite?"

Licking her lips, Taylor nodded. Pierre handed her his tasty dessert and she took a big bite. Always feeling like she had to watch her figure because of her career, she devoured the tasty treat. "Oh my God. This is sooo good, Pierre."

"I know. Now give it back, honey." Pierre held out his hand, and Taylor handed the pastry back to him. Although Pierre was Taylor's talent agent, he was also her good friend. "So. Are you ready to dye your hair red, honey?" He chuckled.

"For three hundred and fifty thousand dollars, I sure am." Holding the hot mug to her lips, the delightful aroma of the gourmet coffee wafted up her nose. Curling her lips around the rim of the mug, she sipped the warm vanilla, sweet orange coffee. *Mmm, Ladurée's gourmet coffee is the best in town.*

"Good. This morning I got two calls requesting your services. One was for a toothpaste commercial and the other was for a hotel billboard. Apparently, some new hotel is being built here, and they're looking for some models. Honey, I tell you...you're hot stuff."

Taylor blushed. "Thanks Pierre. For everything. If it weren't for you, I wouldn't be where I am today. I love you."

Pierre fanned his face. "Ah. Stop it, honey. You're going to make Pierre cry. And Pierre hates crying. What can I say, I love you too, honey. Now let's discuss this toothpaste commercial because that's coming up real soon."

When Pierre had mentioned hotel, Taylor couldn't help but think of Zeke's father, Mr. Colton Balfour's hotel in Hilton Head Island. Although she'd been very young when she'd lived in Hilton Head Island, she'd known that Zeke's father owned a hotel, and was a very wealthy gentleman. However, it wasn't until she'd gotten older that she realized Zeke's father was a billionaire. "When are they looking to do the billboard for the hotel?"

Pierre shrugged. "I don't know. I don't have much information on that yet. According to the advertisement agency, they haven't even started building it, so it's still early in the game."

"Oh. Well about this toothpaste commercial. Who's it for?"

"Colgate baby!"

Taylor laughed when she heard the excitement in Pierre's voice.

INSIDE RUE DES ECOLES BREAKFAST eatery, the waitress lowered Zeke's breakfast plate in front of him. "Is there anything else I can get you at this time?" the pretty dark haired, young lady asked.

Zeke shook his head. "No thanks." Smiling, the waitress turned and walked away. Sitting across from the architecture named Francois, Zeke eyed his plentiful breakfast. Eggs, bacon, sausage franks, and French toast covered his dish. "This looks good."

Francois lifted the ceramic cup of hot green tea sprinkled with black pepper to his mouth. "It is good. Wait until you taste the French toast. It just melts in your mouth."

Zeke blessed his food then forked the French toast into his mouth. A buttery sweet maple flavor burst onto his tongue. "This is delicious."

"I come here all the time just for the French toast. Tried to make it myself, but burned the heck out of it." Francois sipped his tea then lowered the cup to his napkin. "Back to what I was saying earlier...as you requested, I sketched the ceiling for the hotel to reflect an ornamental mural. The cartouche is going to look great painted in acrylics with twenty three gold karat leaves."

"I can't wait to see the final designs."

Leaning back in his chair, Francois crossed his legs at the knee. "If you don't mind me saying, normally the CEO isn't as involved with the minor details such as the arts as you. They normally just hire someone to do it for them."

Zeke agreed. "Normally I wouldn't partake in the minute detail such as this either. However, this hotel is very important to my father. It's a representation of my grandfather and his dream for his legacy. That being said, I'm going to be involved in every single part of the building's structure."

Francois curled a finger over his mustache. "Wow. So this building was your grandfather's dream, huh?"

"Yes." Zeke scooped cheesy scrambled eggs onto his fork then held them to his mouth. "I want the hotel building's interior to reflect the women ancestors in the Balfour family." *Although my mother didn't carry the Balfour name. My father loved her as such. So the penthouse suites will reflect her sweet personality.* "And I want the exterior to reflect the Balfour men...strong, determined, passionate, creative, complicated.

"I think I can handle that." Francois stated.

Enjoying his breakfast, Zeke peered out the window next to where he sat. Zeke found the structures of the surrounding buildings in Rue de Rivoli-Le Marais captivating. Like the Hotel de Ville building across the street. Located in the fourth arrondissement, the building held large receptions, housed local city administrators, and the Mayorof Paris. Yes, all of that was interesting, but so were the many details in the structure. *What a beautiful building.*

Arched windows, thick white columns, tall, spacious, refined with light, Hotel de Ville had taken years to build and he saw why. Wanting the new Balfour Hotel in Paris to have detailed structure like the one across the street, Zeke came up with some great ideas. "Francois."

"Yes." Francois uncrossed his legs and leaned into the table.

Zeke's eyes went back to Hotel de Ville across the street. "See how the roof over there have different elevations?"

Francois nodded. "Let me guess, you'd like something like that for the Balfour. I can definitely come up with something like that. I think that's a great idea. If we paint the roof a nice gold and..."

As Zeke sat listening to Francois, a tall beautiful woman wearing a white long coat, gracefully walked past the window along the sidewalk. Zeke's breath caught. His heart lurched as his eyes followed the woman. *Jesus Christ.* From the side, the woman had a striking appearance to Taylor. A much older Taylor, but still Taylor.

"Excuse me!" Zeke leapt from the table, stormed out of the breakfast eatery, and began following the beautiful woman. Slinking in and out of tourist walking along the jammed sidewalk, Zeke kept his eyes trained to the woman's backside.

Wearing a pair of red high heels, the woman eased her hands into the pockets of her white winter coat. The rich brown curly hair parading down her back blew with the wind.

Trying to catch up with the elegant woman, Zeke's heart beat like drums inside his tight chest. *Oh God. Is that Taylor? No. My eyes must've been playing tricks on me.* Wind whipped at Zeke's cheeks. Anxious to catch up with the woman, his heartbeat escalated. Walking faster and faster, in and out of people, he watched the woman make a sharp left at the corner, and disappear. *Damn.*

Desperate to catch up with the woman, Zeke jogged the long length of the sidewalk. When he reached the end, he made a sharp left turn. *Thank God she didn't disappear.* The beautiful, elegant woman's long hair covered the side of her face as she stood at Jaubalet, a custom made jewelry store, peeping at a piece of jewelry through the window. Head almost touching the glass window, she brought her hands up to the sides of her head, covering her face more.

Heart pounding, Zeke took slow purposeful strides towards the woman. Passing chic shops, he swallowed. From the side, the woman looked every bit like Taylor. His high school love. His one and only true love. The love of his life. But because he hadn't seen Taylor in so long, in years, since he was a young boy, he couldn't be sure if it was her or not. *No way in hell it's her.*

Heart about to pop out of his chest, Zeke now towered the woman. With her hands positioned sideways to the sides of her head, she didn't bother looking up at him, she kept looking at the sparkling diamond ring.

"It's a beautiful piece of jewelry isn't it?" Slowly, the woman turned her head, and gazed up at him. Shock coursed through Zeke's veins. His knees buckled. The pecan brown complexion on her face looked like satin. Curly rich brown hair hung over her shoulders. Sensual caramel eyes glowed. If this woman wasn't Taylor, then she damn sure was Taylor's twin. Zeke's slapped hard hands to his chest. "Oh. My. God...Taylor."

Chapter Nine

"TAYLOR," TAYLOR'S NAME ROLLED OFF the handsome tall man's lips standing in front of her like a whisper in the night. Her head tilted back, Taylor's eyes bore into the man's gorgeous tanned face. Strong and muscular looking, dark brown hair grazed his broad shoulders. As he towered her, a misty sheen covered his brown coffee colored eyes. "It's you. It's really you. My sweet, Taylor."

Shock engulfed Taylor. Stole her breath. Water filling her eyes, Taylor stood speechless. Her limbs weakened. Feeling faint, her eyes remained glued to the man. Feeling like she was dreaming, she cupped the sides of her face. "Zeke," she whispered his name. A tear rolled from her left eye.

A strained chuckle erupted from Zeke's lungs. A single tear rolled down his right cheek. "Oh God, Taylor. I found you. I finally found you." Zeke wrapped his arms around Taylor's shoulders, drew her form to him, and held her tight. "This is the happiest day of my life. I've dreamed of this day for so long."

Head to his chest, Taylor closed her eyes, and sank into Zeke's warm embrace. His woodsy cologne traveled up her nose. Memories of the last time she'd seen Zeke came charging into Taylor's head. It'd been right before she'd been kidnapped.

With her arms draped around Zeke's waist, she sobbed. She held him tight. Continued inhaling his woodsy fragrance. Felt the muscles of his rock hard chest pressing against her face. God, she'd waited forever for this day. Thought it'd never happen, and yet, it had. "Oh Zeke. You're here. You're really here." *I've waited forever for you to come back to me.*

"Let me get a good look at you," Zeke said, prying her from his body. Gently cupping the balls of Taylor's shoulders, Zeke's eyes raked up and down her figure covered by the white trench coat.

Zeke gently palmed the back of Taylor's head with one hand, grazed his knuckles over her left tear covered cheek with the other. "You're even more beautiful than I remember. Are you in a hurry? Can we go somewhere and talk?"

This is a miracle. Taylor swiped at the tear rolling down her face. "Sure. I'd like that," she cried, her gaze dropped toward the ground.

Standing on the sidewalk overwhelmed and crying, Zeke put a finger to Taylor's chin, tilted her head back. Gazing lovingly into her weeping eyes, he cupped her face, then dried her tears with the pads of his thumbs. "I'm here now, Taylor. Regardless of what's going on in your life, I'm going to make sure you're always taken care of." He cupped her head.

Shaking her head in his big strong palms, thin trails of snot ran from Taylor's nose. "My apartment is fifteen minutes away from here. We can go talk there. We'll have to catch a taxi."

Zeke and Taylor walked to the corner of the street across from the traffic light. Constantly staring at Taylor, Zeke flagged down a taxi. The taxi rolled up on the curb. Zeke pulled open the rear door for Taylor, and after she climbed in, Zeke did. Mild conversation took place inside the taxi.

Minutes later the taxi pulled up on the curb in front of Taylor's duplex. Zeke reached into his pocket, paid the cab fare, then exited the vehicle. He hurried to the other side of the taxi to pull open the door for her.

Zeke's passionate eyes held her still as he extended his hand towards her. Taylor placed her hand in his, sparks of electricity shot through her arm. Still disbelieving her eyes, she flung her feet to the concrete, and eased out of the cab.

Listening to her heels click against the ivory marble flooring, Taylor waved at the concierge, then began crossing the small courtyard overflowing with live plants inside her duplex. As Taylor and Zeke ascended the spiral staircase toward her luxurious apartment, silence fell upon them. Whether from Zeke's front, or his back or his side, she couldn't stop gawking at him. And he couldn't stop staring at her either.

Wondering if Zeke was married, Taylor stuck the key in the lock of her apartment's front door, and clicked it open. "Welcome to my home," she said, entering.

Zeke stepped inside Taylor's luxurious apartment behind her. "Wow. This is some apartment. You've done quite well for yourself, I see." Zeke stalked over to the tall floor to ceiling window, and drew back the white sheers covering the view. "This is some view."

After taking off her white trench coat and laying it on the sofa, Taylor walked closer to the window and stood behind Zeke. "I love it. Waking up to this view is what have kept me sane for many years. It's so beautiful and peaceful."

Zeke kept his back to her while he absorbed the breathtaking view. Although, she woke up to this view every day, she could never get enough of it. A former mansion, her upscale apartment had dark wooden parquet floors. Tall floor to ceiling windows. High ceilings. Cream colored walls and golden details sculpted by a French noblesse. Located on a quiet side street near Quai d'Orleans, it had stunning views of the left bank, Ile de la Cite, and Notre Dame. "Look at the structure on the Cathedral." Zeke seemed in awe.

Dressed in a black fitted dress, Taylor folded her arms across her breasts. "It's gorgeous. Sometimes I sit here on the window sill and just stare. Dream. And think."

Letting the sheers slipped from his fingers, he turned from the window, and peered down at Taylor. "Do you ever think of me, Taylor?"

Taylor nodded. "I think of you every day, Zeke."

Remorse filled his pupils. "I'm so sorry for what happened to you. It should've been me. If I could go back and trade places with you, I would. I'd take all the pain you endured as my own. Take all the fear. Erase all the horrible images out of your head."

Taylor sniffled. "He was beautiful. Our son was beautiful, Zeke."

Moisture coated Zeke's eyes. "I hired a private investigator a long time ago to look for you and our son. But after years of trying, the investigator quit. I guess I should've hired another one. Anyhow, ever since I've learned about our son, I've thought of him and you every single day."

Taylor's heart squeezed with grief. "Me too. He's alive, Zeke. Our son Zavier is alive."

A smile came on Zeke's face. "Zavier. That's what you call him? I like that name. Zavier Balfour. He's ten now."

"Yes. Ten. Born right after Christmas, I celebrate his birthday every year. Are you married, Zeke? Children? Family?"

"No Taylor, I'm single. And you?"

Relief flooded Taylor's insides. "I'm single, too. I've never been married."

A rush of air expelled from Zeke's lungs as if he was relieved. "Me either. God, you're so beautiful."

Taylor's lips spread into a smile. "Thanks. You're very handsome, Zeke."

Zeke hearty chuckles floated in the air, enticed her female senses. "I don't know about all that. But hey, thanks for the compliment."

For the rest of the day, Zeke and Taylor stayed in her apartment catching up on each other's lives. Sitting beside him on the expensive couch inside her den, she told him all about how she was discovered as a model. Told him about how she'd modeled for Victoria's Secret, Vogue, Channel, and other elite fashion icons.

Zeke shared with Taylor about how he'd come to Paris to build a hotel at his father's request. In honor of his grandfather. Told her about his time at the University of Oxford, and how he'd been a star football player for the prestigious school. He'd said he was honored to be the CEO of Balfour Enterprises. Although his brother Antonio was pissed, Zeke expressed that he couldn't have been more pleased with his father's wise decision.

They'd both shared their dating experiences over the years. They talked about everything, except for how it'd been hell living with mean Mildred and scary Kelvin. Maybe one day she'd give Zeke a detailed breakdown about that, too. But right now, she didn't want to relive the horrible experience. Right now, she wanted to enjoy the moment of reconnecting with the only man she'd ever loved. And from where she sat at this very moment, she'd always love the kind, and powerful—Zeke Balfour.

As they sat on the sofa conversing, a gleam of interest came into Zeke's eyes. "We have so much catching up to do, Taylor. If you let me, I'm going to spend every minute of my awakening hours pampering you. Making up for lost time. Giving you the life that should've been given to you a long time ago."

Taylor desired to lay her head on Zeke's chest, and let him hold her. "But Zeke. We've only come back together a few hours ago. How could you say you want such things already? I'm not the same sixteen year old girl you remember. I've change. And so have you."

"You're right Taylor. You've changed, and so have I. A lot has changed about me. Except for one thing. One very important thing." Peering into her eyes, Zeke tucked a piece of her hair behind her ear. "And that's how much I love you. I've never stopped loving you."

Flattered by Zeke's admission, Taylor cupped his jaw. *This is too good to be true.* "I've never stopped loving you either, Zeke."

Zeke bowed his head and gently lowered his lips to hers. "A man knows when he's met his mate. I met mine when I was eighteen. Unfortunately, she was stolen from me. But now that she's returned to me, I'm never letting her go. Never Taylor. Never."

Desire radiated Zeke's dark eyes. He cupped Taylor's neck, pulled it forward. Heat swooned inside his eyes as he slinked his think pink tongue into her mouth, and kissed her erotically.

The strong hardness of Zeke's lips caused desire to course through Taylor's veins, set her soul on fire. A hoarse moan rattled inside her throat.

Oh God. Tongues curling, his firm lips gliding across hers felt heavenly. *Please stay true to your word, Zeke,* Taylor thought drinking his saliva.

Zeke broke their heated kiss. "For me to find you in Paris of all places is not a coincidence. It's fate. Fate Taylor. Fate. This is God's doing."

"I agree Zeke. God brought us back together. There is no other explanation."

Zeke ran the pad of his thumb over her swollen lips. "Let me spend the night here with you. We don't have to have sex. All I'm asking is that you let me hold you, Taylor. Just let me hold you all night long, baby. Please." Zeke's husky voice enticed Taylor. Sent chills skittering up her spine. Made her hot, and aroused.

"There's nothing I'd like more than for you to hold me. All...night...long." *My Mr. Right is really here. And he still knows how to make everything in my world right.*

"Yes!" Zeke gathered Taylor in his strong arms, cradled her to his muscular chest, and held her so tenderly for the rest of the afternoon, and all through the night. And Taylor Spelling couldn't have been happier.

Chapter Ten

LYING ON HER BACK SLEEPING, Taylor felt something hard nudge into the thin pajama bottoms she wore. Awakening from a mild sleep, her eyes fluttered open to the wonderful feel of Zeke's hard erection pressing into her sheathed buttocks. With her back to Zeke, he threw a heavy arm over her waist, and snuggled his masculine body into her form.

Wrapped in Zeke's strong arms, loving the feel of his thick erection slapped on her clothed behind, tingles twirled the pit of Taylor's stomach. A dull ache settled at her entrance. Her nipples tightened beneath the thin fabric bra she wore. Refraining from making love to Zeke hadn't been a challenge last night. But that was only because he didn't try to have sex with her. If he'd tried to make love to her, there was no telling what might have happened.

Oh my. Who was she kidding? If Zeke would've made a hot lusty move on her, she would've given in to his demands, and made sweet passionate love to him. What woman wouldn't? After all, Zeke had all the qualities any woman could ever want. He was every woman's dream. At least he was her dream. Always had been her dream. Always would be her dream man.

Zeke stirred. "Taylor, are you awake?"

With all that hard manhood pressed into her behind, of course she was awake. "Yes. I'm awake."

Zeke palmed her shoulder and gestured for Taylor to face him. *Beautiful.* Zeke was simply a beautiful man.

When Zeke caressed the side of Taylor's face, she felt an eager affection coming from him. "How'd you sleep last night?" he asked, a sense of longing in his voice.

"Wonderful. I haven't slept that well in years." *Probably never.* Having Zeke sleep next to her last night had provided her with comfort. Security. Warmth and love. Made her hopeful about her future. Their future. Zeke had said on yesterday that he was there to stay, and for some reason, Taylor believed him.

"What about you? How did you sleep?" Taylor asked.

A heart rending tenderness settled in his gaze. "I woke up a few times last night to make sure you were still here by my side. And you were. I still find it hard to believe that you're here in Paris, with me. That I found you. That God led me to you. Finally."

Using the tip of his index finger, Zeke touched Taylor's forehead. He slowly trailed his finger down her cheek. Traced the outline of her lips.

Gazing into Zeke's sexy dark brown eyes, moisture seeped into her core. My, she wanted him inside her. Wanted to feel his thickness like she used to when she was just sixteen. Imaging Zeke slipping between her slick folds, her walls clenched. "Would you like some breakfast?"

"Sure. But first I want this." Zeke slanted his mouth over Taylor's and kissed her feverishly. Bolts of electricity shot through her veins then blasted straight to her opening. Her clitoris knotted. Twining her tongue with his, her labia fluttered.

Zeke groaned huskily in Taylor's throat and she drank it. His shaft turned to stone against the lower part of her belly. Oh God, how she wanted him to make love to her. Now. Right freaking now. Suddenly, he broke their heated kiss, and left her mouth burning like wild fire.

Husky breaths pierced through the opening of Taylor's mouth from kissing Zeke. "I know this may sound crazy, but although you're here, I still miss you."

His fingers glided along her collar bone. "That doesn't sound crazy at all. I still miss you, too. We have a lot of lost time to make up for. If you're free today, I'd like to start making up some of it right away. I want to spend the whole day with you Taylor."

Yes! Her mind cheered. "What do you have in mind?"

"First, I'd like to take you to the land where I plan on building the Balfour Renaissance Hotel. Afterwards, I want to tour the city with you. Are you gained?"

"Yes. I'm gained." Taylor eased up in bed, turned sideways, then flung her feet to the floor. Looking at her toes, she felt she could use a pedicure. Standing next to her queen sized bed, she grabbed her robe from the cranberry chair, and shrugged her arms through the sleeves.

Zeke flung back the covers then quickly got of bed. "I'm going to take a shower." Walking towards her, he rolled his shirt over his head, then tossed it on the bed. *Lord have mercy!* The muscles in Zeke's chest bunched. His hard biceps looked like ripe plums. With an eight pack and muscles galore, Zeke's body looked as if it'd been sculpted perfectly by a well renown artist.

Water filled Taylor's mouth and her sex clenched as fine behind Zeke walked past her and headed into the bathroom. As Taylor footed towards the kitchen, her mind drifted back to the last time Zeke and her had been together before yesterday.

Right after he'd given her the promise ring they'd made love in the lake. And my, it'd felt so good. Had been so wonderful. Zeke's shaft had been gigantic back then.

If his manhood had been that big at eighteen there was no telling how big it was now that he was a grown man. Gripping the handle of a frying pan, Taylor lowered it to the stove, and turned it on high.

Whipping up some eggs in dish, Taylor smiled. *I can't wait to see how big Zeke's penis is now that he's older. Hopefully, it'll fit.*

HOT WATER SPRAYED ZEKE'S BACK as he scrubbed his chest with a bar of soap. Dying to make love to Taylor, his hard rod stretched down his thigh. Then some more. And some more. The bulging head on his erection threatened to burst with come just from thinking of Taylor.

Taylor had felt so good snuggled up against him last night and this morning. It'd been difficult to keep his hands to himself while in her presence. Been challenging to keep his manhood soft. While he may have been the perfect gentleman thus far, he didn't feel confident that he could keep it up. *Damn, my cock hurts.*

Taylor set him aflame in a way that no other woman ever had. Sure, he'd had sex with women while in college. A few after college. Some one night stands. But that's all it was—just sex.

Zeke placed the bar of soap back in its dish then fisted his erection. Thinking about how he used to flick Taylor's nipples with his tongue, he slowly began jerking himself. Up and down. Up and down. Damn, he needed to be inside Taylor's sex bad. Real. Bad. Groaning, Zeke felt his mushroom head leak with pre-come.

Wanting to save himself for Taylor later on this evening, or until she was ready to make love to him, Zeke released his aching rod, rinsed off, and got out of the shower. Feeling like he had the blue balls, he grabbed the towel from the rack, and began toweling off. He mentally ordered his tool to soften, but it wouldn't. That sucker stayed hard as a pipe.

Pained erection pointing straight out, Zeke began drying his hair with the towel. Back in the day, Taylor used to let him have his way with her body. Make sweet passionate love to her. And boy did he use to enjoy it. Not because he'd wanted to use her. But because he'd loved her. Because he'd connected with her on so many levels. And although he'd just found her, he already knew that she was the woman for him. He'd known she was the only girl for him his entire life.

Sure he'd dated a lot of women. Just recently broke up with a gal by the name of Tessalyn a few months ago. But none of them had even come close to winning his heart. Although he'd been involved with too many women to count, he'd always known that if Taylor Spelling ever came back into his life, he'd drop the woman he was with like a hot cake for a chance to get back with Taylor.

You're the only woman for me, Taylor. I've always known it. After Zeke got dressed, he made his way into the kitchen. When he arrived, his mouth smiled, and so did his heart. Taylor had set the dining table by the window for two—him and her. Fluffy scrambled eggs, English muffins, bacon, and fresh fruits adorned the dishes.

Eyeballing the tasty looking food, Zeke's stomach growled. He pulled out Taylor's chair for her, and after she took her seat, her rounded the table and took his. Admiring her breath taking beauty, he slid his arms across the table, cupped her hands, and said the blessing. "Heavenly father. I come to you this morning to say thank you for the food we're about to receive. May it be a nourishment to our bodies. Bless the hands that prepared this meal, Dear Lord. In addition, please bless this relationship between Taylor and myself as we embark on a new journey. Thank you Dear Lord for giving Taylor back to me. Amen," he said, bring the prayer to closure.

Taylor lifted her bowed head and met Zeke's gaze. "Amen. That was such a lovely blessing." For a brief moment Zeke sat across from Taylor staring at her face, not uttering a single word. "What are you thinking?"

Dullness came into his eyes. "I'm thinking about our son, Taylor. I can't help but wonder what he looks like. Does he look like me? Or you? Who's personality does he have? Who does he sound like when he laughs? It breaks my heart to know he's out there somewhere without me or you."

"I know how you feel. It hurts to know he's out there in this cruel world being raised by someone else. For years I tried to find Zavier. I've hired so many private investigators, but they all came up empty handed. Deep down in my soul I can feel that he's alive." Taylor patted the space over her heart. "I can feel he's alive in here. As long as I'm alive, I'll never stop believing that. I just pray that whoever has our son is taking great care of him. Love him like we would."

Pain riveted on Zeke's face. "I'm going to do everything in my power to try and find our son, Taylor. It's been a while since I've looked for him. I used to look for y'all a lot when I first returned to Hilton Head Island. I even went looking for you at your mother's house when I first came back from college, but by then, you and Veronica had left Hilton Head Island."

"Why didn't you call me back, or reach out to me, after Katherine told you I came to visit you?" Taylor felt he owed her an explanation.

Zeke's head jerked. "I'm confused. What are you talking about?"

"A few days after I was rescued, right after I got out of the hospital, I went to your father's house looking for you. Katherine answered the door. She called you while I was there and left a message on your phone for you on my behalf. She told you to call home because they'd found me, and I wanted to speak with you. I waited years for you to call me, but you never did. What kept you from calling me, Zeke?"

Frowning, Zeke banged his fist on the table causing Taylor's glass of orange juice to spill. "That evil woman. Katherine never told me you called, Taylor. This is the first time I ever knew that you tried to reach me."

Anger boiled inside Zeke about what Katherine had done. *Wait until I get my hands on Katherine.* Right now Zeke felt like he could strangle the life out of Katherine from keeping such important information from him. What kind of person would do such an ugly thing? *An evil one. A very evil one.*

Chapter Eleven

THE FREEZING COLD JANUARY AIR clung to Taylor's face as Zeke and she embraced each other in front of the Eiffel Tower. Being in Zeke's arms like this, seemed unreal. Like she was dreaming. If she was dreaming, she prayed she'd never wake up.

With their noses touching, Taylor's gaze soaked up Zeke's dreary eyes. Smooching his sexy lips together, he pecked her lips. "Doing all this tourist stuff, have I worn you out, yet?" Zeke's husky voice rolled over her, making her nipples tingle.

She dreamed of being made love to tonight. "Not hardly. I'm having the time of my life and I never want it to end."

Zeke's sexy mouth pulled into a grin. "Ditto."

Zeke and Taylor had explored Paris a lot today. They'd had the wonderful pleasure of sightseeing the National Museum of Modern Art, The Louvre, the Arc de Triomphe, and now they stood wrapped in each other's arms in front of the Eiffel Tower.

Wanting to always remember this beautiful romantic moment, Taylor snuggled her head against Zeke's thick chest and looked up at the beautiful Eiffel Tower sculpture.

Purple hues made a beautiful backlash in the sky as evening neared. The fading sun lowered to the horizon. Tourist walked along the grounds, some snapped photos of their surroundings. Being with Zeke like this made Taylor elated.

Struggling not to cry happy tears, Taylor's nose burned. Her eyes moistened. And so did her sex. Yep. It got wet there, too. How could it not? One of the finest men in the world was holding her like he adored her. Like he loved her. Like a wife he could never get enough of. Like a wife he couldn't live without.

"Do you mind if I take a selfie of us?" Taylor wondered.

"As long as you send it to me, go right ahead."

Taylor extracted her cell from her purse, put her cheek to Zeke's, and snapped the photo of the two of them looking madly in love in front of one of the most beautiful pieces of art she'd ever seen. Although she'd seen the Eiffel Tower many times before today, it still felt like it was her very first time. Maybe it felt that way because she now looked at it through a different set of eyes. Eyes filled with love. Hope. And promise. Zeke had given her the gift to look at things differently. For that she'd forever be grateful.

Zeke and Taylor strolled hand in hand along the emerald grass. Making their way toward the street to catch a taxi, Zeke stated, "Would you like to go to dinner tonight?"

She'd much rather be at home in private with him instead, she thought, yet still contemplating. "If it's okay with you, I'd like to pick up something to eat."

"What do you have in mind for dinner?"

"A salad."

"A salad." Zeke chuckled. "What else?" he asked, flagging down a taxi as they stood on a tiny bridge above the Seine. The taxi pulled up on the curb, and slowed. Just as Zeke pulled open the back door of the taxi for her, a romantic Paris cruise ship passed by, sailing the Seine. "A big guy like me needs more than a salad for dinner."

"And a model like me has to keep her figure in shape. So all I'm eating is a salad tonight." Taylor slid in the backseat of the taxi.

Zeke climbed in behind her. After giving the driver Taylor's address, he cupped her hand. Taylor loved how touchy feely Zeke was. In many ways he was still the same old Zeke. In other ways he was a much different person. Either way he was too good to be true.

"Speaking of figure," he broached the subject again, "You have a very nice body, Taylor. I hope you don't sit around worrying about your shape. It wouldn't matter to me if you were a size zero or a size twenty six, I'd still love you, my love. Being in shape is a good thing, but more importantly, I'm concerned with what's in a person's heart. Your heart is good, Taylor. I've never met anyone like you."

Hearing Zeke say he'd love her even if she got big, made her heart squeeze. "I wouldn't care if you lost you figure either."

Zeke chuckled. "That's good to know, because the way I eat," he patted his stomach, "there's no telling what may happen to this body of mine."

"You're so physically fit. You must exercise all the time."

"As a matter of fact, I do. Started in college and haven't slowed down since. Exercising relaxes me. Help me to deal with stress. After I lost you..." Zeke's words trailed off. A sullen expression shown on his face. "Let's think of happy times only, tonight," he quickly changed the subject.

I can't wait to run my hands all over his muscles. Hoping Zeke would try to finally make love to her this evening, Taylor's sex throbbed. She'd never had sex with a man other than Zeke, and that was when she was a little girl. She needed to know what it felt like to have sex as a woman now. Once they made love, she prayed she didn't disappoint him from her lack of sexual experience.

Head over heels for him, she laid her head on his shoulder. Zeke's spicy cologne traveled up her nose, enticing her. Making her more excited.

Bright city lights and billboards radiated brightly throughout the romantic city, flashing sporadically inside the taxi. Long minutes later, the taxi pulled up to her apartment, and dropped them off.

Taylor pushed through the door of her apartment with Zeke towing behind her. His bold presence stalking so closely behind her caused heat to smolder through her bones. From her breasts, to her sex, to her toes, this hunk disturbed her libido in every way possible.

Dropping her purse on the couch, she walked over to the intercom. In the mood for cuddling and hot sex, Taylor pressed the button on the wall. Slow R&B melodies sailed from the speakers, softly resounding throughout her entire apartment.

Linking her gaze with Zeke's, Taylor walked back over to where he stood, in front of the sofa. He delicately pushed her bangs from her forehead, then his fingers slowly undid the buttons on her white, trench coat. "This color coat looks great with your skin complexion. Makes you look soft and elegant."

"Thanks." Shrugging her arms from the sleeves of the thick coat, Taylor turned her back to Zeke. Zeke's big hands wrapped around the fabric of her sleeves and helped to remove the coat from her warm tingling body. *He's such a gentleman,* she thought, her back still to him.

Desiring to turn around and kiss him, Taylor took a step forward. Zeke softly touched her shoulders, seizing her. With her back to him, he pressed his hard length into her rear. Tingles spread through her veins like hot oil. *He's hard. Oh how I want him.*

Caressing Taylor's shoulders, Zeke dropped his lips to her ear, and breathed hotly. "Thank you for spending the whole day with me. I want to make love to you, Taylor. Let me pleasure your body like I used too, but only better. Tonight. Now." His deep voice heightened her arousal. Fire and desire coursed through Taylor's veins. Fluid excreted from her vagina and wet her panties. No one but Zeke had this kind of effect on her.

Taylor slowly turned around to face Zeke. Dark brown wiry hair grazed his shoulders. Heated desire flickered his dark brown pupils. When he swallowed, the ball in his thick neck glided up and down. The man looked as if he could eat her alive, and she hoped like hell he did. All the models bragged about how good oral sex felt, and she couldn't wait for Zeke's long tongue to show her.

Taylor cupped Zeke's jaw. "I've waited ten long years for this, Zeke. Make love to me. Now."

Zeke's mouth descended down rough onto Taylor's. Groaning hoarsely, he thrashed his tongue into her mouth, and twined it with hers. Sucking. Pulling. Tugging. Waves of heat flooded Taylor. His scorching kiss sent new spirals of ecstasy shooting through her.

Keeping his mouth intact with hers, Zeke zipped down Taylor's black pants, and removed them. Rolling her red sweater over her head, he grind his erection into her stomach. Sucking on her tongue, he motioned his head backwards, his juicy tongue slipped from between her burning lips.

Zeke's eyes kissed Taylor's body as she now stood in front of him wearing a hot pink lace bra with matching panties. His hands caressing her arms, love filled his irises.

Suddenly, his hands paused.

He took a step backward. For a moment he said nothing, just stared at her. His gaze left her face, slid down over her perched breasts, lowered to her abdomen. Her hips. Her thighs. Her long legs, and then her toes.

Zeke's appraising eyes climbed back up the length of Taylor's body to her face again. "You're so damn beautiful. Sexy. Mine."

Eyes flickering with heated desire, he closed the distance between them. His lips brushed against hers as he spoke, "Yes Taylor. I'm staking my claim. You're mine. You've always been mine." A lusty groan broke from her mouth, shot into his.

Zeke fully captured Taylor's mouth. He jerked Taylor off her feet. Carrying her to the bedroom, his ravaging mouth never left hers. Lips hard and searching, and exploring, he finally tore away his mouth.

Once inside Taylor's master bedroom, Zeke turned back the covers on her bed, and gently lowered her to the mattress. He glanced back over his shoulder at the fireplace near the wall then back at her. "Mind if I turn the fireplace on?'

Shaking her head, a dull ache formed in her center. "Please do." *Please hurry up and get inside me, I'm hurting. Bad.* Taylor felt as if she could come just from looking at the tall, muscular, stallion.

Zeke stalked over to the gas fireplace and flicked the button on the wall. The ignited logs burst into orange hot flames. He turned around and went and stood at the foot of the bed. Anxious to see him naked, Taylor spread her legs on the cranberry silk sheets, and beckoned him to climb on top of her. Make wild burning love to her. Lick her with his long tongue until she got dry.

Peering down at her, Zeke removed his emerald sweater, and then his navy jeans. *Good Lord.* His erection looked like a big cucumber inside the black, boxer briefs he wore. Waiting for him to remove his underwear, Taylor's heart pounded hard beneath her breast.

Clit throbbing, she eased up on her elbows. Bent her legs at the knees. Watched in yearning for Zeke to take off his underwear.

Keeping his sexy gaze locked with hers, Zeke rolled his underwear down his long hairy legs, freeing his erection. Water seeped from the pores inside Taylor's mouth. Zeke's steely, creamed colored shaft pointed straight out. Starting with his round glorious head, the skin on his thick erection pulled tight. Veins bulged at the sides. Hung like a horse, his round balls looked big, too.

When Zeke took a step forward, his shaft swung. *Oh my.* He huskily stated, "I haven't even touched you yet, and my head is leaking."

Taylor's breathing heightened with erotic anticipation. "Touch me, Zeke. Touch me. Please." Taylor opened and closed her thighs. Opened and closed them again.

Smoldering heat flickered Zeke's eyes as he climbed on top of Taylor. Hovering over her, he reached around to her back, unsnapped her bra, pushed the straps from her shoulders one at a time. Tossing her bra to the floor, he stuck his tongue out, dropped his head, and flicked his delicious tongue over her pea like nipple. Fire and desire coursed through her freaking veins. She groaned huskily.

Sucking gently on her tender breast, his hands moved urgently to remove her panties, and throw them to the floor. Zeke released her lips. His eyes traveled over her belly and stopped when they reached her shaven womanhood. "Your sex is bald. Glistening with juices. I love it." Zeke put his forehead to hers. "Oh Taylor. You got me so worked up, I'm about to burst, my love."

Taylor's labia quivered. "I'm about to come, too."

Zeke nipped at her bottom lip with his sharp teeth. He kissed her right eye then her left. He placed a series of heated kisses on her face. Lips pecking on her neck, his mouth descended downward to her right breast. He cupped her mound in his hand, sucked her nipple into his mouth.

Taylor groaned. Palming the back of Zeke's head, his silky hair strands glided through her fingers as she mashed her sensitive breast into his face. His mouth left her right breast to pay attention to the left one.

Taylor grind her drenched triangular bald snatch against Zeke's muscular abdomen. Groaning, he cupped both of her breasts in his large hands, pushed them together, and alternated flicking the tip of his tongue over each of her nipples. *Oh God. He's going to make me come.*

Devouring her breasts, Zeke's shaft plopped between her wet folds. With her labia at the sides of his hard length, he gyrated vigorously. The head of his shaft knocked against her throbbing clitoris with every rock of his hips.

Zeke slid down her body, leaving her breasts swollen. His face hovering over her vagina, he pulled back the hood of her sex. Anxious for Zeke to suck her clitoris into his hot mouth, her body jerked. Using the tip of his tongue, he flicked at her blood filled clit. Sucked it into his mouth and clenched it with his sharp teeth. Taylor's husky moans filled her own ears.

Curling his tongue over her tight bud, he inserted his finger inside her heat, and twirled. *It's true. It's true. Oral sex is great. Oh God. Great. I'm not ready to come.* Bucking against his face, Taylor's thighs slapped to the sides of Zeke's head and she held him tight.

Wet smacking sounds echoed from Zeke's mouth as he ate her. He inserted another finger inside her, and she just about lost it. Scraping his fingers on her g-spot, Taylor eased up on her elbows, and watched him feast between her legs.

Flicking, sucking, and twirling, Zeke's head motioned up and down between her thighs. Circling her hips, a ball of fire sat at her opening. Any moment she'd explode. Zeke's fingers left her entrance to spread her fluttering lips.

Delicately spreading her labia apart, he thrashed his tongue into her drenched sex. "Zeke!" Taylor's sex erupted on Zeke's tongue as it darted in and out of her opening. Fisting the comforter, her eyes hooked onto the dancing orange flames inside the fireplace.

"Oh. Uh. Uh." Feeling her mind blowing orgasm taper off, Taylor's chest rose and fell. Basking in the aftermath of a good licking, her lips curved up into a smile, and then she fell back on the bed. *I've died and gone to heaven,* she thought, glancing up at the ceiling, and breathless.

Zeke shot up her body to capture her gaze. "You tasted so good, my love."

"Let me see," she said, smooching her lips together. Zeke lowered his mouth to Taylor's and kissed her so she could taste herself. The salty essence of her sex glided from his tongue onto hers. Sweet and musky, she relished the flavor of her vagina. Giggling, she released his mouth. "I do taste pretty good, don't I?"

"The best." Zeke reached down between their bodies, fisted his shaft, then put the engorged head to her opening. "Open wide." Staring into his eyes, she spread her thighs farther apart. Circling the tip of his nose with hers, he rocked his hips. The head of his member inched past the circular nerves of her channel and rested.

Rocking his hips backward, Zeke withdrew his rod, putting the head back to the outer part of her sex. Fisting his tool, he slid his rod up to her clit, and rubbed his hard knob in circles on her clitoris. He then slid the head back down to her entrance, stuck it, then slid it back up to her clitoris again and circled it. "Oh, yes. Yes."

Now twirling the head around the circular part of her canal, Taylor's folded her bottom lip between her teeth, and let him pleasure her. With his flat palms pressed into the mattress, Zeke circled his hips, and pressed forward. As his shaft slowly slid further inside her channel, her stretching walls stung. His massive size caused a ripple of pain to shoot through her, even to her lower spine. *He's too big. Go slow. Keep going slow.*

"It's been a long time, hasn't it?" he asked, working his way toward her bottom.

Her chest heaving, Taylor nodded. "Very long. You're the only man I've ever slept with, Zeke."

Zeke's tender strokes went still inside her. Joy stretched his eyes. "Taylor. Oh God, Taylor. I'm the only man you've ever been with? The only man you've ever made love with?"

Feeling her pain subside, Taylor nodded. "Yes, Zeke. There's been no one but you inside me."

"Thank you." He twirled his tool inside her. "For waiting on me to return." He stroked her gently. "Thank you. For letting me be the only man to ever brand you." Feeling Zeke's shaft pushing at her bottom, she wrapped her legs around his waist. Oh, his strokes were so tender. "And if I have it my way, no man other than me, will ever get inside you." Swirling around in her heat, Zeke captured her lips, and plunged his tongue into her mouth.

Driving into her, his firm lips rummaged over hers. His hard sac repeatedly slapped her rear. Stroking her deliciously, Zeke reached down between their sexes, and rolled the pad of his thumb on her clitoris. Electricity surged Taylor. A husky groan left her throat, blew into his kissing mouth. *I'm about to come again.*

Rocking her g-spot forcefully on his throbbing length, Taylor's mouth shot wide open, and she freaking hollered. Zeke brought his shaft all the way up to her entrance then slammed into her. The whole bed shook.

Lolling her head back, Taylor's eyes rolled. Her center burst into an earth shattering orgasm. "Zeke. Ah. Oh. Ooo. I'm com … ah. Ah. Coming!"

STREAMS OF FLUID LEFT TAYLOR'S canal and coated Zeke's pulsating shaft. Watching her come, watching her eyes roll to white, spurts of hungry desire inched through Zeke's veins. Arousal shot through his system, charging up his rod. Making it harder. Stronger. Tingly.

Taylor's sex wrapped around Zeke's thick erection like a velvety cocoon. Clenched him. Drove him mad. "Come on me, baby. I feel you coming. Keep coming." The last of Taylor's orgasm rocked his tool. Quick breaths left the large opening of Zeke's mouth as he stroked her hard.

Zeke brought Taylor's legs upward placing them over his shoulders. Pounding into her, he cupped her breasts. Flicked his fingers over her nipples.

Taylor's head motioned side to side as if she was about to have another orgasm. Stroking her heat, the headboard banged against the wall. *Knockknockknock.* As his strokes quickened, sounds of the mattress squeaking emanated inside the room. *Squeaksqueak squeak.*

"Open your eyes Taylor?" Zeke requested. Taylor's eyes sprang open. Blinking, her long lashes curled down on her face. "Promise me. That you'll always be mine."

"I promise, Zeke."

"Tell me. What exactly do you promise, Taylor," he asked, listening to the squishing sounds of her sex.

"I promise to always be yours. I promise to always love you, Zeke."

Zeke grabbed the soles of Taylor's feet, brought them to his mouth, and started kissing them. Swirling around inside her, he grunted. "I love you, my love." Starting with the tip of his stem, desire surged Zeke's tool, and he began unleashing inside her. Thick come shot from the eye of his shaft into her slit. Filling Taylor up to the hilt, thunderous groans leapt from Zeke's lungs, and bounced off the walls.

Taylor's sex sucked Zeke's throbbing column hard. Now drained dry, he started softening inside her. Saturated in sweat, he clenched her hips, rolled over to his back, placing her on top of him. With his semi-erection still buried inside Taylor, her eyes gleamed like summer lightning as she held his gaze.

Zeke's hands explored Taylor's perspired back as he shrunk inside her come filled walls. "You were great, Taylor."

Sitting on top of his manhood, she flattened her palms on his chest. "You were great too, Zeke. I swear I must've came like three times."

Zeke had fucked plenty of his women before. But he'd never made love with anyone other than Taylor. It'd taken every fiber within Zeke not to come as soon as he'd entered her body. He hadn't any clue as to how he'd managed such daunting task. But was glad he had because it'd brought the love of his life so much pleasure. "We didn't just have sex. We made love."

Straddling him, she cupped his jaws, put her lips to his. "We made wild, burning, love."

He caressed her arms with his fingertips. "I want you to keep my cock in you all night. Sleep on top of me."

"The pleasure is all mine." Taylor laid her head on Zeke's chest, and then pulled the cranberry colored, silk sheets up over them. Keeping his stem buried inside Taylor's drenched womb, Zeke and Taylor both drifted off into deep slumber.

Chapter Twelve

SLEEPING HARD ON A RIGID board, Taylor felt something growing hard inside her entrance. Whatever it was, it inched all the way past her stomach. Suddenly, her body starting moving. She felt like she was lying flat on her stomach on a hard surf board, riding a strong wave.

Enjoying the pleasurable feelings spreading through her body as she tried to awaken, Taylor moaned. Her eyes fluttered open to find herself still laying on top of Zeke. His tool was still inside her. *I slept like this all night.*

Thrust. Thrust. Oh my. She was riding alright, but it wasn't a wave. It was Zeke's hard rod instead.

Solid like hard wood inside Taylor, Zeke rocked his hips. "Get up sleepy head." Feeling Zeke's hard shaft stroking her channel, a long yawn escaped Taylor. Mustering up her strength, she sat upright on him. Zeke's lips pulled into a handsome grin. "Now this is how a man's supposed to wake up."

This man is making love to me. Oh my. Taylor's lips curved upward. Circling her hips, her nipples tingled. Turned to tiny hard pearls. "Tell me, Mr. Balfour. Exactly how should a man wake up?"

"Every man should have the pleasure of waking up to a beautiful woman riding his cock."

Riding Zeke, Taylor arched her right brow. "Is that so?"

"Yes, my love." Thrusting up inside her, Zeke pushed up on his elbows, and kissed her.

"I need to brush my teeth, Zeke," Taylor spoke around his mouth.

"No you don't. You're fine. Just ride me," he stated huskily in between erotic kisses.

Bucking on Zeke's shaft, Taylor circled her fingers around the headboard. Wanting to give him a taste of his own medicine, she brought her sex up to the tip of his erection, paused, then slammed down on his rod as hard as she possibly could.

Zeke shuddered. "Fuck! I almost lost it."

Taylor snickered. "Good."

Zeke's eyes lit up. "Good my ass. I want to take my time making love to you this morning. You do that again and I can't promise you that I won't come."

"Oh yeah." Feeling mischievous, Taylor lifted her hips, and slid up his length again. Smiling, her center rested on the tip of his erection.

"Taylor, Taylor. Don't do it. I'm warning you." Taylor slammed down on Zeke. *Bam!* "Fuck!" Zeke tensed, his tool detonated inside her. Squeezing his eyes shut, he groaned inside his throat. Milking him, she felt his tool rattle inside her belly. Giggling, Taylor covered her mouth with her hands. Finishing off his orgasm, Zeke's eyes shot open. "I warned you not to do that, didn't I?" he asked, his eyes smiling.

Taylor put her hands on her hips, and playfully rolled her neck. "Yes you did. But you can't do anything about it. Now can you?"

"Wanna bet?" Zeke playfully shoved Taylor and she fell backwards, severing their connection. He got to his knees, smiled down at her. When he clenched her hips and rolled her to stomach, come oozed from her entrance, saturating the linen.

Pressing his chest into her back, Zeke pinned Taylor beneath him. Laughing hysterically, Taylor glanced back over her shoulder at Zeke. Fisting his still hard shaft, he linked his eyes with hers. *Dang, he's still hard. How does he do that?* "Let me go, Zeke." she said, snickering, kicking her legs wildly against the mattress. Loving every minute of it.

"Nope. I'm not letting you go." Chortling, Zeke began spanking her rear with his shaft. *Spankspankspank.* "You've been a bad, bad, girl." Mmmph. Actually, it felt heavenly. In fact, it felt so good until Taylor wanted more.

Egging him on, she writhed beneath him. "Stop Zeke. Stop."

"Your mouth is saying one thing Taylor, but your eyes and body is saying another." Clenching himself at the base, he slipped inside her. "You know you want it. Now admit it."

Loving the feel of him stroking her from behind, Taylor moaned. "You're right."

Zeke twirled his stem inside her. "I'm right about what?"

"You're right about how much I want you inside me." Pushing backward on his length, her eyes drifted closed. Zeke's strokes deliciously swirled her insides. His love making was so tender. Her sex made loud squishing sounds as he thrashed in and out of her. In and out.

Zeke gripped her hips and pulled her upward till her buttocks perched high in the air in front of him. On her hands and knees doggy style, Taylor faced forward, and noticed the fireplace still blazed orange-reddish flames. Zeke's pressed the pads of his fingertips into her behind, and slammed into her.

Taylor's mouth dropped wide open from the intense thrust. Quickening his strokes, he thrust harder. Her breasts slapped one another, making clapping noises. Lowering his sweaty chest to her spine, Zeke reached beneath Taylor, and tweaked the nipple of her right breast. So many sensations shot through her.

Keeping her eyes attached to the burning fire sparkling inside the fireplace, a hot brew stirred in the pit of her belly, and smoked its way down to her opening. Her orgasm built like a raging fire inside her. Hotter than the fire she glared at.

Sliding back and forth on Zeke's rod, she clenched him with her sex. Hard. Held him hostage. Zeke roared like a beast. "Aaaggh."

On the brink of exploding, she arched her back like a feline, tooted her rear further up in the air. Her posture caused his shaft to angle downward inside her canal, scrape her g-spot.

Taylor looked over her shoulder just in time to capture Zeke's face twisting with pleasure. Feeling her orgasm pool at her circular opening, she crashed her sex backwards, fell hard into his lap. Taylor's sex shattered into a million tiny pieces as Zeke's pulsating member unloaded with hot morning come.

Taylor's eyes left Zeke's face to spy the time on the clock. "Oh no!" She jumped from Zeke's lap, flung her feet to the floor, and stood.

"What's wrong?"

"I have a photo shoot this morning with Revlon. If I don't hurry I'm going to be late!" Pensive about coloring her hair red, Taylor ran into the bathroom, and jumped into the shower.

Rubbing the soapy washcloth between her sticky thighs, she hoped Zeke would like her new hairdo after he saw it later on this evening. *I hope it turns out to look good. If not, Zeke may wish he never ran into me after all these years.*

BULLDOZERS DUG DIRT FROM THE earth. Across the way, construction workers wearing bright yellow helmets hammered sticks into the ground. Architects and electricians walked about, pointing, talking, and observing the wide spacious land.

Cold nipping at the back on Zeke's nape, he slid his hands inside the pockets of his wool coat, and smiled. The site he'd selected to build the new Balfour Renaissance Hotel on couldn't have been more perfect. Now that he'd come back in contact with Taylor, there was some minor changes he needed to make to the design, though.

Coming up with the perfect present for Taylor, he waved Francois over. Speaking on his cell standing next to a construction worker, Francois shot over to where he stood. "What's up?"

Francois asked, tapping the button on his cell to end the call.

"There's some changes I want done to one of the penthouse suites."

Francois put his hand on his hip. "Say what? What you've done thus far is already wonderful. Why in the world would you want to change it now?"

"Because, I want it to reflect someone very special to me. And it just doesn't do that now. The design is too hard. Not soft enough. It needs to have more columns. More curvatures. Its design needs to be utmost feminine with a hint of exoticness."

Francois chortled. "Sounds like some woman."

"I do have a woman in mind. But she's just not any woman. She's a very special woman. Taylor is everything a man could ever want."

"That's if you like women," Francois muttered, and Zeke burst into laughter. "Her name's Taylor, huh?"

Zeke nodded. "Yes. Taylor's her name."

Francois tilted his head. "My partner manages a model named Taylor. If your Taylor looks and acts anything like this one, then I see why you're strung out over her."

Surprised, Zeke's lids lifted. "My Taylor is a model. Taylor Spelling."

"Get the heck out! Yes! That's her." Clenching a black binder to his chest, Francois stomped his foot, and cracked up laughing. "Wait till I get home and tell Pierre this. It's a small, small world."

"Maybe the four of us can double date sometimes," Zeke suggested.

Francois flamboyantly twirled his wrist in the air. "You can't be serious. Are you?"

"Yes. Why wouldn't I be?" Zeke gave his shoulders a shrug.

"Ah, it's just that...some people are uncomfortable going out in public with us gays. It's sad that it's that way, but it is."

"The people that feel that way are closed minded. Pay them no mind. Taylor and I would love to hang out with you and..." Trying to recall Francois' partner's name, Zeke snapped his fingers.

"Pierre."

"Yes Pierre. As a matter of fact, I'm planning a big surprise for Taylor tonight, and would love if you and Pierre could be there. If either or you happen to know any of Taylor's friends, please invite them, too. It's going to be at LeMeurice. At my expense."

Francois slapped his thigh and laughed. "Shoot. You ain't got to invite me twice. Should I wear my dancing shoes?"

Zeke chuckled. "Yes, wear your dancing shoes. I have a lot of last minute planning to do for tonight, so I'll catch up with you later."

Excited about his plans for Taylor this evening, Zeke stalked away from the construction site. He pulled open the back door to the black sleek Mercedes, slid in the back, and shut the door.

The driver glanced at Zeke in the rearview mirror. "Where to Mr. Balfour?"

Excitement jumped around inside Zeke as he said, "Jaubalet jewelry store on Rue de Rivoli."

His driver Ricardo smiled at him. "By the look on your face, something very special is about to happen, Mr. Balfour."

Zeke smiled so hard until his jaws ached. "You have no idea, Ricardo. None what so ever."

Twenty minutes later, Ricardo drove the Mercedes up to Jaubalet jewelry store and parked. Ricardo rounded the back of the car to open the rear door for Zeke, but before he could get there, Zeke hastened out the vehicle. Thrilled, he rushed up to the glass window of the store, and spied the huge, emerald cut diamond tucked inside the slit of the silver box. Glee rushed Zeke. "Yes!" Smiling, he spun around. "It's still there Ricardo!" he shouted.

Standing beside the driver's side door of the Mercedes, Ricardo looked over the roof of the car at Zeke. "What's still there Mr. Balfour?"

"The ring!" He threw his hands up in the air. "This shouldn't take long. I'll be back shortly." Zeke flung open the door, and smiling his ass off, he hurried up to the counter.

"How may I help you?" the pretty young woman standing behind the counter asked.

"I want to buy the ring in the window."

"It's quite expensive," she advised.

I'm sure it is. "I don't care how much it costs, it's going home with me today."

Giving him an uncanny look, the lady walked from around the counter, unlocked the glass display, and returned back with the ring. Standing behind the counter, she spread a thin piece of material on the glass counter, placed the box on top, and read the tag. "Its emerald cut, fifteen carats, set on a platinum basket surrounded by a leaf design. It cost three million dollars."

Three million. Taylor's worth it, and then some. Zeke plucked the sparkling diamond from the slit and brought it up to his eyes. The emerald cut diamond sparkled. "I'll take it," he said, handing it back to the cashier.

"Wait a minute. Aren't you that famous celebrity, Zeke Balfour?"

"I'm Zeke. But I'm not a celebrity," he confirmed.

"Well, you're a celebrity to me." The cashier rung up the ring, placed it in a nice silver bag, then gave Zeke his merchandise along with her business card. "If things don't work out with you and your girlfriend, by all means give me a call." Flirting, she winked.

"They'll work out. I'm going to make certain it does." Package in hand, Zeke left.

Chapter Thirteen

GLANCING AT HERSELF IN THE mirror while speaking on the cell phone, Taylor sulked. "I look a hot mess, Pierre!"

Pierre sucked his teeth. "Girl, get a grip. I saw your hair and it looks gorgeous, honey. Absolutely stunning. That red hair you're styling is a hit!"

Red wavy hair hung past Taylor's shoulders and down her back in a big fat, strawberry mess. Wanting to make her red head of hair switch back to dark brown, Taylor closed her eyes then reopened them. Too bad, her hair was still red. *It's the same color as Katherine's.* "Zeke is going to hate my hair, Pierre."

Pierre sucked his teeth. "Girl, please. From what you've told me about that man, he couldn't dislike your hair, or you, even if he tried. The way the two of you came back together after all these years is so romantic, Taylor. Sounds like something in a fairy tale. Francois and I are very happy for you. Speaking of Francois, his birthday is tonight, and I want you to come out and party with us."

"I'm sorry, I can't"

"Can't or won't?"

"Didn't you hear me when I said I look a hot mess, Pierre? I look like a red headed, African American Raggedy Ann doll."

"Honey, please. If you don't get over your hair, I'm going to spank you. Now, you're coming to my man's birthday bash and that's it. Bring Zeke if you want too."

Taylor's lips pouted. "Alright. I guess I put my big girl panties on and sulk it up. I guess things could be worse."

"That a girl. See you at eight. Oh yeah, before I forget, I'm doing it big. I'll be picking you up in a limo."

"Hmmm. I see you're romantic like Zeke."

"Chile please. Your Zeke doesn't have a thing on Mr. Pierre. Bye!"

Giggling, Taylor hung up the phone. Discourage about her new red hair, she walked from the bathroom into her bedroom, and pulled open the closet door. Searching for a nice dress to wear to Francois party this evening, her hands floundered over the hangers, causing the clothes to sway.

She pulled an emerald dress from the closet, walked over to the long mirror leaning up against the wall, and held the dress up to her chest. "Oh god no...I look like a freaking Christmas tree."

Returning the dress to her walk in closet, she stumbled across a beautiful Ivory dress. Zeke had said that the ivory color looked great with her skin complexion. She wondered if he'd still think that after he saw her new hideous hair color.

Now holding the ivory dress up to her chest and gazing at herself in the mirror, she half smiled. Maybe the hair would grow on her. Maybe if she straightened it, she'd like it better. Tilting her head, the corner of her lip hitched. Well, at least she got paid a whole lot of money for doing the commercial. That being said she'd be grateful. And if Zeke hated her hair, then she'd just color it back dark brown.

As Taylor laid the ivory dress on the bed, her cell buzzed on her nightstand. Walking over to answer it, she hoped it was Zeke calling. "Hello."

"Hello beautiful."

I might not be so beautiful to you once you see my hair. "Hi Zeke."

"How did the commercial shoot go today?"

"Good."

"Are you sure? You don't sound like your usual self."

"They changed my hair and it's just taking some getting used, too."

"Oh. I'm sure your hair looks fine. Just like you. I'm not going to be able to make it over there tonight." *Oh no.* "Something came up with the construction and I need to get some things straightened out. I'll be working late tonight, and will call you first thing in the morning."

Taylor released a soft sigh. "My talent agent, Pierre, invited us to his partner's birthday party tonight. Are you sure you can't get away? Just for a little while?" *Please say yes.*

"Sorry. But I can't. Being with you for the last couple of days has me way behind. But I'll see you tomorrow."

"Promise?"

"I promise. I have a phone call coming through. Got to go." Zeke rushed off the phone so fast until he didn't give her chance to say goodbye or she loved him. Tapping the end button on her cell, insecurities developed inside her.

What if Zeke had someone else and that's why he couldn't see her tonight? What if he'd changed his mind about the two them? What if he had a girlfriend in Hilton Head Island? Of course, he had to have a woman back home. At least something. No man like Zeke could really be single. Not completely alone. Realizing she'd been a complete and utter idiot, she slapped her forehead, and tried her hardest to think she was overreacting.

Hours later Taylor stood inside the foyer of her apartment building, waiting for Pierre and Francois to arrive. "You look absolutely stunning this evening, Taylor. Love the new hair color, too," the concierge, Hank, stated as he stood behind the desk.

Taylor smiled. "Do you really like the hair? You wouldn't lie to me would you, Hank?"

"No. Taylor. The red hair suites you."

"Thanks Hank."

A sleek black limo pulled up in front of her building and parked. The driver of the limo exited the vehicle, rounded the rear. Wearing her usual white, trench coat, Taylor's Christian Louboutin's heels clicked against the pavement as she made her way to the chic ride.

"Good evening Ms. Spelling. I was told to advise you that Pierre and Francois are waiting for you at the restaurant so you'll be riding by yourself this evening." He pulled the door open for her.

"Okay. Thanks." Finding it strange that Pierre failed to call her and abreast her of his change of plans, Taylor slid in the backseat of the fancy limo. As the limo drove down the dark road, Taylor's cell buzzed inside her sparkling diamond clutch. Extracting her cell, her heart longed for Zeke.

Bling. Looking at the screen of her cell, she had a text message.

ZEKE: Sorry I couldn't join you tonight. I'll make it up to you.

TAYLOR: I completely understand. You don't have to make it up to me. Can't wait to see you tomorrow.

ZEKE: If I finish up early, maybe I'll swing by if it's not too late.

TAYLOR: I'd like that.

ZEKE: Will you?

TAYLOR: Will you what?

ZEKE: Will you let me lick your pussy if I come over tonight?

Typing, Taylor burst into a fit of giggles.

TAYLOR: Of course, I will. Try hard to come.
ZEKE: Come? I definitely plan to come inside you. Good night.
TAYLOR: Good night.
ZEKE: Meant, I'll see you soon.
TAYLOR: Ok.

Hot and bothered from the text messages, Taylor smiled. Thinking about the way she'd slept on top of him last night, a delicious shudder heated her body. She tossed her cell in her clutch.

The limousine pulled up to the restaurant, and halted. Gazing out the window at the white grand building of LeMeurice, Taylor wondered if Pierre was about to pop the question to Francois. Very expensive and grandeur, LeMeurice sat in the heart of the city. *Zeke is going to miss out big time.* The driver pulled open the back door of the limo and Taylor stepped out into the cold night air.

As Taylor mounted the steep stairs to the eloquent building, strong winds blew from the direction of the Seine, causing her hair to brush across her lips. Swiping the long strands from her lips, she stepped inside the warm building. *Whew. It's so cold out.*

"Are you here for a party?" the gentleman at the hostess desk asked.

"Yes."

He pointed to his left. "Down that hallway. Last door to the right."

"Thanks." *Gosh, this is some fancy hotel,* Taylor thought, making her way down the hallway. When she reached the end, she turned into the room to find it dark inside. Suddenly, the lights flicked on.

"Surprise!" A group of people shouted.

Taylor jumped. Startled, she clenched her heart. Momentary panic shot through her. Mouth wide open, her eyes slowly traveled around the room to find Zeke there along with several more of her friends. Pierre, Francois, Sofia, and even her first roommate Ivey was there.

Confused, she finally pressed her lips together. A woman to her right gestured for her to remove her coat so she did, and then handed it to her.

Standing at the front of the room, Zeke held out his hands toward Taylor and beckoned her to him. As Taylor walked toward Zeke, she noticed a live band on a stage to her right.

"What's going on Zeke?" she asked, coming to a stop after she reached him.

Wearing a navy blue suit and red paisley tie, Zeke looked gorgeous. Cupping her hands, his eyes danced with merriment. Everyone encircling them had big wide smiles on their faces.

"Taylor. Ever since you walked into my life twelve years ago, I've loved you. Even when we were apart, I always loved you. At a very young age, I felt in my heart you and I were meant to be. And now that I'm older, I want us to spend the rest of our lives together."

Zeke reached into his pants pocket, pulled out a silver box, and got down on one knee. Taylor slapped a hard hand to her trembling lips. Ooos and ahhs emanated from the crowd. Tears welled up in her eyes.

Gazing up at her, loved flickered Zeke's pupils. He popped back the lid on the box. She gasped. Inside the box lay the emerald cut diamond she'd been looking at on the day they'd rediscovered one another. *Oh. My. God.* The tears dripped like raindrops from her eyes.

Zeke gently took Taylor's right hand into his. "Taylor Spelling. I want you to be my wife. Will you marry me?"

Sniffing, Taylor nodded profusely. "Yes! Yes Zeke. I'll marry you." *I'm finally going to marry the right man for me—my Mr. Right.*

Applause erupted inside the room.

Zeke slid the sparkling ring up Taylor's wedding finger. The humungous rock covered her entire knuckle. Zeke rose to his feet, draped an arm around her waist, and drew her to him. "I love you so much, my love." With his chest pressing into hers, Zeke slanted his mouth over Taylor's, and French kissed her. Overwhelmed, Taylor fought to stop all that darn crying.

"I'm going to be Taylor's maid of honor!" Pierre shouted.

Snickering, Taylor broke her kiss with Zeke. She pointed at Pierre. "You knew about this all along, didn't you?"

Pierre clapped his hands together. "Okay. I'm guilty."

Zeke laughed richly. "Thanks Francois and Pierre. I couldn't have pulled this off without the two of you. Before the night begins, I just want to thank all of you for coming out to support Taylor and I."

"Yes. Thank you all so much for coming." Taylor placed a hand to her chest. "Your attendance at my engagement party means so much to me."

Zeke nodded at the man standing at the microphone and the band began playing a slow rendition by John Legend. Tugging her hand, he led her to the dance floor. Swaying side to side, she twined her arms behind his neck.

Slow dancing, Zeke's shaft pressed into Taylor's belly. His eyes studied her face. "I can't wait to marry you, Taylor. I can't wait for you to have my last name."

Taylor gazed the twinkling lights in Zeke's eyes. A silken cocoon of euphoria wrapped around her. "I can't wait to be Mrs. Balfour. You've made me the happiest woman in the world."

"I'm glad."

"Please don't take what I'm about to say the wrong way, but I think the ring is too much. Too expensive."

"Nothing's too much for you, baby. If I could, I'd buy you the world. From this day forward, I'm going to spoil you rotten. Whether you like it or not, I'm going to make sure you're treated like the queen you are."

Taylor slid her fingers into the dip at the front of her dress, grasped the diamond ring circled at the end of her necklace, and pulled it out. She held the silver promise ring Zeke had given her on the day she'd been kidnapped up to his eyes.

Zeke's body went rigid. "You still have the promise ring I gave you?"

"Yes. Ever since you gave it to me, I've kept it with me everywhere I go. It's what kept me alive. Every time I looked at the ring it gave me hope. Hope that someday you'd come back to me. So you see Zeke, having a big expensive ring doesn't matter to me. I'm fine with this."

Zeke wrapped his hand around hers and kissed the promise ring. "Taylor," he said on a shaky voice. "As long as you marry me, I don't care what you wear on your finger."

"Maybe I'll wear both." She tucked the ring necklace back inside the top of her dress.

"I'd like that. I just feel in my heart you're supposed to have the ring I gave you this evening. It's the ring you were looking at when we reconnected. It's a symbol of our reunion."

Well, when he put it that way, she knew he was right, therefore, she'd keep the beautiful emerald cut diamond. "You're right. It does symbolize our reunion." She smiled. "I'll keep the ring, Zeke." She glanced down at the emerald cut stone on her finger again. "It's so beautiful," she said, peering back up at him.

The slow song faded and upbeat tempo began playing. "It's beautiful just like your red hair."

Holy smoke! Taylor's mouth parted. She'd been so caught up in the moment until she'd forgotten all about her red ugly hair!

Chapter Fourteen

KNUCKLES RASPED ON THE DOOR of LeMeurice Hotel penthouse suite where Zeke had proposed to Taylor last night. Apparently hearing the knocking, Taylor emerged from the bathroom door with a white, fluffy towel clenched around her torso, and pulling her hair up into a high pony tail. "Did I hear someone knocking on the door?"

Sitting in bed clenching the newspaper in his hands, Zeke glanced at her over the edge of the paper. Looking like an exotic model with her new red hair, Taylor had told Zeke she didn't like her new hair color, but he did. He didn't care if she colored her hair green, he'd love it. Hell she could color her hair purple, and he wouldn't give a damn.

"Yes. I'll get it." Zeke laid the paper on the bed, and footed toward the front door. Considering Taylor and him had made love seven times last, he shouldn't have a hard cock right now, he thought, mentally willing his shaft to soften. *Guess we're making up for lost time. I can never get enough of her. She's going to be my wife. Wait till I tell Richmond and Braylon about this. My father is going to be shocked like hell. And Katherine—she's going to have to answer to me for failing to tell me that Taylor paid me a visit after she was rescued. Damn you Katherine. Why would you keep such important information from me?*

Feeling sour about Katherine's inexcusable reckless behavior, Zeke opened the door of the immaculate penthouse suite Taylor had fallen in love with to find the bellman standing there. Wait until Taylor found out he was designing a penthouse suite with her in mind at the new Balfour Renaissance Hotel in Paris.

"Good morning," Zeke said, stepping to the side.

"Good morning." The bellman walked past Zeke pushing a cart containing their breakfast.

"You can put it by the window." Zeke tipped the Bellman, closed the door, and then headed back into the bedroom to join Taylor.

"Who was at the door?" she asked, wearing a pair of white satin panties, and snapping her bra in the front. Her pointed nipples pressed into the lace. He could see the big circles of her dark areolas beneath the thin lace material. Taylor looked sexy and elegant. Growing aroused, his shaft grew inside his drawers.

"The bellman. I ordered room service for us."

"Thanks. I'm so lucky to have you."

"And I'm lucky to have you, too." Zeke stalked up to Taylor, and kissed her brown enticing lips. "Take the bra off." Cupping her behind with one hand, he unhooked her bra with the other, and tossed it to the floor. Dying to get inside her this morning, he pressed his hard erection into her stomach. "It wants you."

Taylor slid her hands inside Zeke's underwear, wrapped her warm fingers around his shaft, and squeezed. Zeke groaned. "And I want it." Taylor jerked him up and down. *Damn that feels good.*

Zeke's heavy balls ached. As hungry as he was, he was hungrier for sex than for food. "Let me hit it from the back real quick."

Without uttering a single word and braless, Taylor walked to the foot of the bed, and bent over. *Hell yeah.* White satin panties stretch over the sexy curves of her tooted rear. Curly long hair paraded down her bare back. Taut black nipples grazed the gold silk comforter of the mattress.

Standing behind Taylor, Zeke pulled his sweatpants down, letting the cotton fabric puddle at his ankles. Forgoing to remove his underwear, he pulled out his hard stem, spit in his hand, and smeared his saliva on his aching member.

Zeke's eyes caressed his soon-to-be-wife. Arched spine. Buttocks perched. Legs spread apart. Taylor's sexy posture tantalized Zeke. He fisted his saliva coated rod, and motioned the skin up and down. He edged her panties to the side, inserted his finger in her heat, and twirled her essence. A long hum eased from her mouth.

Taylor's sex slid back and forth on his finger. Ah, her pussy was slick. And hot. "Give it to me, Zeke."

"You're so wet, Taylor." Keeping her panties pushed to the side, he put the head of his penis to the top line of her butt crack. Using the head of his shaft, he traced the line all the way to her center. "Let me get inside this good stuff," he uttered, slipping inside her velvety channel.

Thrusting in and out of Taylor, her hot moisture swam around his tool like a hot sauna. Pressing his fingers into her sexy, brown buttocks, he drove deeper into her slick womb. His testicles slapped her rear, intensifying the pleasure. "Lord this some good, good pussy."

"That feels so good baby," Taylor purred. Gyrating her hips, her sex clenched his tool, and held it. Hips still, she squeezed him hard. Her inner wet muscles pulsated. Sucked him deep.

Hands to her delicate waist, Zeke lolled his head back. Frozen, he locked his gaze on the ceiling. Limbs locked, knees weakened,

Taylor's inner wet muscles heaved come from his stem in loads. "Aarrggh."

Taylor hissed. "Oh Zeke. I love when you come inside me."

After Taylor and Zeke took quick showers, Zeke warmed their breakfast in the microwave, then joined Taylor for breakfast at the table by the window. Lowering the plates to the table, he took a sea across from her. Holding her hands, he blessed the food.

"Amen," they said in unison.

Enjoying the seasoned hash browns, Zeke peered out the window next to him. Beyond the balcony, sailboats cruised the Seine. Tourists walked to and fro. Taxi's and luxurious vehicles drove along the road.

Although he loved Paris, he had no intentions to make the beautiful city his permanent home. Knowing this, he wondered how Taylor would feel about moving back to Hilton Head Island. Paris, France and Hilton Head Island were like night and day. So different.

What if Taylor didn't want to move back to Hilton Head Island? Then what? After all his love had been through, he could definitely see why she'd be reluctant to return home. But considering her mother had moved back there, and his family and friends lived there as well, he felt it'd be a perfect place for them to live, and raise their children. Children needed to be around family and grandparents. And considering his father was ill with prostate cancer, Zeke wanted to spend as much time as possible with him. Maybe he should've talked to Taylor about permanently residing in Hilton Head Island before he asked her to marry him. He cursed inside his head. Well, regardless of her answer, he still planned to marry her. He loved her just that much.

Zeke hefted his glass of orange juice to his lips, sipped, then lowered it back to the table. "Taylor, we need to talk."

"Uh oh. Why the serious look?"

"Because what I want to ask you is serious, and it's a lot to ask of you." Looking elegant in the black, silk robe he'd bought her on yesterday, she lowered her fork to her napkin.

"What do you want to ask me, Zeke?"

Apprehensive, Zeke slid his hand across the table, and cupped her hand. "We need to discuss when we'll get married. Where we'll get married. And where we'll live after we get married. I'd like to marry you right away. I see no point in waiting."

He couldn't help but notice the tingle of excitement in her irises as she spoke. "How do you feel about a small wedding? Here in Paris?"

"I'm cool with getting married here in Paris." Taylor's brown lips pulled into a soft smile. "Let's get married next week."

"Next week!"

"I know it's fast, but I don't want to shack up as girlfriend and boyfriend. You deserve better than that, Taylor. You deserve a husband who loves you. That'll give his life for you. I can give you that. I want to give you all of me. And I want to do it right away." Living without her had been pure hell over the last ten years, and Zeke saw no reason to delay their wedding union. God wanted them to be together, and so did he. Taylor was his life. Now it was time she became his wife. "Will you do me the pleasure of marrying me next Saturday?"

Smiling her behind off, Taylor nodded. "Yes. Next Saturday will be great. I guess you're moving in with me then, huh?"

Here goes. "I really would like to make Hilton Head Island our permanent home. How do you feel about that?" Silence settled in the atmosphere. Dark disapproval resonated in Taylor's caramel eyes. She diverted her gaze from Zeke and peered out the window. "Look at me Taylor."

Taylor returned her disturbing gaze to Zeke. "How do you feel about a long distance marriage?" she asked, obviously not thrilled about possible moving back to Hilton Head.

"Taylor, the thought of not being with you everyday bothers me. I want to spend my every awakening moment with you. All my free time with you. We've already been separated for years, I *need* you by my side when I wake. *Need* you by my side before I go to bed." He'd staked his claim on her and had branded her, and the thought of being without her for a long length of time made his gut coil. "I know Hilton Head has some ugly memories for you. It does for me, too. But I think if we're together, in time, we can get passed it, and live very fulfilling lives there. And since I'm building a new hotel here in Paris, you can come back to visit often."

"I don't know, Zeke. I love Paris. And Hilton Head scares me."

"With me by your side, you won't have anything to be scared of. I'll protect you." *I wish someone would try to hurt her, I'll break his fucking neck. Kill him dead.* "I'll put security cameras around our home. I'll hire a security guard to watch you all day, and night. I'll do everything in my power to make sure you're safe and happy."

Taylor's lips turned under as she softly asked, "Why are you so adamant about moving back to Hilton Head Island?"

Zeke's chest caved. "Because my father may be dying."

Taylor's eyes grew wide. "Oh God, Zeke. I had no idea. I'm so sorry to hear that. What's wrong with your father?"

Zeke sighed. "He has prostate cancer. He may not live long Taylor. I want to spend as much time as I possibly can with my father while he's alive. Say you'll move with me. Please baby. I need you by my side."

Taylor grabbed Zeke's hand, placed it on her cheek, and nodded. "Okay. You win. When do we leave?"

Zeke's heart jostled. "After the wedding."

"I'll be ready. I still can't believe we're getting married so quickly. To be truthful, it's almost frightening, Zeke."

"Don't be scared. Our marriage is quick, but it's meant to be. You and I are made for each other Taylor. With God in the mix of our marriage, we'll be just fine." Zeke kissed the back of Taylor's palm.

Later on that day, Zeke stood at the registration desk of the hotel checking out. Clad in a red wool coat and black Dutch hat with flowers, Taylor looked absolutely stunning and elegant. Like the model she was. Making their way towards the entrance of the hotel, the heels of Taylor's long boots clinked against the marble floor.

The bellman pushed open the door for Zeke and Taylor, and they stepped outside of the hotel into the cold afternoon air. Before they could descend the steps, Paparazzi besieged them. Caught them off guard. Tourists stood at the foot of the steps looking up at them as if they were celebrities.

Standing in front of the golden doors, Zeke clutched Taylor's glove covered hand, and they began descending the steps. Paparazzi snapped photos of them. Camera men filmed footage. It looked like a damn circus outside of LeMeurice Hotel.

"How in the hell did our relationship get leaked?" Zeke muttered.

Halfway down the stairs, a reporter ran up to them, got in Taylor's face, and shouted, "Taylor Spelling, tell me, how does it feel to be engaged to an heir of a billionaire?" Smiling, the gentleman stuck the microphone to her lips.

Putting her gloved hand to her chest, Taylor's face flushed. "I couldn't be happier."

The reporter put the microphone to his mouth and continued. "I hear your story is quite one of a fairy tale." He stuck the microphone back in Taylor's face.

Taylor looked at the reporter enigmatically "Yes it is."

Keeping the microphone to her lips, he then asked. "To have had your baby stolen must've been a nightmare."

Zeke's gut knotted at the mention of his son's Zavier's name. His lips pressed into a hard line. "That's enough. Get out of our way. Move!" Tugging Taylor's hand, he shoved the photographer out of the way, and forced his way through the crowd.

Chapter Fifteen

Hilton Head Island

KATHERINE'S BUTLER, DELBERT, WALKED INSIDE the den carrying a tray in his hands. "Here's your lunch Mrs. Balfour," Delbert denounced gracefully, slightly standing behind the couch where Katherine sat.

Keeping her gaze fixated on her favorite soap opera, *Young and the Restless*, Katherine didn't bother turning around to look at Delbert. "Place it on the table, Delbert."

"Yes, Madam."

Actor Victor Newman spat, "You must take me for a damn fool!"

Actress Nicki Newman's lips folded under as she looked at her on screen husband, Victor. Nicki parted her lips and said, "But Victor. I had no choice."

Excited about what was about to happen next, anticipation charged Katherine. Clasping her hands, she leaned forward. "Tell her to hall ass Victor." Katherine felt a figure towering her. She glanced back over her should to find Delbert still standing there. "Is there something else, Delbert?"

"No. I just wanted to see what Victor is going to do that's all," Delbert replied.

Nodding, Katherine returned her gaze to the soap opera. If Delbert hadn't been so good to her, she would've told his behind to leave, and go finish his work. After all, there was so much to be done around the house. But considering all the things Delbert had done for her, and the secrets they shared, she had no choice but to be nice to him, and pay him a fortune to work for her. If Delbert ever told anyone about what she'd done in her past, she could go to prison. For a very long time. *For the rest of her life.*

Face crinkled, Victor pointed to the door. "Get the hell out of here! And don't you ever come back! Do you hear me?!"

Ecstatic over the ending, Katherine's exulting cheers belted from her lungs. "I'm glad he kicked Nicki out. Old drunk."

"Me too. Mrs. Balfour, you look lovely today as you do every day. However, must you always dress so formal just to sit at home and do nothing?" Delbert asked, laughing.

Glancing up at Delbert, Katherine chortled. "Yes I must. I learned a long time ago to always look your best. Always act your best. And always be your best because you never know who's looking at you when you least expect it."

Delbert gave his head a hard shake. "Lord I pray to God that no one was looking when we—"

Katherine flung her hand up in the air, stopping Delbert from uttering another single word. Her brows dove downward. "Don't you dare bring up the past, Delbert. Now, please get back to work."

"Yes, Madam." Delbert left the room.

Damn, we should've picked someone braver than Delbert to help us commit the perfect crime. Eager for the Bold and the Beautiful soap opera to come on next, Katherine stood. Dressed in an elegant, long red dress, she walked over to the rectangular wooden table, and looked out the long bay window at the woods and lake. Hating that Delbert was about to spill some beans, an eerie chill swept over Katherine. Goosebumps pimpled her arms as she looked down at her lunch.

Eyes lingering over her tasty meal, her mouth watered. Brocolli cheddar cheese soup, club turkey sandwich piled with tomatoes, and sliced caramelized pears for dessert, her lunched looked delicious. She pulled out the chair at the head of the long table, smoothed her hands over the buttocks part of her dress, and sat.

Just as Katherine scooped up the broccoli cheddar cheese soup and put it to her mouth, the phone rang. Short seconds later, Delbert reentered the room. "Telephone, Mrs. Balfour." He extended the phone towards her, and she took it. He turned and walked away.

Can't he see I'm trying to enjoy my lunch? "Thanks Delbert," Katherine said after him. "Hello."

"Turn to CNN right now!" the man on the other end exclaimed.

"Why?!" Katherine wondered.

He sucked his teeth. "Just do it. You're not going to believe your ears. Or your eyes." "Interrupting my soaps, this better be good." Katherine hefted the remote and started flipping through the stations.

The man on the other line grumbled then shouted, "Got damn it, this if a fucking nightmare!"

When she reached CNN, a picture of Zeke and Taylor standing in front of some fancy hotel building in Paris was on the screen. Katherine's heart rate pitched. Her nerves jittered. The remote went tumbling into her soup. Cheese splattered her face and dress. Shaking her head, her bottom lip quivered. "No. No. No."

Sarcasm was loaded in the man's voice when he uttered, "Yes. Yes. Yes. Zeke found Taylor. After all these years, your son found her."

Unable to tear her gaze away from Zeke's and Taylor's picture on the television, Katherine spat, "Don't you dare refer to Zeke as my son. He's not my son. Nor will he *EVER* be my son."

The man's tone turned cold as he barked, "Son. Zeke. Call him whatever you damn well please. You just better pray to God, or whoever the hell you believe in, that Zeke don't bring his fiancée back to Hilton Head Island. One look at you, and Taylor may come to realize that you had her son stolen."

Irritated by his cold tone, Katherine felt sick on the stomach. "Zeke and Taylor's son is far away from Hilton Head Island. They wouldn't be able to find that little boy no matter how hard they tried."

"For your sake. My sake. And for Delbert's sake, you better be right. I'm not going down for this. Do you hear me, Katherine?! I'm not going down with you!" *Click.* The line went dead.

Still looking at Zeke's and Taylor's photo on television, hard tremors shook Katherine's body. Pushing her lunch to the side, she propped her elbows up on the table, dropped her forehead in the palms of her sweating hands. "Please don't let them move back here."

Yeah. She'd had Taylor's baby kidnapped. Taken away from her. For a damn good reason, too. It was no way in hell she was going to let another bastard child get their hands on her husband's fortune. If she'd had any doubts before, she definitely didn't have any now.

When Colton made Zeke the CEO of Balfour enterprises, he'd proved her to be right about which son he favored the most—Zeke. Colton loved Zeke way more than he loved Antonio and Bane. And he proved it by making Zeke the CEO of Balfour Enterprises.

Antonio was the oldest. The smartest. He had her blood and Colton's blood. Therefore, Antonio should've been the CEO, not Zeke, the son of an adulterer. *The son of Colton's fucking mistress,*

Bridget. I'm glad Bridget is dead. Glad I killed her. Katherine felt someone had a tight fist around her heart, crushing it.

Nauseated over Zeke's and Taylor's engagement, Katherine placed a hand to the lower part of her stomach, and stood. Bile scratched the back of her throat as she climbed the staircase, rounded the corner, and headed into her bedroom.

Sick to the stomach, she turned back the covers on her king sized bed, and slid beneath the covers. "Cheating with my husband, Bridget got what she deserved." *And when Colton dies of cancer, everything he has will belong to me. I will own Balfour Enterprises and run it the way I see fit. The first thing I'm going to do, is make Antonio CEO of Balfour Enterprises. The second thing I'm going to do, is be just like Victor Newman and throw people out on their hairy asses. Zeke, my dear, will be the first person I fire.*

A wicked smile titled Katherine's lips as she glared up at the ceiling. Dozing off, she looked forward to the day she became owner of Balfour Enterprises. To the day her sons finally was treated like Balfours, and not like they were the one's who'd been born of a mistress—Bridget.

Stomach churning, Katherine's eyes blinked. And blinked. And blinked. She slowly doze off to sleep.

Thunder crackled. White sheets of rain poured from the dark sky. Parked along the side of the dark road across the street from Bridget's home, Katherine sat inside her car weeping. She cried because her no good cheating husband had lied to her. Again.

Colton was supposed to be hanging out with his friends tonight, Drake and Russell, but he'd somehow managed to find his way at his mistress, Bridget's home, instead. As Katherine sat inside her car waiting for Colton to come outside so she could confront him, her eyes traveled up to the second level of the Bridget's home. The expensive home Colton had bought for her.

Suddenly, Colton and Bridget appeared in the window. Katherine grabbed the binoculars from the seat beside her, cradled them in her hands, and placed them over her watery eyes. Because there was no drapery covering the window, Katherine had a clear view of the two traitors.

Colton draped his arms around Bridget's waist as she twined her arms around his neck. Gazing into Bridget's eyes as if he didn't have a wife at home, Colton's mouth crashed onto Bridget's, and the two of them started tongue sexing.

Suddenly, Colton jerked Bridget off her feet, carried her over to the bed, and jumped on top of her. Dropping her head on the steering wheel, Katherine wailed. "This is the last time the two of you will make a fool of me," Katherine cried on a shaky voice.

Katherine sat in her car for a whole hour for Colton to come out. Finally, he did. Standing in the doorway, Colton kissed Bridget on the lips, then walked out into the rain. Apparently hating to see Colton leave, Bridget stood in the doorway waving goodbye to him as he backed up out of the driveway.

Terribly upset, Katherine snatched her purse from the seat, and hurried out of the car. Rain pounded her head as she darted across the street. Thunder clapped the sky. A flash of white lightning struck the sky.

Bridget had to learn the hard way that Colton Balfour was off limits.

Standing on Bridget's doorstep dripping wet, Katherine lifted her finger to ring the doorbell, but suddenly decided against it. Taking a chance that the door may be unlocked, she grasped the doorknob, twisted, and the door clicked open.

Careful not to alarm Bridget, Katherine softly pushed the door open then entered. Inside the house was dark. Warm. Inviting. Unlike anything Katherine felt.

Katherine felt hatred. Betrayed. Foolish. Foolish for trusting Colton. Stupid for believing her husband would never cheat on her. Dumb because she never saw this coming. His ugly betrayal.

Water streamed from Katherine's clothing as she made her way into the kitchen. In a daze and unfamiliar with the house, she pulled a blade from the utensil holder, then headed upstairs.

Katherine's heart thudded hard inside her chest when her foot left the last step at the top. Walking down the hallway, she heard Bridget singing. She turned into Bridget's master bedroom and heard the shower running.

Knife in hand, Katherine hated what she was about to do, but couldn't stop herself. Potent anger coursed through her veins. Listening to Bridget sing while taking a shower, Katherine stood on the other side of the wall. Quickly, she inched her head inside without Bridget noticing.

Bridget stood inside the shower looking beautiful. Tilting her head back to wash Colton's scent off of her, water streamed through Bridget's silky blonde hair. Water drizzled over her big, perky breasts, down her flat abdomen, her toned thighs. No bigger than a size four, she had a tiny waist, too. Having seen enough, Katherine quickly flicked off the lights inside the bathroom.

"Who's there?" Bridget asked. With her back pressed to the wall just beyond the bathroom, Katherine clenched the handle of the blade tight. "Oh, the rain must've caused the electricity to go out."

Bridget's bare wet feet slapped the tile as she walked closer to where Katherine stood. Waiting for her to enter the dark bedroom, Katherine shook violently. Mumbling to herself, Bridget said, "Oh Colton. The lights are out and here you are, having to run home to her. You don't love her. You should be here with me, making love to me."

As soon as Bridget's right foot touched the carpet of her bedroom, Katherine stepped in front of her clutching the sharp blade. Wet hair matted to Katherine's head, she frowned. "You're wrong, bitch. Colton does love me." Katherine plunged the knife into Bridget's stomach.

Bridget's mouth dropped. Her eyes sprang wide. Wrapping her wet hands around the handle of the blade as it pressed into her stomach, she dropped to the floor, and died.

"Wake up. Wake up, Katherine." Katherine's eyes sprouted open to find Colton hovering her. "I have some wonderful news to share with you."

Oh hell, I was dreaming about killing Bridget. Vividly remembering her dream about what she'd actually done to Bridget, Katherine mouthed. "What's going on Colton? Is it your health?" *Please don't tell me he's getting better.*

Colton peered down at her with a glad look on his face. "No. This has nothing to do with my health."

Katherine eased up in bed until her back rest against the headboard. She shrugged. "Then what are you so happy about?"

Colton chuckled. "Don't you watch anything other than the soap operas during the day? Zeke found Taylor in Paris. Can you believe that? Paris! I knew when I made him CEO and sent him to Paris something good was going to happen. But in a million years...I could've never predicted this. Hot damn, Zeke found Taylor!"

Katherine said an expletive inside her head. "That's great news, Colton."

Still smiling, Colton shoved his hands in his pockets. "You ain't heard the best yet."

"Oh yeah. What's the best?" she ripped out the words impatiently.

Colton's hands flew up in the air. "Zeke and Taylor are getting married and moving back here...to Hilton Head. But it gets better." *Like hell it does.* "I insisted that Zeke and Taylor move in with us until their dream home is finished being built." Colton kept smiling, something he rarely did around her. "Having them live with us is going to be great, Katherine. Absolutely great."

It's going to be a disaster. Oh God, I think I'm going to be sick. Bile bubbled at the surface of Katherine's belly. Stomach churning and burning, she flung back the covers. Ran to the bathroom, hopped on the toilet. Clenching her abdomen, a loud explosion erupted from her rear.

Chapter Sixteen

AT ZEKE'S PERSISTENCE, ZEKE AND Taylor had returned to Hilton Head Island for their big wedding debut. Standing on the balcony at the *Balfour Hotel & Resort* on the ocean, Taylor curled her fingers over the railing, and glanced out at the blue, shimmering sea. A strong breeze blew from the ocean, descended down on her, making her shiver. Cold nipping at her cheeks, a smile crossed her face. "Just think no one knows that Zeke and I got married in Paris," she mumbled to herself. *And I plan on keeping it that way.*

On Saturday afternoon while in Paris, Zeke and Taylor had had a private wedding ceremony just for the two of them at a nice elegant chapel. She'd worn a simple white chiffon dress and Zeke had worn a plain white collar shirt with a black pair of slacks. The secluded wedding had been romantic, and would've been enough for her.

But Zeke, or *Mr. Right* as Taylor sometimes called him, had felt she deserved a big fancy wedding. He'd felt they should share their special day with all their family and friends. Therefore, he'd convinced her to get married *AGAIN* in Hilton Head Island at his family's ocean front hotel—Balfour Hotel & Resort. Glancing out at the big beautiful sea, Taylor was glad she'd obliged.

Wanting to get out of the cold weather, Taylor pulled open the sliding glass door, and walked back inside. Hilton Head Island brought back so many memories. Some good. Some horrible.

Horrid images of the night Taylor's son had been stolen from her entered Taylor's mind as she lowered her body to the foot of the bed to pray. To praise God for this beautiful day. Her *second* wedding day.

Although Taylor was thankful and happy to be marrying the man of her dreams for a second time in one year, in less than two weeks, an aching hole resided in her heart. It was a void that could never be replaced. A void that only her son, Zavier, could fill.

This day would be perfect if Zavier was here. On her knees at the foot of the bed, Taylor longed to hold her baby. She longed to see his face. Longed to know what and who he looked like. Part of her happy, part of her sad and longing, she brought her hands to her lips, and put them in a prayer symbol.

"Heavenly Father. Thank you for all the blessings you've bestowed upon me. Thank you for my career. Thank you for my husband, Zeke. And thank you for my son, Zavier. Although Zavier is not here in person to see his father and me get married, he's here in spirit. It is my greatest hope, Father, that you will someday bring Zavier back to me, just as you did his wonderful father. In Jesus name, I thank you. I give you praise. Thank you. Amen."

Clapping hands resounded in Taylor's ears just as her lids lifted. "Amen, honey. I'm gone need you to teach me how to pray like that." Giggling, Taylor stood, then turned to look at Pierre. Blinking, he touched the bottom part of his eye. "Look at me. I'm already crying and the wedding hasn't even started yet."

"Me too," Taylor's mother, Veronica said, entering the room. As soon as she looked at her mother, coming home finally felt right.

Like she belonged here with her mother. Like she should be here with some of her other relatives and good childhood friends, too. But most of all, she belonged here with Zeke.

"I'm about to cry, too," Taylor said, walking over to the oval shaped mirror. Oh for heaven's sake, please don't let her cry. She'd ruin her beautiful makeup. "Is Zeke here yet?"

Pierre nodded his head adamantly. "Yes, he is. And he's looking absolutely stunning. Now let's hurry up and get your dress on. Girrrll, you definitely don't want to keep a man like Zeke Balfour waiting at the alter."

"I agree. Zeke looks mighty handsome." Taylor's mother lightly put her hands on her daughter's shoulders. "My precious angel is getting married today. I hope your marriage to Zeke is everything you ever wished for, and then some." Veronica kissed her daughter's cheek. "Like Pierre said, let's not keep Zeke waiting any longer to get his beautiful—"

"Dashing bride!" Pierre's excitement made his voice hitch. Veronica and Pierre helped Taylor to get her wedding dress on. Tilting his head, standing behind her looking in the mirror as well, Pierre clamped Taylor's shoulders. "Oh Taylor, you look fabulous. You're the prettiest Bride I've ever seen. And I've seen lots."

Veronica cupped her mouth. "My. You look beautiful." Veronica touched her heart area. "My baby girl is getting married today. I can hardly stand it I'm so happy."

Water wet Taylor's eyelashes as she stood in front of the mirror looking at herself. Trying to remain modest, she felt as if she looked like a beautiful princess. Thank God she'd colored her hair back to dark brown because if she hadn't she'd look like a candy cane today. "Oh, Pierre. Thanks for helping me pick out this dress."

Pierre twirled his wrist in the air. "You can never go wrong with wearing a Chanel wedding dress, honey."

Taylor's eyes roamed over her white wedding dress. Diamonds adorned a sweetheart line all the way to her waist. Satin material with a long white trail made up the rest of the dress. Her dress sparkled a lot that's for sure. And it was a lot fancier than the dress she'd worn for her first wedding back in Paris. "I love the way I look."

"Zeke is going to love the way you look too. But if you don't hurry up and get down to the ballroom and marry him, he's going to have issues with you before you have a chance to say I do." *I'm already married*, Taylor thought, giggling inwardly. Pierre placed her red rose bouquet in her hands, and led her out the hotel suite.

Nervous, Taylor stood in front of the gold ballroom doors of the elite Balfour Hotel & Resort on pins and needles. Nerves on edge, Taylor glanced at her mother's brother, her uncle Louis, standing next to her. Her lips turned up into a smile.

"Gee whiz, you look beautiful niece," Louis complimented. "Zeke is a lucky man."

Taylor flushed. "Thanks for coming, Uncle Louis."

Louis eyes appraised her. "Are you kidding me? I wouldn't have missed this for the world. Besides Veronica, that sister of mine, would've had a fit if I didn't walk you down the aisle. But the pleasure in all my niece. You and Zeke are meant for each other."

"Are you ready?" The wedding planner asked Taylor.

"Yes." Taylor hooked her arm through Louis's. As the wedding planner and helper pulled open the heavy ballroom doors, Taylor's heart pounded beneath her breast. *Here goes.*

Taylor's eyes went to the front of the room and linked with Zeke's. Warmth infused her heart. Dressed in a black tuxedo, Zeke looked handsome. Gorgeous. She couldn't wait till marry him again. To promise to love and cherish him for all eternity in front of all these people. All of their family and friends.

The wedding march began playing. Thankful for this day and smiling, Taylor strolled down the aisle with her uncle beside her. Eyes roaming over the audience, she noticed Zeke's father, Antonio, Bane, and Katherine in attendance. Now smiling at her own mother, Taylor paused when she got halfway down the aisle.

MY WIFE. WHEN THE DOORS had opened a few minutes ago, Zeke had swallowed a deep breath. The striking sight of Taylor had stolen his breath away. Nearly knocked the wind out of him. She'd looked pretty last week when they'd gotten married at the chapel, and she looked equally pretty today. *My wife is beautiful.*

Zeke stood in front of the wedding arch smiling at his wife, the beautiful Taylor Spelling-Balfour. Taylor looked elegant and stunning in her white wedding dress with sparkling diamonds at the top. Deep red lipstick painted her lips. Wearing a long white veil, her dark brown hair was pinned up with curls hanging down the sides of her face.

Carrying beautiful red roses in her hands, she slowly made her way down the aisle of the ballroom. *I'm going to be the best husband Taylor could ever wish for. She's my heart. Means the world to me. Feels good to be marrying her again. I can do this year after year, after year.*

Zeke met Taylor halfway down the aisle and took her hand into his. Holding her hand, they proceeded to walk towards the flowery wedding arch. Face to face with Taylor, unconditional love filled Zeke, and he knew he'd love Taylor to the day he died.

Even with Katherine's unwanted presence in attendance, the wedding went smoothly, Zeke thought as the pastor pronounced them husband and wife. "You may now kiss your bride," The pastor stated.

Taylor's red lips pulled into a pretty smile. "I love you, Taylor." Noticing her eyes watering, Zeke lifted her veil from her face, then slanted his mouth over hers. Oh, God he loved this woman.

Applause echoed inside the room.

Standing behind Taylor, Pierre cleared his throat. "Alright you two. You do need to breathe, you know?" he laughed, and so did the crowd.

Zeke surrendered Taylor's soft succulent lips. With his wife by his side, Zeke cupped Taylor's hand and lead her out of the ballroom. The first people to greet him and Taylor after they'd gotten beyond the ballroom were Taylor's mother, Veronica. Next to come up and approach Zeke and his dashing new bride were Richmond and Kayla. Zeke politely made the introductions between Taylor and his friends.

When Taylor extended her hand towards Kayla, Kayla threw her arms around Taylor's shoulders as if she'd know her before this afternoon. "You're so pretty," Kayla told Taylor, releasing her.

Taylor professed to Kayla, "Thank you for coming. I've heard so much about you and Richmond."

"All good things I hope," Kayla said.

Taylor nodded. "Yes. All good—"

All smiles Braylon and Sandella walked up to where Zeke, Taylor, Richmond, and Kayla stood. Again, Zeke made the introductions. "We finally get to meet the bride. Man you told me Taylor was pretty, but you were wrong. She's beautiful." He jutted a thumb at Zeke. "What do you want with him?" Braylon joked. "I'm just teasing, Zeke is a great guy."

"Don't I know it," Taylor admitted. "I'm very blessed."

Sandella chimed in, "You're beautiful, Taylor. And so was the wedding. I'm looking forward to getting together with you for double and triple dates with our husbands and some girl's night out."

Taylor nodded. "I'm looking forward to it, too. Thank you for attending our special day."

Richmond laughed. "We're glad to be here and finally have the wonderful pleasure of meeting you Taylor."

Zeke watched Taylor's eyes roam around the luxurious area of the Balfour Hotel where he was the proud CEO. Like she was taking their very special day in for a second time. When his gaze relinked with Taylor's, something tugged in Zeke's heart.

To have all his family and friends in attendance for his big wedding celebration, Zeke couldn't have been happier. Yeah, the small wedding they'd had in Paris had been fantastic. Something he'd appreciated. Something he'd always cherish. But he loved Taylor so much until he wanted to share their union as husband and wife with the people that meant the most to him—his family and friends.

"Congratulations," Colton said, giving his son a big bear hug.

"Thanks father." Considering his father had so much going on with his health, Zeke didn't expect him to come. But here he was in the flesh. Alive and kicking.

Colton smiled. "I'm glad you decided to have the wedding here in Hilton Head, son. It was beautiful."

"Me too," Antonio exclaimed. "I'm glad you had the wedding at home, bro." *Yeah right.*

"Ditto," Bane stated.

Zeke looked inside the ballroom and spotted Katherine heading their way. *Oh boy. Here comes the drama queen.*

"Good afternoon everyone," Katherine said in her most proper tone as she swayed out of the ballroom. Clad in a white long, beaded pearl dress as if she was the bride, Katherine twirled her wrist in the air, showing off her glittering diamond bracelet. "Oh Taylor. You look marvelous, darling." Smiling her behind off, Katherine threw her arms around Taylor's shoulders, and accidentally got makeup on her dress. "I can't wait till you move into the mansion with Colton and me. I already have the guest house prepared. Oooo. I'm so excited!"

Taylor's eyes twinkled. "Thanks Katherine. I'm looking forward to moving in at the estate. I appreciate your kindness."

Zeke stated, "It's not going to be for too long. Just until our dream home gets built."

Katherine waved her hand in the air. "Well, feel free to stay as long as you like. Delbert will be at your beck and call."

Taylor gave Zeke a curious stare. "Who's Delbert?"

Katherine patted Taylor's shoulder. "Why he's the butler, darling."

Distaste for Katherine roiled Zeke's gut. Now call him negative, but Katherine's overly uplifting demeanor seemed a bit phony to Zeke. Maybe he just felt that way because Katherine had failed to tell him that Taylor had paid him a visit after she'd been rescued. Taylor had asked Katherine for a forwarding address as well, and she'd never bothered to give it to her. In fact the mean woman had even pretended to call him in front of Taylor.

Katherine can't be trusted. That being known, Zeke planned on keeping an eye on Katherine's bourgeois behind. No make that two eyes, Zeke thought, ready to get the wedding pictures over with so he could go upstairs and make wild burning love to his beautiful wife.

Chapter Seventeen

INSIDE THE GUEST HOUSE AT the Balfour's estate Zeke wrapped his arms about Taylor's shoulders. Squeezing her, he kissed the top of her head. "I'm glad you're adjusting to being back in Hilton Head." Zeke caressed the hair covering her back, released his strong hold on her.

"Returning home is not as bad as I thought it'd be. Living here in the guest house isn't bad either." Taylor's eyes traveled around the spacious guest house at Colton and Katherine's estate.

Katherine had great taste when it came to decorating. Golden painted walls. Dark chocolate furniture. Two bedrooms and two bathrooms. The guest house overlooked a dense wooded area and a nice wide lake. Fully equipped kitchen, the guest house had to be at least two thousand square feet, big enough to be a house.

Zeke rubbed his hands up and down Taylor's arms. "I knew you'd adjust once you returned."

Taylor tilted her head. "How did you know? I didn't even know that being here would come as easy as it had thus far."

"I knew you'd adjust because I know you. You're a strong woman, Taylor."

I miss Zavier, Taylor thought, longing for her son every second on the day now that she'd come back to Hilton Head. "I don't feel so strong at times, Zeke."

"Well you—"

"I want to hire a private investigator to find our son," Taylor blurted. Nodding, Zeke grabbed her hand, and led her over to the couch in front of the window in the family room. As they sat side by side gazing in each other eyes, a whimsical feeling rose inside Taylor, giving her hope. "Zavier is alive, Zeke. I know he is."

Zeke cupped Taylor's hands. "I believe he's alive, too. That's why I'm one step ahead of you. I've already hired a private investigator to help us find our son. He's on his way over here as we speak. His name is Donald McQuade. Goes by the name Don. He helped Richmond find out who killed his wife, Salina."

Killed! Taylor shivered. "Richmond was married before Kayla?"

"Yes. He was married to a beautiful woman named Salina. Unfortunately, Richmond's father murdered Salina. Salina was dying and she asked Richmond's father to help her commit suicide. Salina left a letter and video saying she wanted to die. In her letter, Salina pleaded to Richmond to forgive her and his father for killing her."

Taylor hated hearing such sad story. "That's horrible, Zeke. Well, did Richmond forgive his father?"

Zeke shrugged. "I don't think so."

That's awful. "I can't say that I blame him."

"Me either. But as I was saying, Don is a great private investigator. If anyone can find Zavier its Don. I've already briefly spoken with Don via telephone, and he should be here any minute now—" The telephone rang. Zeke rose from the sofa to go answer it. "Hello. Yes. I'm expecting him. Please send him to the guest house. Thanks Delbert," Zeke stated, then placed the cordless phone on the receiver. "Don just arrived to the main house."

"Thank for taking the initiative to do this." Ever so grateful Zeke and she were on the same page, Taylor watched Zeke walk back closer to her.

Zeke towered Taylor as she remained sitting. "You don't have to thank me for hiring Don. Zavier is my son, too. As his father, it's my responsibility to find him. I'll never stop searching until I do. And when I find out who took my son, who did this to you, to him, to us… I'm going to kill them with my own fucking hands." Zeke's bold throaty voice held anger.

Imaging Zeke snapping someone neck's in half, Taylor cringed. She knew her husband meant every single word he'd just said. If Zeke ever found out who kidnapped her and their son, Zeke would kill him.

The doorbell rang. "That's Don." Zeke stalked toward the door and pulled it open. Standing, Taylor observed the private investigator from where she now stood. Round chubby jaws, double chin, scraggly brown hair, and wearing a pair of black square glasses, Don looked like a detective. Looked very smart, cool, and collective. "Thanks for coming, Don," Zeke stated.

"The pleasure's all mine," Don said. Pushing his black square glasses up the bridge of his nose and carrying a black briefcase, he stepped over the thresh hold, and entered.

After Zeke made the introductions between Don and Taylor, he gestured for Don to sit in the chair opposite the window. Glad to be taking the first step in finding her son since she'd returned home, Taylor steepled her hands in her lap, and prayed inwardly. *God, please give Don the wisdom to help find my son.*

Don reached inside his briefcase, pulled out a note pad, and tape recorder. "Taylor, I'm going to ask you some questions that may require you to relive your past. More specifically, the day you were kidnapped and everything thereafter. If at any point you get uncomfortable or upset, let me know and we can stop. Okay?"

Taylor nodded. "Okay."

Don continued. "But keep in mind, in order for me to do my best job, you must tell me everything. Even things you think aren't important, I need to know about them. From the smallest detail to the biggest, tell me everything you can remember about the day you were kidnapped." He pressed the button the recorder, "You can start now."

"Where should I start?" Taylor asked.

Zeke caressed Taylor's knee. "How about you start from the time you left me, right after seeing the treehouse I'd built for you," Zeke suggested.

Tension tightened Taylor's chest. *I can do this. I can do this. I have to.* "Zeke had taken me in the woods close to this estate to show me the treehouse he'd built for me. While doing so, he'd given me a promise ring. Right when I was getting ready to tell Zeke I was pregnant, I heard Katherine shouting his name. She sounded like she was mad so I took off running."

"Why do you think Katherine was mad?" Don questioned.

Zeke spoke up. "She was mad because Taylor's mother had just informed her that Taylor was pregnant."

Don asked, "Did she make any suggestions as to what you should about the pregnancy?"

Zeke nodded. "Yes. She wanted Taylor to get an abortion."

Taylor's eyes rounded with sadness. "I never knew Katherine wanted me to have an abortion until now. I would've never agreed to it."

"Me either," Zeke replied.

"What happened after you left Zeke, Taylor?" Don prompted.

Memories of the day she'd been kidnapped assailed Taylor's mind. Stabbed her heart. "It was getting dark…" her words trailed off, and then she finally told Don everything.

Gazing down at the sparkling promise ring Zeke had given her, Taylor crossed the railroad tracks leading towards her home, and smiled. Zeke had said the promise ring was a token of how much he loved her. Placing her hand to the bottom part of her pregnant belly, Taylor had smiled.

Feeling blissful and hopeful about her future with Zeke, Taylor wondered if Zeke knew she was pregnant by now. Close to her home, darkness fell upon Taylor. Burning wood smelling like a bon fire wafted up her nose. Gazing down at the ground, she kicked at a rock, and looked at her promise ring again.

Suddenly, Taylor felt a shadow towering her from behind. Just as she whirred, someone covered her head with a bag. Clawing at the hands squeezing her neck, the locket necklace around her neck snapped, and fell to the ground. Losing her breath, she plummeted to her hands and knees.

Scurrying away with the bag covering her head while on her hands and knees, the crazy man yanked her off the ground. Unable to see, she screamed. She kicked, and punched, and jerked harshly in the strong man's arms. "Let me go! Let me go!"

"Shut up. You should've thought about your consequences beforehand," the man had said.

Crying her eyes out, Taylor heard bleeps from a car as if her abductor was unlocking it. He tossed her, and she landed hard on something. Bam! Sounded like a door had slammed close.

Frightened on wits end, Taylor snatched the bag from her head to find herself trapped inside the trunk of some man's car. Laying on her back, surrounded in sheer darkness, she felt the car rock and shimmy over the railroad track. Short moments later a train's whistle resounded throughout the night's air, and sailed into the dark trunk of the horrible monster's car.

Kicking and banging on the trunk's roof, Taylor wailed. He's going to kill me and my baby. Oh God, please help me. "Somebody help meeee!"

A single tear slid down Taylor's left cheek as she brought her past nightmare to a close. "I thought he was going to kill me."

Don exclaimed, "Your abductor knew you were pregnant and he was mad about it."

"What makes you say that?" Taylor queried.

Don stated, "Because he said you should've thought about your consequences beforehand. He was referring to the pregnancy. Besides your mother, Katherine, and Zeke, who else knew you were pregnant Taylor?"

Taylor thought back to who she'd told she was pregnant. Gosh, that'd been so long ago. "A few of my girlfriends from high school knew."

"What's their names?" Don questioned.

"Amber Peterson and Tiera Langston."

Don offered her a different perspective when he said, "How did Amber and Tiera feel about your pregnancy?"

Taylor shrugged. "From what I could tell at the time—they were happy for me. What does my kidnapping have to do with Amber and Tiera?"

Don stopped the recorder and gave her a peculiar stare. "Maybe nothing. Then again, it could mean everything."

"You don't think they had anything to do with me being kidnapped, do you?" Taylor wondered.

"That's what I'm here to find out. And I will find out. I've been an investigator for twenty something years, and I've had success with all my cases, except for one. Zeke and Taylor. I'm going to find your son," Don adamantly stated. He placed his items back into his briefcase, stood then walked over to the front door.

Zeke shook Don's hand as he stood in front of the opened door. "Thanks for coming, Don."

"Yes. Thanks."

Don released Zeke's hand. "No problem. You two have a wonderful day. I'll be contacting you very soon." He turned and headed back pass the main house.

Soft hope wandered through Taylor. Something inside her told her Don would do exactly what he promised—find her son. *Just please let Zavier be alive, and doing well.*

After Don left, Zeke called up to the main house. He asked Delbert to fix a nice lunch for them, and then he sent Taylor up to the main house to get it. Taylor grabbed her coat from the hangar, slid her arms through the sleeves, then walked outside.

Greenery lined the concrete sidewalk on either side. Huge oaks shielded the path that Taylor walked along as she headed towards the main house thinking about what Don had said about Amber and Tiera. *No.* Her girlfriends from high school couldn't have had anything to do with her kidnapping. Could they? God no. What if Amber had wanted Zeke for herself? Or what if Tiera had been jealous of her and she'd never known it? Maybe one of their fathers had arranged for her to be kidnapped. Who wouldn't want their daughter to marry into a billionaire family? Taylor opened the back door of the mansion, and entered the warm family room.

"How it'd go?" Katherine asked, as soon as Taylor entered the rear of the house.

"How'd what go?" Taylor wondered as she walked further inside the den.

With her red hair pulled back in a tight bun, the huge diamonds in Katherine's ears sparkled. Wearing a long flowery dress,

Katherine stood and met Taylor in the center of the room. "How it go with the private investigator?"

"I think it went pretty well," Taylor responded.

Katherine's green eyes gleamed. "Oh great. Does the investigator have any leads?"

I wish. "No. Not yet."

Katherine gave Taylor a soft stare. "For what it's worth, Taylor. I hope Don finds your son. I'm praying for you and Zeke."

"Thanks Katherine. Zeke and I need all the prayers we can get."

Delbert entered the family carrying a tray in his hands. "Oh, you finally got here," Delbert said as if the mansion was far away from the guest house. "I was just about to bring your lunch out to you. I didn't want it to get to cold. Hope you like fresh blackened salmon, herb pasta, and Ceasar salad." Delbert extended the tray topped with two covered dishes to her.

Taylor retrieved the tray from Delbert. "Thanks for cooking lunch, Delbert. I love salmon. However, this sounds like a lot for lunch."

Delbert fanned the air. "I forgot. You models eat very little."

Clenching the tray, Taylor snickered. "Actually, I probably eat more than you think."

Delbert's gaze raked up and down Taylor's body. "If you do, I can't tell. Your figure is perfect. I know women who'd kill to be shaped like you. Now if you'll excuse me, I need to go clean the kitchen," Delbert said, then began walking away. "Zeke has married a model. Now how about that?" Delbert talked to himself then disappeared into the kitchen.

"Speaking of modeling. Now that you're back here in Hilton Head, do you think you'll get many jobs?" Katherine asked.

"Yes. My agent, Pierre, looks out for me. He'll be sure to keep me busy. Normally, I get more jobs in the spring and the summer than I do in the winter. Once the spring gets here, I'll probably hardly see you. Or Zeke."

"Considering you have a busy schedule and travel all the time, are you sure you want to find your son?" Katherine's question stunned Taylor. Made her uneasy.

"What does my busy schedule have to do with finding my son?" Taylor felt restless and irritable.

Katherine placed her hand on Taylor's shoulder. "I'm just wondering how you'll be able to fit your son in your busy schedule if you find him. With Zeke being the CEO of Balfour Enterprises, and you traveling the world, I'd hate for you to take him out of a stable home and put him into one where his parents spend very little time with him."

What an idiotic thing to say. Taylor gritted her teeth in annoyance. "Let's get one thing straight, Katherine. My son is *not* in a stable home. He was kidnapped. The home he's living in is a lie. And for all I know, it may not be a stable one. We have no clue as to how he is living." Katherine opened her mouth to speak, but Taylor cut her off. "Another thing. I'll never be too busy for my own son. When Zavier comes home to me, I'm going to love him. Spoil him. And spend every awakening moment with him. How dare you suggest to me that my son will be a burden to me?" Furious, Taylor spun on her heels and flung open the back door.

Katherine hurried up behind her. "Oh Taylor. I'm sorry for upsetting you. I didn't mean it the way you took it."

Yeah right. Tempted to throw the salmon in Katherine's face, Taylor slowly turned around. "What you said offended me, Katherine."

Red hair hanging over her shoulders, worry shone in Katherine's green pupils. "I'm sorry, Taylor. I was out of line. Please don't tell Zeke about our disagreement."

Taylor purposely narrowed her eyes at Katherine. "Why don't you want me to tell Zeke about our conversation? Let me guess...you want me to keep our disagreement from him, just like you didn't tell him I came to see him after I was rescued." Katherine's eyes grew wide. "That's right, Katherine. Zeke knows that you pretended to call him on the day my mother and I paid you a visit all those years ago. For whatever reason, you purposely didn't tell Zeke I'd come to see him, and that I was alive. My husband and I don't keep secrets from each other. We tell each other everything. And you can bet your bottom dollar he's going to know about this!"

Chapter Eighteen

ZEKE AND TAYLOR WALKED ALONG the dirt path, making their way through the woods not far from the Balfour estate. Holding his wife's hand, Zeke brought the back of her hand up to his mouth, and kissed it. When her pretty mouth split into a lovely smile, his heart tingled, and so did his shaft. Marrying Taylor had been the best thing Zeke had ever done.

Yeah, being CEO was great. And yes being extremely wealthy was great, too. But being married to the love of his life, Taylor, was truly what made him happy. All that other stuff wouldn't mean a thing if he didn't have Taylor to share it with.

I wonder what Taylor's thinking. "You're quiet. Look nervous. We don't have to do this if you don't want too. If you want, we can turn around," Zeke offered, knowing seeing the treehouse he'd built for her all those years ago may trigger an uncomfortable feeling inside her.

Taylor looked relaxed in her purple winter coat and blue jeans. "I'm good, Zeke. I want to see the treehouse." Her voice came out sweet and gentle.

"Good." Pines scented the woods. Leaves scattered on the ground, a branched broke beneath Zeke's shoe.

A soft laugh escaped Taylor's mouth. "If it weren't so cold, I'd suggest we go skinny dipping for old time sake."

Zeke's brows hiked. "Would you really go skinny dipping at this age?"

"With you. My husband. You bet I would. It's not like anyone comes out here. Your parents own this land, and they have a big no trespassing sign stuck in the ground."

"Parent," Zeke corrected her. "Katherine's never been a mother to me."

"Why do you feel that way about Katherine? Is it because she didn't tell you about me?"

Resentment for Katherine floored Zeke. "Yes, it's that. But she's done other things, too. When growing up, Katherine treated me like I was some bad stepchild." *I tried so hard to please her, but it never worked.* "For example, Katherine would attend Banes and Antonio's sporting events, but she never attended any of mine. Not one. When it came to household chores, my brothers, well they didn't have any. Like in the movie Cinderella, I did all the work. Even though we had a maid and Delbert, Katherine worked me like a dog. Treated me like a slave."

Pity for Zeke developed in Taylor's eyes. "Did your father ever say anything about Katherine's unfair behavior towards you?"

All the time. "Yes. He did. But I think he felt so bad for having an affair with my mother until he let a lot of Katherine's bad behavior slide."

"Oh. I see."

Zeke and Taylor paused when they reached the big oak with the treehouse at the top. The wood on the treehouse had decayed some. "Let's go inside," Zeke suggested.

Anxious for her to see the surprise he had waiting for her, Zeke mounted the worn ladder on the tree, and entered the treehouse. On his hands and knees, he reached for Taylor's dainty hand, and helped to pull her inside.

Taylor's eyes swept over the romantic setting he'd quickly put together. "Oh Zeke. When did you find time to do all this?" Taylor asked, smiling.

Lanterns burned in all four corners. A small floor heater warmed the inside. He'd gotten a new blue rung to cover the planks of the floor.

"While you were napping earlier today, I ran out and picked up a few things."

Taylor pinched Zeke's chin then smacked his lips with hers. "You slick rascal. This is so romantic. Thanks."

Sitting with his back aligned to the wall, Zeke patted the empty space between his legs. "Sit here."

Taylor climbed between Zeke's legs. Enjoying Taylor's behind pressed against his shaft, Zeke tenderly held her.

Every day his love for Taylor deepened and intensified, he thought, cuddling her. "My father told me that he and my mother were high school sweethearts like you and I were. He met my mother way before Katherine came into his life. Actually, my father and my mother were engaged when he met Katherine. One night while he was at a bar, hanging out with his friends, he ran into Katherine, and ended up getting stupid drunk. One thing led to another, and Katherine ended up getting pregnant with Antonio that night. When Dad found out Katherine was pregnant, he told my mother, and she ended their engagement. If my mother wouldn't have ended things with my father, I think the two of them would've gotten married."

"Your parents eventually found their way back to each other, huh?

It felt wonderful to be able to share his past with someone who wouldn't judge him, or his mother, or his father. "Yes. But by then, Dad was married to Katherine. Dad told me that although he'd married Katherine, he never stopped loving my mother. I believe him. It almost killed him when my mother was murdered." Zeke was trapped by the memories of his father balling his eyes out while sitting in his recliner when he thought no one was looking.

Taylor shivered in Zeke's arms. "Thank God you hadn't been there when she'd been murdered."

"I wish I had been there, Taylor," he said, remembering he'd spent the night at a friend's house that terrible stormy evening.

"Why?" Taylor asked.

Talking about the day his mother had been murdered caused Zeke grave turmoil. "So I could know who killed her. Living with not knowing who murdered my mother is just as torturous as not knowing where or who has Zavier."

"Oh Zeke. You've been through so much." Taylor's concern sounded genuine just like her.

The light inside the lantern flickered orange. Zeke put his cheek to Taylor's. "We've both been through a lot in our lives. But now that we're married we have each other. Together we can get through anything. We can move mountains. Build an empire. In addition to the hotel industry, I want to have many businesses just like my father."

With her back to his chest, Taylor gently laid her head on his chest. "I like the sound of that. Do you have any specific type of business in mind?"

Zeke took a moment to think. "Well, there're many. But right now, one in particular comes to mind. I presently volunteer at a group care facility, and would like to start a non-profit organization for the children there. Maybe I can start a scholarship fund for children in need. Or maybe I can start an organization to help build their careers. Give them a start, you know? Or prep them for college. I tell you Taylor, of all the things I do business wise, working at the group care facility with those needy kids makes me the happiest. By far it's the most rewarding."

"Volunteering the way you do with kids, God's going to bless you, Zeke. I bet the children love you."

"It seems that way. Some of the kids come from horrible living situations. It breaks my heart to hear some of their stories. I just hope Zavier is in a good, clean home, and is treated fairly. Hope he's getting all the love he needs." Ill feelings about Zavier's whereabouts dredged up inside Zeke.

Taylor blew out a deep breath. "Me too, Zeke. Don sounded really positive about thinking he can help us find Zavier."

Zeke swallowed hard. "He'll find him, Taylor. Don will find our son. Or he'll die trying. You heard the man, he's never lost but one case, and he sure as hell don't plan on making ours number two." Zeke suddenly remembered his other surprise. "Oh yeah, before I forget," he reached into the pocket of his jacket, pulled out a square box. "There's something I want to give you," he said, handing her the hot pink, velvety box.

"What's this?" she asked, holding the tiny box.

She's going to love this present. "Open it up and see?"

Taylor popped back the lid of the box and inside lay a silver locket Zeke had especially made just for her. On the outside of the silver locket the letters **ZTZ** for Zeke, Taylor, and Zavier was scribbled in cursive. "It's a locket, made especially for you." When Taylor opened the jewelry to look at the inside, her hand touched her lips. The left part of the locket had a picture of the two of them on their wedding day in Paris. And on the right, Zeke had his son's name Zavier printed. "Oh Zeke, this is so thoughtful. Beautiful. Thank you." Her voice trembled.

Zeke squeezed Taylor tight in his embrace. "When Zavier comes home to us, you can put his picture on top of his name."

"Thanks," she said, sniffling. After Zeke hooked the locket around Taylor's neck, she shifted sideways in his lap and looked over her shoulder at him. "It's so cozy in here. Coming here to cuddle, this was a great idea. Bring back so many memories."

Zeke grinned naughtily. "Who said all I wanted to do was cuddle?"

Taylor's brown lips pulled into a sweet smile. Her eyes gleamed. "Why Mr. Balfour, whatever else do you have in mind for us to do?"

The skin on Zeke's rod stretched as it grew long, and hard inside his jeans. "Not us. You."

Taylor touched her gloved covered hand to her chest. "Me?"

Stiff rod pressing into the jeans covering her fine buttocks, Zeke nipped Taylor's bottom lip with his teeth. "Yes you."

A subtle light danced in his wife's eyes. "Your every wish is my command. Just name what you'd like for me to do husband."

Zeke's right brow hiked. "Anything?"

Taylor touched a finger to Zeke's lips. "Yes. Anything."

He sucked her finger into his mouth. Pulling her finger from between his lips, Taylor moaned. "Do you think I can get a blow job?" Zeke could already envision her curling her lips around his hard cock.

"Now? In here?"

Hell yeah in here. "I'm hurting, my love. Bad." Zeke put his fingers to Taylor's lips. "I need you to take your pretty sexy mouth and soothe the pain between my legs." Removing his fingers, he kissed her lips. "Take the pain away, please."

"I'd love too, husband." Smiling, Taylor got on her hands and knees, and turned around to face Zeke. Locking her gaze with his, she zipped down his fly. The sound of his zipper ripped in the air.

"I want to feel your thickness in my hands," she said, removing her gloves, then placing them by her side. In a doggy position, her tongue dabbled her bottom lip and then she fisted his erected tool.

Aroused, a strong bolt of hot electricity surged Zeke. Taylor's hot hand squeezed him hard. Fluid oozed from the tiny eye of his swollen head, then slid beneath the deep circular groove of his throbbing shaft. When Taylor squeezed him hard again, more pre-come seeped from his slick slit. Zeke groaned, "Taste me, Taylor."

Taylor perched her sexy lips to Zeke's knotted head then slid her hot mouth all the way down to his base. Coating him with her hot saliva, Zeke shuddered. The inside of Taylor's mouth felt hot, wet, and tight. *Jesus, that's feels good.*

Back to the wall, hands flattened on the planks, Zeke watched Taylor give him one hellified blowjob. She brought her sexy lips up to his pulsating tip, then slowly mashed them back down his tingling shaft. His round testicles tickled. *Fuck yeah.* Motioning him up and down in her tight fist, Taylor's head bobbed up and down. Up and down. She swallowed him whole.

Taylor's wrist twisted vigorously as she clenched Zeke's stem tight, sucking him at the same time. Zeke's shaft wiggled like a slithering snake inside his wife's wet mouth. Taylor scraped her manicured nails on his scrotum, driving Zeke mad. Pushed him over the edge.

Mouth clenching, jaws sucking, her curly brown hair grazed his gyrating lap as Zeke gently pound Taylor's sweet mouth. Still looking at her talented performance, Zeke thrust upward, saliva poured from Taylor's puckered mouth, and slid down the sides of his tool.

Fisting him, she angled his dick downward, brought those damn sexy lips of hers to the top of his tool again, and hummed a song around his pulsating head. About to shoot, Zeke shut his eyes and let Taylor take him on one hell of a sexual exploration. *Oh yeah. Sing on it. Talk on the microphone.*

Taylor sucked his head. Massaged his hard sac. Softly sliding back and forth between her soft lips, Zeke felt her teeth graze his length. A hot ball of fire shot through his system. His eyes shot open.

Gripping the sides of Taylor's head, Zeke mashed himself to the back of Taylor's tight throat. Sperm shot up his length, rested at his throbbing tip. *I'm about to come. Got...*

On the verge of unleashing inside Taylor's mouth, Zeke grabbed his shaft, and snatched it from her clenching lips. *Plop!* His manhood popped loudly from her mouth. Harsh breaths whipped from Zeke's mouth. "That was close. I almost came in your mouth." Sperm bubbled at the top of Zeke's engorged, blood filled erection.

Eyes lustrous, Taylor's lips were so swollen and wet. "I'll swallow if you want me, too."

"Let me make love to your tits."

"How do you do that?"

"Here. Let me show you." After Zeke took off Taylor coat and removed her shirt and bra, he laid her on her back. Curiosity shone in her sensual eyes as he climbed on top of her.

Knees pressing into the wood, Zeke clenched his shaft and slapped it between the alcove between Taylor's breasts. Beholding her tender gaze, he scooped her swollen mounds with erected nipples in his hands, starting grinding. "This is called titty-fucking, my wife," he said, his stem sliding back and forth between her boobs.

"I like it, Zeke." Taylor placed her small hands on the outside of Zeke's, and helped him mash her breasts harder to his rod. Breasts clutching his tool tight, Zeke's squeezed his butt cheeks.

Zeke's balls tightened. The head of his erection popped from the top of her breasts, and knocked into her chin, then disappeared back between her smothering boobs. His bulbous head protruded from the top of her tits again hitting her chin. His member burned into her tingling skin. "I'm. Oh. Uh. Arrrgh!" Hot come shot from Zeke's shaft onto Taylor's chest. His spunk came close to hitting her face.

Taylor cracked up laughing. She looked at the white sperm clinging to her chest. "Ooo. You had a lot in you."

Damn, that was good. Zeke's shaft started shrinking. "Thanks for letting me make love to you in here. I know it's not the most ideal place, but it's——"

"Adventurous. Spontaneous. Romantic." She playfully hit his arm. "You done got me horny, babe."

"Oh yeah. I can fix that."

"How?" she asked, easing up on her elbows. Zeke's white come rolled down the crack between her breasts to her stomach. He pulled a tissue from his pocket, wiped the sticky sperm off.

He tossed the tissue to the corner. "I can show you better than I can tell you." Zeke rolled Taylor's jeans and panties down her thighs then tossed then placed them aside. Putting a hand to her shoulder, he gestured for her to lay back down.

With his head positioned over her vagina, Zeke pulled back the hood of her plump sex. His mouth watering, he stuck out his tongue, and licked her delicious center. Taylor writhed. "Mmm," she moaned. Bucking on his face, she grabbed the sides of his head, and said, "I sure do love you." Groaning, she wrapped her legs around his head, scraping her erected clitoris on his teeth.

"I bet you do love me." Zeke curled the tip of his tongue over her clitoris, inserted two fingers in her heat. *Mmm.* She tasted good. A salty and sweet taste coated his probing tongue. Circling her hips, Taylor panted. Her juicy labia fluttered softly against his lips. Slick juices slipped from her opening onto his tongue. His nose. His chin.

He could eat this pussy all day every day, Zeke thought, his dick elongating down his thigh. "Oh Zeke. I'm coming. Oooo." Cooing and bucking on his face, Taylor squeezed the sides of his head hard. She sucked in a bout of air. "Ahhh." Licking her from clit to slit, a load of liquid squirted from Taylor's channel and soaked his face.

"You were horny," Zeke said, coming up for air.

Taylor snickered. "Whew. I guess I had a lot in me, too."

Zeke dragged his hand over his drenched mouth to wipe it. "Yes. You had more than me."

"Liar!"

Chapter Nineteen

NOISE FILLED OCEAN COAST GROUP care facility about thirty minutes away from Hilton Head in a small town called Beaufort. Inside the facility near Paris Island, Zeke sat at a table tutoring a high school teenager by the name of Jaheem Parker. Using his fingers to count, Jaheem reworked the math problems on the test he'd failed.

Elbow on table, Zeke stared at the handsome African American kid with a mini afro. *Handsome young fellow.* Zeke stated, "Why don't you try using mental math like I showed you on Monday?"

Sixteen year old Jaheem sucked his teeth. "Man after the day I had in school, my mental ability is shot to fucking hell."

Zeke's brows dipped into an affronted frown. "Hey, what your language. Use better words when you talk to me."

Jaheem's lips turned under, his eyes rounded with regret. "Sorry, Mr. Balfour. I promise I'm going to work on my language. Okay?"

He looks like he's really sorry. "Alright. I hear you. I told you that you can call me, Zeke."

Holding the tip of his pencil to his math paper, Jaheem nodded. "You come here all the time, Zeke. You tutor me, and you come to my basketball games. Why are you so nice to me?"

Warmth filled Zeke's heart as he looked at Jaheem. "Because you deserve it. You're a good kid, Jaheem."

Fingers spread out before, Jaheem kept counting his fingers. "Don't nobody think I deserve help, but you. Everybody, especially my teachers, think I ain't gone be shit when I grow up."

"Watch your language," Zeke reminded Jaheem. *This kid have a serious cussing problem.*

Eyes wide, Jaheem slapped his hand over his mouth, then lowered it to the table. "Sorry. I mean, they think I'm not going to be anything when I grow up. But I'm going to do what you told me to do. I'm going to work real hard prove all the naysayers wrong. I'm going to study my behind off and earn a scholarship."

"As long as you keep that attitude, you'll be successful, Jaheem. Always remember, with hard work and determination, you can do and be anything you want to be." Zeke held out his fist and Jaheem bumped it with his own fist.

Jaheem's dark lips smiled across his face. "Man, you a good role model. When I become rich like you, I'm gone volunteer and donate to shelters, too. Just wait and see. I'm gone——"

"Kiss my ass!" A young kid shouted.

Zeke looked up to find a chair flying over his head. He ducked, and the chair crashed into the wall in front of him. *What the hell!* Instinctively, Zeke bolted from the table, and ran up to the young kid.

Tempted to snatch the little young boy standing in front of him pouting up, Zeke's fists balled. Zeke glared down at the honey brown complexioned kid with big curly hair. "Hey kid, you almost cut my head off with the chair. What's your problem?"

Frowning, the kid sucked his teeth, and took a bold step forward. "It's gone be you dude if you don't get out my way. I just kicked Torrance's ass, and I'll kick yours, too!"

"Oh, it's like that, huh?" Zeke snapped. *I'll put his skinny behind over my lap and snap him in half.*

Sticking his tiny chest out, the young boy jutted his chin. "Yeah. Move mister."

Zeke had to calm his nerves down before further speaking to the kid who was obviously determined to have an argument tonight. *Count backwards Zeke. Ten, nine, eight...Calm your nerves. The kid may have a good reason to behave like this.* Zeke's temper quickly dissolved. "Look, I don't know what happened to get you this fired up, but—"

"There you are!" Marva Donaldson yelled, scampering toward them, pointing her finger at the kid in front of Zeke. "Evan! Come here?! You're in big trouble."

Evan stumped his foot. "Man, I hate it here!"

Marva fisted her hips and pointed in Evan's face. "Now you look here young man, I know times have been hard for you, but that doesn't give you the right to punch someone in the face, and call people names."

Evan rolled his eyes. "Torrance hit me first. You just happened to catch me hitting him back."

Marva took a deep breath. "What started the fight?"

Evan yelled, "He called me an Oreo, and I got mad."

Marva stated, "That's nothing to get mad about, Evan."

Anger burned inside Evan's brown eyes. "It is if you're mixed."

"Mixed with what?"

Big tears settled on the rims of Evan's dark brown eyes, making Zeke feel sorry for the young boy. "Black and white. Just in case you haven't noticed lady, I'm biracial! Ever since I got here they've been teasing me about my complexion. And I'm tired of it. Fucking tired!" Evan took off running down the hallway.

Marva threw her hands up in the air. "Evan! Come back here! They don't pay me enough to do this job." *Hell, I don't get paid anything to be here, but you don't see me complaining.* Eyes peering down the hallway, Marva shook her head. "Now I got to go find him."

"I'll go speak with Evan," Zeke offered.

Marva sighed. "Thanks, Zeke. He could probably use a man to speak with. Thanks."

"Don't mention it. I'm happy to help." Zeke jogged down the hallway, rounded the corner, and went to the end of the hallway. Standing next to a closed door, Evan's soft cries sailed inside Zeke's ears. Zeke pulled open the shut door of the closet to find Evan sitting in the dark, crying his eyes out.

"Go away!" Evan yelped.

Sorrow dulled Zeke's heart. Praying for God to give him some encouraging words to share with the kid named Evan, he walked inside the closet, shut the door, and sat beside him. Zeke cleared his throat. "I'm sorry for the way the kids treat you here. I can't even imagine what you're going through. But I'd like to listen to how you feel if you want to share."

Evan sniffed. "I said go away. They already told me that you were rich, so you could never understand what I'm going through. Never."

Zeke stated, "I may be rich, but like you, I've had problems."

Evan clucked his tongue. "Yeah, right. What happened to you? Your maid didn't bring you any tissue to wipe your ass?"

This kid is a lot like Jaheem was when I first started mentoring him. Tough and angry, he uses bad language, too. "No. My problems were worse than that." Zeke pulled his cell from his pocket, and turned on the light. The dark closet vaguely brightened.

Evan lifted his wet face from his palms. His sniffles slowed. Legs bent at the knees, back to the wall, he laced his hands behind his head. "Like what?"

Thinking about his son Zavier, Zeke's body tensed. "Like I had a son, and some cruel person kidnapped him. I never got a chance to see my son's face before he was stolen. But if I had seen his face, I bet he'd look a lot like you."

Evan's face scrunched. Wet pupils, he looked Zeke up and down. "Oh, no. Your son wouldn't look nothing like me, mister."

"I disagree."

Evan's head jerked back. "How you figure that mister? You're all white!"

Zeke chuckled. "Yeah, but the woman that had my son was a black lady. So you see, my son, wherever he is, is biracial like you."

Evan's voice lowered as he said, "So you never found your son, mister?"

Zeke's chest ached. "No. He's still missing."

Evan released a heavy sigh. "You're right. We both have problems. Both of us are fucked up."

At first Evan's forwardness made Zeke cringe. Then out of nowhere Evan's admittance threatened to make him chuckle. "Hey. Let's make a deal."

Seemingly still aggravated, Evan rolled his eyes. "I don't make deals."

"Well, you've probably never been made a deal like this." Evan gave a nonchalant shrug. Zeke continued. "The deal is…if you come out of the closet with your head held high, and try your hardest to ignore those fools teasing you, I'll come here and pick you up on Saturday, and take you wherever you'd like to go."

Evan's eyes brightened. "Really!"

Zeke offered Evan a sincere smile. "Yes, really."

Evan folded his arms across his chest. "Even if I want to go ice skating to the new arena all the kids are talking about, you'll take me there?"

Zeke ruffled the dark brown curly hair on Evan's round head. "Yes, I'll even take you ice skating," he said, holding out his hand.

Evan gave him a firm shake. "We've got a deal, Mister."

"HOW DARE TAYLOR TREAT ME like crap in my own house, questioning me," Katherine muttered under her breath as she descended the staircase inside her mansion. The mansion that every woman in Hilton Head Island and around the world wish they had the privilege of living in. The home that every living woman wished they'd someday acquire, and leave to their children. And their children's children.

Damn right I didn't tell Zeke that she was alive. It wasn't my place. Furry burned Katherine's insides. Turning inside the kitchen, the bottom of her long dress swept the floor. *Insinuating I should be worried if she tells Zeke. Apparently, Taylor doesn't know who she's messing with.* A wicked thought entered Katherine's mind. "I guess I'm going to have to teach the prissy bitch a lesson."

"Talking to yourself again, I see." Colton snuck up behind Katherine.

She whirled.

Quiet stillness lurked in the air as Katherine looked at her husband, Colton. The man who'd once been the love of her life. Until recently, he'd been the love of her life, all her life. But when he made Zeke CEO of *Balfour Enterprises*, the love she had for her husband vanished. No one treated her son Antonio like a bastard. Zeke was the bastard, not Antonio.

Clearly able to see it was a thin line between love and hate, disdain for Colton stabbed Katherine's heart. "Yes, I'm talking to myself," she shrugged, "And?"

"And did you answer yourself, too? They say if you answer yourself, you're certifiable crazy." Colton teased.

I can show you how crazy I am. Keep messing up. "Don't you ever have anything nice to say about me?" Katherine asked.

Colton stalked up to Katherine and pecked her lips. "Yes. I love you."

Katherine rolled her eyes. "Yeah right. The only person you love is Zeke."

"Here we go." Colton pulled open the refrigerator, grabbed his medicine, and a bottle of water. Popping the cap off the water bottle, he shook his head negatively.

"Don't you here we go again me. It's true. You proved who you love when you made Zeke CEO. What you did hurt Antonio to the core, Colton. To the freaking core. Antonio hasn't been himself since you put him second in charge and not first. It's not too late for you to go back and change it if you want."

Colton tossed his medication in his mouth, and gulped down the entire bottle of water. Releasing a loud belch, he tossed the empty bottle in the trash can. "You said that magic words, Katherine. If I *want* to change it I can. Well, I don't want to put Antonio in charge. Nor will I. Zeke is the CEO of Balfour now. The sooner you and Antonio accept my decision, the better off this family will be."

Curses swooned around inside her head. "You're so cold and heartless, Colton."

"Snap it shut, woman." At the sound of his stern voice Katherine briefly snapped her lips together.

You're going to regret your decision Colton. "You still love her, don't you, Colton?"

Colton shook his head. "Please don't start with that again."
Bing. Colton's cell chirped, signaling a text had just come through.
He pulled the chair from beneath the dining table, pulled his cell
from his pants pocket, and using his thumb, he tapped the screen.

Sick and tired of being sick and tired, Katherine marched up to
Colton, snatched the cell from his grip, and held it high in the air.
"You're not getting your cell until you answer my question."

Colton gave Katherine a hostile stare. "You seriously don't
want to do this Katherine. Now give me my cell back."

She kept the cell held high above his head. "Why are avoiding
the question? Will you for once in your pathetic life just answer me?
Admit it. You still love Bridget. Don't you? You're in love with a
dead woman. I'm glad Bridget is dead."

Colton leapt from his seat and lounged forward. Face twisted,
he fisted the top of Katherine's dress, and wagered his big manly
finger in her face. "Watch your gotdamn mouth. Take it back. Take
it back gotdamnit!" The bridled anger in his voice vibrated inside
his thick neck.

"Look at you, Colton. You want to hit me." Tilting her head
back, she turned her cheek to him. "Go ahead. Do it Colton. Hit
me because I meant what I said." Katherine clenched her teeth
together. "I'm glad Bridget is dead." Bringing her neck forward,
Katherine spit in Colton's face.

Twisting Katherine's clothing in one hand, Colton raised his
fist above her face, and started shaking. Chest heaving, his face
scrunched. "You're not even worth it." Releasing her dress, his fist
lowered to his side. "I've never hit a woman before. Never even
came close to it. What you said about Bridget disgusts me." The
muscles in his jaws flickered. "But to answer your question. Yes. I
still love Bridget. I'll always love her. I'm sorry if I hurt you for
saying it, but it's true. And although I've said it a million times
before, I'm sorry for cheating on you with her. It was wrong. I was

wrong. But I shouldn't have to spend the rest of my life paying for it." Tears welled in Katherine's eyes. *Hmmph.* Colton continued. "Believe it or not, I love you too Katherine. I really do. I'm willing to get marriage counseling if you'll come with me."

"Marriage counseling won't change how you feel about Bridget. You'll grieve that dead woman till the day you die." *And the sooner you die the better.*

"I'm not taking all the blame for how things turned out. You bare some of the responsibility for what happened, too. You knew I was engaged to Bridget when we met. I was set to marry her. From what I heard, you knew I'd be at the bar on the evening we hooked up, and you planned to be there just to seduce me."

Katherine huffed. "You sure think highly of yourself, Colton."

"Well, somebody has to because you sure don't think much of me. I'd only had a few drinks that night. It wouldn't surprise me if you drugged me. Gary told me he saw you fooling around with my drink when I went to the bathroom. But I was too naïve to believe him back then. I sure as hell hope Gary was wrong. Because if he wasn't, I'm as dumb as they come. A stupid fool." Spittle flew from Colton's mouth.

Yes she'd drugged him, but so what? It wasn't like she was the first woman to put something in a man's drink to secure her future. "Gary lied. He always had a thing for me, and you know it."

Colton rolled his eyes. "Yeah. Yeah. Whatever. I'm going to bed." When he reached the family room, he turned back to look at her. "Again, Katherine. I'm sorry. Let's get some marriage counseling please. I really want to save our marriage. I know I may not be the best husband. But I sure am willing to try." Colton dropped his head between his shoulders and walked out of the room.

The kitchen door leading to the garage swung open and Antonio emerged inside the kitchen. "I could hear the two of you arguing all the way outside."He removed his coat draping it on the back of the chair. "It was about me, wasn't it?"

Katherine nodded. "What your father did to you is just downright wrong. I could just kill him sometimes."

Antonio cupped his mother's shoulders. "Don't go getting anything bad inside that pretty head of yours, Katherine."

Katherine hit Antonio's arm. "What did I tell you about calling me Katherine? You sound like Zeke. Not only did he put Zeke in charge, but he offered him and Taylor to come live here without asking me first. I'm starting to hate your father. I hate to say it, but it's true."

"Shhh." Antonio hastened over to the family room, then the living room, and back over to Katherine. "Mother. You can't just say whatever come to your mind. Dad could've overheard you."

Katherine waved her hand in the air. "He can't hear me, he's hard of hearing." She pulled a box of cigarettes from her cleavage, grabbed a lighter from the kitchen drawer, and lit the tip. As she inhaled a long drag, a single tear rolled down her cheek. Pooching her lips in the air, smoke spiraled from her pursed lips. Katherine said, "Taylor's hell bent on finding her son. Her and Zeke. If they find that child, we're doomed."

Antonio's glowered at Katherine. "Oh no. I'm not going to jail, Katherine. We have to make sure that Zeke and Taylor don't find their son."

Katherine thumped the ashes in the sink beside where she stood. "You said their son was far away from here. Are you sure?" Smoke spiraled from her mouth.

"Yes Katherine, I'm positive. I paid Kelvin a lot of money. Trust me the damn kid is probably in Germany or somewhere."

Katherine puffed on her cigarette again. "Kelvin ain't never been that bright. But then again, he was convincing. He convinced you to join the *Southern Mafia* gang when y'all were teenagers.

Whatever you do, please don't ever take off your shirt. Why did you let them boys in that gang burn your chest with the letters SM?"

"That's the past, Katherine," Antonio said, rubbing his covered chest area where the big SM branded him. Colton didn't even know he'd burned his flesh with those initials.

"Yeah, but if anyone finds Kelvin, see his chest and then yours, they'll know you knew him. I wish you would've killed Taylor when you had a chance. I told you to make sure they killed her after she had the baby. Why couldn't you get it right, Antonio? Huh? Why?" Feeling her life falling apart, she turned, and as she started walking away, her oldest son palmed her shoulder.

Antonio's squeezed her shoulders and the knots beneath her flesh rolled. "I did my best, Katherine. It's not too late for me to take care of Taylor. All you have to do is tell me what you want me to do to her."

I want Taylor dead. Stressed, Katherine folded her arms beneath her breast, and refaced Antonio. "You know what I want when it comes to Taylor, Antonio. It's the same thing I wanted on the day you had her kidnapped." Eyes bugging, Antonio's finger flew to his mother's mouth.

Meaning every single word, Katherine strolled out the room, her dress dragging on the floor with her.

Chapter Twenty

DELBERT PUSHED THE DINNER CART inside the formal dining room, parked it by the wall, and one by one he lowered a hot plate in front of each Balfour family member. As usual, Colton sat at one end with Katherine at the other. Zeke, Taylor, Antonio, and Bane surrounded them. Feeling nauseated, Taylor spied her dish covered with fried barbeque chicken, braised collards, and macaroni and cheese.

Lately, Taylor hadn't been feeling well. It seemed like every time she ate, she got sick. She didn't know if she was pregnant, or had the flu, or maybe Delbert's cooking just didn't agree with her.

Sourness rolled inside Taylor's stomach. Hot, perspiration wet her forehead. After Colton blessed the food, Taylor stabbed the chicken with the fork, then sliced the tender meat in half.

Holding the sweet smelling piece of meat to her mouth, Taylor stomach cramped. She just knew she'd puke in any minute. *I need some Tums antacid. I can't eat this chicken.* Wanting to excuse herself without alarming anyone, she lowered her fork to the side of her plate.

Sitting to her right next to his father, Zeke rubbed circles on Taylor's back. "Are you okay, my love?"

Chewing on some collards, Katherine gave Taylor a strange look. Knowing Katherine, she was probably wondering if she'd told Zeke about their conversation a few days ago. Well, she'd decided not, too. The last thing Taylor wanted or needed was to have Katherine mad at her while she was living under her roof. Some things were just better left unsaid.

"I don't feel too well," Taylor drawled.

Katherine's face lightened. "You're not pregnant are you? It'd be so much fun to have a little Zeke running around here."

"Or a little Taylor." Colton lowered his glass of lemonade to the table. "It'd really be something is if y'all had twins."

"Or triplets," Bane interjected.

Antonio forked macaroni in his mouth, then snapped his eyes up. "They don't need to have any kids yet. They just got married," his tone was clipped.

"What's got you in a bad mood?" Bane asked.

Antonio shrugged. "Who said I was in a bad mood?"

Bane stated, "I know you, and something's bothering you. I hope you're not still upset about not being CEO. If you are, get over it."

Antonio dropped his fork to his plate with a clink. "I said," much emphasis was on the word said, "there's nothing bothering me." Antonio scooted his chair back from the table, stood, and glared down at Bane. "Some people need to mind their own damn business around here."

I hope Antonio doesn't start a fight. I'm not in the mood, Taylor thought, her stomach curdling.

Bane stood to meet Antonio's harsh stare. "Having a bad attitude about the situation is not going to solve anything. Dad made his decision about the CEO position, now just accept it."

Colton dragged his napkin over his mouth, then balled it in his hand. "All right you two, that's enough. Y'all are two grown men, now act like it."

Eyeballs to eyeballs, neither of Antonio or Bane moved.

"You better be glad you're my brother," Antonio stated.

Bane's eyebrows dipped. "Or you'll what?"

"Trust me little brother, you don't want to know. You have no idea what I'm capable of, so if I were you, I'd keep my damn mouth shut from this day forward about who's running the company. Everyone is on Zeke's side, except for Momma. She's the only one that has my back."

Taylor's stomach burned with pain. Bile rushed up her esophagus. *What's wrong with me?*

Finally having had enough of the bickering, Zeke ordered, "Both of you need to do as Dad said and stop arguing. Sit back down and enjoy this delicious dinner Delbert cooked."

"Everybody got my side except for Momma," Bane whined, mocking Antonio.

Antonio punched Bane in the face. Gripping his split cheek, Bane's stumbled backwards. "Punk!" Bane lounged into Antonio. Antonio's body slammed into the table. Plates of food went flying into the air. Bane rose his fist above his brother's face. "I ought to bash your brains in!"

Zeke clutched Bane's shoulders and pulled him off of Antonio. "Don't stoop to his level. Be the bigger man, Bane."

Bane touched his red split cheek. "Easy for you to say. You're not the one that got punched in the face." Furious, Bane stormed out of the room then left.

Afraid to speak, Taylor glanced up at Zeke. "Can we leave now?"

Katherine exclaimed in a proper tone, "But you haven't touched your food."

Taylor put her hand to the lower part of her stomach. "I don't have an appetite."

"I'll wrap up your food for you and you can take it home." Katherine's kind offer made Taylor feel as if their relationship was headed in the right direction. Maybe the two of them could become good friends one day after all.

"Thanks Katherine. I'd like that—" Taylor hopped out of her seat, ran to the bathroom in the hallway, and purged in the toilet.

Towering her, Zeke patted her back. "Is there anything I can do for you?"

Wiping her mouth with the back of her hand, Taylor rose from her knees. "No. Let's go."

Zeke's worried dark eyes clung to her face. He put his flat palm to Taylor's stomach. "Is it possible that you're pregnant?"

"Yes. It's possible. How would you feel if I am?"

"Nothing would make me happier than for you to be pregnant with my child." Zeke grabbed Taylor's hand and after she got her to go box from Katherine, they returned home to their guest suite behind the main house.

SEVERAL WEEKS LATER TAYLOR'S HANDS curled around the steering wheel of the Audi Zeke had given her on their *second* wedding day. Not much into cars, she loved the Audi. Shiny black paint on the outside. Orange-brown leather on the inside, the Audi RS was the finest and most luxurious car she'd ever owned.

Turning the corner, Taylor headed down Ocean drive. Passing *Balfour Hotel & Resort*, the ocean to her right glistened. Sunrays beamed down through the windshield onto her face. She reached into her console for her white Bvlgari, designer sunglasses and slid them on her face.

"You have reached your destination. Your destination is to your left," the lady on the GPS announced.

Taylor slowed her Audi and glanced at the building in front of her. *SugarKanes.* "This is a very nice building." She drove into a vacant parking space, placed the gear in park, and cut the engine.

Toting her clutch, the cool March air bristled Taylor's face as she walked along the pavement across the street from the ocean. Hoping she wasn't too dressed up in her red blazer, skinny jeans, and black Christian Louboutin shoes, Taylor pulled open the door, and entered.

Glad Kayla had invited her to her baby shower, a delicious caramel flavor sailed up Taylor's nostrils upon entering *SugarKanes. Mmm. Must be one of those caramel pecan pies everyone rants and raves about,* she thought, admiring the beautiful decorations.

Baby blue balloons floated in the air. A three tier white cake encircled with blue rattles sat centered on the table in the corner.

"Taylor!" Kayla hopped up from the table and wobbled over to Taylor. A pregnant Kayla threw her arms around Taylor and hugged her like they were already best friends. "I'm so glad you could come," Kayla said, smiling, releasing her.

Taylor smiled back. *Kayla is so beautiful.* "Thanks for inviting me." Taylor waved at her mother sitting over there in the corner talking her behind off. "Thanks for inviting my mother, too. Wow. You look so pretty, Kayla."

Kayla caressed her protruding belly. "I'm glad you and your mother Veronica could come. Thanks for the compliment. With this big old belly, big thighs, and heavy breasts, I sure don't feel pretty."

Excited to be amongst the presence of such nice women, Taylor felt grateful. "But you are pretty. Wait until I tell you about the phone call I received. You're not going to believe your ears."

Belly hard and round, Kayla put her hands to her hips. "Well, don't keep me in suspense tell me now."

Taylor shook her head. "Today is about you. So let's just focus on you."

"Get over here, you two!" Sandella waved for them to come and sit.

After Kayla introduced Taylor to Willa and Leslie and the rest of the women, they played a few games, and ate a delicious lunch prepared by one of Sandella's chefs. As the women sat indulging in the sweet strawberry cake with cream cheese icing, Kayla opened her presents. Lord knows she had a lot of them, too.

"So Taylor," an older woman by the name of Willa started, "how does it feel to be back in Hilton Head Island?"

"Actually, it feels great. I'm happy to be here," Taylor responded, meaning it.

Leslie exclaimed, "I bet it's a lot different from Paris, isn't it?"

Taylor nodded. "Paris and Hilton Head are in no way alike. They're totally different."

Kayla tore the sparkling blue paper off the square package. "I'm glad to hear you're adjusting, Taylor."

Crossing her legs at the knees, Leslie said, "With a man like Zeke for a husband, what woman wouldn't adjust?"

Willa high fived Leslie. "Ain't that the truth, Leslie! Zeke so fine women would travel the world to and fro just to be with him. I did the same thing for my Drake when we first met. Shoot, good men are hard to find."

"Tell me about it. I wish I had a good man," Leslie admitted.

"Even at your age, you want to date?" one of the other women asked Leslie.

Leslie said, "Hell yeah. I may be old, but I ain't dead." She looked down between her legs. "It's still hot and jumping down there. Of course I want a man to date." Clapping her hands, Leslie cracked up laughing, and so did the rest of the women.

After the baby shower ended, Taylor, Willa, Leslie, and Veronica remained at *SugarKanes* to help Sandella clean up.

Sweeping the floor, Taylor glanced over at Kayla as she sat in the chair tucked in the corner by the glass display. Rubbing her belly, Kayla's face wrinkled. The broom stilled in Taylor's hands. "Are you okay?"

Rubbing her belly, taking a deep breath, Kayla nodded. "Yes, I'm fine. Oh yeah, before I forget what did you have to tell me?" Kayla inquired.

"Sandella come here," Taylor called her over to where she stood speaking with Kayla. Rounding the glass display, Sandella came and stood beside Taylor. "I have something I want to share with y'all. Before I say anything, just know that this idea is just food for thought."

"Okay," Kayla and Sandella said in unison.

"What are y'all over here talking about?" Willa stopped wiping the tables and joined the small circle of women. A moment later, Leslie and Veronica joined them as well.

Gleeful, Taylor continued. "I got a phone call from a producer in Charleston and he proposition me with an idea concerning the three of us," Taylor said, referring to her, Sandella, and Kayla.

Sandella's eyes smiled. "A producer contacted you regarding Kayla and me, and you?"

Taylor nodded. "Yes. He's interested in the three of us doing a reality television show called The Brides of Hilton Head Island."

"Oh my goodness. I'm too shy to something like that," Sandella said.

"Because we all have different personalities, it'd be great." Taylor waited for Kayla to respond. "What's your take on it Kayla?"

Sitting in the chair, Kayla spread her thighs apart. "My life is too boring. No one would be interested in following me."

Laughing, Leslie shook her head in disagreement. "Like hell your life is boring, Kayla. Your father-in-laws girlfriend tried to kill you! And don't forget that stupid Russell paid your ex to pretend like he wanted you back. All that drama makes for an interesting television series in my opinion."

"No, try movie." Willa laughed.

"I'll think about it," Sandella stated.

Veronica exclaimed, "I'm single. I'd love to get married and be a bride of Hilton Head Island."

Kayla's face contorted. "Ooouch! I think I'm in labor! Somebody call Richmond!"

"Call me for what?" Richmond asked, pushing through the front door of the bakery.

A second later Zeke and Braylon entered behind Richmond. Braylon shouted, "We're here to crash the party."

"Do y'all need any help cleaning up?" Zeke kindly questioned.

Kayla's eyes squeezed tight "Ahhh! Richmond, it hurts. Help!"

"Are you in labor?" Richmond's voice echoed.

Kayla nodded her head over and over. "Yes. Yes."

Like a strong warrior, Richmond scooped Taylor up in his arms. Gush. Water splattered from Kayla's entrance saturating her dress. Taylor's body tensed as she watched the scene unfold. Kayla squirmed. "Put me down! I feel the head coming! The head is coming!"

Richmond lowered Kayla to the floor on her back, hiked her dress to her hips, and spread her legs. "Oh God. I see the head!"

Scared out of her mind, Taylor snatched her cell from her purse, and dialed 911.

Ten minutes later the paramedics arrived and hurried inside.

Taylor, Sandella, Zeke, Braylon, and Willa stood outside of the bakery, eagerly awaiting the birth of Richmond's and Kayla's baby. Upon Kayla's request, she'd wanted her mother-in-law Leslie to remain inside the bakery with her.

While waiting outside for Kayla to give birth, a part of Taylor hoped Katherine and she would become close like Leslie and Kayla someday. Over the last couple of weeks Katherine had been really nice to her, making her feel there was indeed hope for the two of them.

Thinking she needed to go buy a pregnancy test today, Taylor prayed Kayla was doing okay inside the bakery. "What's taking them so—"

Richmond burst from the front door with a huge smile on his face. "It's a boy!"

Taylor, Zeke, and the rest of the crew cheered.

Chapter Twenty-One

BOUNCING THE BASKETBALL IN HIS hand inside the gym, Zeke longed to teach Jaheem and Evan a good lesson—although Zeke was older, he still could whip their little young behinds in basketball.

Running down the court bouncing the basketball, Zeke juked past Jaheem, and then Evan. Showing them who was boss, he shot the ball in the air. The ball plummeted through the net.

In victory, Zeke punched the air. "Yes! You two can't touch me!"

Smiling handsomely, Jaheem faked coughed. "The only reason you scored was because I'm sick with a little something, something."

Evan's handsome little face smiled, melting Zeke's heart. "Oh, I let you score. If I had some better shoes to play in, I would've beat you big time, Mister."

Zeke's gaze fell to Evan's worn shoes. Torn and dirty, Evan needed some new shoes bad. "How about I take you to get some news shoes?"

Evan's brown eyes widened. "Mister, are you serious?"

Zeke patted Evan's back. "You should know by now that when I say something I mean it. A real man always keeps his promise."

"What else does a real man do?" Jaheem queried.

Zeke sat on the bleachers to tie his sneakers. Jaheem sat to his right while Evan sat to his left. "Well, for starters, real men take care of their families. They also honor girls and treat them with the upmost respect. A real man puts God first, family second, and everything else thereafter."

"I want to be just like you when I grow up," Jaheem said.

Zeke's heart warmed from the way Jaheem admired him. "Thanks for the compliment Jaheem. But there's nothing wrong with you being you. I see the good young man you are. I see your potential. It's time for you to start seeing your own potential, and believing in yourself."

Jaheem nodded. "I'm gone try to believe in myself."

"Don't try. Just do." Zeke touched Jaheem's forehead with his index finger. "As long as you have your mind, and you work hard, you can do anything in life you want to. The ability to think for yourself gives you power. Don't let anyone put negativity in your mind. Believe in yourself and be your own man."

Jaheem nodded. Leaning forward, he then looked over at Evan. "You gone tell him or what?"

Concerned, Zeke looked at Evan. "Tell me what?"

"I told you to keep your big mouth shut, Jaheem." Frowning, Evan huffed. "I got my progress report today, and..."

"How did you do?" Zeke questioned.

Evan reached into his pocket, retrieved a folded sheet of paper, and handed it to Zeke. "I did horrible."

Zeke unfolded the paper. As his eyes scrolled over Evan's progress report, he knew he had to do something to help this poor kid out. "All F's. Tell me how does someone make all F's?"

"Because..." Evan's words trailed off.

"Because what?" In order to help Evan, Zeke had to get to the root of the kid's problems.

Jaheem told Zeke, "Because he can't read."

Zeke's heart dropped. *Whoa.* "Evan. Is it true that you can't read?"

Eyes getting watery, Evan nodded. "Yes, Mister. It's true."

"How does a child get in the fifth grade and can't read?" Zeke wondered, looking at Evan.

Evan shrugged. "I don't know."

Zeke draped his arm around Evan's shoulder. "Well, you may not be able to read today. But it won't always be that way. If it's the last thing I do, I'm going to teach you how to read."

Jaheem smiled. "I told you he'd help you, big head!"

"Yo momma got a big head!" Evan retorted.

Jaheem came back with, "Well, at least I know my momma and she come visit me."

"Yeah. But she look like a walking stick. A freaking crack head. My momma don't have a car so she can't come visit me," Evan stated.

Suddenly, both Jaheem and Evan laughed, but Zeke didn't see a darn thing funny. They joked about each other's mothers as if it didn't bother them in the least bit.

"Hey ease up on the momma jokes," Zeke warned.

Clapping his hands, ignoring Zeke, Jaheem said, "Your momma so nasty until even the roaches won't eat at her house."

Evan cracked up laughing. "Oh yeah, your momma so nasty until when she open her legs she smell like fish sticks!"

Oh no Evan didn't. Laughter eased from Zeke's lips. He put his hands over both of their mouths. "No more jokes. Now let's go shopping."

WHILE AT THE SHOPPING MALL, Zeke bought Evan a pair of brand new white Jordan's and bought Jaheem a pair of red ones. He'd also bought them two hoodies a piece, two shirts with collars, which they didn't want, and a pair of jeans each.

"Thank you Mister," Evan said, licking his vanilla ice cream cone.

Walking along the sidewalk at the outlet mall, Zeke patted Evans's shoulder. "You're welcome. If you bring your grades up, I promise to bring you back here again and take you on a bigger shopping spree."

Evan's brown eyes rounded with amazement. "A shopping spree bigger than this one?! I'm gone try so hard to learn how to read. I'm gone study all day and night. I think all I need is for someone to take time with me."

"Well, like I said earlier today, I'm going to teach you how to read. I promise." Zeke looked forward to tutoring Evan.

Jaheem spooned butter pecan ice cream into his mouth and swallowed. "My teacher, Mrs. Lane says no one should pay you to make good grades. She said you should do it because you want too."

Zeke thought before her responded to Jaheem's teacher's statement. "You're teacher is right, Jaheem. However, there's nothing wrong with being rewarded from time to time for doing something good. You and Evan have had very hard lives, and deserve to be treated well for your hard efforts."

Evan shook his head. "You're right about that, Mister. I've had a real hard life. My mother used to beat the skin off me." Evan pulled up his shirt, exposing his side. "Look what she did to me."

Zeke's heart clenched when he saw the long permanent scar on Evan's side torso. "What happened to make your mother do something like that to you?"

Holding the end of the ice cream cone, melted ice cream dripped down Evan's small hand. "She just hated me because I was born I guess. My mother is mean. She treated my brothers and sisters better than me if you ask me. All I had to do was look at her, and she'd beat my butt."

Upset, Zeke wondered what kind of person would beat a child to that degree. "Your mother should be ashamed for how she treated you."

Evan licked his ice cream cone. "Tell me about, Mister."

"How about we go to the park and play a round of football before I take you back to the shelter?" The boy's cheers resounded in the air. "Let's go—" Zeke's cell rung and he fished it from his pocket. "Hello."

"Hello Zeke. This is Don. I have something I need to share with you. As soon as you get a moment, I need for you and Taylor to swing by my office." A sense of urgency was in Don's voice.

Zeke's heart pounded inside his chest. "I'm all the way across town right now. How late will you be in your office today?"

"What I have to tell you is important. So I'll stay until you get here," Don offered.

"We'll be there around five," Zeke confirmed.

"I'll be waiting." Don hung up, leaving Zeke wondering if he'd found his son Zavier.

As promised, Zeke took the boys to the park, and the three of them played football. The entire time they were there, Zeke had problems focusing.

On the wide spread grass at the park by the ocean, Zeke gripped the end of the football and threw it in the air. Running sideways, Evan leapt up in the air and caught it. Evan had natural athletic ability, and so did Jaheem. Shoot if someone invested enough time in these boys, it wasn't no telling what they could do.

Zeke felt he had to be the one to invest time in these two boys, who had become a regular part of his life. More than that, Jaheem and Evan had become a major part of Zeke's heart. For the rest of the day the boys and Zeke played football, then he later took them to the shelter and dropped them off.

RIGHT AT FIVE PM, ZEKE steered his Porsche SUV into the parking lot of Don's office and parked. Pulling his key from the ignition, Zeke glanced over at Taylor, her eyes met his. His wife looked distraught.

Zeke reached over the console and cupped Taylor's hand. "Regardless of what Don tells us, I'll be here for you."

Strain shone on her face. "I'm so nervous, Zeke."

"I know. I can look at your face and tell." Zeke grazed Taylor's cheeks to find them rather warm.

"You feel hot." He placed the back of his hand to her forehead. "You're burning up, Taylor."

"I know. I haven't felt like myself in a very long time. I thought I might be pregnant, but as you know, unfortunately, I'm not. If this continues, I'm going to see a doctor."

"Let me know when you make your appointment, and I'll come with you." Taylor gave her head a slight nod. More than concerned about his wife's constant illness, Zeke pushed open the SUV's door, then walked around to get the door for his loving wife. He pulled the door open for her, and Taylor stepped out onto the pavement. "Oh by the way, the contractor called, and they started putting the stucco up for our home today." Taylor stepped to the side, he shut the door.

Her eyes smiled. "Now that's some very good news. I can't wait to see what it looks like."

"I can't wait till it's finished being built so we can move in it."

Zeke and Taylor emerged inside Don's office to find him sitting behind his desk writing on a yellow legal pad. When Zeke cleared his throat, Don lifted his eyes. He then stood to greet them, and shook their hands.

"Have a seat," Don gestured to the chairs in front of his desk.

Zeke and Taylor sat. Waiting on Don to explain why he'd called a last minute urgent meeting, worrisome chewed away Zeke's insides. Determined not to let Taylor see him bothered, he pushed back his shoulders, and made sure he sat upright in his chair. Regardless of what Don told them, he would remain strong for his wife.

Don steepled his hands together. "Thank you for dropping everything to come here this evening."

"You're welcome," they said in unison.

"I called you here because I have some good news and some bad news to share with you. Which one do you want first?" Don asked, looking over the rim of his black square glasses.

"I want to hear the good news first," Taylor said, and Zeke agreed.

Don continued. "I was able to get a hold of all the evidence inside your kidnapper's house were you were held hostage. Inside the bag was a peculiar looking key. Come to find out, the mysterious key belonged to a locker at the train station in Walterboro. I drove to Walterboro to see if the key still worked in the locker and it did. There was cash inside the locker, and passports for Mildred and Kelvin." Don turned his computer toward Zeke and Taylor. On the screen was a picture of Taylor that she'd taken when she was a little girl. Don stated, "This picture of you was inside the locker at the train station, too."

"I took that picture in the eighth grade," Taylor confirmed.

"Where is all this leading, Don?" Zeke wondered.

"Mildred and Kelvin had a photo of Taylor in their locker. This confirms that Taylor's kidnapping wasn't random. Taylor didn't just happen to be a few weeks pregnant, walking along the train tracks, and then some mysterious man just jumps out of the woods, and grab her. No." Don's eyes traveled to the computer screen. "Someone gave Kelvin this picture. The money in Mildred and Kelvin's bank accounts, and the money at the train station...added up to half a million dollars."

"Half a million dollars!" Zeke shouted.

"Yes half a million dollars," Don reiterated. "Both Mildred and Kelvin were unemployed and disabled. The sudden large deposit to their bank accounts happened the day after Taylor vanished from Hilton Head. Someone hired Mildred and Kelvin to kidnap you, Taylor. And that someone knew you were pregnant. Whoever paid to have you abducted, either didn't want you to have the baby, or they wanted the baby for themselves. Now the questions are...who wanted your baby and why?"

Raw hurt appeared in Taylor's eyes. "Because I was so early in my pregnancy, and not many people knew I was pregnant, I always thought that maybe I was in the wrong place at the wrong time. That maybe Mildred and Kelvin kidnapped me because they wanted me to be a slave to them. Having this new evidence means that whoever paid Mildred and Kelvin to take me, knows me, and they were watching my every move."

Don swallowed. "Yes Taylor, you're exactly right. This is where the bad news comes in. Whoever in Hilton Head paid to have you and your baby stolen, is probably still watching your every move."

Taylor gasped. "Oh my God. This is frightening."

Zeke's heart plummeted to his gut. He reached over and grabbed Taylor's hand to find it scorching hot. "Don't worry. I'll protect you," he said, squeezing her hand.

Until now Zeke had never wondered if he'd made a mistake by bringing Taylor back to Hilton Head. *Jesus Christ. What have I done? Maybe I should've left her in Paris.*

Knowing Taylor's abductor may still reside in the area, Zeke shifted uncomfortably in the chair. If anyone hurt Taylor, he'd never forgive himself. First thing tomorrow morning he was going to go buy himself a gun. And if anyone tried to hurt his wife, he'd blow their ass to pieces and wouldn't feel bad about it.

Chapter Twenty-Two

FINALLY HOME ALONE, KATHERINE DESCENDED the staircase, and strolled inside the living. Red hair hanging over her shoulders, she wore a yellow spring dress that she'd had custom made by a famous designer in New York. She pulled back the sheers on the large bay window and peered out at her front yard. Gazing out the window, she thought about her day today.

Earlier today while Zeke was visiting the dumb group care facility instead of running Balfour Enterprises like he was hired to do, Katherine had gone to the guesthouse to take Taylor her lunch prepared by Delbert. Right as Katherine had raised her hand to knock on the door at the guesthouse situated behind her mansion, she'd noticed it ajar.

Standing beyond the slightly parted door, clenching a tray with Taylor's lunch in her hands, Katherine eavesdropped on Taylor's telephone conversation with Kayla. At first ungrateful Taylor had chatted with Kayla about how Kayla had given birth inside Sandella's bakery, SugarKanes.

Then the two women had started talking about how it'd be fun to have a reality tv show called The Brides of Hilton Head Island.

While Taylor sat giggling on the phone with Kayla, Zeke had called, and Taylor had rushed to end her conversation with Kayla so she could click back over. And what Katherine had heard next had bothered her all day.

Reliving the conversation between Zeke and Taylor, Katherine's nerves jittered.

While on the phone with Zeke, Taylor had said, *"Well, hello Mr. Right. About time you give your wife a call. When are you coming home?"* Silence. *"Don wants to see us? Today?"* Silence. Taylor continued. *"Don has something to share with us? Oh Zeke, I hope he knows where our son is."* More silence. *"Why doesn't Don want us to let anyone know that we're meeting with him?"* Pause. Pause. Taylor eventually said, *"Well, you don't have to worry about me saying anything. I get it Zeke, don't say anything. Especially not to Katherine."*

Still gazing out the window, Katherine shuddered. "Especially not to Katherine, why didn't Zeke want Taylor to tell me about their conversation? Why did Zeke emphasize my name?" Had Don linked the kidnapping back to her? Katherine wondered. Where the police going to come and arrest her soon?

Disturbed, Katherine turned from the living window, and strolled up to the brick fireplace inside the family room, and pondered. Looking over her left shoulder, and then her right shoulder, she reached high up in the fireplace. Searching for the murder weapon she'd used to kill Bridget, her hand floundered over the dirty soot wall. "There," Katherine said, hand gliding over the handle of a blade.

Biting hard on her molars, Katherine yanked the blade from the fireplace and now held it in her dirty hand. Black soot smothered the sharp blade. Tempted to hide the murder weapon used to kill Bridget somewhere different, her mind flashed back to the way Bridget's mouth had popped open when she'd stabbed her.

Colton's admittance about how he still loved Bridget came rushing inside Katherine's head, instantly giving her a headache. "Colton is still in love with a dead woman. I done heard it all."

"Mrs. Balfour." Delbert called Katherine's name. "I'm here."

Katherine hurriedly replaced the knife back inside the fireplace. Hands filthy and black, she ran to the bathroom down the hallway, and washed her hands. Glancing at her reflection in the mirror, she felt like she'd lost herself. Like she didn't know who she was anymore. Like it was her up against the world. Up against Zeke. Up against Taylor. But worse of all, up against Bridget. A freaking dead woman.

With her stomach pressed against the bathroom counter, Katherine dropped her head in her palms. Her brain swirled. Jumbled. "I'm losing it."

If Colton hadn't had an affair with Bridget, her life would be so different. If her unfaithful husband just would've kept his dick in his pants, Zeke would've never been born. And she would've never had all these insecurities. One thing having led to another, she would've never felt the need to have Antonio arrange for Taylor to be kidnapped and her son to be sold. All the horrible ugliness she'd done had been brought on by one man—Colton Balfour. And now knowing Don had something to tell Zeke and Taylor, her past just may be catching up with her.

Trying hard to pull herself together, Katherine lifted her head from her hands, pulled open the bathroom door, and waltz to the kitchen. Delbert stood at the stove stirring a spoon into a small pot when she arrived.

"What's for dinner?" Katherine asked, forgetting what Delbert had said he was cooking for dinner this evening.

Delbert lifted his gaze from the pot, looked at her face, and frowned. "You have something black on your face, Mrs. Balfour." *Soot!* "I'm cooking fried smothered pork chops with mushrooms, cabbage, Mexican cornbread, and rice pilaf. And I'm cooking chicken gnocchi soup for Taylor. Earlier, she put in a request for something healthy and bland. You know Taylor, she loves eating healthy."

Katherine drawled, "She's not footing the grocery bill so she needs to eat whatever you fix."

"Oh, I don't mind cooking separately for Taylor. I hope you don't want any soup because I only made enough for her."

"I need more than a bowl of soup for dinner." *Let me go get this soot off my face.* Tires rolling over gravel entered Katherine's ears. She walked to the living room, slightly parted the sheers on the window, and looked out to the driveway.

Bright lights blazed from Zeke's Porsche. Sitting in the passenger seat of the SUV, Taylor leaned over to kiss Zeke's cheek. She got out the car, and headed toward the guest house. Dropping Taylor off, Zeke backed the vehicle out of the driveway, and left.

After Katherine washed the black soot off her face, she returned to the kitchen, and Delbert had a glass of red wine waiting for her. While making small talk with Delbert and sipping the flowery fragrant wine, Delbert's cell rung. "Excuse me. I need to take this call," he said.

"Go ahead," Katherine told him, and couldn't have been happier that someone had interrupted their conversation.

Delbert left the kitchen through the back garage door.

Head still aching, Katherine reached into the pocket of her dress and retrieved a small orange, bottle. Standing over the stove, she twisted the white cap off the bottle. She sprinkled the white powdery poison into Taylor's soup then stirred.

Sliding the bottle back into the pocket of her dress, Katherine strolled over to the table and sat as if she hadn't done a darn thing. *I'm killing Taylor slowly. She's dying and doesn't even know it.*

Talking about she thought she was pregnant. Maybe if she died, Zeke would forget about finding his son.

Delbert emerged back inside the kitchen and walked over to the stove. He stirred Taylor's soup, poured it into a bowl, and after making Taylor a fresh tossed salad, he put her food items on a tray. "I'll be right back to fry those pork chops after I drop this off to Taylor."

Finishing off her glass of delicious red wine, Katherine said, "Take your time. The men are at the office. According to Colton, they all will be working late tonight." *It'll just be me and the prissy bitch outback at home tonight.*

Chapter Twenty-Three

"THANKS DELBERT."

"It's my pleasure," Delbert said, closing the door to the guest house.

Sitting on the barstool inside the kitchen, Taylor hefted the remote, aimed it at the television inside the family room, and pressed the power button. Steve Harvey's face appeared on the television screen. Listening to Steve Harvey host Family Feud, Taylor lifted the lid off her soup. A mild chicken flavor wafted up her nose. "Mmm. This looks delicious."

Spooning the soup into her mouth, Taylor thought about what Don had said earlier. The person who had kidnapped her may still be watching her. Savoring the soup, the scary thought made her shiver. Thank God, Colton and Katherine were gracious enough to let Zeke and her stay here at the estate with them and with Antonio. Bane had his own place. With a family this large, someone was always at home or visiting. With her kidnapper still out there, the last thing Taylor wanted was to always be alone.

Sucking the soup from the spoon into her mouth, the warm chunky food glided down her throat. "This is pretty good, Delbert."

Completing her soup and salad, Taylor longed for her husband's company. Longed for him to return home and make sweet love to her. Longed for him to lick between her legs with his long, thick tongue. Imaging Zeke feasting between her legs, Taylor's sex clenched. Her nipples tingled.

Taylor placed the empty bowls in the sink, walked to the family room, plopped down on the couch. She wished she was plopping down on Zeke's hard shaft instead.

Lonely, Taylor decided to do something she thought she'd never do, but probably should've done a long time ago. Invite Katherine to the guest house for some girl talk.

Hoping she don't regret her decision, Taylor stabbed the intercom with her French manicured nail, and called up to the main house.

"How may I help you, Taylor?" Delbert answered in a friendly tone.

Lord, please don't let me regret this. "Hi Delbert. Is Katherine around? I'd like to speak with her."

"Yes, she's sitting right here. Hold on."

"Yes," Katherine answered in her ever so proper voice.

"Hi Katherine. I'm about to watch the Atlanta Housewives show and wanted to know if you'd like to join me."

"Sure! I'm on my way." Katherine hung up the phone, and a few seconds later, Taylor saw her walking up the pathway, making her way to the guesthouse.

Taylor pulled open the front door to find Katherine looking fabulous in a simple yellow dress, and holding a tiny bowl in each hand. "I brought dessert for us to enjoy while watching tv," she said, handing Taylor the dish in her right hand. "Fruit with a small dollop of whip cream."

"Oh, that sounds good. Thanks for coming, Katherine."

Katherine walked past Taylor and waltzed straight into the family room. "Thank you for inviting me. This is going to be fun. I love watching these housewives shows."

Taylor giggled. "Me too. I didn't watch much television while in Paris, but since I've been here, that's all—" A sharp pain sliced Taylor's belly. She flinched.

Katherine placed a gentle palm on Taylor's shoulder. "Are you okay?"

The pain quickly faded. Taylor took a deep breath, and then put the television station on Bravo. "Yes. I'm fine." Taylor dropped down on the couch, and Katherine sat beside her. She pulled the foil off the fruit bowl, picked up the little spoon that Delbert had put inside, and began enjoying the sweet fruit. The juicy strawberry covered in whip cream squirted on her tongue. "I love fruit."

Eyes on the television, Katherine spooned some fruit into her mouth. "Me, too."

"How would you feel if I starred in a reality show?" Taylor wondered.

"It wouldn't bother me any," Katherine said flatly. "You're a grown woman. You can do whatever you please."

"I'm surprised to hear you say that."

Katherine shrugged. "Why?"

"Being married to a billionaire, I know image has to be important to you."

"Yes. It is." Katherine agreed.

"Image is important to me, too. That's why I turned down the offer to do a reality show for the producer in Charleston."

Katherine's gasp of surprise smacked Taylor's drums. "You were offered the opportunity to do a reality show and you turned it down?"

"Yes. But not just because of the whole image thing, I just didn't see how It'd fit in my schedule. My Agent, Pierre, got me a gig in Paris for a small movie role. Hopefully Zeke and I can wrap up a few things here real soon, so I can return to Paris for a while to do the movie."

"What kind of things do you need to wrap up here?" Katherine asked.

"Oh nothing. We—" Gut wrenching pain knotted Taylor's belly and shot to her chest. Clenching her stomach, Taylor placed the fruit bowl on the end table, and ran to the bathroom. Stomach roiling and burning, she clenched the sides of the toilet, and vomited.

Katherine rushed inside the bathroom behind her. "Are you okay?"

Sweat developed on her forehead. "I've just been so sick lately. I'm going to the doctor tomorrow." Chest tightening, Taylor's head throbbed. Feeling weak, she struggled to stand.

Katherine hooked her hands under Taylor's armpits. "Here, let me help you. You need to go lay down." Katherine assisted Taylor to the bed inside her master suite then turned back the covers for her. Taylor climbed onto the mattress and laid on her back. Peering down at Taylor, Katherine pulled the covers up over her body to her chin. She placed her hand to Taylor's cheek. "You're burning up. You must have a fever. I'll be right back." Katherine turned, leaving her all by herself.

A few minutes later, Katherine returned with a bottle of fever reducing medicine. Katherine placed a cold white washcloth on Taylor's forehead, poured the purple liquid onto a Tablespoon and fed it to her twice. "Thanks for help me, Katherine. Having you here means so much." *She's not so bad after all.*

Sitting on the mattress beside Taylor, Katherine cupped her hand. "I'm just happy you let me take care of you. Do you want me to call Zeke?"

Her lids drooped. "No. I'll be fine. But thank you for offering. Katherine, will you please do me a favor?"

Patting the back of Taylor's hand, Katherine nodded. "Sure. Anything."

"Will you stay here with me until Zeke gets home?" Uncertain what may happen to her body while she was sleep, Taylor didn't want to be alone.

"Of course I will, Taylor. I'm going to run up to the guest house, see Delbert off, and I'll be right back." Katherine took the washcloth on Taylor's forehead, and wiped the sides of her sweating face. She then went into the bathroom, put more cold water on the washcloth, and then replaced it on her forehead.

"Thanks." Taylor's limbs felt weak. Her body ached. She must have the flu.

Katherine turned and left.

Taylor's eyes slowly drifted. Putting her hand to the top of her cramping stomach, she moaned painfully. *If this pain doesn't go away, I'm going to the emergency room.* Eyes closing and opening, closing and opening, she turned her head toward the window.

The full moon gleamed brightly in the dark sky. Sparkling stars twinkled. Suddenly, Antonio appeared in the window. A deadly look was in his pupils, the outlines of his face hardened. Feeling threatened by his haunting glare, Taylor's body jerked.

"I'm back!" Katherine shouted. Taylor tore her gaze from Antonio to look at the entrance to her bedroom then looked back at the window. Antonio had vanished. "Are you feeling any better?" Katherine asked, peering down at Taylor.

Why was Antonio looking at me like that? "Not really. Did you see Antonio outside? He was looking at me through the window."

Katherine dabbled the washcloth along the edges of Taylor's hairline. "I just got off the phone with Antonio. He's at work.

You're seeing things because you're sick, darling. Close your eyes and go to sleep. I'm sure you'll feel better in the morning."

ZEKE'S EYES WANDERED AROUND HIS immaculate new office at Balfour Hotel & Resort as he sat behind his oak wooden desk. Navy blue couch against the wall, dark brown furniture, book shelf filled with business books, and a big shark tank beside the sofa, this was how a CEO's office should look. Determined to make his father proud, a huge smile came on Zeke's face.

Carefully studying the shark swimming inside the humungous tank, Zeke put the tip of the pen to a legal document. In deep thought, images of Taylor snuck into his mind.

Tall and lean with a small waist, Taylor's firm breasts and succulent body always enticed him. Between her legs smelled fresh and flowery. When aroused, she smelled thick and salty. Envisioning his tongue tracing the outline of her dark areola then flicking her black nipple, Zeke's shaft hardened. His balls tingled. The tip of his head leaked inside his underwear. *I can't wait to get home so I can make love to my beautiful wife.*

Knockknockknock. Zeke's eyes traveled from the shark tank to the door, and in walked his older brother Bane.

Bane lowered a file to Zeke's desk then slid it toward him. "I think you need to take a look at this, bro."

"What is it?" Zeke asked, having a bad feeling.

"It a hard copy of our financial report from last month." Obvious irritation was in Bane's tone.

Zeke opened the manila folder to read the financial reports. Noticing one deficit after another, frustration rattled him. He lifted his gaze to Bane. "The numbers are off."

Bane frowned. "Exactly. It looks like someone is stealing money from Balfour."

"And a lot of it."

Bane sighed. "Where's Antonio? I've been looking everywhere for him."

I'm getting sick of Antonio coming to work whenever he damn well pleases. "That's what I was about to ask you. Did you try calling Antonio's cell?"

"Yes. But it sent me to voicemail."

"Someone's in the finance department is stealing from the company. We need to have an emergency meeting about this." Zeke hefted the phone from the receiver and dialed Antonio. Antonio's cell went straight to voicemail. "Hey Antonio. It's me, Zeke. An emergency has come up and we need to meet right away. I know it's getting late, but this can't wait. Meet up at the office asap." He hung up. "I told him two weeks ago that we were meeting tonight, so there's no excuse for him not being here."

Bane nodded. "My thoughts exactly. I don't know if it's me or what, but he's been acting rather strange lately. I understand his frustration about not getting the CEO position, but then again, I don't. I mean, just look at the little stunt he's pulling tonight. His ass should be here—"

"Talking about me behind my back, I see." Antonio stalked inside Zeke's office with a snide look on his face. "Yeah, I'm late." He shrugged. "But at least I'm here. Let's get this meeting started, and over with." He plopped down in the navy chair in front of Zeke's desk, crossed his legs at the knee.

Shaking his head, Bane took the seat in the chair next to Antonio. "Just rude," Bane grumbled.

Zeke felt where Bane was coming from in regards to Antonio. "I agree. Before the meeting begins, let's get one thing straight Antonio. If you're going to work for me, you must be on time from now on. Do I make myself clear?" Zeke's firm tone must've made Antonio upset.

Uncrossing his legs, Antonio leaned forward. "You just became CEO and you're already trying to dictate and change things around here. You and Bane both know I've never been on time, and I come and go as I damn well please."

Frustration entered Zeke's system. "Not anymore, you don't. For now on you need to be on time. Our father may have put up with your rudeness, but he and I are two different men. I'm looking to grow Balfour by leaps and bounds. Take it to heights our father could only dream of."

Antonio crossed his legs at the knee, his blue eyes turned cobalt. "Balfour is already successful. So this is more for your ego than for the good of the company."

Zeke didn't have time for idle bullshit. He definitely wasn't going to explain himself. "Just have your ass here on time for now on. Discussion over with. Now let's get on to more important matters like who's stealing from the company."

"Before we begin, let me just ask you something," Antonio changed the subject. "What exactly do you plan to do to me if I'm late?"

He's trying my patience. "Well, dear brother. That's a very easy question to answer. If you're late again, I'm going to fire you and toss you out on your scrimpy ass." Despair shone on Antonio's face, but he didn't say a word. *Thought so*, Zeke gloated internally.

THREE LONG HOURS AFTER HIS meeting with Bane and Antonio, Zeke pushed open the door to the guesthouse to find Katherine asleep on the couch. *What is she doing here?* Taken by surprise, Zeke walked over to Katherine, and gently patted her shoulder.

Katherine's eyes slowly peeled open. Blinking, she sat upright on the sofa. "What are you doing here, Katherine?"

Katherine yawned. "Taylor invited me over to watch television with her, but she ended up getting sick. She asked me to stay here with her until you got home."

Why didn't someone call me? "She hasn't been feeling herself lately. Was her sickness real bad?"

Katherine stood. "I don't think it was too bad. Sounds like she has a cold or a virus. There's been some kind of bug going around. My girlfriend Lolita got it, and she's doing much better now. Give it a couple of days, and I'm sure Taylor will be feeling much better."

Worrisome about his precious wife consumed Zeke. "I hope so. Thanks for staying with her, Katherine. I really appreciate it."

"You're welcome. Call me if you need anything. Good night." Katherine pulled open the door then headed up to the main house.

Apprehensive about his wife, Zeke entered the master bedroom, stalked over to their king sized bed, and pulled the beaded string on the lamp. The room vaguely brightened. Looking down at Taylor, his heart swelled.

Sleeping on her back, rich brown hair lay past shoulders. Her brownish-mauve lips set in a straight line. Her cheeks looked a rosy red.

Zeke touched Taylor's face with the pads of his fingers to discover her flesh hot to the touch. A ball of sorrow exploded inside him from seeing how sick she'd gotten since he'd dropped her off earlier.

Stroking her hair with his fingers, he softly uttered her name. "Taylor. Wake up, baby. Wake up." Taylor's body looked rigid as a board. Zeke gently shook her shoulder. "Taylor. Wake up."

When Zeke kissed Taylor's cheek, her eyes finally peeled open. The white part of her eyes were a scary red. "Who. Are. You?"

Zeke's gut swirled. "I'm your husband, Zeke baby," he choked out. He snatched the covers off Taylor, scooped her seething hot body into his arms, and rushed her to the emergency room.

Chapter Twenty-Four

THREE DAYS LATER TAYLOR SAT upright in the hospital bed watching Judge Mathis on television feeling better than ever. Clad in a cotton white hospital gown, she glanced at Zeke as he slept sleeping in the chair beside the bed. Ever since he'd brought her to the hospital, he hadn't left her side.

Taylor cell buzzed in her lap. Spying the caller ID, a smile covered her face. "Hi Momma. How are you?"

"I'm fine. How's my baby girl doing?" Veronica sounded chipper.

"I've never felt better. Thanks Momma."

"Is there anything I can do for my baby girl?"

Taylor giggled. "Momma. You just left here five minutes ago. Nothing's changed since you left. I'm good. Thanks for asking, though."

"Okay. Well, you just make sure you call me if you need me. I know you said the doctors may release you today. Keep me posted. I love you."

"I love you too, Momma." Taylor pressed the button on her cell to end the call.

Feeling like her old self again, Taylor whispered her husband's name as he remained sleeping in the chair propped against the wall in the corner. "Zeke."

Zeke's body stirred. His eyes opened. Stretching his arms and legs in the recliner, he sat upright. Yawing, Zeke brought his watch up to his eyes. "The doctor was supposed to be here by now."

Taylor's stomach growled. "I hope he comes soon because I'm getting hungry."

Zeke patted his stomach. "Me too."

Just as Zeke stood Dr. Mason Papotto entered the room. "Good afternoon, Taylor. Are you ready to go home yet?" Clenching a small lap top in his hands, the physician smiled down at her.

"Good afternoon, Dr. Papotto. I've been ready to go home. I'm getting out of here today, right?"

"If your vitals are still good, I don't see any reason why you can't home this afternoon." Dr. Papotto lowered the lap top to the bed, washed his hands, then placed the cool metal of stethoscope to Taylor's chest. "Breathe in and out." Taylor inhaled deeply then released it. Dr. Papotto removed the stethoscope from her chest area and placed it on her back to listen. "Everything sounds and looks good."

Zeke gave the doctor a strange look. "So you still don't know what caused her to get sick?"

"Like I said before, my guess is she had a stomach virus."

Your guess. "Well, I feel all better now. Thanks Dr. Papotto."

"The nurse should arrive with your dismissal papers shortly. The two of you have a great day."

Yes. I'm going home. "You have a great day, too, doctor."

An hour later Taylor walked across the parking lot of the hospital feeling stronger than ever. Brand spanking new. That virus had got her down and out. But now, stronger than ever, she felt like she could run a marathon. Felt like she could have sex with Zeke for days.

Zeke opened the door to the Porsche SUV for Taylor, she climbed in. He shut the door then rounded the car and mounted on the driver's side. Sitting behind the steering wheel, he gazed over at her, then leaned inward. "I'm so happy you're doing better." Clenching the steering wheel with one hand, grazing her collar bone with the other, he slanted his mouth over hers.

Taylor moaned deep inside Zeke's throat as she tongue kissed him. Tongues twining, a dull ache formed in her center. Moisture crept into her panties. Hot fire spread through her bones.

Zeke broke their erotic kiss. "I thought maybe we could swing by the lot to take a look at the progress of our house, and then afterwards, maybe we can swing by Ruth Chris and get something to eat."

Feeling like her old self, Taylor looked forward to seeing the progression of her new home. "Sounds good to me. Let's go."

Zeke cranked the engine, put the car in reverse. Smiling over at Taylor, he put the gear in drive then drove out of the packed parking lot of the hospital.

Fifteen minutes later Zeke made a right at the long end of Ocean, drove down another long road, made a left, then parked the SUV on the road in front of their ocean front lot.

Zeke and Taylor met at the front of the truck then walked along the dirt up to their white stucco home. Evening approaching, darkness began to settle in the late afternoon sky.

"It'll be finished soon," Zeke said with tremendous joy in his voice.

"It gets prettier and prettier every time I see it." Bright sun rays shinned down on the glistening, blue sea treading behind the white, huge mansion. Seagulls spread their wings flying over the roof of the two story home. "Fifteen thousand square feet, what are we going to do with all the space?"

Zeke gave Taylor a serious look. "Let me ask you something, Taylor. What are your thoughts on adopting?"

Adopting? "I'm open minded about adopting."

"Is that so?"

"Yes. Until you came back into my life, I dated, but I never had a true serious relationship. For a long time, I never thought I'd get married and have my own children again. So often I thought about adopting. There's so many kids out there that needs adopting, and could use a good home. We definitely will have the space if that's something we wanted to do. What makes you ask me about adopting?"

Zeke's complexioned lightened. "There's these two kids that I've become extremely close with at the shelter."

Taylor saw exactly where this was headed. "You mean Jaheem and Evan?"

"Yes, I talk about them so much until you even know them by name now." Smiling, Taylor nodded. Zeke said, "I don't know what it is about those two little boys, but I'm drawn to them. Even when I'm not with them, I think about them. Think about what activity we'll do next. About how I love tutoring them."

His face lights up when he talks about Jaheem and Evan. "I can see in your eyes that those boys mean a lot to you. If you want to adopt them, I definitely would consider it, Zeke."

Zeke cupped Taylor's cheeks. "Do you really mean it, Taylor? You'd really do that for me?"

Taylor nodded her head in his hands. "Well, it wouldn't be just for you. It'd be for me too. I love children. I've always wanted a big family with you. With all the money we have, we can adopt Jaheem and Evan and we can some children of our own."

Zeke pulled Taylor's face forward. "You're the best, my love." He pecked her lips. "Once this house is finished being built, I'm going to make love to you in every single room." *I can't wait!* Zeke grabbed Taylor's hand, and placed it on the bulge beneath his jeans. His stem wiggled on her hand.

Taylor jumped. "Oh my. Your penis is gigantic."

Arousal glowed inside Zeke's irises. "And it's all yours, wife."

Taylor squeezed his tool hard. "When are you going to give it to me?"

"You can have it right now if you want. Come." Zeke tugged Taylor's hand, and led her toward the parked Porsche.

When they reached the SUV, he opened the back rear door, and led her inside. Sitting next to her in the back seat, Zeke zipped down his jeans, freeing his juicy looking erection. His creamy column lay hard and rigid to his stomach.

Sex throbbing, Taylor dropped her mouth on his thick stem.

Zeke groaned huskily. "I wasn't expecting you to do that."

Taylor slurped around his rod. *Me either. It just looked so good. And tasty.*

Thrusting his tool inside her squeezing mouth, Zeke's moans filled her ears. Salty pre-cum oozed from his slit onto her tongue. Licking him like a vanilla popsicle stick, the thick veins of his shaft throbbed against her tongue.

Zeke gripped the sides of Taylor's head and pulled it upward. Her mouth released him with a loud pop. "Ride me." His request sounded more like an order.

Taylor climbed on top of Zeke's lap and straddled him. Breathing like a wild animal, he hiked her dress up to her hips, pushed her panties to the side, then flicked his finger over her tingling clitoris.

Falling forward, Taylor clenched Zeke's bottom lip with her teeth, chewed gently, then sucked it into her mouth. Sucking and pulling on his bottom lip, she felt him put his head to her wet entrance. He twirled the outline of her core with the hard knobbed flesh.

"Put it in, Zeke. Put it in, now," Taylor begged. "Hurry."

Clenching himself at the base, Zeke pitched upward. Taylor circled her womanhood downward on his tool. "You're pussy is soaked."

"Mmm. Hmm." Rocking her sex roughly on his rod, Zeke reached inside the v-front of her spring time dress, scooped out her left breast, and sucked the nipple into his mouth. Taylor winced in sheer pleasure.

Rocking her hips back and forth, Taylor's clitoris knocked repeatedly against Zeke's steely length. Flicking his tongue wildly over her nipple, he cricrossed his arms over her back, clutched her shoulders, and stroked her hard. Pumped vigorously. Stuck it good.

"Yes, my wife. Ride me. Fuck me good." Zeke's pole punched Taylor's sex. Swung side to side. Pound all around. Hit her walls deliciously. Hot sensations coursed through Taylor's veins. Lit up her body.

Orgasm nearing, she lifted her hips, brought her snatch up to his tip, and slammed down hard. "Zeeekkkeee!" Her sex exploded in a fiery orgasm.

"Keeping fucking me, my wife." Zeke clenched her hip rough, then he stroked. His member pulsed inside her womb, then began spurting hot come. "Aarrrgh!"

The hard beats of Zeke's stem slowed. "I can't believe I just had sex with you inside a truck. Having sex in public like this, I should be ashamed of myself." Taylor had to catch her breath.

Zeke gently brushed the hair on Taylor's back with his hands. "There's nothing for you to be ashamed of, my wife. We're married. Besides there's not another house around for at least three miles down the road. I love the adventure we just partook in."

"Me too." Taylor climbed off Zeke, hot come leaked from her sex, slid down her thighs. Her cell rang inside her purse in the front seat. She hopped up to answer it. "Hello."

"How are you, honey?!"

Excitement kicked up inside Taylor. "Hi Pierre! Long time no hear!"

"Sorry about that, but Pierre's been super-duper busy with work, and with Francois. Look honey, in addition to the movie, Colgate is requesting that white bright smile of yours. For an advance of three hundred thousand, they want to shoot you in Paris."

Ohmygoodness. Taylor shrieked. "When?"

"Now see. That's where the problem comes in. They'd initially scheduled another model to do the shoot, but she came down with the chicken pox. That said, honey, they want you in Paris in two days."

"Two days!"

"Don't get mad at me, I ain't the one that makes the schedule." Pierre chuckled, and so did Taylor.

"Hold on." Looking at Zeke stuff his tool back inside his underwear, Taylor covered the speaker of her cell. "It's Pierre. Colgate called him, and they want me to do a shoot for them in two days. If it's okay with you, I'd really like to do it."

"Taylor, you don't have to get permission from me to do anything your heart desires. I'm your husband, and I support you in everything you want to do. Go to Paris. I'll be here waiting on you when you return. I'll get the company jet ready for you and make all the arrangements."

Taylor mouthed Thanks to Zeke. "Pierre."

"Yes honey?"

"I'll see you sometime tomorrow."

"Oh, goody!"

Chapter Twenty-Five

GLANCING OUT AT THE OCEAN from inside his office, Zeke missed Taylor terribly. Because of the short feature film she had to do, Taylor's six weeks to Paris had turned into two months. And just the other day, she'd gotten an offer to do some print work for a fashion magazine. When she'd called him to share her good news, the excitement in her voice had come through the phone. And he couldn't have been happier for her.

Longing for the scent of his wife's flesh, Zeke locked his computer, stood, and headed for the boardroom. Weeks ago he'd scheduled Balfour's monthly meeting today. Top executives from several Balfour hotels would be in attendance. Due to complications with the prostate cancer, his father couldn't make the meeting today.

Speaking of his father, Colton had looked weak and pale while sitting at the breakfast table this morning. Before he left to come to work, Zeke had stood behind the wall, and quietly watched Katherine spoon oatmeal into Colton's mouth. She'd looked like she really did love the man for once. Maybe she'd changed after all.

Zeke opened the door of the conference room and headed for the seat at the head of the table. The seat where the boss sat. The seat were important decisions were made. A seat he'd worked his ass off to earn.

Zeke's eyes traveled around the room at the men and gentleman in attendance. "Good afternoon, everyone."

"Good afternoon." The voices of Balfour's most influential executives filled the room.

"Thank you all for coming today. There's going to be a lot of changes at Balfour Enterprises. I hope you all consider them good changes. So without further due, let's get started."

Taking his seat, Zeke's eyes traveled around to each of his executives. Everyone one of them were present except for Antonio. Angry emotions flared inside Zeke. *Antonio better have a good excuse for not being here. He better not come in here late, embarrassing me, or himself either.*

Throughout the presentation, Zeke's administrative assistant, Patricia Belle, sat beside the podium working the slide presentation. Standing at the podium, it took Zeke thirty minutes to explain and share Balfour's rising growth with his stellar executives from around the country. He explained to them how the hotel being built in Paris was just the beginning, the icing on the cake. He'd planned on building five star hotels in China, Japan, Brazil, and even Africa.

Zeke observed his employees faces, smiles plastered many of their mouths. Ready for the next slide, Zeke nodded at Patricia. She tapped a key on the laptop, and a new slide appeared on the screen.

"This screen is comprised of many salaries for Balfour employees. Being that it's personal, only you should know your salary. Find the range of your salary, then look at the number to its right. That's your bonus for taking time out to come here today. Thanks for coming. I appreciate you all."

Heartfelt joy from his executives spread throughout the room. After the meeting, many women and men came up to Zeke, shook his hand, and graciously thanked him for their enormous bonuses. One by one, executives exited the room, leaving him alone with Patricia and Bane.

"Have you spoken with Antonio today?" Zeke asked Bane in disappointment.

"No, I haven't seen him, or spoken with him," Bane conferred.

"He better have a good reason——"

Patricia interjected, "I saw Antonio right before the meeting started. He was walking down the hallway heading toward the spa."

"He wouldn't," Bane said.

He's taking me and his job for granted. "Knowing Antonio, he did. Patricia have you had a chance to draw up those papers I asked of you yet regarding Antonio?"

"Yes. I have them right here." Patricia pulled an envelope out of her briefcase and handed it to Zeke. Zeke pulled the paper out of the envelope, signed it, then stuck it back in the envelope. Extending his hand, Zeke smiled at Bane. "Congratulations Bane."

Bane's brows hiked. "For what?"

Zeke smiled. "You just got promoted, my brother."

Bane looked perplexed. "Promoted? I didn't know we were hiring."

"We will be, right after I fire Antonio." Holding on to the envelope, Zeke turned on his heels, and left.

No one tries me like this, Zeke thought, marching down the hallway towards the elevator. He pressed the button and the elevator doors glided open. Fuming, Zeke stepped inside and hit the button for the ground level where Balfour's upscale spa was located.

A few moments later, the gold elevator doors glided open. Temper rising, Zeke stepped out onto the ground level floor with the envelope in his hand. Marching down the hallway of the dimly lit spa, Zeke searched in and out of rooms for Antonio. Thus far, Antonio hadn't been anywhere in sight. Having checked everywhere for him except for the sauna, he turned and headed in that direction.

Zeke's hard dress shoes traipsed along the tile floor of the sauna room. Hot steam rose above his head, clouding the moist air. Zeke pulled open the door to sauna number one, and it was empty. Sauna numbers two and three were empty, too.

Perhaps Antonio had left the spa by now. Zeke wrapped her fingers around the silver handle of the last sauna on the end, and yanked it open. Anger surged Zeke.

Some woman had her face in Antonio's lap giving him a blow job. Zeke cleared his throat. Antonio's eyes sprang open. The lady's head shot up from his brother's thrusting lap. "How dare you do this in a place where the customers come?"

The blond haired woman snatched the towel from the bench, wrapped it around her body, then hastened out of the sauna. Wearing a dress shirt and bottomless, Antonio frowned. "I'll call you later," he called out after the blonde. *Who wears a shirt while in the sauna?* Antonio jumped to his feet. "What I do is my business."

"You're exactly right. What you do is your business. And what I do is my business. That being said, I have something for you." Zeke extended the envelope to Antonio.

"What's that?"

"Just take it and read it." Antonio snatched the envelope from Zeke's grip, unfolded it, and began reading it. "As Donald Trump would say…Antonio Balfour you're fired! Pack your things and leave!"

Seemingly shocked, Antonio's mouth dropped. Finally, he snapped it shut. Eyes narrowing, he bald the pink sheet in his fist.

Shoulders pushed back. Head held high. White steam swirled above Zeke's head. Glad to be rid of the lazy pompous ass man, Zeke turned, and victoriously stalked away.

"Fuck you Zeke!"

Good ridden asshole. Needing to get some fresh air, Zeke exited the hotel from the spa exit, and stepped outside. Walking along the side of the building, he took some very much needed deep breaths.

Reaching the parking lot, he pressed the button on his key fob, and the locks to his SUV popped up. His temper tamping down, he slid between the seat and steering wheel, stuck the key in the SUV's ignition, and turned. The engine of the vehicle buzzed to life.

Clearly understanding Antonio wasn't going to take getting fired lightly, Zeke pulled out on ocean drive, and decided to go take a look at his home under construction. When he'd last spoken with the contractor, he'd mentioned his home should be completed in two to three weeks. Although that may have seemed quick to some, it wasn't to him. Money could buy you almost anything. Money, was the root to all evil. Mildred and Kelvin had kidnapped Taylor, and stolen their son for money. *Money.* People would do anything for money. And now Antonio wasn't making any.

"You got what you deserved, brother." Zeke pulled up alongside of the road and stared at his and Taylor's future home. The stucco, white ocean front mansion looked spectacular. Green shrubbery planted the grounds beneath the long bay window. Taylor had done such a wonderful job designing the outside until he felt confident she'd do the same thing with the inside, too.

Remaining inside the SUV, Zeke rolled down the window, and took a picture of the recently embedded shrubbery and flowers with his cell. He then sent the photo to Taylor via text.

Rolling up the window, his cell buzzed in his hand. Taylor's picture came up on his screen. Smiling he swiped the phone. "Hello, my wife."

"Hi, my husband. I see they planted the shrubs and the flowers. From the looks of the picture, I'm very pleased. Are you?"

Oh, how he missed her. "Yes. It looks great."

"I miss you so much, Zeke. I'm so ready to come home."

"I'm miss you too. When will you be finished?"

"Hopefully, in a few days. I——"

Zeke's cell buzzed. Pulling the cell from his ear, he quickly glanced the caller ID. "Baby, sorry to interrupt you, but an important phone call just came through. I'll call you right back."

"Okay."

Zeke clicked over. "Don. How are you today?"

"Doing rather good. Are you alone? Do you have a second to talk?" Don seemed to rush the words from his mouth.

"Yeah. What's going on?"

Don stated, "I stumbled across something I know you'll find interesting. Mildred's son, Kelvin, attended high school here in Hilton Head Island. Up until the day Taylor was kidnapped, he frequently visited this area. But that's not what has me riled up, Zeke."

"What has you riled up, Don?"

"According to my sources, back in the day, David belonged to a bad boy gang called *Southern Mafia*. While in high school, any boy that joined *Southern Mafia* had to be branded on their chest with the initials SM. Since the members of *Southern Mafia* have gotten older, they really don't commit crimes anymore. However, from time to time they still get together. Go hunting. Fishing. Hang out at the local bars."

"I don't get it Don. What does this have to do with Taylor's kidnapping?"

"One of the guys in the gang by the name of Broderick Whitefield wife was pregnant ten years ago. Well, a week before Taylor went missing, Broderick's wife miscarried. She was seven months pregnant when she lost the baby."

"Whoa."

"But here's the kicker, Zeke. Our bad boy Broderick still lives right here in Hilton Head. Broderick is now a multimillionaire cosmetic surgeon…a respectable doctor in the community. He has money coming out of his ears! Broderick has enough money to have hired Mildred and Kelvin. Braced yourself." Zeke's body tensed. Don continued. "Broderick and his wife have a ten year old son. Their son is the same age as yours. This is progress, Zeke. Progress!"

"Oh God, Don. If your theory proves correct, this means Taylor and my son lives right here in Hilton Head."

"Exactly!"

Don and Zeke ended their conversation.

Still sitting inside his SUV, Zeke felt elated about the news Don had just shared with him. *Dr. Broderick Whitefield may have my Zavier.* Overly excited, Zeke called Taylor back and filled her in on everything.

While on the phone with her, she'd gotten so overwhelmed, and had started crying. More than anything, Zeke had wished he could've been with Taylor in Paris when he'd told her what Don had said. Been there to kiss her cheek. To dry her tears.

After Zeke got off the phone with Taylor, he drove to Charlie's steak house for a rib eye and loaded baked potato. Finishing up a quick dinner, he then drove way to Beaufort to tutor Jaheem and Evan.

Now at the group care facility sitting at a table beside Evan, Zeke read the book *Letters to a Young Brother* by Hill Harper to the little kid. Clenching the inspiring book in his hands, Zeke's words trailed off. He turned to look at Evan. "We'll finish the rest of the book tomorrow."

Evan turned his palms up and shrugged. "But Mister, we're just getting to the good part of the book. Will you please keep reading to me?"

Zeke was glad that Evan found the book interesting. "I will. But, you must get your homework and studying done first."

"Okay. Oh yeah. I have something to give you. It's not much, okay, Mr. But it's the best I can do for now." Evan reached inside his pocket, and handed Zeke a folded sheet of paper.

Zeke unfolded the sheet of paper. On the paper was a beautiful drawing of a little boy and a grown man. The lines, the tinted coloring, and the shapes in the drawing were perfect. Looked like a perfectionist artist had drawn it. "This is beautiful, Evan. Who drew this?"

"I did Mister. I drew it. Oh, I forgot something." He took the drawing from Zeke. By the little boy in the drawing he wrote the name Evan. By the older guy's name he wrote Zeke and in parenthesis he wrote Mister. "Here." Evan threw his arms around Zeke and gave him a big hug. "Thank you for trying to teach me how to read. I finally made a C on my spelling test."

Chuckling, Zeke patted Evan's back. "A c is good. Improvement. I'm so proud of you. Thanks for the drawing. I'm going to buy a frame for it and put it up in my office."

"Can I— Nah, never mind. You gone say no." Evan shook his head.

Zeke prompted, "Go ahead, and ask me. You never know what I'm going to say if you don't ask."

"Can I come see what your office looks like one day? Is it big?"

Zeke chortled. "I'd love to bring you to my office."

Evan threw a fist in the air, then yanked it to his chest. "Yes! I don't mind earning my visit either. Maybe I can sweep your office for you once I get there." Evan stuck out his hand. "Deal."

Zeke shook his hand. "Sure. Deal."

Just as Evan finished the last of his homework, Marva strode up behind Zeke and shared some positive new about Evan with him. "I spoke with Evan's teacher today. She said he's making so much progress with his grades and effort. She also said that his attitude has improved. Tell me, Evan, what has inspired you to do better?"

"Mister here. He's been so nice to me. He's the first person that has ever believed in me." Evan's caring words threatened to make Zeke's eyes water. Determined not to let this kid see him shed a tear, Zeke sniffed. "Hey, Mister. Please don't tell me you about to cry cause I ain't never seen a grown man cry!"

Marva and Zeke laughed synchronously. Yeah, he was about to cry alright. Cry because he'd just made the final decision to go ahead and adopt Jaheem and Evan. Giving two deserving boys the Balfour last name sounded like music to Zeke's ears. *Jaheem and Evan Balfour. I like the sound of that.*

Chapter Twenty-Six

WIND BLOWING FROM THE FAN brushed curly strands of hair across Taylor's face as she sat on the floor with her bare feet kicked up in the air. Modeling a short red skirt, short sleeve yellow jacket, and white tank for Asture Fashion Summer Magazine, she parted her lips. Striking graceful poises, long hair tickled her tongue.

Snapsnapsnap. Lights flickered from the camera. "Get the hair out of your mouth," the photographer requested, cradling the camera in his hands. Taylor tossed her hair behind her shoulder. "Thanks. Now let's take pictures standing."

As Taylor stood next to a tall live plant, Lance threw her a hat, and she caught it. Lowering the black summer hat to her head, she slightly shifted sideways. *Snapsnap.* Putting a finger to her chin, she titled forward. *Snapsnap.* Hand on hip, she arched her spine. Perched out her breasts.

The breeze from the fan gently whipped at Taylor's face. Her mind drifting to Zeke's call a day and a half ago, she slid a hand in her left pocket, and relived their conversation inside her head as she modeled.

"Taylor! Guess what, my wife? I think Don has found our son! He's alive Taylor! Zavier is alive!"

"Zeke, are you sure?!"

"Not exactly. Don is going to put in a court order requesting a paternity test for the people he think may have Zavier."

"I don't want to get my hopes up, Zeke. Only to be disappointed."

"I have a good feeling about this Taylor. I think Broderick Whitefield has our Zavier!"

Lance snapped his fingers in front of Taylors face, snapping her out of her daydream. "Where were you just now? You completely zoned out, Taylor."

"Sorry Lance. I have so much going on inside my head."

"That's okay. We're done."

The long photo shoot left Taylor exhausted. "Time flew by. Well, if that's it, I guess I'll be headed home. Thanks for everything."

"When you say home, are you talking about your apartment here? Or your home in Hilton Head Island?"

"I'm going home, home. Home to my husband." Taylor snatched her clutch up from the table, and couldn't get out of the building fast enough.

"Have a safe trip." Lance waved goodbye.

FORTY-FIVE MINUTES LATER, TAYLOR'S heels clicked against the pavement as she walked across the concrete at the airport. Mounting the steps of Balfour's company jet, the ends of her hair twirled in the light breeze beneath the black, stylish hat she wore. *Oh Zeke, I can't wait to get home, and see you.*

"Welcome aboard," the handsome African American pilot said, stepping to the side.

"Thanks."

Taylor's eyes roamed over the small company aircraft. Buckling her seatbelt, she pulled out her phone and dialed Zeke.

"Hello," Zeke answered.

His deep voice stirred her libido. "Hi babes. I just boarded the plane and will be taking off shortly."

"Okay, thanks for calling. Have a safe flight."

"I miss you so much baby." Taylor felt a tall presence come stand behind her. Turning her head, she glanced upward. Surprise, her mouth separated. "Zeke!" fingers working quickly to unbuckle her seatbelt, Taylor jumped out of her seat, and threw herself into Zeke's husky arms. "This is the best surprise ever!"

Brown eyes luminous, Zeke had a big hearty smile on his handsome tanned face. "I miss you too, my wife. Missed you so much until I just had to come here to pick you up."

Heart tinkering, Taylor jumped up in Zeke's lap, wrapped her legs around his waist, twined her arms around his neck. "Now that you're here, what do you have in store for me?"

"Some good, good loving." Using his strength to carry her, Zeke walked to the back of the aircraft, and headed into the bedroom. Standing at the foot of the bed, he dropped Taylor on the mattress.

Taylor's hands moved urgently to remove her shirt and bra as Zeke yanked off her skirt. Butt naked on the bed, she spread her legs wide. As Zeke peered down at her hot sex, she opened and closed and opened her legs.

Labia quivering, she purred. "Is this what you miss?" She slid her own finger in her heat, caressed her g-spot, then put her wet finger to his lips. Zeke suckled Taylor's slick juice from her finger. Tingles spread through her bones. Her clitoris curled.

Lifting off the ground, the jet's engine hummed, and shot in the air.

"Yes, I missed it." Groaning, he removed his shirt and jeans. His hard erection pointed forward. He climbed on top of the bed, slid his finger in her heat, scraped her sensitive g-spot. "I'm about to show you just how much I missed it, too."

Entering Taylor's channel, Zeke scooped up her leg, put it over his shoulder, and drove deep into her womb. Taylor put her toes on her free leg to his lips. Driving deliciously into her, one by one Zeke sucked the joints of her toes.

Stroking. Kissing. Teasing. Her husband set her body aflame. Pushed her over the edged. It'd been months since he'd been in her. Too long.

Taylor's spine arched. "Oh Zeke," she cooed, her jism splattering on his shooting length. Coming together had never been better.

Hilton Head Island

KATHERINE STOOD AT THE BAY window inside her family room cringing as she listened to Colton and Antonio argue. Her husband's and son's loud voices escalated inside of the mansion. Looking out at the lake, it took everything inside Katherine to refrain from grabbing a frying pan out the kitchen and bashing Colton's skull out. *Where's your backbone Colton?*

"I'm not going to undue Zeke's decision!" Colton's angry voice echoed throughout the house. "He fired you and I respect that!"

"I've worked at the hotel with you since I was a little boy. Doesn't that count for something?!" Antonio fired back.

"Antonio, for years I paid you a salary for something you didn't do. Often times while you were supposed to be at work, you were running around town getting into trouble with the law, or two timing women. Well, there's a new captain on board now, and I guess he's decided to not put up with your horrible work ethics.

There's certain requirements that comes with being Vice President for a major hotel conglomeration. Being on time is one of them."

Antonio grumbled. "I ain't believing you! You have the power to right Zeke's wrong and you're not going to do it. You're not going to help me get my job back. What am I supposed to do for money?"

"As much money as I paid you to do nothing, you should have some saved. Not to mention you're a grown ass man and live here rent free! If you don't have any money, that's just too damn bad!"

Anger stomping her chest, Katherine marched inside the living room. "I let you give Zeke the CEO position. But I'll be damned, Colton, if I let you allow Zeke to throw my son out on his ass."

Colton jumped from the seat at the head of the table and stepped to the side. His face contorted. "Let me! Let me! Balfour Enterprises is my damn company. My ancestors built Balfour from the ground up and passed it down to me. You don't let me do shit Katherine. I do as I damn well please. You spoiled Antonio rotten. Gave him everything he ever wanted. He had no chores. No responsibilities. Even when I tried to give him some duties and responsibilities, you went behind my back and either did them for him, or hired someone else to do his work. It's your fault that Antonio is sorry ass hell."

"Fuck you old man!" Antonio bellowed.

Colton lunged at Antonio throttled his ass. Antonio fell to the floor. "I might be old. And I might be sick. I might even be dying, but I'd rather die, than to have a child of mine disrespect me." Lying on the floor holding his jaw, Antonio's eyes narrowed at Colton. The wicked look frightened Katherine. "I'm about to leave before I do something I may regret. Pack your shit and get out." Colton stomped abruptly towards the front door.

About to trip over her long dress, Katherine had to walk fast to keep up with him. His hand grasped the doorknob, she clenched his elbow. "You can't kick Antonio out of the house Colton. You can't do this."

Colton glanced over his shoulder back at Katherine. Grave disapproval embedded his pupils. "Why don't you go with him, you no good for nothing, woman." Tone colder than ice, Colton stalked outside, and slammed the door behind him.

The picture on the wall of Colton and Katherine on their wedding day some umpteenth years ago fell to the floor, and shattered.

Hearing the glass breaking, Katherine's heart crumbled. *My life is falling apart. This is all Zeke's and Taylor's fault. Oh God, Antonio.* Fisting her dress at the hips, Katherine ran back into the dining room, and then into the kitchen.

Antonio sat at the kitchen table holding an ice pack to his bruised jaw. "Dad is low down and dirty. He don't have a single ounce of love for me in him. He gave my job to his mistress' son. I wouldn't be surprised if he's taken me out of his will."

Katherine patted Antonio's back. "No. He wouldn't do a thing like that."

Antonio gave an evil chuckle. "You're fooling yourself, Katherine. Dad is just as ruthless as that man named Victor that you love watching on television every day."

Katherine picked up her crocodile Hermes Birkin purse off the counter and clutched the handle. "I'll be back."

"Where are you going?" Antonio looked at her inquisitively.

I should've done this a long time ago. For all I know Colton may try and change his will behind my back. "To see an attorney. If Colton Balfour thinks he's going to die and leave me and my children out of his will, he's a damn fool. I have rights. Please be gone by the time your father gets back. The last thing I need is for the two of y'all to get into a fist fight."

"Where am I supposed to go? I can't even stay at the hotel."

Katherine reached into her wallet and handed Antonio five crisp one hundred dollar bills. "You can stay at my parent's old house off the main road in the woods if you want, too. Bye." She entered the garage from the back kitchen door. Just as Katherine slid inside her snow white Mercedes, a black BMW pulled up on the side of the road, and parked on the curb.

The Caucasian gentleman driving the BMW was none other than Dr. Broderick Whitefield. Apparently not noticing her, Broderick got out of the BMW and stalked toward the front door of the estate. *What is Broderick doing here?* Katherine wondered, her mind flashing back to the gang he'd been in along with Antonio.

Broderick and Antonio had both been a part of a gang called *Southern Mafia* back in the day. But now that Broderick was married and a successful cosmetic surgeon, Katherine had no idea he still kept in touch with Antonio. *What in the hell is Broderick doing here?* she wondered, belatedly exiting her car.

Katherine put her ear to the garage door to see if she could hear voices. She didn't. Curious as to why Broderick had paid Antonio a visit, she quietly reentered the house through the kitchen to find them standing in the living room.

"Let's talk in the library," Antonio said. Unaware of Katherine's presence, Antonio led Broderick down the long hallway towards the library. After they entered the library, Katherine came from out of hiding.

Tiptoeing down the hallway, Katherine had a bad feeling her world was about to come crashing down on her freaking head. Praying she was wrong, Katherine put her ear to the closed door of the library. Antonio's and Broderick's voices droned inside the room, and she heard them clearly.

"So what do I owe this pleasurable visit?" Antonio asked.

"What happened to your face, man?" Broderick question

"Fell off the ladder while cutting the hedges," Antonio lied. *No you didn't. Your daddy socked you in the face.*

"You make enough money to hire a gardener to do the lawn for you, man." Broderick cleared his throat. "Anyway, I'm here because a detective by the name of Don paid me a visit today, and questioned me about you and your mother."

Ear pressed tight to the door, Katherine's heart dunked.

"What kind of questions did Don ask you?" Antonio asked in a cool tone, but Katherine knew he had to be worried.

Broderick said, "At first Don asked me about my son. He wanted to know if Sarah and I legally adopted him? When I told him yes, he asked me if Sarah and I would subject our son to a DNA test. When I asked him why, he said he suspects that our son was stolen, and belongs to a couple that misses him dearly."

"How does this relates to me?" Antonio asked.

"That what I was wondering. Don told me he knew I'd been a member of the *Southern Mafia* gang back in high school. He asked me to give him the names of the other gang members. He wanted to know if any of the gang members were capable of kidnapping. Right when I got ready to tell Don to leave my house, my cell phone rang, and I had to excuse myself."

Antonio sounded worried when he said, "Please tell me you didn't tell Don I was part of *Southern Mafia*."

"No I didn't."

Antonio released a deep breath. "Good. It's none of his business."

"But I think Don figured out, anyway."

Antonio's voice deepened as he asked, "What do you mean Don figured it out?" Eavesdropping, nervous tension rushed Katherine.

Broderick continued. "After I finished my phone call, I returned back to the living room, and Don was gone. And so was the photo album I had on the coffee table. Inside the photo album was a picture of me, Kelvin, Jack, Paul, Stephen, and you from back in the day. We had our shirts off and was pointing to those stupid SM initials we'd gotten on our chest. Don now knows who the *Southern Mafia* gang members were. Are any of the old gang members or you in some kind of trouble?"

"No man, I'm not in any kind of trouble. I stop being a bad boy a long time ago. Thanks for stopping by and filling me in. Things are good here," Antonio lied.

Don knows Antonio was a gang member. It's only a matter of time before he puts two and two together. Or maybe he already has. I have to stop him from telling Zeke. Or Taylor. Or the police. Katherine bustled away from the door, ran upstairs to her bedroom, and yanked open the bottom drawer of her nightstand.

Her silver shiny pistol with glossy pink handle lay beside her bible. Hands shaking, she hefted her gun, and placed it inside her purse. Grabbing her black curly wig from the top shelf of her closet, Katherine hopped in her car, and left.

Chapter Twenty-Seven

FLUFFY WHITE CLOUDS FLOATED PAST the tiny window of the aircraft as it glided smoothly in the bright sky. Tucked beneath the cotton sheets of the jet's comfortable bed, Zeke held Taylor's in his arms. Madly in love, Zeke kissed the top of Taylor's head. "It's going to be so good having you home."

Taylor's finger teased Zeke's nipple. "It's going to be good being home. Speaking of home, I can't wait for our home to get finished being built so we can move in."

"That reminds me, I spoke with the contractor today. Our home will be move in ready next week."

Her head shot up from his chest. Eyes twinkling, Taylor's lips curved upward. "Next week?" Zeke nodded. "Oh that's wonderful. I can't wait."

He twirled his finger around the end of her long curly hair. "Me either. How's your health been lately?"

"Great. Ever since I've left the hospital, I've felt wonderful. Have you given any more thought about adopting Jaheem and Evan?"

Hearing the two young boy's names made Zeke's insides jump with joy. Traveling his fingers along Taylor's collar bone, he said, "Yes. If you're truly on board, I'd like for you to meet them when we get back. If you feel they're a right fit for our family, I want to adopt them as soon as possible."

Tilting her head, Taylor's eyes glistened. "I'm definitely on board, Zeke. If Jaheem and Evan are a good fit for you, then I know they'll be a good fit for me as well. As my husband, I trust your decision. I can't wait to meet them."

Zeke appreciated the way Taylor trusted him to lead her right. "You're going to love Jaheem and Evan. There are such great kids. I can't explain it, but I have a deep connection with both of them. But if I'm being honest, I feel especially connected to Evan for some reason. Don't get me wrong, I love them both equally. But there's just something about Evan to where I feel really drawn to him. Maybe it's because he's the same age as our Zavier. Maybe it's because I've always imagined Zavier having the same honey brown complexion as Evan. As the same brown eyes as him."

"What does Evan's hair look like?" Taylor asked.

"It's dark brown and curly—" Zeke's cell buzzed. He lifted it from the end table to spy Don calling. "It's Don." Seeing hope buried in Taylor's eyes, Zeke swallowed then answered his cell. "Hey Don. How's it going?"

"Zeke! I have something very important to tell you. Are you sitting down?" Seriousness laced Don's voice.

"Yes."

Don cleared his throat. "I paid Dr. Broderick Whitefield a visit today. To avoid court legalities and media attention, Broderick agreed to let us test his son's DNA to see if it matches with yours and Taylors. While I was visiting with Broderick, I stumbled across a photo of the Southern Mafia gang members. Kelvin and Broderick is in the photo along with—who's there? Oh God no!"

At the sound of Don's horrifying voice, Zeke bolted up in bed. "What's wrong Don?"

"Put down the gun! Please don't' do this!" Don begged.

Pow! A gunshot blasted in Zeke's ear then the phone line went dead.

"Don! Don! Don!"

ONE WEEKS LATER DON MCQUADE lay in the hospital bed in a deep coma looking dead. Pale skin, bloated face, the doctor had stated it was a miracle that Don was still alive. In critical condition from a gunshot wound to the head, bandages wrapped around his skull. Intubated, his chest rose and fell.

Zeke and Taylor stood beside Don's bed looking down at him and holding hands. "God, I can't help but wonder if the person who did this to Don, did this to stop him from telling me who has our son. Maybe Broderick's son isn't ours. Zeke put his mouth to Don's ear. "Fight for your life, Don. Fight."

Taylor cupped Don's hand. "Don, it's me Taylor. God is in control over your situation. He's revealed to me that He will see you through this so hang in there."

Hard shoes clacked against the floor causing Zeke and Taylor to turn around and look toward the entrance of the room. Braylon, Sandella, Richmond, and Kayla entered the room then walked up to Don's bedside.

"How's he doing," Richmond asked.

Zeke replied, "There hasn't been any changes."

"I feel so sorry for him," Sandella said just above a whisper.

"Me too. I feel sorry for him, and his family," Kayla acknowledge, tears pooling her pretty eyes.

"Although I'm a criminal investigator for the Marines, I've still been doing my own investigation regarding Don. I've been working around the clock trying to figure out who committed this crime," Braylon said.

"Braylon will catch them," Sandella stated, confident in her husband's work abilities.

Hating to see Don fighting for his life, Zeke's heart was filled with sorrow. "It's good seeing you guys, Taylor and I are about to head out. We're moved into our new home yesterday. Once we get settled in, we're going to invite you guys over to have dinner with us."

Sandella's face beamed with joy. "I can't wait to see your new home, I know it's beautiful."

Kayla said, "Let me know if you need any help unpacking, Taylor."

Taylor spoke, "Thanks for offering, Kayla. But Zeke hired someone to unpack our things for us."

"I'll be in touch." Zeke placed his hand on the lower part of Taylor's spine and steered her out of the room. Seeing his friends had cheered him up some. And when he saw Jaheem and Evan in a short while, he was certain he'd feel even better. *My sons.*

Zeke steered the vehicle down the street and headed toward his brand new home on the ocean. It'd taken over an hour for Zeke along with Taylor to drive to Beaufort to pick up Jaheem and Evan, and then head back to the other side of town.

When Taylor had first laid eyes on Jaheem and Evan while at the group care facility, she'd wrapped her arms around both the boys like she loved them with all her heart. A very affectionate woman, Taylor had arrived at the shelter bearing gifts for all the children. Books, toys, socks, and t'shirts, she'd spent a small fortune at Walmart after they'd left the hospital to see Don.

With Jaheem and Evan in the back seat of his SUV and Taylor in the passenger's seat, Zeke drove the Porsche up the long driveway of their new home on the ocean, and parked.

"Who in the heck lives here?!" Jaheem asked.

Zeke looked at Jaheem in his rearview mirror. Jaheem's mouth was wide open. "This is Taylor and my home."

Evan slapped his hands to his honey brown cheeks. "I've never seen a house this big in my whole life! This is two mansions, Mister!"

Zeke and Taylor both chuckled. Taylor asked, "Would you guys like to see the inside?"

"Yes!" Jaheem and Evan said in unison. At the same time, they quickly hopped out of the car, slammed the doors, and scurried up to the front door, leaving Taylor and Zeke sitting in the SUV.

Zeke watched Jaheem and Evan as they stood on the porch waving for him and Taylor to get out of the car. "I think they're going to like their new home. I can't wait to tell them that we want to adopt them."

Taylor's eyes radiated. "I think they're going to love it here, too. You said they were adorable Zeke, and they are. I can't wait to see their faces when we tell them we want to adopt them." Taylor placed her hand over her heart. "I've fallen in love with them already. When can we make them officially ours? I want to adopt them right away."

"After we speak with them today, I'll call the attorney, Gar, and have him to draw up the paperwork ASAP."

Her features became more animated. "I can't wait. I'm too excited."

Zeke and Taylor climbed down from the SUV, walked up to the heavy glass door of their mansion. Turning the key in the lock, Zeke winked his eye at Taylor.

Jaheem laughed. "Stop flirting, Mr. Zeke."

"You caught me, huh?" Zeke chuckled.

Jaheem pointed at his own eyes. "These eyes don't miss nothing."

Zeke stepped to the side to let his family in first. Standing in the foyer, he closed the door behind them. Upon entering the mansion, the oversized living room offered a great view of the wide blue ocean.

Jaheem's eyes traveled around the spacious area. "Wow. Look at this house."

Evan put his fist on hips and titled his head. "Are you some kin to Jay-Z, Mister?"

Zeke chortled. "No Evan. I'm not related to Jay-Z."

Evan threw his hands up in the air. "I heard you were rich. But I didn't know you was this rich."

After showing Jaheem and Evan the house, Zeke took them to the family room, and sat them on the couch between Taylor and him. "Jaheem...Evan...there's something Taylor and I want to discuss with you."

"Oh-uh. This sounds serious," Jaheem stated.

"Tell me about it. I've been good lately, Mister." Shaking his head, Evan held his hands up to his chest level. "So whatever they say I did, it wasn't me."

Taylor giggled. "Your teacher gave us a good report on you, and we know you've been good, Evan."

Zeke exclaimed, "What Taylor and I want to talk to you two about is serious. Over the last few months, I've spent a lot of time with both of you. I've bragged on the two of you over and over to Taylor. After hearing how wonderful you are, she and I decided we'd like to adopt both of you."

Taylor caressed Evan's back as love filled her eyes. "We love both of you and want you to be our sons."

Zeke caressed Jaheem's back. "How do you guys feel about that?"

Jaheem burst into tears.

Sniffing, Evan folded his arms over his chest.

The two boys looked at each other and smiled.

Jaheem's teary voice shook as he cried, "I never thought I'd see this day come. Never thought anybody would ever love me. Normally, no one wants the older kids. I'd love for you to adopt me."

Evan's tiny little finger shot up in the air. "Me too!"

Zeke's heart swelled. "Then it's settled. The four of us are going to live here, and be one...big...happily family."

Zeke and Taylor sat on the long couch, glancing out at the sea, embracing their soon-to-be-children.

Chapter Twenty-Eight

FOURTEEN DAYS LATER, TAYLOR STOOD upstairs in the hallway of her home with Jaheem on her left and little Evan on her right in front of a closed bedroom door. Anxious for the boys to see what she'd done to each of their soon-to-be bedrooms, Taylor's insides jingled.

The boy's presence gave Taylor so much joy. "This is your bedroom Jaheem. Are you ready to see what it looks like?" Smiling, Jaheem nodded his head. "I hope you like it." Taylor opened the door, and the three of them walked inside.

Jaheem's mouth dropped. His eyes spread wide. "Whoa! This is my room? I even have my own bathroom?" Standing in the center of his bedroom, Jaheem started dancing. Snapping his fingers, his feet shuffled.

Taylor and Evan started laughing. *Having these boys here is going to be so much fun,* Taylor thought, noticing Jaheem had a lot of soul and rhythm.

Because Jaheem had mentioned he loved the Florida Gators football team, Taylor had selected a Gator theme for his room. Blue walls, orange sofas, white curtains with tiny alligators, desk against the wall, by the amazed look on Jaheem's face, she felt he loved his room. "Do you like it?"

Jaheem finally stopped dancing. "Like it? I love it! Thank you so much, Ta—" He stopped speaking midsentence. "Is it okay if I call you, Mom?" His white teeth accentuated the dark brown complexion of his smooth skin.

Taylor's heart melted like butter. "Sure Jaheem. I'd love for you to call me, Mom."

Evan patted Taylor's shoulder. "Can I call you, Mom, too?" he asked.

Taylor ruffled her hand over Evan's brown, curly hair. Looking down at him, she noticed his honey brown skin held a red tint, and he looked feverish. He'd said earlier that he hadn't been feeling well. "Yes, Evan. I'd love for you to call me mom, too. Are you ready to see your room?" she asked, Evan. *He looks sick.*

Evan nodded. "Yes."

Taylor and the boys exited Jaheem's room and rounded into Evan's bedroom. Evan was a huge fan of the Miami Heat. So Taylor had had a basketball themed mural painted in the center of the wall above Evan's full size bed. On the basketball court itself, Evan's name was painted in black, bold letters. A play basketball goal stood tucked in the corner across from his bed. Maroon and black bean bags sat on the floor beneath the window.

Evan's eyes were as big as the Mississippi river. "This is soooo beautiful." He wrapped his arms around Taylor's waist and gave her a big hug. "Thank you so much, Mom. When I get a job, I'm going to take good care of you, and pay you back for this."

Rubbing his knuckles over his eyes, Evan walked up to the window, and plopped down on the bean bag. Smiling up at the ceiling, he crossed his legs at the ankles, and spread his arms toward the ceiling. "Dear Lord, if I'm dreaming, please don't ever let me wake up."

Taylor and Jaheem both laughed at the precocious kid. After Evan explored his bedroom a little, she showed her sons their loft filled with two arcades, a play station, and a pool table. As Taylor sat on the sofa watching Jaheem and Evan play with their play station, her heart rejoiced.

She thought Zeke had fulfilled her, and he did, beyond her wildest fantasy her husband did. But having Jaheem and Evan gave her a different kind of fulfillment. A sense of pride. Accomplishment like she'd done something to help others. She couldn't explain it, but like Zeke, she felt so close to them. She loved them so much. And she'd do everything in her power to protect them, and make sure they never went without.

Thank you God for giving me these two precious little boys. I don't know why you blessed me with them, but thank you. Thank you.

Thunder crackled. Grey clouds hung over the ocean. Raindrops suddenly poured from the sky. Bringing her feet to the sofa, Taylor's cell vibrated against her hip. She pulled it from the clip attached to her jeans and answered it. "How is the world's greatest husband doing?"

"Bad." Zeke's deep voice sounded troubled.

Disliking the frustrating sound of Zeke's voice, Taylor straightened her back on the sofa. "What's wrong?"

"I have some bad news, Taylor." *Oh no, please don't tell me Don died.* Zeke continued. "It's about Evan. His mother is protesting the adoption. She claims she now wants to raise him."

"Hold on for a second." Tears quickly crept into Taylor's eyes as she stood, and left the loft. Descending the staircase, her feet hit the floor on the first level. "I'm back. Zeke no. We can let Evan's mother take him from us."

Zeke's sigh came through the phone. "Evan was never legally ours, Taylor."

237

Taylor's heart crackled. "Isn't there something you can do? I love Evan. I know I've only spent a few weeks with him, but in those few weeks I've grown so attached to him. He feels like my own. If I didn't know any better, I'd think he was mine." *He looks just like he could be ours.*

"I know, baby. I feel the same way too. But his mother wants to keep him. She's changed her mind about letting us adopt him."

A hot tear rolled over Taylor's cheek as she stood at the window in her family room glaring out the window at the dull rolling sea. Dark grey clouds hung in the air over her home. The ocean tides grew higher. "I bet his mother doesn't even want him. She's probably knows we're rich and wants us to offer her some money."

"That thought came across my mind, too. Evan's mother is going to pick him up today after you drop him off at the group care facility."

Disappointed, Taylor fought not to burst into tears. "Today? Evan has been at the group care facility for months, and not once has his mother visited him. How could someone just drop their baby off and never come back to see him?" *Oh God, why is this happening?* "Offer her some money, Zeke. I bet that'd get her attention. Get her to change her mind. I don't care how much you have to pay her, just do it. Evan is meant to be my son. There's nothing anyone can say or do to make me feel any different. I love him," she choked out. *How did I get so attached to him so soon?*

"Oh baby, don't cry. Please don't cry. I'll promise, I'll make Evan's mother a monetary offer. One that she won't be able to refuse."

"Thanks, Zeke. I love you so much."

"I love you, too, my wife."

Zeke and Taylor ended their call. Drying her weeping eyes, Taylor continued looking out at the rolling ocean. Waves crashed up against the beige sand then rolled back into the sea. *I can't lose you, Evan.* She wanted to adopt Evan more than anything in the world. If she lost him, it'd kill her.

"I'm not going back to her," Evan's said, sneaking up behind her. *Oh no, he overheard me talking on the phone with Zeke.* Taylor slowly turned to face Evan.

Dread filled his dole like brown eyes. "I know you don't want to go back. I don't want you to go back either. But she's your mother—"

"She's not my mother! You're my mother. That old lady don't want me. She's never even liked me. All she do is beat me. I'm tired of her beating me." Tears dripped rapidly from Evan's eyes. "Please don't send me back. If you do, I'm going to run away."

Taylor tried so hard to hold back her tears, but it was useless. "I'll fight to get custody of you, Evan. But I don't know if it'll work. As much as you don't like your mother, she has certain rights—"

Evan flung open the sliding glass door and took off running down the beach. Taylor chased after him. Bare feet twisting in the wet sand, rain pelted Taylor's scalp. "Evan! Come back here! Please Evan!"

The beach stretched for miles. Thunder roared. Zig-zag lighting struck the sky. White sheets of rain saturated Taylor as she scurried as fast as she could after Evan. How could his mother do this to him? Originally she'd agreed to give him up for adoption. Why did she all of a sudden want him back? Chasing after Evan, Taylor wept.

Evan halted. Shoulders motioning up and down, he turned to look at Taylor. Just a she reached him, his red stained eyes stretched wide.

Gasping for air, Evan gripped his throat. He fell to the ground. Eyes rolling to white, his body jerked wildly. Foam bubbled from his opened mouth.

Taylor dropped to her knees beside Evan as he lay on the ground writhing. Hunched over, she touched his shoulder with one hand, and his face with the other. "Evan! What's wrong? What's wrong baby?" Taylor snatched her cell from the clip attached to her hip. Her fingers quivered as she dialed 911. "Oh God what's wrong with my baby!"

Chapter Twenty-Nine

Two Days Later

ZEKE DRAPED HIS ARM AROUND Taylor's shoulder and peered at Evan through the glass window of the intensive care unit at the hospital. Tubes in Evan's mouth, nose, and veins, grief pricked at Zeke's chest like sharp needles. Suffering from kidney failure, Evan needed to have a kidney transplant in order to live. Brain working overtime, Zeke swallowed. His eyes grew watery. *God, please pull Evan through this. I'm begging you God. Please help this poor, innocent kid.*

Zeke groped inwardly. How could a kid's kidney be failing and nobody knows? How could it get to the point where it'd become life threatening? Were there any signs before two days ago? Any symptoms? Did the people at the group care facility notice anything different about him and just ignored it?

Right now Evan was on a waiting list to receive a kidney. On yesterday Zeke had informed Evan's doctor he'd like to donate his kidney to Evan. Doctors explained to Zeke and Taylor that Zeke first had to be tested to see if he was compatible. Because Zeke and Evan weren't blood related, the chances of him being compatible was slim. Taylor had offered to donate her kidney to Evan as well, but Zeke had told her under no circumstances would she do such thing. If he'd lost her due to surgery complications, he'd die. Literally.

After Zeke had told Taylor that under no circumstances would he let her donate her kidney to Evan, she'd gotten angry, and tight lipped. If she loved Evan just as much as he did, Zeke understood why she'd gotten so upset over his hard stand on the whole organ donation thing.

Taylor folded her arms beneath her breasts. "Look at him, Zeke. He so precious. His skin is so pale. He looks so tired."

"After all he's been through, he has to be tired, Taylor. There's only so much a kid like him can take. Child abuse. Sent to the shelter to live just because you were born."

Stress pulled the lines on Taylor's face tight. "Considering Evan's mother said she wanted to keep him, I'm in disbelief she hasn't paid him a visit yet."

"Evan's mother turned down the money I offered her to let us adopt him. But something in my gut tells me she's going to change her mind. His mother, Muriel, is broke. My friends in Beaufort tells me Muriel has never liked the kid. Trust me, she's just waiting to see if I up my offer—"

"My baby!" A loud scream coming from way of the receptionist desk made Zeke's eyes divert from Taylor to the lady standing at the circulation desk. Severely upset, the crying woman nodded as she spoke with the nurse. Sitting behind the circulation desk, the nurse handed the lady a tissue, then pointed her in their direction.

Grey hair and flowery dress, the wide hipped woman with thick legs walked in their direction. Obese, she more like wobbled toward Zeke and Taylor. When she reached the doorway to Evan's room, she gave Zeke and Taylor a sad look, then she looked at Evan from the doorway. Head tilting, the woman's bottom lip poked out. She put her hand over her ample bosom. "Oh, just look at my baby boy."

Astounded, Zeke thought he'd heard the lady wrong. "Are you Evan's mother?" Zeke asked the old, Caucasian woman. All that screaming she'd just did, yet the woman hadn't a single tear in either of her eyes. What a performance?

"Yes, I am." *Dear Lord, she looks old enough to be Evan's grandmother. She must've had him in her late fifties.* "Seeing him like this just breaks my heart." The woman slowly walked inside Evan's room to go stand beside his bed. Fake crying, her shoulders shook as she looked down at Evan.

"She doesn't look anything like I expected." Taylor seemingly read his mind.

Zeke remained outside the room, observing Muriel from the glass window. "I was thinking the same thing." *Where are the tears lady?*

"Evan doesn't even look anything like her," Taylor acknowledged.

Evan must look like his father. "I know. But according to the documentation, Muriel Elliott is Evan's birth mother."

Taylor's vexation was evident. "He must look like his father. I think Evan looks more like me than he does her."

"I agree. Let's go introduce ourselves to her," Zeke said, leading Taylor inside the cool temperature room. Zeke's attorney had told him Evan's mother, Muriel, had given birth to Evan right at this very same hospital. With Don fighting for his life two doors down, and Evan fighting for his life on the same hallway, Zeke fought hard to remain strong.

Broken hearted, Zeke wanted to shake the hell out of Muriel as she stood over Evan's hospital bed pretending to love him. From what he'd heard, Muriel didn't have an ounce of love for Evan in her heart.

Evan looked so at peace, even with all those tubes running every which way in his body.

Tired of listening to Muriel's fake crying, Zeke cleared his throat. "Muriel."

Muriel met Zeke's gaze. "I'm Zeke Balfour. The man who—"

"Wants to adopt Evan." Dry eyes, Muriel sniffed.

"Yes. I want to adopt Evan. This is my wife, Ta—"

"Taylor. Your attorney has told me all about you two. Nice meeting both of you in person. And thanks for your kind offer to adopt Evan. But he's not for sale. Even if he were, he'd be worth way more money than you offered." She placed a hand to her right, hefty bosom then transferred her gaze back at Evan. "Worth a whole lot more."

She wants more money. Zeke chuckled nastily inside his head.Muriel's hand lingered up and down Evan's arm. She put her lips to Evan's ear, and whispered. "Evan, its Momma. I'm here now."

Disgusted with Muriel's fake performance, Zeke fixated his eyes on the vital machine beside Evan's bed. His heart jostled wildly. The green numbers on the vital machine started dropping quickly. The green line going up and down on the machine flattened. *Beeeep.* A loud bleep came from the machine.

"What's going on, Zeke?" Taylor's voice cracked.

Zeke's heart collapsed. "He's coding. Hang in there Evan."

"Code blue East 516. Code blue East 516." The emergency warning came over the intercom system. Seconds later an emergency team of doctors and nurses scampered inside the room. The doctor said, "We need you to leave so we can work on him."

"I'm not going anywhere," Muriel stated, standing still.

"Oh, yes you are." Furious, Zeke jerked Muriel off her feet and carried her heavy behind out of the room. *Oh God, she's heavy.*

"Put me down you crazy fool!" Grumbling, Muriel kicked up a storm.

Zeke's back hurt from carrying the overweight woman. *I'm about to drop her.* Once they got outside the room, Zeke gladly lowered Muriel feet to the ground. He pointed his finger in Muriel's face. "This is all your fault!"

Muriel touched her chest. "My fault. How is this my fault? He was with Taylor when this happened, not with me."

Zeke looked over his shoulders at Taylor. Balling, she stood at the glass window watching the doctors and nurses try to bring Evan back. Other than Katherine, he'd never desired to slap the hell out of a woman.

"Evan didn't start coding until he heard your voice, Muriel. Doesn't that tell you anything?" Muriel parted her lips to speak, but Zeke held up his hand, stopping her. "The boy doesn't feel love from you. He doesn't want to go home with you. Do us all a favor, and give Evan up for adoption. Taylor and I love him, and we want to raise him."

Muriel's weight shifted. "If you want Evan, you can have him. But it's going to cost you more than a million dollars."

Thought so. "How much more do you want for Evan, Muriel?"

Not in the least bit concerned about Evan possibly dying inside the intensive care room, Muriel's eyes traveled to the ceiling then back down to Zeke's face. As if she was thinking, she curled a finger over her top lip. Her left brow arched. "How about five?"

"Five what?"

"I'll let you adopt my Evan for five million dollars."

"You're pathetic lady. I'll call up my attorney, have him to draw up the paperwork, and I'll be more than happy to pay you five million dollars to adopt Evan. As of today, I want you to stay out of Evan's life—forever. If you even think about showing your face to him after I pay you and he legally becomes my son, I'll have you arrested for stalking."

A smirk was on Muriel's chubby white face. "I promise to stay away. Please make sure you tell your attorney to put this in the contract—I get the money even if Evan dies. Good bye. He's all yours." Not even bothering to wait to see if Evan would pull through, Muriel began walking away.

Watching Muriel walk past the circulation desk, Zeke felt like taking off his shoe, and throwing it at her grey round head. *Good ridden, Muriel.* Katherine and Muriel would make great friends. The two of them acted much alike. Only difference, one was skinny and the other was hefty.

Struggling to pull himself together, Zeke walked over to stand beside Taylor. "Evan's going to pull through this, Taylor."

With an entire medical team trying to bring him back, the doctor gripped the handles of the defibrillator, placed the metals on his chest, and shocked him. Evan's tiny little chest rose violently them slammed back onto the bed.

The green light on the vital machine spiked upward.

Taylor ran inside the room. "Is he going to be okay?"

The doctor nodded. "He's stable for now. He's a very strong little boy."

"Yes. He is. He's like me, his father." When Zeke called himself Evan's father, mixed emotions stirred him. Glad that Muriel had agreed to let him and Taylor adopt Evan, he was also sad because the little guy was lying in a hospital bed fighting for his life.

After the physicians and nurses left the room, Zeke stood on the left side of Evan's bed while Taylor stood on the right. Zeke put his mouth close to Evan's ear, and whispered. "Evan. It's Zeke. Your father, Zeke. Muriel has agreed to let Taylor and I adopt you." Taylor's watery eyes widened, her lips curved into a smile.

Zeke continued. "If you want to come live with me, Taylor, and Jaheem, you have to try and get better. You have to fight for your life. You can do it." Aching inwardly, Zeke cupped Evan's hand and squeezed it.

Evan's free left hand lying on the bed jerked.

Taylor gasped. "His hand moved." Blood shot eyes, Taylor pointed at Evan's hand. "Evan. If you can hear me, wiggle your fingers."

Evan's fingers wiggled. Taylor let loose a wet chuckle. "Thank God. You're going to be all right, Evan. I love you so much. Mommy loves you so, so, so much."

Zeke and Taylor lifted Evan's hands to their lips and kissed his hands.

Long moments later, Zeke rounded the foot of the hospital bed, walked up to Taylor, and whispered, "I'm going to go spend a little time with Don. Afterwards, I'm going to stop by the attorney's office to make sure he takes the paperwork to Muriel today. I want her out of Evan's life as soon as possible."

"Okay. I'll see you later at home." Taylor smooched her lips together and Zeke kissed them.

Shoulders knotted, Zeke stalked down the hallways, and rounded into Don's room. Still on life support, Don's chubby face had turned darker since he'd seen him on yesterday. All alone inside the cold room, stress punched Zeke's gut.

"Don, man. I'm here again. I wish you'd tell me who did this to you." Too sad to describe, Zeke's eyes roamed over Don's face.

Don had said on the phone right before he'd been shot, that he had a photo of the members in the Southern Mafia gang. Well, when the police arrived at Don's office, the photo was nowhere to be found. Since then, he and Taylor had taken a DNA to see if Broderick's son was theirs, and it turned out that the little boy wasn't in any relation to them.

Whoever did this didn't want me to find out who has Zavier. Don is here because of me. Because I hired him to take on my case to find my son. Damn. "I'll be back tomorrow, man."

Weighted down with problems, Zeke stalked out of the room. Something inside his mind told him he needed to hire a security guard to protect Taylor when he was not around. He needed to install cameras inside the house for her protection as well. As soon as he got a chance, he'd do exactly that.

Chapter Thirty

"HOW DOES THAT FEEL?" ZEKE asked, driving his stem into Taylor's drenched opening as she lay on her stomach the following afternoon.

"Wonderful," Taylor purred. Circling her hips, Taylor slid her hand between the mattress and her hairy sex. She slipped her fingers to her tingling clitoris and began rubbing circles on the engorged substance.

Flat hands pressed against the mattress, Zeke's slow, deliberate strokes soothed her insides. Made her hot sex pulse. Clench with need. Desire to explode on Zeke's rod.

Pinching her blood filled clit, squeezing Zeke's rod with her channel, Taylor turned her head sideways on the mattress and captured the beautiful sunrays shinning down of the shimmering ocean. A spring breeze blew from the balcony through the opened sliding glass door to the inside of the bedroom, ruffling the white sheers on either side of the sliding glass door.

Feeling the gentle breeze caress her arm and face, Zeke's hoarse groans filled Taylor's ears. He dropped his firm lips to her shoulders, placed a series of kisses all over her. Pushing her hair from her nape, he twirled his thick tongue in her ear. Hot breath whipping into her ear, chills skittered up her spine.

"Yes, my wife. Fuck me. I need this." Zeke spread Taylor's butt cheeks, traced a finger around her rear, then slipped it inside.

Finger twirling inside her back door, Taylor moaned. She never knew the sensual act could feel so good. Desire flooded her veins.

"Oh, Zeke. It's been, too long since we've made love."

"It's only been two days." In one quick fluid movement, Zeke slid his arms between her torso and the mattress, scooped her up in his arms. Still driving deep into her womb while behind her, starting at her right shoulder, his fingers trailed down her arm.

Taylor's knees pressed into the mattress. Circling her hips, she grabbed her sensitive breasts, and squeezed. With one knee pressed into the mattress, Zeke bent his other leg at the knee. He hooked an arm beneath the underside of her kneecap, brought her leg upward, and placed it over the bent part of her leg. Gosh, you definitely have to be flexible for this position, Taylor thought, feeling the hard knob of Zeke's shaft thrust deep inside her.

To keep her balance, Taylor curled her fingers around the bedrail and mashed backwards. And what happened next was simple remarkable. Pushed her over the edge. "Hold on tight," Zeke demanded. He lifted her other leg upward to his waist. Now both of her legs was wrapped around his waist as he slowly thrust in and out of her from behind.

Sex noises resounded through the air. Breathless, she looked back over her shoulder at Zeke. Linking her gaze with his, Zeke's face twisted. Grunting, he stroked her something delicious.

"Keep going slow. Oh. Uh. Ooo," Taylor oohed, and ahhed.

Zeke's tool twirled in slow delicious circles inside Taylor. Air got into her canal, and as he twirled her entrance, it made loud popping sounds. *Pop. Pop.* "I'm making that pussy pop, my wife."

"Yes, Zeke. Hit it slow, baby. Right there."

"Like this?" Clenching her hips, he gently stroked her.

"Yes. Yes. I'm coming." Her sex burst into an intense orgasm.

Zeke pushed hard. His body tensed. Come erupted from his tool soaking her. "Unh. I'm coming, too."

Ring. The house phone rang. Zeke lowered Taylor's legs to the mattress, slipped out of her entrance. Hot come spilled from her opening onto the linen. She reached over to the nightstand, lifted the phone to her ear. "Hello."

"Hell Taylor. This is Dr. Howard. The kidney compatibility results are in. I need for you to drop whatever you're doing and come to the hospital right away." A sense of urgency was in the doctor's voice, frightening Taylor.

"Okay, we're on our way." Taylor hung up the phone and looked at Zeke who was now lying on his back motioning his still hard shaft up and down in his hand. "That was Dr. Howard. She wants us to come to the hospital right away."

Zeke's hand froze on his hard erection. "Is Evan okay?"

"I didn't ask. She sounded funny. Let's hurry, Zeke."

Zeke and Taylor hopped in the shower together. He stood under one shower head while she stood under the other. Hurrying to bathe, they didn't utter a single word. Praying for the best, they hopped out of the shower, threw on their clothes. Zeke drove like a bat out of hell to the hospital.

DR. HOWARD'S GAZE LIFTED FROM the manila file clenched between her hands when she heard Zeke and Taylor enter her office. She stood, walked over to the door, and shut it. "Please have a seat." Dr. Howard sat back down in the black leather chair behind her desk while Zeke and Taylor took plopped down in the chairs in front of her desk. "Thank you for coming so quickly."

"No problem," Zeke said.

Worried sick over what Dr. Howard had to tell them, Taylor's stomach churned. Oh God, what if neither of them were a match for the kidney transplant? Then what? As severe as Evan's case was, he could die while waiting on a kidney. *God, please let Dr. Howard have some good news to share with us.*

Dr. Howard's expression was hard to read. "Where do I start? Well, as you already know, both of you were tested to see if you'd be compatible to give Evan a kidney. To my surprise, both of you are a perfect match."

Zeke burst into laughter. "This is great news."

Taylor's mouth dropped wide open. "Oh my God. Are you serious? How can this be?"

"That's exactly what I wanted to know. For both of you to be compatible is nothing short of a miracle unless there's more to the story. And there is."

Zeke looked at Taylor then back at the doctor. "What do you mean there's more to the story, doctor," he said.

"More to the story. I'm confused," Taylor stated.

Dr. Howard said, "So was I at first. Knowing your two history and remembering reading about the kidnapping that'd happened to Taylor many years ago, I decided to run a DNA test on Evan to see if his DNA matched with the two of yours. And it did." Dr. Howard's lips pulled into an endearing smile. "Zeke ... Taylor ... Evan is your son."

Grabbing the sides of her head, Taylor just stared at Dr. Howard. "What did you just say?"

Zeke bolted from his chair. "What did you say?" he mocked, Taylor.

Dr. Howard's eyes beamed. "I said, Evan is your son. Evan is the baby that was stolen from you all those years ago."

Glancing up at the ceiling, Zeke threw his hands up in the air. "Are you sure? Thank you God. Thank you God."

"Oh God. Oh God," Taylor cried. "Oh God, thank. Thank you. Are you sure, Dr. Howard?" Taken by complete surprise and overwhelmed, Taylor rose to her feet.

Dr. Howard nodded. "I had the test run four times to be certain. I'm one hundred percent positive. There's no doubt in mind or in any of the other doctor's minds around here that Evan Elliott belongs to the two of you. Zeke and Taylor you are Evan's biological parents."

Zeke threw his arms around Taylor. "Baby, Evan's ours. God sent him back to us." He kissed the tear running down her cheek. "I always felt so connected to him, but couldn't explain it. Now I know why."

Swallowing, tears streamed down Taylor's face. "Me too. From the very first day I laid eyes on him, I felt like Evan was a part of me. I felt like if I let him go, I'd die. Felt like I had to be crazy to feel such strong feelings for a child I barely knew. But I felt that way because he came out of my body. I gave birth to him. Zeke, I gave birth to Evan. This is a miracle."

Zeke looked at Dr. Howard. "Yes it is a miracle. Doctor, I'll be the one to give Evan a kidney."

Smiling wide, Dr. Howard nodded. "Okay. There's some more great news."

"More?" Zeke asked.

Dr. Howard said, "Yes. Evan is finally awake."

Taylor cupped her mouth then released it. "Oh God. Let's go see him, Zeke and tell him the good news."

"Okay. But let me make a phone call first." Zeke dialed his attorney. "Hey Gar. Have you given Muriel the check yet? She's on her way over there now to pick it up?" Zeke laughed. "Don't give it to her. In fact, do me a favor, and tear it up in her face. I'll explain the details later."

After Zeke got off the phone with the attorney, he put a quick call in to one of his good friends—the chief of police. He filled the chief in on Muriel and he'd promised Zeke he'd take care of Muriel right away.

Zeke and Taylor got off the elevator, past the nurses station, and walked into Evan's room. Upon their entrance, a nurse stood at Evan's bedside, hand feeding him. In total shock and disbelief, Taylor and Zeke walked up to their son's bedside.

Honey brown skin, curly brown hair, dimples in his cheeks, Taylor always knew Zavier looked like a lighter complexion of her mixed with hints of Zeke. "I'll finished feeding him," Taylor told the nurse and she left. "How are you feeling?" Taylor asked Evan or Zavier.

Evan put a hand to his stomach. "Not good. I feel sick. Why am I in here?"

Zeke told Evan, "You need a new kidney."

Evan's face scrunched. "A new kidney? Am I going to die? If so, I'm not scared. It'll be much better than going back to live with mean Muriel."

Zeke stated, "You're not going to die, Evan. I'm going to give you one of my kidneys."

Evan's lids looked hooded. "I see you still being nice, Mister. If you give me one of your kidney's I'll never be able to pay you back. I'm going to have to sweep your office till the day I die to pay you back for a kidney. Maybe I can cut the grass, too."

Taylor's face creased with a slow smile. "You don't have to pay us back for anything we do for you. We love you, Evan." *Oh, Evan. You're my biological son, Zavier Balfour.* Taylor encircled her arms around Evan as best as she could. Squeezing her eyes, tears slid down her face. She pried herself from her son and just stared. And stared and stared.

"There's something we have to tell you," Zeke said. "Remember when I told you that I had a son and he was kidnapped?"

Evan nodded. "Yes."

Zeke took a deep breath. "Well, to make a long story short, the doctors ran some test on Taylor and I to see if we'd be a match to give you one of our kidneys...and...um...well." Unable to hold back his emotions, Zeke let the situation get the best of him. A few thin tears left his eyes.

"What is it, Mister? Why are you crying?" Evan reached out and wiped the water from Zeke's face with his tiny fingers. "It'll be okay."

Zeke sniffed hard. "Evan...you are Taylor and my son. You're the little boy that was kidnapped from us. I'm your real father and Taylor is your real mother."

Evan's brows furrowed. "Man, you ain't been drinking have you? Are you sure about this?"

Taylor giggled. "He's sure. The doctors looked at our blood and it matches yours perfectly." Caressing Evan's arms, Taylor looked up at Zeke, smiled, and then hooked her gaze back on Evan. "You're our son."

Evan slapped his forehead. "You mean to tell me I've been putting up with Muriel's shit all these years and she ain't even my momma?!"

Zeke shook his head. "I'm going to let you slide with the cussing this time my son, but from this day forward if you use profanity, you're going on punishment." Zeke ruffled the hair on top of Evan's head.

"Sorry for cussing, Mister. I mean...mom and dad. I'm so happy you're my REAL parents. Wait till the kids at the shelter hear about this. Especially Jaheem!"

Taylor's heart grew big beneath her ribs. "Please, call me mom again?"

Evan's lips kept smiling. "Mom."

Taylor's heart twirled. "Say it one more time, please?"

"Mom. Mom. Mom." Evan got teary eyed. "So what's my real name? Is it Evan?"

Taylor caressed the soft, honey brown skin of Evan's face. "No. It's Zavier. But you can keep the name Evan if you like. I'll leave it up to you. As long as you're happy that's all I care about."

Evan thumped his finger to his cheek. "I think I'll go with Zavier. Zavier Balfour."

Never wanting to leave her son's side, Taylor said, "I love the name Zavier Balfour." Taylor caressed his shoulder. She couldn't wait to get him home and hold him. Squeeze him. Kiss him. Make up for lost time.

"I like the name, too. I'll be back later." Zeke stood.

"Where are you going?" Taylor already had a feeling she knew the answer.

"To the police station to make sure Muriel was arrested. I'm going to make sure she spends the rest of her miserable life behind bars." Zeke stalked out of the room.

Taylor pulled her cell from her purse and dialed the one person she knew who'd be just as happy as her to learn about Zavier's safe return—her dear sweet mother, Veronica.

Dialing her mother, Taylor's eyes spied the clock on the wall. *Ohmygoodness.* With everything that was going on she'd almost forgotten that she had a lunch date with Katherine today as well as important doctor's appointment with her OBGYN, Dr. Sauer.

I wonder how Katherine is going to feel about having two step grandsons, Taylor thought, waiting for her mother to answer the phone.

Chapter Thirty-One

BEFORE ZEKE WENT TO THE police station, he stopped by Don's room for his usual daily visit. Zeke's eyes roamed over Don's body as he lay in the hospital bed clinging to his life. Chapped lips, Don's beard and mustache had thickened. Other than his facial hair not much had changed. Well, that wasn't exactly true. Don's complexion did look a tad bit lighter.

Praying Don would someday wake up, Zeke patted the hospitalized man's shoulder. "You're going to get through this. I can feel it, Don."

Suddenly, Don's eyes slowly peeled open. *Jesus Christ!* In a daze, Don's eyes blinked. And Blinked. Zeke waved his hand in front of Don's face. "Don. Don. Can you hear me?"

Don's eyes bulged as if he suddenly recollected who Zeke was. "R, r, agh." His chapped lips babbled around the tube buried inside his throat.

"You're in the hospital. You were shot. Who did this to you, Don? Who?"

Don's chubby fingers wiggled. "Wr…Wr…"

"Huh?"

"Wri—"

"Wr...wr...oh write. You want something to write with?" Zeke hurried to the nurse's station right outside Don's room, retrieved a pen and note pad, and rushed back. At first he'd been tempted to tell the Nurses Don had awaken, but he needed to get some life alternating information from him first.

Zeke put the pen in Don's hand and held the notepad beneath the pen so he could write. "Write down who shot you."

With the tip of the pen on the pad, Don wrote, ant. Don's lids drooped then closed. Just that quickly, he'd fallen to sleep.

Zeke cursed then stuck the notepad with the letters *ant* into his back jean pocket. "Glad to see you woke up, man. Hope you feel better." Zeke alerted the nurses that Don had briefly woke up, then he went to the police station to make sure old behind Muriel had been arrested for stealing his damn son.

The early evening fell upon Zeke quicker than he'd realized. Anxious to confront Muriel for stealing his son, he drove up to the police station, and parked. Pushing through the entrances' double doors, fury burned Zeke's insides, and he couldn't stop thinking about the initials *ant* that Don had written on the notepad.

"Ant," Zeke mumbled. Had Muriel hired someone by the name of Ant to shoot him? Maybe a thug named Ant? Well, one thing was for certain, Muriel had taken Zavier, and sooner or later she'd spill the beans as to who she hired to shoot Don so he'd keep his mouth shut.

An officer showed Zeke into Chief Shelton Wallace's office. Peppery hair, broad shoulders, and tanned complexioned, Shelton's eyes diverted from the computer screen to look at Zeke. "Zeke, come on in." Shelton jumped up from his seat, hurried over to Zeke, and the two men shook hands. "We got her, man. I had

Muriel arrested right after I got off the phone with you earlier." He shut the door to his office. "Have a seat."

Exhausted, Zeke flopped down in the chair Shelton gestured to. "Did Muriel admit to kidnapping my son?"

Shelton stated, "Not initially. But after I ran a background check on her, and interrogated her ass, she started singing like a damn bird. Come to find out Muriel and Mildred are twins. According to Muriel, her twin sister Mildred and nephew Kelvin dropped Evan off on her front door step the same night Taylor gave birth to him. Muriel claim's Kelvin had threatened to kill her if she ever told anyone what he and Mildred had done. And after she saw how badly her sister's face had been burned, she'd gotten scared for her own life."

"Yeah right. I'm sure Kelvin gave Muriel a lot of coins to keep her big mouth shut. They're all crooks. Did she tell you where Kelvin and Mildred are?"

Shelton leaned back in his chair. "Muriel claims she doesn't know. Claims she hasn't spoken with them since the night they dropped off your son. Don't worry, though. We're going to keep interrogating her. If that doesn't work, we'll offer her clemency. One way or the other, I'm sure she'll eventually spill the beans. I got to tell you, Zeke...this is about to hit the news. So get prepared."

Zeke extended his hand towards Shelton. "Thanks for your help, Shelton. Find Kelvin and Mildred. I want them to rot in hell for kidnapping my son. Keep me posted on what you find out."

"I'm glad this story has a happy ending. Good luck with everything."

"Thanks I appreciate it."

The afternoon sun smacked Zeke in the face as soon as he pushed open the door at the police station. Heading for the parking lot, tremendous joy tugged his heart. *Evan is my son. Zavier Balfour has finally come home to Taylor and me.*

Aiming his key fob at his SUV, he popped the locks. Sliding between the steering wheel and the seat, Zeke prayed the kidney transplant with Zavier would be successful. After that, he could get his son home for good.

Driving down the long road heading towards his father's home, Zeke hit the buttons on the door. Both the driver and passenger side windows rolled down. Wind blew inside the car, whipping at the hair on his nape. *Thank you God. Thank you. Thank you. Thank you for putting it in Dr. Howard's mind to run a paternity test on Evan. I mean Zavier.*

For the first time since he'd lost Taylor and Zavier, Zeke felt whole. Like his life was complete. Had a full purpose. Had a full meaning. Now that he had Taylor and Zavier and Jaheem in his life, he was never letting them go. Not ever. And if things went as he planned, he was going to get Taylor pregnant, and adopt more children.

A vivid image of the ugly scar Muriel had put on Zavier's side made Zeke's lips twist. While Muriel was in prison, she better hope no one beat her like she used to beat his damn son, Zavier. She better pray no one marks up her skin from whips and belts. Zavier had been through so much while living with Muriel so he definitely had to make sure he got his son counseling. They all would get family counseling.

Zeke turned the Porsche into the driveway of his father's estate. Parking the vehicle, he couldn't wait to see the look on his father's and Katherine's face when he told them that Zavier had been found. Not only that, that he'd been tutoring him at the shelter for many months now. How ironic?

Now that he didn't live with his father anymore, Zeke rang the doorbell out of respect. While he was sure his father wouldn't mind him using his key, Katherine on the other hand may have a problem if he used it. The door cracked open.

Holding the door open, Delbert smiled. "You're just in time for dinner. I cooked one of your favorites. Stewed tomatoes with shrimp and sausage over jasmine rice."

"Delbert my man! Wait till you hear my great news!" Zeke crossed over the threshold and entered the living room. A spicy aroma hit him in the nose. With Delbert following him, Zeke made his way to the family room. His father and Katherine were sitting on the couch watching television together. "Father, Katherine, good you're both here." Zeke's tone pitched with happiness.

Watching Katherine's favorite television show, Divorce Court, both Colton and Katherine turned around to face him.

Colton's mouth turned upward. "Hey son, come on in and join us. We miss having you around here."

Wearing a fancy dress as usual, Katherine's lips turned upward. "We sure do. When are we going to get the invite to visit your new home?"

"Oh, dad's already been by to see the house. I told him to bring you by when we first moved in." Zeke filled her in.

Katherine frowned at Colton. "Colton, I've been asking and asking you to take me to see Zeke and Taylor's new home, and you never mentioned that you'd already went. I guess I have to take myself."

Colton's face remained expressionless. "I guess so. If you can't go to marriage counseling with me, then don't go anywhere with me. Final answer," he said as if he was a contestant on *Who Wants to be a Millionaire.*

Crossing her legs at the knee, Katherine sucked her teeth. "Act that way then."

Delbert stood at the dining table holding a black kettle. Pouring hot tea in a tiny mug, Delbert cleared his throat, and looked at

Katherine. "Excuse me Mrs. Balfour, but would you like some lemon in your tea?"

Katherine's hand caressed her throat. "Sure, Delbert. Thanks."

"How's Taylor doing, son? Is her health still good?" Colton asked.

Warmth spread inside Zeke's chest. Rolled around in his gut. Ticked hard inside his heart. "Taylor is doing great! In fact, we're both doing great! We've never been better!"

"By the look on your face she must be pregnant," Colton stated.

Jaws hurting from smiling, Zeke's pulse raced. "No. It's not that. You're not going to believe your ears. Hold on to your seats because what I'm about to tell you, is going to blow your minds."

Colton put his elbow up on the curb of the couch and fisted his chin. "Well don't keep us in suspense as to why you're smiling like that. Just spit it out already."

"We found our son!" Zeke rejoiced. He threw his hands up in the air giving God praise. "Zavier Balfour is alive!"

Colton's jaws parted. "My God!"

Katherine gasped. Clenching her chest, her eyes darted back and forth. "No. What did you say—"

The hot cup of tea in Delbert's hand slipped from his grip and splattered the floor. "Dear God." Delbert stuck his finger in his ear and wiggled. "Did I hear you right?"

"Yes. Yes. The little boy that Taylor gave birth to is alive. He lives right here in Hilton Head Island. And get this…I've been tutoring him for the last few months. This is a miracle."

A glassy look appeared in Colton's eyes. Severely ill, he managed to push himself up from the couch. "I've prayed for this day. Over and over and over, I've prayed for this day. I always knew you'd find him, and that's why I put him in my will. Like you, I want my grandson to someday run Balfour Enterprises. Thank God, for this day!"

Remaining sitting on the couch, Katherine burst into tears. Her shoulder's rocked violently. Delbert stood over Katherine patting her back. "I'm so glad they found my grandbaby. I couldn't be happier. Thank you. Thank you God," Katherine said.

Delbert nodded at Zeke. "I'm happy for you and Taylor, Zeke."

Zeke hefted the remote from the end table and switched the channel to CNN. "The story has made worldwide news."

Katherine lifted her weeping face from her hands to gaze at the news. Taylor's face was on the screen.

The newscaster stated, "Apparently, Mildred left little Evan on her twin sister's doorstep in Hilton Head Island ten years ago and vanished. At this present time Muriel Elliott is in police custody. There are still no known whereabouts of Mildred and Kelvin at this moment. I tell you Fred, I'm just extremely happy for Zeke and Taylor Balfour. To be reunited with their son after finally finding one another is definitely an act from a higher power," news anchor Alicia Bivens said.

Fred smiled back Alicia and stated, "Yes Alicia. What a fairy tale ending."

Zeke clicked off the television, slapped a hand to his chest, and took a deep breath. "I can't wait for you to see Zavier, Dad. You too Katherine and Delbert. He's a great kid. Real funny, too. He looks just like Taylor. Has a little bit of me in him, too."

"How did this all come about?" Katherine asked, seemingly shaken.

"Well, I'm not sure if dad told you or not, but Taylor and I have been spending a lot of time with the kids at the group care facility. While doing so, we decided to adopt two of them...Zavier is one of the kids we wanted to adopt. Long story short, while visiting us a few days ago..."

Colton interjected, "Evan got sick on the beach, had a seizure, and ended up in the hospital."

Katherine rolled her eyes at Colton. "You knew about this, too? And didn't tell me?"

Colton responded, "Didn't think you'd be interested."

"Well I was. And you should've told me!" Katherine shouted.

Zeke's cell buzzed at his hip. He pulled the cell from his clip to find a text message from Taylor on the screen. He clicked on the text message and a picture of Taylor and Zavier lit up his screen. Made his heart catch with love. Made him smile. "Taylor just sent me a picture of Zavier and her. Here take a look." Proud father, Zeke held the picture up to Colton's face. Colton's face split into a grin. Then he put the cell in Katherine's face so she could see the picture, too. Katherine's face looked gloomy. "I thought I knew what love was, but I didn't know what it fully was until today."

With a hand to her stomach, Katherine's face turned crimson. "I'll be back later." Dress switching over her behind, she hastened away.

"Where are you going?" Colton questioned as Katherine hurried out of the family room.

Katherine shouted out, "I'm going to go have lunch with Taylor. Then afterwards, I'm going shopping for Zavier, my precious grandson."

"I'll be in the kitchen finishing up dinner." Delbert's mood seemed laid back under the circumstances.

Colton took the cell from Zeke's hand and just stared at the photo of Taylor hugging Zavier. Eyes watering, Colton released a hearty chuckle. "Zavier does look like Taylor. Your wife is a beauty you, know? I see some of you in him, too, though." When Colton handed Zeke his cell back, he slid it back into the clip at his waist. "As soon as Zavier gets better, I want you to bring him over here so I can take him fishing."

"I'm sure Zavier would love that. Enough about me, how's your health?"

Shaking his head, Colton sat on the sofa. "Oh. Let's not talk about me."

Zeke sat on the sofa next to his father. "Is there something you're not telling me?"

Tears welled in Colton's eyes. "What I'm about to tell you, I haven't told anyone. This is for you ears only...I'm dying, Zeke. The doctors have given me three months at the most to live."

Zeke's heart crumbled.

Chapter Thirty-Two

FINGERS CURLED AROUND THE STEERING wheel, Katherine sucked in huge bouts of air. Face beat red. Chest tight with cramps. Terror riveting through her, Katherine struggled to breathe. With her stomach balled in knots, she signaled a right with her blinkers, and merged into traffic.

Katherine had just left lunch with Taylor, and all she talked about was how she'd found that damn son of hers. When Taylor had gotten up and gone to the bathroom during their lunch date, Katherine had sprinkled some poison in her drink. *Ooh, I can't stand that woman. Bragging about that boy. She just found out Zavier was her son, and acts like he's all of that. Like he's perfect.*

"How in the hell did this happen? Antonio promised me he'd take care of the Taylor and the baby. He fucking promised."

Antonio had promised her that Taylor's baby was far, far away from Hilton Head Island. And the damn baby had been here all along. Damn Antonio, Katherine thought, driving down the road. She couldn't count on her oldest son like she thought she could. How could Antonio be so damn irresponsible? How? How?

Pissed at Antonio beyond measure, Katherine glanced in the rearview mirror at the car behind her, then back at the road in front of her. "Damn you, Antonio. I now see why your father thinks you're irresponsible. You can't do shit right."

Angry, she banged her fist on the steering wheel. *I should've taken care of the kidnapping and Taylor myself. Just like I took care of Don. I should've got my damn gun and killed Taylor. Knocked her off. If Muriel tells the police where Mildred and Kelvin are, they will tell the cops about Antonio. Which will lead the police to me.*

Katherine felt like she couldn't trust her own son now. Right after she paid Antonio a visit, she may just have to get her passport and get the hell out of Hilton Head Island. As much as it'd kill her to leave behind the wealth, it'd kill her even more if she ended up in prison. *I'd never survive in prison.* If she did decide to leave, before she left, she'd make sure to transfer every darn dime from Colton's and her savings to an account overseas somewhere. The last time she'd checked, Colton had well over fifty million in one account that had her name on it. "Damn, Antonio. You can't do nothing right."

Enraged at her son, Katherine pulled off the main road, and steered the car into the woods. Driving along the dirt path surrounded by tall trees, the car rocked and shimmied. "Look how he's living. Out here in the damn woods like some poor pathetic human being. Like a damn wolf."

The brown, wooden home Katherine's parents had grown up in came into view. Three rusty rocking chairs on the porch, two windows with decayed wood, and a raggedy screen door, it looked like Old Mother Hubbard could live out here.

Katherine threw the gear in park, cut the engine, and flung open the door. Marching along the dirt ground toward the weathered looking home, her right high heel shoe got stuck in the grimy dirt, causing her to trip, and fall flat on her face. "Ahhh!"

Inhaling the unpleasant odor of the bowel smelling mud, Katherine flattened her palms on the ground, and stood. Livid, she wanted to kill someone. Not someone, Taylor. And Antonio. And Zeke.

Had Taylor kept her legs closed all those years ago, and didn't get pregnant, she wouldn't be in the mess she's in today. Covered in gooey dirt, Katherine yanked off her high heels, then proceeded in her pursuit.

Cool, moist dirt pressed into the soles of Katherine's bare feet as she stomped along the grounds of Antonio's now stupid looking home. Particles of dirt felt grimy between her teeth.

Feeling like stabbing something, Katherine mounted the worn steps. The planks creaked beneath her feet. Knocking on the door, it squeaked.

"Coming!" Antonio yelled from the other side of the door.

A moment later the door squealed open. Antonio stood shirtless inside the house. Katherine's eyes snagged on the initials SM branded on his chest.

Antonio's face split into a grin. "Katherine. What do I owe this pleasant surprise?" Clenching her shoes to her chest, Katherine gripped the handle of the screen door, and swung the hell out of it. Nose scrunching, she slapped the hell out of Antonio. "Ouch! Why in the hell did you do that?"

"Don't you watch the news?!" She shoved her ignorant son's chest and stormed past him into his living room, then threw her dirty shoes on the floor.

Rubbing his hairy jaw, Antonio shut the door. Katherine looked around the small, unkempt home. Brown carpet, green sofa, roof caving downward, the home her parents once lived in looked like a dump. A stinky, filthy, dump.

Antonio's reddish-blonde hair spiked on top of his head like he hadn't combed it in days. "I haven't had time to watch the news today. What's going on?"

In her ever most proper tone, Katherine sarcastically stated, "Hmm. Other than Zeke and Taylor finding their son after all these years, nothing else is happening here in little old Hilton Head Island." Just looking at stupid Antonio here irked the crap out of Katherine.

Antonio's blue eyes widened in shock. "No. No. You're lying."

Katherine pointed a finger at her own frowned up face. "Does it look like I'm lying?! It's been all on the news! Zeke and Taylor's son has been found. They arrested Mildred's twin sister, Muriel for kidnapping him. It's only a matter of time before Muriel tells the cops where Mildred and Kelvin are. Once they police find them, Mildred and Kelvin are going to point the police right back to you! You can't do anything right can you?!"

Huffing and puffing, Antonio snatched the remote from the coffee table, aimed it at the television, and clicked it on to the local news. Then he clicked to the next station, and the next, and the next. Every news station out there covered the story about Zeke and Taylor's son.

Antonio threw the remote across the room and it hit the wall. "We're doomed Katherine! Doomed!"

Katherine slapped Antonio upside his head. "Get it together, fool!" she snapped. "Get it together right now. We're not doomed. You're doomed. Even if the police finds out about your involvement, you better not mention my name in any of this mess." She pointed her finger at Antonio. "I mean it. For once in your life, you better man up! Man up and do the time for the crime. You're so damn stupid. Dumb. I gave you one thing to do, and you couldn't even get it right. Just dumb!"

Antonio's cobalt eyes bugged from their sockets from fury. "You think the police aren't going to figure out that you were the one to shoot Don? Huh?" Katherine's mind spun. She hadn't told anyone she'd shot Don. Not even Antonio. "You didn't know I knew about that did you? Yeah, Mom," he uttered. Using the quotation mark symbol with his fingers, he muttered, "Not only do I know that. I also know that you killed Bridget—Zeke's birth mother. Calling me dumb. Hmmp. How dumb is it of you to keep the murder weapon in the damn fire place?" Antonio chuckled nastily. "Here's the deal. You're going to give me twenty-five million dollars by tomorrow evening to keep my mouth shut about you. If you don't and the police come looking for me, I'm going to tell them everything I know about you. I may be dumb, but I'm not as dumb as you think I am. I smart enough to get some damn money and flee my ass from Hilton Head Island." His square jaw tensed visibly.

Oh God. He knows I killed Bridget. Katherine couldn't afford to fold under the pressure, but she started crumbling anyway. "How? How did you find out about what I did to Bridget?"

Chortling angrily, Antonio tossed his head back, then snapped his eyes at Katherine. "The night you followed dad to Bridget's house, I followed you. I was driving back then, remember?" His eyes narrowed. "I saw you come out of Bridget's house trying to look as cool as a cucumber, but guilt was written all over your face. When you got home, you tried to act like you hadn't done a thing. Except you had. You'd murdered dad's mistress. You killed Zeke's mother." Hard lines appeared on his face. Right hand on his hip, Antonio pointed his finger in her face, making her feel like the kid for once. Making her feel smaller than a mouse. Defeated. Raw hurt appeared in her son's eyes. "For years I've been protecting you, supporting you behind closed doors. You owe me, Katherine. Big time." Heart twisting like a rope inside her tight chest, Katherine felt like she was losing her damn mind. "Now as I was saying a few moments ago, get me the money. I tell you what... for five million more, not only will I keep my mouth shut about everything you partook in, but I'll kill Taylor, too." Katherine inwardly beamed with delight. "Once and for all, I promise you I'll kill Taylor, Mom. But I'm going to need your help." An evil glint flashed his eyes.

"My help? How?" Katherine felt like he really meant it this time.

"Find a way to keep Zeke busy tomorrow night."

A cold shiver rushed her. "I think I can handle that. I'll get you the money by tomorrow. You'll get half upfront, and the other half you'll get after you get rid of Zeke's bitch." Eagerly anticipating Taylor's demise, Katherine picked her high heels up from the ugly carpet, pulled open the front door and got the hell out of them damn woods.

Chapter Thirty-Three

THE GLOWING MOON PERCHED AMIDST twinkling stars in the dark sky above the serene sea behind Zeke and Taylor's ocean front mansion. Leaning against the white column on the deck while on the phone with her mother, pallid sounds of ocean waves crashing against the edge of the earth assuaged Taylor's ears. Salty scents of the beach streamed up her nose. Finally at peace because Zavier had been returned to her, a soft smile came to her face. Her heart smiled.

Taylor's mother's snickers came through the phone and sailed inside her ear. "I had a blast visiting my grandson. I'm going to spoil Zavier rotten. God is so good, Taylor."

Love for her family simmered inside Taylor's system. "Yes he is, Momma. I just got off the phone with Zavier a few minutes ago and he can't wait for you to come back and see him again. Zeke, Colton, and Katherine are at the hospital now visiting with him. Zeke and I agreed we'd take turns spending time at the hospital. We don't want him to ever be there alone."

"I think that's a good idea. I don't want Zavier to be there by himself either. As his grandmother, I'm going to go sit with him, too. That way you and Zeke can get a break. And after you adopt Jaheem, I'll be more than happy to baby sit the boys for you anytime."

The phone chirped in Taylor's ear. "Thanks Momma. Sorry to cut you off, but this is Sandella calling. Let me see what she wants. I'll talk to you later."

"Tell Sandella I said, hi," Veronica stated.

"Okay. Good night." Ending the call with her mother, Taylor clicked over. "Hi Sandella. How are you?"

"I'm good. Having your son back, I know you must be on cloud nine." Sandella spoke in a cheerful tone.

"Sandella, words can't explain how I feel. One moment I'm laughing. The next I'm crying. I can't explain it, but I never gave up on finding Zavier. I always knew he was alive and would come back to me one day."

"You kept the faith. I'm so happy for you and Zeke. Braylon and I send our well wishes. If there's anything we can do to help, please don't hesitate to let us know. I baked a welcome home cake for Zavier. If it's okay with you, I'd like to drop it off for him tonight."

Beaming inwardly, Taylor pulled open the refrigerator, and grabbed a bottle of red wine. "Oh. You baked him a cake? That's so sweet of you, Sandella. I'll be here all night so drop it off whenever you feel like it."

"I'll see you shortly."

"Okay." Taylor lowered the cordless phone to the receiver. Everyone had been so nice and kind to her, Zeke, Zavier, and Jaheem.

Standing to the side of the sink, Taylor reached into the cabinet above her head to retrieve a wine glass. Placing the glass on the counter, she tilted the bottle to the glass, and poured herself a drink.

Taylor raised the drink to her nose and inhaled the sweet, flowery alcohol liquid. Taylor curled her lips around the edge of the glass as she sipped the delicious red wine. Mounting the staircase while sipping on her drink, her empty hand glided along the iron rail.

Ding dong. The doorbell rang. *Oh, that must be Sandella.* Taylor descended the staircase, placed her wine on the dining table, and pulled open the door. Looking like a ball of pretty sunshine, Sandella's lips hitched. "I'm not going to come in," Sandella said, handing Taylor a box with the cake inside. "It's chocolate with butter cream icing. Let me know how Zavier likes it. I'm making a cake for Jaheem, too. I'll bring Jaheem's cake over after the adoption becomes finalized."

Appreciation spread through Taylor's bones. "This is so kind of you, thanks Sandella."

"Oh yeah," Sandella reached in her purse, pulled out a bag of whistles, matches, and candles, and then handed the items to Taylor. "I got these for the boys, too. I know it's not their birthday, but after everything they've been through, they deserve to make a wish."

Taylor's face smiled. "Thanks, Sandella. This is so thoughtful of you. I'll be sure to let the boys make a wish. This house is going to get noisy real fast with two boys and a bag of whistles. I'm sure they'll love them." Holding the bottom of the box with one hand, Taylor slid the whistles, candles, and matches into her back pockets.

"Willa has been watching Logan for me all day, girl. So let me hurry up and get my behind home." Sandella turned and headed for her car.

Taylor watched Sandella back her car out of the driveway then finally shut the door. Back inside the kitchen, Taylor lowered the cake box to the counter, and opened it. "Oh, this cake is so pretty," she said, eyes roaming over the beautiful blue and white cake with welcome home written on it. The scent and appeal of the cake made Taylor's mouth water.

Folding the lid on the box to recover the cake, the doorbell rang again. "Sandella must've forgotten to give me something," Taylor mumbled beneath her breath as she headed for the front door. She picked her glass of wine up from the decorative table against the wall, and pulled open the door. "Antonio."

Antonio's mouth split into a wide handsome smile. "Congratulations on getting your son back."

Taylor smiled. "Thank you so much, Antonio." Taylor's eyes traveled to the driveway to find it empty. "Where's your car?"

"Down the street. It broke down on my way here. Is Zeke home? I need a lift."

"Zeke's at the hospital. But I can give you a ride if you need me too."

Antonio's face split into a grin. "That'd be great."

Holding the frame of the door, Taylor stepped to the side. "Please, come in. Let me get my purse."

Antonio's eyes gazed up at the thirty foot ceiling then they roamed over the wide spacious area of the living room. "Wow! This is some fancy beach home you have?"

She sipped at her delicious wine. "Thanks. Zeke and I designed it together. Believe it or not, your brother has some good taste."

"The moment he told me he was marrying you, I knew he had good taste." Antonio's eyes raked up and down Taylor's body. An uncomfortable feeling faltered Taylor's excitement. Silly her. Antonio was just admiring her, that's all. "Would you like a quick tour of the home?"

"Sure."

Taylor showed Antonio the downstairs first, including the outdoor patio, then she led him upstairs where majority of the bedrooms were. After showing him Jaheem's room, she showed him Zavier's room. As she stood in the doorway of Zavier's room, she looked at the name Evan she'd had drawn on the wall.

Still holding the glass of wine in her hand, Taylor glanced up at Antonio. "Zavier wants me to take down the name Evan and put his real name up. Now that it's starting to sink in that he was kidnapped, I think he wants to forget his past."

"I can't blame him. What Muriel and Mildred did to him was horrible. I hope they rot in jail for what they did to my nephew." Antonio's throaty voice had depth.

"My purse is in my bedroom. I'll be right back." Taylor left Antonio inside Zavier's room and went to grab her purse. Inside her bedroom, she strapped the purse over her shoulder, picked up her keys. Walking back down the long hallway, she sipped at her wine.

When she reached Zavier's room, Antonio walked out, and they accidentally bumped into each other. The red wine flew from her glass and splattered his white dress shirt. "I'm so sorry Antonio. I didn't know you were still up here."

Antonio's hand brushed the red stained fabric of his collared shirt. "Yeah. I was checking out Evan's room."

"Zavier. He wants to be called Zavier. Would you like for me to get you one of Zeke's shirts to wear?" She offered.

Antonio waved a hand in the air. "No, that's okay. Is it okay if I use the restroom in Zavier's room?"

"Sure. I'll meet you downstairs."

Antonio headed for the bathroom inside Zavier's room as Taylor made her way downstairs. Halfway down the staircase, she turned, and headed back upstairs. *I ruined his shirt with the red wine. I'm going to get him one of Zeke's shirts to wear.*

Once back inside her master suite, Taylor pulled open the drawer to Zeke's armoire, retrieved one of his folded t-shirts. Right before Taylor exited the bedroom, her cell phone rang. She tucked the shirt beneath her armpit, and grabbed the phone from her purse. It was Dr. Sauer...her OBGYN. "Hello."

"Hello Taylor. This is Dr. Sauer. Sorry to call you so late, but there's something urgent, I need to speak with you about," Taylor's OBGYN stated. She hadn't told anyone, not even Zeke. But after she'd had lunch with Katherine the other day, she went straight to her doctor's office. Because she was thinking about trying to conceive, Taylor had had Dr. Sauer to do an extensive exam on her, including bloodwork.

"What is it, Dr. Sauer." Pressing the phone to her ear, Taylor held the empty glass of wine in her free hand, and started walking down the hallway towards Zavier's room so she could give the clean shirt to Antonio.

Dr. Sauer sighed. "You may want to sit down for this."

Taylor's nerves jittered. *Oh God, please don't tell me I can't have children.* "What's wrong Dr. Sauer?"

Disliking the sound of Dr. Sauer's voice, Taylor entered Zavier's room to find the door to the bathroom slightly ajar. Antonio stood at the sink washing his hands looking in the mirror.

Unnoticing her peeping through the crack of the door, Antonio grabbed the white towel from the rack, wet it, then dabbed at the red stain on his shirt. Unable to get the stain out completely, he unbuttoned his shirt to wipe the red liquid from his chest.

Dr. Sauer said, "Unfortunately, I have some very disturbing news to share with you. The lab called and reported that they found an enormous amount of arsenic in your blood. It looks like someone is trying to poison you."

Someone's trying to poison me! Taylor's heart clenched. Her eyes snagged on the bubbly skin on Antonio's chest with the initials SM. *SM? Southern Mafia!* Shock hit Taylor like a ton of bricks. Her mouth dropped. Pressing the cell to her ear, the glass slipped from her other hand and shattered the floor.

Antonio's eyes snapped in her direction. He quickly looked down at the permanent branding on his chest then back up at her face. Wicked evilness darkened Antonio's eyes as he took slow purposeful strides towards Taylor.

Throat clogging, Taylor took a few backward steps, then took off running. "Call the police!"

"Come back here!" Antonio chased after Taylor.

Taylor ran down the hallway. "Dr. did you hear me?!" The line went dead in her ear. Terrified, she scurried down the stairs. Right when Taylor's foot his the last step of the staircase, Antonio fisted her hair, and yanked it hard. Hands flailing, Taylor's feet slipped from under her, and she fell flat on her back. Her cell went flying in the air.

Losing her balance, she plummeted to her back, head banged hard into the floor. Laying on her back on the stairs, Taylor's brain throbbed. Pain stabbed her spine. Her temples ached.

Antonio pulled a gun from his waistband, raised it above her face. "Please. No. No." Bones aching, she felt crippled.

Antonio's face twisted with a psychotic look. "I never did like you." The handle of the gun came crashing down on Taylor's head. Eyes rolling, she blacked out.

Chapter Thirty-Four

"I TELL YOU MAN, ZAVIER'S a soldier. Got his strength from Taylor and me. Got his good looks though from his mother." On the phone with Richmond, Zeke steered the Porsche into the driveway of his beach home, and parked.

Richmond laughed. "I'm glad you said Zavier got his good looks from his mother because the last time I checked, you weren't that good looking, man." Richmond teased.

Zeke chortled. "My wife would beg to differ with you, man."

"Nah, I'm just teasing. Kayla had a field day shopping for Evan today. Man she's super excited for you and Taylor. And so am I. We can't wait to meet Zavier and Jaheem."

"Feel free to stop by the hospital anytime to see Zavier. He'll love that. Let me know when you go by, and I'll try to make sure Jaheem is there so you can meet him, too." Zeke inserted the key in the front door, pushed it open, then closed the door behind him.

"Are you sure it's okay if I stop by the hospital?" Richmond asked tersely.

Tired, Zeke headed toward the kitchen. "Yeah man, I'm sure. You and Kayla are like family. Hey, I home now. Tell Kayla I said hi."

"Will do my brother."

The two men hung up with each other. Looking forward to spending time with Taylor, Zeke was glad Veronica had come to the hospital to sit with Zavier.

Hungry beyond measure for sex and food, Zeke pulled open the refrigerator. "Taylor!" Dropping his keys on the kitchen counter, his stomach growled.Imaging Taylor's hot sex sliding down on his hard rod, the head of his shaft rounded into a bulging knot. His shaft grew. Inched down his thigh. *I can't even think about Taylor without getting horny as hell.*

Walking around with a hard on, Zeke opened the *SugarKanes* box on the counter to find a nicely decorated cake inside. He read the cake: *Welcome Home Zavier.* "Nice gesture, Sandella. Zavier is going to love this. Taylor! I'm home baby!"

Ready to eat his wife's pussy, Zeke's testosterone kicked up a notch. Wondering where in the heck Taylor was, he left the kitchen, and headed for the staircase. As soon as Zeke lifted his foot to ascend the staircase, he noticed Taylor's purse along with dark blood on the step. *Blood.* He stooped, swirled his finger in the slick substance, and then held the slippery fluid up to his nose. *Jesus Christ!* It was blood alright.

"Taylor!" Heart drumming against his ribs, Zeke cantered up the staircase. Searching in and out of every room, his heart thudded harshly inside his chest. Unable to locate Taylor, he darted inside Zavier's room. Shattered glass was on the floor. A dirty red rag was in the sink.

"Something's wrong." He bustled downstairs, ran through the kitchen, and yanked open the back door. Taylor's car was still there, but she wasn't anywhere to be found.

Panic stricken, Zeke whipped out his cell, and dialed his wife. He was sent straight to Taylor's voice mail. Zeke ran back to the staircase, pulled open Taylor's purse. Searching for her cell, his hands floundered around the many items inside her purse.

Just as Zeke got ready to call Chief Shelton Wallace, his cell buzzed in his sweating palm. "Hello."

"Hello Zeke. This is Dr. Sauer. Taylor's OBGYN. Is Taylor with you? Do you know where she is?" Panic was in her voice.

"No. And I can't find her anywhere."

"Dear Lord. I called Taylor several minutes ago and told her that the lab discovered high levels of arsenic in her blood. And it looked like someone was trying to poison her. While on the phone with her, she screamed for me to call the police, and then I heard a man shout come back to her. Suddenly, the line went dead."

Holding the phone to his ear, bile rose to the surface of Zeke's stomach. "Ohmygod. Jesus. Did you call the police? Yes. I gave the police the address Taylor had on record with our office. If it's correct, the police should be to your home any minute now."

Police sirens blasted the night air. Zeke flung open the front door of his home. Red and blue flashing lights emanated from a swarm of police cars as they sped up in his driveway. "They're here. Did Taylor tell you who was with her? Did she scream a name?" The officers jumped out of their cars. Standing behind the doors of their police vehicles, they drew their weapons, and pointed them at Zeke.

Dr. Sauer said, "No. She didn't have time. The line went dead all of a sudden."

Zeke glared at the weapons aiming at his head. *Please don't let them shoot me.* "If you think of anything else please call me." Holding his hands up in the air, Zeke's cell slipped from his grip. He dropped to his knees and sobbed. Surrendering to the police like he was a criminal, he lolled his head back, and bellowed. "Oh God. Oh God. Oh God! My wife. Who has my wife?!"

HEAD THROBBING, TAYLOR FORCED HER eyes open to find herself immersed in darkness. Thoughts swooning, vision blurry, she touched her paining head to find it slick with something wet. *Blood? Where am I?* Dizzy, her aching body bumped and rolled inside a cramped space.

Rocking and bouncing, horrid thoughts ran inside Taylor's head, terrifying her. *Oh, God. Antonio. Antonio took me.* Remembering the branded SM initials on Antonio's chest, and Dr. Sauer saying someone had poisoned her with arsenic, Taylor smartly put two and two together.

Antonio had had her kidnapped all those years ago and Katherine probably had orchestrated the whole thing. *Katherine poisoned me.* She'd just had lunch with Katherine the other day right before she'd gone to Dr. Sauer's office to have an exam and some extensive blood work done on her. Katherine must've put some poison in her food when she'd gotten up and gone to the bathroom. No wonder she felt sick every time she ate Delbert's cooking, Katherine had been poisoning her.

"Let me go! Help! Help!" Taylor banged her fists on the roof of the trunk. The car rocked and shimmied over what felt like hard gravel. Suddenly, the car slowed. The engine halted. *Slam!* The door shut. He's coming. *Oh God. Help me.*

The trunk popped open revealing Antonio's hateful glare. Pointing a big black gun at her face, he spat, "Get out the car!"

"Why are you doing this, Antonio?" Her voice trembled.

"I don't owe you an explanation." He put the cool metal of the barrel to her cheek, yanked on her arm, almost tore it off. "Last warning. Get your ass out now."

Taylor climbed out of the trunk. Checking out her surroundings, she realized she must be at Antonio's home. Big oaks, dirt road, tiny brown house with a small porch, Zeke had told her Antonio lived somewhere off one of the main road in the woods. In a home that used to belong to Katherine's parents.

Antonio put a hand to Taylor's shoulder and spun her around so she'd be facing his wooden, brown house. "Move it." Afraid, Taylor walked slowly toward the dark secluded house shielded by dense forestry. Antonio put the gun to the lower part of her spine, gave her a hard shove, she stumbled. Almost fell on her face.

Right when Taylor lifted her leg to mount the steps of his home, Antonio fisted the back of her shirt, shoved her sideways. Stumbling, she fell to the ground on her knees. "You're not welcome in my home. Go to the garage." Her eyes wandered over to the unattached garage several feet away from the home. Stalling, Taylor slowly stood.

Horrified, Taylor took slow strides toward the garage located to the side of the old, worn home. Eyes darting back and forth, trembles shook her to the core as she looked for something to strike Antonio with. Looking for a way to escape, she spotted a wire fence behind the garage. A *BEWARE OF DOG* sign hung on the silver gate.

Antonio gripped the rusty handle on the old garage and lifted it. The rusty chains churned as the door rolled backwards. A strong gasoline odor attacked Taylor's nostrils upon entering the junky area. Inside the garage tools hung on the walls on either side. In the corner sat a lawn mower. A raggedy blue Honda with a missing rear bumper and shattered back window sat parked in the center.

Evil glazed Antonio's eyes. "When you got pregnant with Zeke's baby you signed your own death certificate."

Screw you Antonio! "I love my son. We never done anything to you or Katherine."

Antonio let loose a nasty chuckle. "You're no different than Zeke's mother Bridget. Bridget tried to take everything from my mother," Antonio pressed the barrel of the gun to Taylor's chest.

Petrified, she flinched. "No! Please Antonio! Please don't shoot me. I'm sorry okay?"

Head tilting, Antonio put the tip of the weapon to Taylor's forehead and trailed the cool metal down the side of her face, let the black glock rest at the base of her throat. "Bridget had a bastard child just like you. She tried to take everything from Katherine. Bridget wanted my mother's husband. Her life. Her wealth." Laughing Antonio slapped his forehead with his free hand. "But the bitch got nothing but murdered. Katherine killed Bridget." Taylor shuddered. Nausea burned at the base of her throat right where the hole of the gun still pressed. "Now, I'm going to kill you." Antonio's voice was thick and unsteady.

Taylor felt like spitting in Antonio's face. *He's a psycho path.* "Zeke is going to find me and when he does you're going to rot in jail for the rest of your life."

Keeping the gun trained on her face, Antonio stooped. He gripped the latch by his sneaker, and lifted, revealing a deep cave in the ground. "Get in," he ordered.

Taylor's eyes lowered from Antonio's evil glare to the big dark whole in the ground. Shaking like a leaf, she lifted her gaze back to his hard lined face. Pulse rate up, she took off running out of the garage.

"Come back her bitch!" Antonio fired his weapon. The hot bullet grazed her arm, shot past the tree. Taylor kept running. If Antonio wanted her, he was going to have to catch her. She wasn't going down without a fight. She had two sons and a husband who loved her to fight for. To live for. *Run Taylor run!* her mind screamed.

Antonio fired his weapon three more times. Scurrying around a tree, bullets flew past Taylor's head. Fast on his feet, Antonio caught up with Taylor. He fisted her hair and pulled. "Ahhh!" she bellowed. Falling backwards, she landed hard on the ground.

As Antonio dragged Taylor back toward the garage by the shirt, her body twisted along the cold dirt, her right tennis shoe slipped from her foot. Scraping her nails into the skin on his arms, her feet kicked wildly.

"You're one tough bitch," Antonio said, lulling her body back into the garage. With her back on the ground, a shivering Taylor looked up at Antonio. He raised his foot over her heaving chest then crashed it to her breasts. *Crack!*

"I said get in!"

Taylor hollered. Pain submerged her ribs, they felt shattered. Gripping her aching chest, she cried. "You're going to pay for—"

As Taylor lay on the ground helpless, Antonio crouched down beside her. "Shut up. I'm tired of your threats." Putting his hands to her injured side, Antonio tossed Taylor into the deep cave. Legs flailing, scratching the air, Taylor landed hard on her back with a resounding thump. Air momentarily left her body, and she couldn't breathe.

I can't breathe. Can't breathe. Laying on her back glaring upward at Antonio's contorted face, struggling for air, she inhaled deeply. Air rushed into her lungs and she started breathing again. Her bones ached.

Antonio stood at the top of the cave inside the garage peering down at her. His lips spread into a wicked smile. "Next I'm going to take care of Zeke and then your son Zavier. No one's getting my father's money except for me. Rot in hell, Taylor. Rot in fucking hell!"

Antonio slammed the door and the entire cave went pitch black. Seconds later Taylor heard the engine of the car gurgling over the latch. It sounded like Antonio had parked the car over the entrance of the cave so no one would notice the hidden entrance.

Laying in darkness, Taylor prayed hard. Lashes blinking at the darkness, a small circular light appeared at the top of the cave. Inside the circle she saw Jesus's face. "I'm not ready to die, Dear Lord. Please let me get to know my sons Zavier and Jaheem before you bring me home."

Chapter Thirty-Five

ZEKE'S HEART CLENCHED WITH FEAR. Gripping the steering wheel of his Porsche SUV, he circled to the back of the gas station, spied the green dumpster. Having no clue as to where Taylor was, he threw the gear in park, hopped out his SUV, and flung open the lid on the dumpster.

Rotten spoiled food assaulted his nostrils. His eyes roamed over the trash in search of Taylor. Frustrated, he slammed the lid, and jogged back over to his white SUV.

Driving down the long dark road beside the ocean, Zeke choked on his cry. "I'm going to find you Taylor. And when I get hold of the bastard that took you, I'm going to break his fucking neck. Rip his heart from his fucking chest."

His mind traveled back to what Don had wrote on the paper...*ant*. "Ant. What were you trying to tell me Don?"

Losing his freaking mind, Zeke made a sharp left, and drove down another long. A tear rolled from his eye and he swiped at it. Coming upon Spaulding Drive, he thought about how he'd planned to take Taylor, Zavier, and Jaheem to ride Lord Balfour at the

Equestrian one day real soon. *Bangbangbang.* He repeatedly banged his fist on the steering wheel.

Needing to get himself under control, Zeke pulled over to the side of the isolated, dark road. Leaving the engine running, he put the SUV in park. He brought his hands up to his face and put them in a prayer position. "God. You're the only person who can help me find my wife. I can't do this by myself. I need your help. In life, a man is supposed to be obedient to your Lord. Supposed to serve God. Find a wife. Protect his wife. If I don't find Taylor, it'll kill me. Please help me."

Putting his balled fist to his nose, Zeke squeezed his eyes shut. He inhaled a deep breath then slowly blew the pent up breath from the circle of his mouth. Damn, his chest ached. Stomach cramped.

"Thank you for helping me. In Jesus name I pray…amen." Having enormous faith in God, Zeke slowly opened his eyes and read the green street sign in front of his SUV. *Spaulding Drive.*

Memories of how Richmond's father, Russell, had killed Richmond's wife, Salina, stormed inside Zeke's head. "Some people can't trust their own family." As soon as the words left his lips, a terrifying thought struck up inside Zeke's head.

Hands on steering wheel, Zeke shuddered at the awful possible realization. *Ant?* "Antonio? Was Don trying to write Antonio? Antonio no. Dear God, my brother? No he wouldn't."

If you took my wife, you will pay Antonio. I will kill you with my own bare hands. Zeke's mouth twisted wryly. He yanked the gear to drive, sped out onto the road, and headed for Antonio's house.

Eighteen minutes later Zeke pulled off the main road onto a dirt road leading to Antonio's house. The SUV shook violently as it traveled along the unpaved earth. Full moon perched high in the sky, thick trees lined either side of the road.

Nerves on edge, Zeke steered the SUV up to Antonio's house, and parked it beside his brother's BMW. *Antonio's home.* This house had once belonged to Katherine's parents before they died. Zeke studied his eerie surroundings. Worn rooftop, raggedy porch, a dim lamp glowed on the other side of the living room window.

Zeke shrugged open the door with his shoulder, clambered out. His heart thudded hard in his chest as he walked along the dirt ground. Bats flew overhead. Crickets chirped. Bullfrogs burped. Humid air clung to the bare flesh of his arms as he mounted the steps to the porch. Ready to eat Antonio alive and spit his ass out like rotten tobacco, Zeke banged his fist on the door.

Several minutes passed. Zeke banged on the door again. "Open up! I know you're in there!" Tired of waiting, Zeke grasped the door handle, and swung the hell out of the screen door. Loosening the hinges, the screen door dropped sideways.

Ready to kill, Zeke barged inside Antonio's house to find him sitting on the sofa talking on his cell. "Where is she?!"

Antonio bolted to his feet. Shoving the cell in his front jean pocket, he rushed up to Zeke and got in his face. "Fuck you coming in here like this?"

Zeke eyes darted around the room. "Where's Taylor? I know you have her."

Hands on hips, Antonio rolled his eyes. "Man, you stupid. What would I want with your wife?" He shrugged. He fanned the air. "I ain't got time for this shit, bro. I'm going to sit my ass back down. Feel free to take a look around if you want." Antonio flopped back on the couch, threw his legs up on the coffee table.

"Taylor! Taylor!" Zeke headed down the dark hallway. Not believing one word Antonio had said, he went inside his evil brother's bedroom, and checked under the bed for Taylor. He then headed inside the tiny bathroom. Standing beside the tub, he snatched back the curtain to find it empty. After he checked the pantry, he checked Antonio's closet, and every single room inside the stale, gloomy house.

Call him desperate, but Zeke felt Taylor's presence nearby. He pulled open the back door of the kitchen, walked outdoors, and dismounted the creaking steps. "Taylor! Taylor!"

Walking past the retention pond, Zeke glanced back over his shoulder just as Antonio came and stood in the back door of the kitchen. "She's not hear idiot! First you take my damn job! Then you fire me! Now you're accusing me of taking your wife? Kiss my hair white ass, bro!" Antonio slammed the back door.

Marching along the grounds Zeke headed over to the garage. He hooked his hand on the garage handle, lifted it, and entered. Fisting his hips, Zeke's eyes raked over the open area. A lot of tools, a lawn mower, and a raggedy car was inside. Nothing abnormal caught his attention.

Why do I feel her soul here? "Taylor! Taylor! Taylor!"

Turning on his heels, Zeke ran and jumped in the pond. Water splashed upward drenching his face. Not caring if a water moccasin bit him, Zeke's hand floundered around inside the pond. A fish swam by the jean area of his knees. *I know Antonio has something to do with Taylor's disappearance.*

"TAYLOR!" BACK AGAINST THE WALL of the dark cave, Taylor sat on the muddy ground, thinking she'd heard Zeke call her name. Going delirious, Taylor pulled her legs up to her chest, wrapped her arms around her knees.

"Taylor! Taylor! Taylor!" She heard Zeke call her name loud and clear.

Sharp prickly pains shot through Taylor's chest as she struggled to stand. Back to the cave's wall, she cupped her hands to the sides of her mouth, and tried to scream. "Zeke I'm down here. I'm down here." It hurt to breathe. Waiting for Zeke to respond, silence filled her ears. "Zeke come back. I'm here in the cave."

Maybe she didn't hear him. Maybe she was losing her mind, Taylor thought, sliding her hands in her back pockets to find them filled with items Sandella had given her earlier. Taylor plucked the whistles, candles, and matches from both of her pockets. *Whistles? Blow the whistle.*

Finger fumbling with the matches, Taylor struck it. The cave vaguely lightened. Spotting a piece of paper on the ground at her feet, she picked it up, lit the end, then placed it in the corner to give her temporary light.

Putting the plastic bag filled with whistles to her teeth, Taylor ripped the bag open. Sweating profusely, Taylor put the whistle to her mouth, and blew as hard as she could. The loud shrills filled her ears, bounced off the walls of the cave. "Zeke!" Shaking vigorously, her cheeks contracted and expanded as she blew the whistle again. And again. And again. Over and over, and over.

SOAKING WET, ZEKE LEFT THE pond and stalked toward his car smelling like a big wet fish. When he reached the garage, he heard a loud whistle noise. Shaking his head, his shoulder length hair slapped at his face. *I'm hearing shit.* Knowing he was mentally going nuts, he ignored the whistle ringing in his ear, rounded the corner of Antonio's house.

Antonio stood on his front porch with a smirk on his face. Folding his arms across his chest, Antonio leaned against the porch column. His right brow hitched. "Found her?"

Dripping wet, Zeke headed for the porch. On his way there, he spotted Taylor's sneaker laying in the grass. Pretending as if he didn't see her shoe, Zeke kept his eyes hooked on Antonio's face. *This crazy sonofabitch has my wife.*

Standing at the bottom of the porch, Zeke grind his back teeth. He balled his fist, and took a hard swallow. Glaring upward at his evil brother, Don's words from a while back rang loud in Zeke's ears. *"Kelvin was part of a gang called Southern Mafia. As part of the gang initiation the boys had to get branded with the initials SM,"* Don had once said.

Remembering what Don had said about the branding of the chest for the Southern Mafia gang members, Zeke demanded, "Take off your shirt."

The smirk on Antonio's face turned to stone. Leaning on the column, Antonio stood erect. "Man, I ain't taking off my shirt for you."

Palms up, Zeke shrugged. "Why not? I tell you what, if you take off your shirt, I'll give you your job back at Balfour Enterprises." He held up a finger. "I'll even go one step further. I'll resign as CEO and make you the CEO. All you have to do to become CEO of Balfour Enterprises is take off your shirt."

Antonio frowned. "Go fuck yourself. I don't want to work at Balfour anymore."

Zeke's heart sliced with hatred. "Have a good night, Antonio." Anger flaring, Zeke coolly walked to his SUV, pulled open the door, and climbed inside. "He must think I'm a damn fool. A weak as pussy," he grumbled to himself, keeping his eyes stuck on Antonio. "You're going to pay for taking my wife. No one takes the best thing that's ever happened to me away."

Knowing for sure it was Taylor's sneaker he saw laying on the ground, fury coursed through Zeke's veins. Just as Zeke cranked the engine, his cell chirped. He pulled the cell from his clip. "Hello."

"Zeke thank God you answered. Chief Shelton Wallace here. I'm leaving the hospital. Don just woke up and told me that Antonio is part of the Southern Mafia gang. Don stated Antonio had had

Taylor kidnapped all those years ago. According to Don, your mother in law Katherine is the person that shot him. Police are on their way to Antonio's and Katherine's homes to arrest them as we speak."

Zeke and Antonio glared each other down, kept their haunting gazes connected. "I'm already here at Antonio's. He has my wife, Shelton." *I'm going to handle Antonio myself. I don't need the police.*

"Don't do nothing stupid Zeke. Let the police handle Antonio."

Still standing on the porch, Antonio's furious gaze narrowed at Zeke's. Pure hatred carved Zeke's heart in half. Disgust ran through his bones. Muscles flicked in Zeke's jaws.

Sliding his hand towards his back, Antonio's eyes shot daggers at Zeke.

Zeke yanked the gear in drive, clenched the steering wheel. Remembering the sounds of the whistles, he bet Taylor was locked in the trunk of the car, or worse. *You're about to pay, dear brother. No one takes my fucking wife and gets away with it.*

Antonio whipped a gun from his pocket, aimed it straight at the driver's side of Zeke's windshield.

"Do or die motherfucker!" Zeke clicked on his bright lights, blinding Antonio. Gritting his teeth, Zeke flooded the gas. The SUV sped forward.

Brows dipped, face scrunched, Antonio's finger squeezed the trigger. Orange fire blasted from the metal hole of the black, weapon. Rounds of gunfire exploded in the night air, cracking the windshield.

A hot sensation coursed through Zeke's body. He'd been shot! Eyes on his prized enemy, Zeke raced the SUV up the steps like a freaking mad man. The SUV rocked, almost flipped over.

Infuriated, Zeke crashed the big driving machine into Antonio. Bam! Antonio's body flew backwards into the inside of the house, slammed into the wall inside the living room, then plummeted to the floor.

Eyes spread wide, blood slipped from the cracks of Antonio's lips.

Smoke billowed from the hood of the Porsche as it now parked inside Antonio's living room. The horn blasted. Potent scents of gasoline assaulted Zeke's nostrils.

Injured, Zeke's legs ached. Felt like his bones had shattered. Bleeding profusely, his arm stung.

Zeke pushed the door open, climbed out. He staggered over to Antonio, reached into his brother's jean pocket, and grabbed his keys. Blood gulped from Antonio's mouth. Gasping for air, his blue eyes bugged, his head tilted.

Needing to see Antonio's chest, Zeke grasped the top of his shirt, and ripped it in half. The buttons flew off. Zeke yanked the material of Antonio's shirt to the side. *SM.* The initials SM was indeed branded on the sorry man's chest.

"Help...me." The barely audible words left Antonio's mouth.

Zeke looked heavenward then signaled a cross over his heart. "God...let your will be done."

"Bastard." Antonio's eyes rolled to a white then closed.

Numbness in regards to Antonio filled Zeke's heart. He turned and walked away.

Dragging his left leg behind him, Zeke half way walked and halfway limped toward the garage. Holding Antonio's keys in his fist, the loud whistling sound pierced Zeke's drums. "Taylor," he groaned out, grimacing in excruciating pain.

Standing at the rear of the car parked inside Antonio's garage, Zeke's arm stung like it was on fire. He took off his shirt, ripped it in half, and tied it around his bleeding arm where he'd been shot.

Pain rippled through Zeke. He inserted the key in the trunk of the car to find it empty. Hearing the whistling clear as day, he dropped to his knees, and spotted a latch beneath the car. *A secret cave?* "Jesus Christ!" He ran and jumped inside the driver's side of the car.

Zeke's fleshy arm burned as he sat behind the steering wheel of the blue car fumbling with the keys. He jammed a key in the ignition, but it was the wrong one. Then he jammed another one to find that it fit perfectly. He cranked the engine, put the car in reverse, and zoomed it out of the garage.

Heart about to jump out of his chest, Zeke hopped out of the car, grabbed the handle of the wooden door on the ground, and yanked it upward.

Taylor stood inside the dark cave blowing on the whistle. "Zeke!" Taylor screamed. "Zeke!"

"Taylor! Hold on! I'm coming, baby." Zeke ran over to the wall to retrieve the ladder. Standing over the dark hole, he lowered the ladder in the ground. "Climb up." As Taylor hurriedly climbed up the ladder it wobbled.

Reaching the top, Zeke grabbed Taylor's shoulders, and gently pulled her out. He cupped her neck. "Oh God. Did he hurt you, Taylor?"

Crying, Taylor nodded. "Yes. He stomped his foot into my chest. I think my rib might be fractured or badly bruised. But that's it."

"Well, he paid for it."

"How?"

"I killed him."

Police sirens blasted the humid night air. Flashing red and blue lights lit up the forest. Chief Shelton Wallace jumped out of his unmarked sedan, and ran up to Zeke and Taylor. "Looks like a damn war took place here," Chief Shelton Wallace barked.

Zeke wrapped his arms around his wife's shoulders, helped her to her feet, then hefted her into his arms. "I'm taking you straight to the hospital."

Taylor's fingers touched the side of Zeke's cheek as he carried her. As he stalked across the ground towards the police vehicles, she pecked his lips. "Thank you for saving my life. I love you Zeke."

Zeke's heart swelled. "Don't thank me. It's my job to protect and save you. I love you too, my wife."

Chapter Thirty-Six

KATHERINE STOOD AT THE SINK inside her luxurious bathroom, brushing her long red hair. Admiring the long black nightgown she wore, Katherine's lips curled upwards. She'd been on the phone with Antonio long minutes ago, and he'd told her that he'd thrown Taylor's behind in the cave.

Yes. "Antonio finally killed Taylor. This calls for a celebration," Katherine softly uttered.

Colton ailed and pale entered the bathroom. "Are you talking to yourself again?" he asked, on death's bed. Hell, if she stayed around long enough and waited for him to die, she could end up a billionaire. Now with Taylor dead and gone, she'd decided that's exactly what she'd do. Right after Colton died, Katherine had big plans for Zeke. She was going to toss him out on his head, and make Antonio CEO of Balfour Enterprises.

Happiness burst inside Katherine. "Yes, darling. I'm talking to myself."

Colton walked over to his side of the bathroom, looked in the mirror. He flattened his hands on the counter, dropped his head between his shoulders, and groaned. "This cancer is eating me alive,

Katherine. I don't have much time to live. We need to sit down and go over my finances and some other things before I die." Colton lifted his head from between his shoulders and turned to face her. Death embedded his pupils. "I don't want there to be any misunderstandings about what my expectations are after I'm gone, so I'm calling an emergency meeting. First thing tomorrow morning I want you, Bane, Zeke, and Antonio to report to Balfour Hotel."

"I'll be there." Katherine strolled over to Colton, cupped his face, and gave him a kiss.

"What brought that on?" Colton asked, his lids drooping.

I'm pre-celebrating your death, Katherine thought, smiling. "I love you, Colton. I know I may not act like it sometimes, but I do. I'm going downstairs to have a drink, do you want to join me?"

Colton a groan filled with irritation. "No thanks."

Never happier, Katherine strolled to the doorway of the bathroom, and paused. Perfectly manicured hand on the frame, Katherine swung her hair, and looked over her shoulder at Colton. "Colton, if it's still on the table, I'd like for you and I to get marriage counseling."

Despair shown on Colton's face. "Katherine, I'm going to be upfront with you. I'm not interested in saving our marriage anymore. When I die, I want to die a happy man. Being married to you doesn't make me happy."

Katherine whirled. Tilting her head, she put her hands on her hips. "What are you trying to say, Colton?"

"Well, I was saving this for tomorrow, but since you asked, I'll go ahead and tell you now. I'm divorcing you, Katherine."

Stunned, Katherine's hand flew to her chest. Never did she think Colton would have the balls to divorce her. Especially not while he was sick and dying with cancer. This man had bigger balls than she'd known or ever imagined. "So you were going to call me in a meeting on tomorrow and tell me you wanted a divorce in front of our children?"

Colton's mouth was grim. "You and I both know you have a bad temper. I wasn't going to tell you in front of them to embarrass you, I was going to tell you in front of them so you could remain calm."

"We're not getting a divorce, Colton," Katherine managed to reply through stiff lips.

Colton closed the distance between them and wagered a finger in Katherine's face. "Yes we are getting a divorce. You've been stealing from me woman! Millions of dollars are gone from my account and I know you took it. Took it without my permission." Colton looked as if he could choke the life out of her.

A tremble touched her lips. "I shouldn't need permission to withdraw money from our account. Your money is my money."

"Not anymore! I'm divorcing you, Katherine the thief." Colton stormed past Katherine.

Terribly mystified, Katherine descended the staircase of their mansion. Feeling like getting her gun and shooting Colton, she marched inside the dining room, walked over to the bar, and poured herself a stiff drink.

Katherine held the glass of alcohol up to her lips and gulped. The bitter alcohol burned her throat as she drank it. *If Colton Balfour thinks he's going to divorce me and leave me out of his will, I'll have him killed before I go out like that. Kill him myself.*

Peeping around the dining room, Katherine's anger got the best of her. Outraged, she waltzed inside the kitchen, pulled open the refrigerator, and took hold of Colton's prescription bottle.

Standing at the sink, she reached into the pocket of her nightgown, retrieved the silver container containing the arsenic. She popped open Colton's last two capsules, poured the cancer medication into the sink, and then refilled the capsules with arsenic.

She then dropped the tiny silver bottle containing arsenic into the pocket of her gown, and replaced the prescription bottle back into the refrigerator.

Pissed beyond measure, Katherine picked up her drink and wrapped her lips around the edge. *I'm going to make sure Colton dies before he changes his will. If he thinks he's going to die and leave me nothing, he has another thing coming.* Colton walked into the kitchen, looked at her, and just shook his head. When he pulled open the refrigerator and reached for his medicine, Katherine's insides jumped with joy. Giving her the silent treatment, Colton grabbed a bottle of water, and walked over to the cabinet carrying his medicine.

Standing at the sink beside her, treating her like a damn dog, Colton twisted the cap off the medication, and retrieved the poisoned capsule. Tilting his head back, Colton held the medicine to his lips and—

Knuckles rasped harshly on the front door.

Take it. Take it. Swallow the poison. Katherine's mind rallied for Colton to swallow the capsule touching his thick lips.

Knuckles banged brusquely on the door again.

Damn. Who could that be? Katherine thought, desperate for Colton to eat the poison.

Colton put the medication back into the prescription bottle. "I'm not going to take my medicine anymore. Are you expecting company?"

Damn, he didn't take it. "No."

Colton's eyes traveled to the time on the microwave. "Me either. It's kind of late for visitors."

"Maybe it's Antonio. I spoke with him earlier today and he said he wanted to come by and apologize."

Colton's mouth thinned with displeasure. "Antonio should've apologized a long time ago."

"Is there anything I can do to change your mind about the divorce, Colton? Please, I'll do anything?" Katherine begged.

"I'm done with you, Katherine. Love don't live here anymore. I'll get the door." Colton turned and stalked out of the kitchen.

Katherine's eyes landed on the knives. Eager to see Colton dead, she envisioned herself stabbing him in his back.

Wondering who'd come to her home this late in the evening, Katherine walked to the end of the kitchen, and peeped her head around the corner. Colton grasped the doorknob, and pulled open the door. Chief Shelton Wallace stood on their porch along with two more officers.

Katherine's heart pumped wildly in her chest. *What is Chief Wallace doing here?*

Chief Wallace said, "Sorry to interrupt you this evening, Colton. Is Katherine home?"

Colton nodded. "Yes, what's this about Shelton?"

Shelton held a sheet of paper to Colton's face. "I have a warrant for Katherine's arrest and to search the house."

"Arrest? For what?" Shock resounded in Colton's deep voice.

Shelton stepped inside the house and caught Katherine peeping at him from around the corner. Katherine's heart dunked.

Shelton Wallace quickly closed in on Katherine while the other officers began searching the house. Now standing in front of Katherine, Chief Wallace pulled handcuffs from his security holster. Fear squeezed the breath out of Katherine as the Chief grabbed her arms, twisted them behind her back, and slapped handcuffs on her wrists.

About to puke and sweating, Katherine flinched. "Ouch! Take these handcuffs off me!"

Shelton stated, "Katherine Balfour you're under the arrest for kidnapping, murder, and attempted murder." Shelton began reading Katherine the Miranda Act.

Hot flashes surged Katherine. "Kidnapping! Murder! Attempt to murder! Why this is absurd!"

Colton gripped his chest. "Kidnapping? Murder? Attempt to murder? Are you sure, Shelton?"

Shelton yanked on the cuffs slicing into her wrists, and nodded. "Colton, you and I have known each other for years. I'm sorry to have to do this. But your wife broke the law. Police have proof that your wife, Katherine here, had your daughter-in-law and grandson kidnapped. Not only that, Katherine shot Don McQuade and killed Bridget. Police found Mildred and Kelvin in Missouri, and they've since confirmed Katherine's involvement."

Colton clenched his chest. His knees buckled. "Is this true, Katherine?"

Tears flooded Katherine's eyes. "They're lying Colton. Please call our attorney. Go call Gar now. Gar can fix anything."

The other officer walked up to where they all stood. "Look what I found hidden inside the fireplace," the cop said, holding up the knife she'd used to kill Bridget.

"Antonio killed Bridget! Not me!" Tears dripped on Katherine's robe.

Shelton's eyes rounded with concern. "Speaking of Antonio. I'm sorry to have to tell you this, but your son is dead."

Katherine's heart burst into millions of tiny pieces.

Chapter Thirty-Seven

Months Later

THE PIPING HOT SUN SHINNED down on the glistening blue ocean behind Zeke's and Taylor's white, stucco mansion. Waves crashed against the edges of the beige sandy beach. A hot summer breeze rolled off the ocean, and brushed Taylor's skin as she walked along the beach looking for shark's teeth.

"Zavier, I don't think we're going to find many shark teeth out here. How about we look for seashells instead?"

Wearing a white shirt and white shorts, Zavier held up his beach bucket. When Zavier bedazzled her with a handsome smile, Taylor's heart melted. Just wilted like a flower in the blazing sun. God, she loved Zavier. "But I already have enough seashells," her precious son exclaimed.

Deep chocolate skin, Jaheem's mouth split into a white grin. Taylor's heart tingled from that handsome smile of his. Man oh man, she loved Jaheem so much. Although she didn't give birth to Jaheem, she loved him the same as she loved Zavier.

Wearing white shorts and a white shirt, too, Jaheem said, "Collecting seashells is for girls, man. Throw them back into the water, Zavier."

Zavier shook his head. "Collecting seashells is for both girls and boys. Isn't that right, Mom?"

Having a great time on the beach with her boys before their coming-together-as-a-family celebration took place, Taylor snickered. "He's right, Jaheem. Both girls and boys collect seashells."

Jaheem said, "Okay, if you say so."

"Taylor! Jaheem! Zavier! Our guests have arrived." Zeke shouted, standing on the back deck of their home.

"Last one to the deck has to do the dishes for a week," Jaheem said.

The boys took off running toward the back of the estate. Walking slowly along the beach, Taylor grabbed the locket draped around her neck, and opened it. The right side of the locket had finally been filled with a picture of Jaheem and Zavier smiling. She'd always known deep down inside the right side of the jewelry would be filled with a picture of Zavier one day. Lucky for her she got two boys instead of one and couldn't be happier with her outcome.

Taylor finally had everything in life that she ever wanted. A husband—her *Mr. Right.* Two sons. Good friends. A great modeling career. But most importantly, she had God. God had done so much for her. And if it hadn't been for Him, she wouldn't be where she was today.

Taylor extended her arms toward the sky. "I never could have made it with you God. Thank you. Thank you for allowing me to see this day with my husband and children."

Smiling, Taylor mounted the steps to the back of her deck. Zeke draped his arms around her waist, and kissed her cheek. "Did you find any shark teeth?" Zeke asked.

"No. We can look again tomorrow."

"You look beautiful in your all short, white dress. You're gone let me make love to you in the dress after our guess leave, right?"

Taylor playfully hit Zeke's arm. "Is that all you think about, Zeke?"

"Stand in front of me. Hurry." Facing the sliding glass door, Zeke clenched Taylor's hips and hurried to place her in front of him. "Don't move. Stay there for a second," he said.

Baffled, Taylor asked, "Why can't I move? And why can't you turn around?"

Zeke drew his lips in a sexy smile. "Because my dick is hard and I don't want the guest to see me like this."

Taylor's eyes lowered to Zeke's white pants. His erection pushed hard beneath the zipper of his pants. "Oh my. You're hard as a brick." Taylor giggled. "I haven't even touched you."

"You don't have too. Just seeing you look so damn fine gets my cock hard." Peering out at the ocean, Zeke kept quiet for a few seconds. He sucked in a deep breath. "It's going down. Okay. I'm good."

"I've never been this happy in my entire life." Taylor reached down and squeezed his shaft then burst into laughter.

"Taylor!" Zeke chortled. "I'm going to get you for that."

Taylor touched Zeke's lips with her index finger. "I can't wait till you make love to me tonight."

"Keep playing with my shaft like that, and I'm gone send everyone home so I can bend you over and make love to you right now." With a flaccid penis, Zeke pulled open the sliding glass door.

Taylor stepped inside to find all of her family and friends there to celebrate Jaheem's adoption and Zavier's safe return. Glee filling her, Taylor's eyes roamed over all of her guests standing inside her den.

"About time you two come inside," Richmond joked.

Veronica, Bane, Colton, Willa, Drake, Sandella, Braylon, toddler Logan, Richmond, Kayla, baby Richmond II, and Leslie all were inside the family room dressed casual.

"Thanks for waiting. Zeke had a little issue he needed to take care of," Taylor snickered.

Chuckling, Zeke nudged Taylor. He then stated, "Anyway, thank you all for coming here today to help us celebrate the reunion of our family. As you all know, Taylor and I are thrilled to have Zavier and Jaheem become a permanent part of our lives. Jaheem, Zavier, come stand beside your mother and me."

Jaheem went and stood by Zeke and Zavier stood on the other side of Taylor. Clad in all white, in Taylor's mind, the four of them looked like the perfect family. Zeke continued. "In life what matters most is family. I cherish my family. Everyone here today is family to me. Thank you all for coming to share in our beautiful reunion celebration. I love each and every one of you."

Loud applause filled the room. After the Pastor said a prayer and blessed their family, the photographer snapped photos of them dressed in all white attire.

"Now let's eat!" Jaheem said, laughing.

Zavier exclaimed, "I can't wait to tear the ribs up!"

Now with the kidney transplant successful and behind them, and the adoption with Jaheem behind them, Taylor felt like for once in her life she had total peace. Yeah she was wealthy, and yeah, she had a great career. And yeah she had the most gorgeous man in the entire world by her side. But it'd all mean nothing if she didn't have love, respect, and most of all peace.

There's nothing like peace, Taylor thought, hugging each and every single guest.

The doorbell rang. Taylor pried herself away from Kayla's tight embrace, walked toward the living room and pulled open the door. He heart dropped past her knees.

"Pierre! You came!"

Dressed in a hot pink sheer shirt, and summery green pants, Pierre was working his outfit. "Honey, I sure did come. Francois is coming too. His slow behind is getting out of the cab. The company jet Zeke sent for us was something else. Just fabulous."

Taylor threw herself in Pierre's arms and squeezed him tight. "I love you Pierre!"

"Pierre loves you too, honey. Now let me go so I can tour this mansion." Pierre chuckled.

the end

ABOUT THE AUTHOR

Sabrina Sims McAfee is your writer of women's fiction, romantic suspense, and contemporary romance. She loves writing about strong men, and sexy strong women, and the adventurous journeys they travel. She lived in Florida for most of her life, but now she's a current resident of Myrtle Beach, SC. She lives there with her husband and two teenage children. In her leisure she likes spending time with her family, reading, traveling, and watching reality and suspense TV shows.

Sabrina's goal is to someday produce one of her books into a movie. As she strives toward her dream, she plans to study the craft of writing, take writing risks, and try her hardest to bring her readers great satisfying stories.

She loves hearing from her readers so please feel free to email her at Sabrina@sabrinasimsmcafee.com or visit her online at www.sabrinasimsmcafee.com

FROM THE DESK OF
SABRINA SIMS MCAFEE

A Writer at Heart
Visit me at my website:
www.sabrinasimsmcafee.com

Dear Readers,
Thanks a million for reading *Marrying Mr. Right*. I hope you
enjoyed reading the book just as much as I enjoyed writing it.
Reviews, comments, and likes are greatly appreciated. Favorable
reviews greatly help authors so thank you.
Fondly,
Sabrina

Also, if you enjoyed the book, please remember you can share it
with a friend via the lending feature. In addition, you can help
readers find it by recommending it to friends and family, reading
and discussion groups, online forums, etc.

Website: www.sabrinasimsmcafee.com
Email: Sabrina@sabrinasimsmcafee.com
Twitter: www.twitter.com/sabrinamcafee
Facebook: www.facebook.com/sabrina.mcafee.10

Made in the USA
Middletown, DE
04 August 2015